PRINCES OF EUROPE

Torn between love and royal obligation…

by Rebecca Winters

Vincenzo and Valentino are determined to fulfil their
duty to their beloved kingdoms by taking royal wives,
but they haven't counted on the revolutions taking
place in their hearts caused by two
captivating commoners.

When these two charming princes risk everything to
win the trust of the women they love, they soon find
the true meaning of commitment and honour, proving that sometimes fairytales do come true—
and in the most unexpected ways!

EXPECTING THE PRINCE'S BABY
Available May 2014

and

BECOMING THE PRINCE'S WIFE
Available June 2014

BECOMING THE PRINCE'S WIFE

BY
REBECCA WINTERS

MILLS &
BOON

Published in Great Britain 2014
by Mills & Boon, an imprint of Harlequin (UK) Limited,
Eton House, 18-24 Paradise Road, Richmond, Surrey, TW9 1SR

© 2014 Rebecca Winters

ISBN: 978-0-263-91289-0

23-0614

Harlequin (UK) Limited's policy is to use papers that are natural, renewable and recyclable products and made from wood grown in sustainable forests. The logging and manufacturing processes conform to the legal environmental regulations of the country of origin.

Printed and bound in Spain
by Blackprint CPI, Barcelona

Rebecca Winters, whose family of four children has now swelled to include five beautiful grandchildren, lives in Salt Lake City, Utah, in the land of the Rocky Mountains. With canyons and high alpine meadows full of wildflowers, she never runs out of places to explore. They, plus her favourite vacation spots in Europe, often end up as backgrounds for her romance novels, because writing is her passion, along with her family and church.

Rebecca loves to hear from readers. If you wish to e-mail her, please visit her website: www.cleanromances.com.

To my four wonderful, outstanding children:
Bill, John, Dominique and Max.

They've had to put up with a mother whose mind
is constantly dreaming up new fairytales
like the one I've just written.

Their unqualified love and constant support
has been the greatest blessing in my life.

CHAPTER ONE

As Carolena Baretti stepped out of the limousine, she could see her best friend, Abby, climbing the stairs of the royal jet. At the top she turned. "Oh, good! You're here!" she called to her, but was struggling to keep her baby from squirming out of her arms.

At eight months of age, little black-haired Prince Maximilliano, the image of his father, Crown Prince Vincenzo Di Laurentis of Arancia, was becoming big Max, fascinated by sights and sounds. Since he was teething, Carolena had brought him various colored toys in the shape of donuts to bite on. She'd give them to him after they'd boarded the jet for the flight to Gemelli.

The steward brought Carolena's suitcase on board while she entered the creamy interior of the jet. The baby's carryall was strapped to one of the luxury leather chairs along the side. Max fought at leaving his mother's arms, but she finally prevailed in getting him fastened down.

Carolena pulled a blue donut from the sack in her large straw purse. "Maybe this will help." She leaned over the baby and handed it to him. "What do you think, sweetheart?"

Max grabbed for it immediately and put it in his mouth to test it, causing both women to laugh. Abby gave her a hug. "Thank you for the gift. Any distraction is a blessing! The only time he doesn't move is when he's asleep."

Carolena chuckled.

"So you won't get too bored, I brought a movie for you to watch while we fly down. Remember I told you how much I loved the French actor Louis Jourdan when I was growing up?"

"He was in *Gigi,* right?"

"Yes, well, I found a movie of his in my mother's collection. You know me and my love for old films. This one is called *Bird of Paradise.* Since we'll be passing Mount Etna, I think you'll love it."

"I've never heard of that movie, but thank you for being so thoughtful. I'm sure I'll enjoy it."

"Carolena—I know this is a hard time for you, but I'm so glad you decided to come. Vincenzo and Valentino need to discuss business on this short trip. It will give you and me some time to do whatever we want while Queen Bianca dotes on her grandson."

"When Max smiles, I see traces of Michelina. That must delight her."

"I know it does. These days it's hard to believe Bianca was ever upset over the pregnancy. She's much warmer to me now."

"Thank heaven for that, Abby."

"You'll never know."

No, Carolena supposed she wouldn't. Not really. Abby Loretto had offered to be a surrogate mother to carry Their Highnesses' baby, but they'd both been through a trial by fire when Michelina was suddenly killed.

Carolena was thrilled for the two of them who, since that time, had fallen deeply in love and weathered the storm before marrying. Now they had a beautiful baby boy to raise and she was glad to have been invited to join them for their brief holiday.

Today was June fourth, a date she'd dreaded every June for the past seven years. It marked the death of her fiancé, Berto, and brought back horrendous guilt. She and Berto had shared a great love, but it had come to a tragic end too soon. All because of Carolena.

She'd been too adventurous for her own good, as her own wonderful, deceased grandmother had always told her. *You go where angels fear to tread without thinking of anyone but yourself. It's probably because you lost your parents too soon and I've failed you. One day there'll be a price to pay for being so headstrong.*

Tears stung her eyelids. How true were those words.

Berto's death had brought about a permanent change in Carolena. Outside of her professional work as an attorney, she never wanted to be responsible for another human life again. Though she'd dated a lot of men, her relationships were of short duration and superficial. After seven years, her pattern of noncommitment had become her way of life. No one depended on her. Her actions could affect no one or hurt anyone. That was the way she liked it.

Dear sweet Abby had known the date was coming up. Out of the goodness of her heart she'd insisted Carolena come with them on this trip so she wouldn't brood. Carolena loved her blonde friend for so many reasons, especially her thoughtfulness because she knew this time was always difficult for her.

As she strapped herself in, several bodyguards entered the body of the jet followed by black-haired Vincenzo. He stopped to give his wife and son a kiss before hugging Carolena. "It's good to see you. Gemelli is a beautiful country. You're going to love it."

"I'm sure I will. Thank you for inviting me, Vincenzo."

"Our pleasure, believe me. If you're ready, then we'll take off. I told Valentino we'd be there midafternoon."

Once he'd fastened himself in and turned to Abby with an eagerness Carolena could see and feel, the jet taxied to the runway. When it took off into a blue sky, it left the Principality of Arancia behind, a country nestled along the Riviera between France and Italy.

Before heading south, she could see the coastal waters of the Mediterranean receding, but it was obvious Abby and Vincenzo only had eyes for each other. Theirs was a true love story. Watching them was painful. There were moments like now when twenty-seven-year-old Carolena felt old before her time.

Thank goodness she had a movie to watch that she hadn't seen before. The minute it started she blinked at the sight of how young Louis Jourdan was. The story turned out to be about a Frenchman who traveled to Polynesia and fell in love with a native girl.

Carolena found herself riveted when the volcano erupts on the island and the native girl has to be sacrificed to appease the gods by jumping into it. The credits said the film had been made on location in Hawaii and used the Kilauea volcano for the scenes.

As the royal jet started to make its descent to Gemelli, she saw smoke coming out of Mount Etna, one of Italy's volcanoes. After watching this film, the thought of it erupting made her shiver.

The helicopter flew away from the new hot fumarole in the western pit of the Bocca Nuova of Mount Etna. The fumarole was a hole that let out gas and steam. After the scientific team had observed an increased bluish degassing from a vent in the saddle, they sent back video and seismic records before heading to the National Center of Geophysics and Volcanology lab in Catania on the eastern coast of Sicily.

En route to the lab the three men heard deep-seated explosions coming from inside the northeast crater, but there was no cause for public alarm in terms of evacuation alerts.

Once the center's helicopter touched ground, Crown Prince Valentino waved off his two colleagues and hurried to the royal helicopter for the short flight to Gemelli in the Ionian Sea. Their team had gotten back late, but they'd needed to do an in-depth study before transmitting vital data and photos.

Valentino's brother-in-law, Crown Prince Vincenzo Di Laurentis, along with his new wife, Abby, and son, Max, would already have been at the palace several hours. They'd come for a visit from Arancia and would be staying a few days. Valentino was eager to see them.

He and Vincenzo, distant cousins, had done shipping business together for many years but had grown closer with Vincenzo's first marriage to Michelina, who'd been Valentino's only sister. Her death February before last had left a hole in his heart. He'd always been very attached to his sibling and they'd confided in each other.

With his younger brother Vitale, nicknamed Vito, away in the military, Valentino had needed an outlet since her death. Lately, after a long day's work, he'd spent time quietly partying with a few good friends and his most recent girlfriend, while his mother, Bianca, the ruling Queen of Gemelli, occupied herself with their country's business.

As for tonight, he was looking forward to seeing Vincenzo as his helicopter ferried him to the grounds, where it landed at the rear of the sixteenth-century baroque palace. He jumped out and hurried past the gardens and tennis courts, taking a shortcut near the swimming pool to reach his apartment in the east wing.

But suddenly he saw something out of the corner of his eye that stopped him dead in his tracks. Standing on the end of the diving board ready to dive was a gorgeous, voluptuous woman in a knockout, fashionable one-piece purple swimsuit with a plunging neckline.

It was just a moment before she disappeared under the water, but long enough for him to forget the fiery fumarole on Mount Etna and follow those long legs to the end of the pool. When she emerged at the deep end with a sable-colored braid over one shoulder, he hunkered down to meet her. With eyes as sparkling green as lime zest, and a mouth with a passionate flare, she was even more breathtaking up close.

"Oh— Your Highness! I didn't think anyone was here!"

He couldn't have met her before or he would have remembered, because she would be impossible to forget. There was no ring on her finger. "You have me at a disadvantage, *signorina*."

She hugged her body close to the edge of the tiled pool. He got the impression she was trying to prevent him from getting the full view of her. That small show of modesty intrigued him.

"I'm Carolena Baretti, Abby Loretto's friend."

This woman was Abby's best friend? He'd heard Abby mention her, but Vincenzo had never said anything. Valentino knew his brother-in-law wasn't blind... Though they hadn't told him they were bringing someone else with them, he didn't mind. Not at all.

"How long have you been here?"

"We flew in at two o'clock. Right now the queen is playing with Max while Abby and Valentino take a nap." A nap, was it? He smiled inwardly. "So I decided to come out here for a swim. The air is like velvet."

He agreed. "My work took longer than I thought, making it impossible for me to be here when you arrived. I've planned a supper for us in the private dining room tonight. Shall we say half an hour? One of the staff will show you the way."

"That's very gracious of you, but I don't want to in-

trude on your time with them. I had a light meal before I came out to swim and I'll just go on enjoying
myself here."

He got the sense she meant it. The fact that she wasn't
being coy like so many females he'd met in his life
aroused his interest. "You're their friend, so it goes
without saying you're invited." His lips broke into a
smile. "And even if you weren't with them, I *like* an
intrusion as pleasant as this one. I insist you join us."

"Thank you," she said quietly, but he had an idea she
was debating whether or not to accept his invitation,
mystifying him further. "Before you go, may I say how
sorry I am about the loss of Princess Michelina. I can
see the resemblance to your sister in you and the baby.
I know it's been devastating for your family, especially
the queen. But if anyone can instill some joy into all of
you, it's your adorable nephew, Max."

The surprises just kept coming. Valentino was taken
aback. The fact that she'd been in Abby's confidence for
a number of years had lent a sincere ring to this woman's remarks, already putting them on a more intimate
footing. "I've been eager to see him again. He's probably grown a foot since last time."

An engaging smile appeared. "Maybe not quite another foot yet, but considering he's Prince Vincenzo's
son, I would imagine he'll be tall one day."

"That wouldn't surprise me. *A presto,* Signorina
Baretti."

Carolena watched *his* tall physique stride to the patio
and disappear inside a set of glass doors. Long after

he'd left, she was still trying to catch her breath. When she'd broken the surface of the water at the other end of the rectangular pool, she'd recognized the striking thirty-two-year-old crown prince right away.

Her knowledge of him came from newspapers and television that covered the funeral of his sister, Princess Michelina. He'd ridden in the black-and-gold carriage with his brother and their mother, Queen Bianca, the three of them grave and in deep grief.

In a recent poll he'd been touted the world's most sought-after royal bachelor. Most of the tabloids revealed he went through women like water. She could believe it. Just now his eyes had mirrored his masculine admiration of her. Everywhere they roved, she'd felt heat trail over her skin. By that invisible process called osmosis, his charm and sophistication had managed to seep into her body.

But even up close no camera could catch the startling midnight blue of his dark-lashed eyes. The dying rays of the evening sun gilded the tips of his medium cut dark blond hair and brought out his hard-boned facial features, reminiscent of his Sicilian ancestry. He was a fabulous-looking man.

Right then he'd been wearing jeans that molded his powerful thighs, and a white shirt with the sleeves shoved up to the elbows to reveal hard-muscled forearms. No sign of a uniform this evening.

Whatever kind of work he did, he'd gotten dirty. She wondered where he'd been. There were black marks on his clothes and arms, even on his face, bronzed from being outdoors. If anything, the signs of the working man intensified his potent male charisma. He wasn't just a handsome prince without substance.

Carolena was stunned by her reaction to him. There'd been many different types of men who'd come into her life because of her work as an attorney; businessmen, manufacturers, technology wizards, mining engineers, entrepreneurs. But she had to admit she'd never had this kind of visceral response to a man on a first meeting, not even with Berto, who'd been her childhood friend before they'd fallen in love.

The prince had said half an hour. Carolena hadn't intended to join the three of them this evening, but since he'd used the word *insist,* she decided she'd better go so as not to offend him. Unfortunately it was growing late. She needed to hurry inside and get ready, but she wouldn't have time to wash her hair.

She climbed out of the pool and retraced her steps to the other wing of the palace. After a quick shower, she unbraided her hair and swept it back with an amber comb. Once she'd applied her makeup, she donned a small leopard-print wrap dress with ruched elbow-length sleeves. The tiny amber stones of her chandelier earrings matched the ones in her small gold chain necklace. On her feet she wore designer wedges in brown and amber.

The law firm in Arancia where she worked demanded their attorneys wear designer clothes since they dealt with an upper-class clientele. Abby had worked there with her until her fifth month of pregnancy when she'd been forced to quit. After being employed there twenty months and paid a generous salary, Carolena had accumulated a wonderful wardrobe and didn't need to worry she wouldn't have something appropriate to wear to this evening's dinner.

A knock at the door meant a maid was ready to take her to the dining room. But when she opened it, she received another shock to discover the prince at the threshold wearing a silky charcoal-brown sport shirt and beige trousers.

He must not have trusted her to come on her own. She didn't know whether to be flattered or worried she'd made some kind of faux pas when she'd declined his invitation at first. Their eyes traveled over each other. A shower had gotten rid of the black marks. He smelled wonderful, no doubt from the soap he used. Her heart did a tiny thump before she got hold of herself.

"Your Highness— This is the second time you've surprised me this evening."

He flashed her a white smile. "Unexpected surprises make life more interesting, don't you think?"

"I do actually, depending on the kind."

"This was the kind I couldn't resist."

Obviously she *had* irritated him. Still, she couldn't believe he'd come to fetch her. "I'm honored to be personally escorted by none other than the prince himself."

"That wasn't so hard to say, was it?" His question brought a smile to her lips. "Since I'm hungry, I thought I'd accompany you to the dining room myself to hurry things up, and I must admit I'm glad you're ready."

"Then let's not waste any more time."

"Vincenzo and Abby are already there, but they didn't even notice me when I passed by the doors. I've heard of a honeymoon lasting a week or two, even longer. But eight months?"

Carolena chuckled. "I know what you mean. While we were flying out, they were so caught up in each other, I don't think they said more than two words to me."

"Love should be like that, but it's rare."

"I know," she murmured. Vincenzo and Michelina hadn't enjoyed a marriage like that. It was no news to Carolena or Valentino, so they left the subject alone.

She followed him down several corridors lined with tapestries and paintings to a set of doors guarded by a staff member. They opened onto the grounds. "We'll cut across here past the gardens to the other wing of the palace. It's faster."

There was nothing stiff or arrogant about Prince Valentino. He had the rare gift of being able to put her at ease and make her feel comfortable.

She looked around her. "The gardens are glorious. You have grown a fabulous collection of palms and exotic plants. Everything thrives here. And I've never seen baroque architecture this flamboyant."

He nodded. "My brother, Vito, and I have always called it the Putti Palace because of all the winged boy cherubs supporting the dozens of balconies. To my mother's chagrin, we used to draw mustaches on them. For our penance, we had to wash them off."

Laughter rippled out of her. "I'm afraid to tell Abby what you said for fear she'll have nightmares over Max getting into mischief."

"Except that won't be for a while yet." His dark blue

eyes danced. No doubt this prince had been a handful to his parents. Somehow the thought made him even more approachable.

"With all these wrought-iron balustrades and rustication, the palace really is beautiful."

"Along with the two-toned lava masonry, the place is definitely unique," he commented before ushering her through another pair of doors, where a staff member was on duty. Their arms brushed in the process, sending little trickles of delight through her body. Her reaction was ridiculous. It had to be because she'd never been this close to a prince before. Except for Vincenzo, of course, but he didn't count. Not in the same way.

They walked down one more hall to the entrance of the dining room where Abby and Vincenzo sat at the candlelit table with their heads together talking quietly and kissing. Gilt-framed rococo mirrors made the room seem larger, projecting their image.

Valentino cleared his throat. "Should we come back?" He'd already helped Carolena to be seated. The teasing sound in his voice amused her, but his question caused the other two to break apart. While Abby's face flushed, Vincenzo got to his feet and came around to give Valentino a hug.

"It's good to see you."

"Likewise. I'm sorry I took so long. It's my fault for leaving work late today, but it couldn't be helped."

"No one understands that better than I do. We took the liberty of bringing Carolena with us. Allow me to introduce you."

Valentino shot her a penetrating glance. "We already met at the swimming pool."

Carolena felt feverish as she and Abby exchanged a silent glance before he walked around to hug her friend. Then he took his place next to Carolena, who still hadn't recovered from her initial reaction to his masculine appeal.

In a moment, dinner was served, starting with deep-fried risotto croquettes stuffed with pistachio pesto called arancini because they were the shape and size of an orange. Pasta with clams followed called spaghetti alle vongole. Then came the main course of crab and an aubergine side dish. Valentino told them the white wine came from their own palace vineyard.

"The food is out of this world, but I'll have to pass on the cannoli dessert," Carolena exclaimed a little while later. "If I lived here very long I'd look like one of those fat Sicilian rock partridges unable to move around."

Both men burst into laughter before Valentino devoured his dessert.

Carolena looked at Abby. "What did I say?"

Vincenzo grinned. "You and my wife have the same thought processes. She was afraid pregnancy would make her look like a beached whale."

"We women have our fears," Abby defended.

"We certainly do!"

Valentino darted Carolena another glance. "In that purple swimsuit you were wearing earlier, I can guarantee you'll never have that problem."

She'd walked into that one and felt the blood rush to her cheeks. That suit was a frivolous purchase she wouldn't have worn around other people, but since she'd been alone... Or so she'd thought. "I hope you're right, Your Highness."

His eyes smiled. "Call me Val."

Val? Who in the world called him that?

He must have been able to read her mind because his next comment answered her question. "My brother and I didn't like our long names, so we gave ourselves nicknames. He's Vito and I'm Val."

"V and V," she said playfully. "I'm surprised you didn't have to wash your initials off some of those putti."

Another burst of rich laughter escaped his throat. When it subsided, he explained their little joke to Vincenzo and Abby.

Carolena smiled at Abby. "I'd caution you never to tell that story to Max, or when he's more grown up he might take it into his head to copy his uncles."

"Fortunately we don't have putti," Vincenzo quipped.

"True," Abby chimed in, "but we do have busts that can be knocked over by a soccer ball."

Amidst the laughter, a maid appeared in the doorway. "Forgive the intrusion, Your Highness, but the queen says it seems the young prince has started to cry and is running a temperature."

In an instant both parents jumped to their feet bringing an end to the frivolity.

Wanting to say something to assure them, Carolena said, "He's probably caught a little cold."

Abby nodded. "I'm sure you're right, but he's still not as used to the queen yet and is in a strange place. I'll go to him." She put a hand on Vincenzo's arm. "You stay here and enjoy your visit, darling."

At this point, Valentino stood up. "We'll have all day tomorrow. Right now your boy needs both of you."

"Thank you," they murmured. Abby came around to give Carolena a hug. "See you in the morning."

"Of course. If you need me for anything, just phone me."

"I will."

When they disappeared out the doors, Carolena got to her feet. "I'll say good-night, too. Thank you for a wonderful dinner, Your Highness."

He frowned. "The name's Val. I want to hear you say it."

She took a deep breath. "Thank you…Val."

"That's better." His gaze swept over her. "Where's the fire?"

"I'm tired." Carolena said the first thing that came into her head. "I was up early to finish some work at the firm before the limo arrived to drive me to the airport. Bed sounds good to me."

"Then I'll walk you back."

"That won't be necessary."

He cocked his dark blond head. "Do I frighten you?"

Your appeal frightens me. "If anything, I'm afraid of disturbing your routine."

"I don't have one tonight. Forget I'm the prince."

It wasn't the prince part that worried her. He'd made her aware of him as a man. This hadn't happened since she'd fallen in love with Berto and it was very disturbing to her.

"To be honest, when you showed up at the swimming pool earlier, you looked tired after a hard day's work. Since it's late, I'm sure you'd like a good sleep before you spend the day with Vincenzo tomorrow."

"I'm not too tired to see you back to your room safely."

"Your Highness?" The same maid came to the entrance once more. "The queen would like to see you in her apartment."

"I'll go to her. Thank you."

He cupped Carolena's elbow to walk her out of the dining room. She didn't want him touching her. The contact made her senses come alive. When they passed the guard and reached the grounds, she eased away from him.

"After getting to know Vincenzo, I realize how busy you are and the huge amount of calls on your time. Your mother is waiting for you."

"I always say good-night to my mother before retiring. If our dinner had lasted a longer time, she would have had a longer wait."

There was no talking him out of letting her get back to her room by herself. "What kind of work were you doing today?" She had to admit to a deep curiosity.

He grinned. "I always come home looking dirty and need to wash off the grime."

She shook her head. "I didn't say that."

"You didn't have to. Volcanoes are a dirty business."

Carolena came to a standstill before lifting her head to look at him. "You were up on Mount Etna?"

"That's right."

His answer perplexed her. "Why?"

"I'm a volcanologist with the National Center of Geophysics and Volcanology lab in Catania."

"You're kidding—" After that movie she'd watched on the plane, she couldn't believe what he'd just told her.

One corner of his compelling mouth lifted. "Even a prince can't afford to be an empty suit. Etna has been my backyard since I was born. From the first moment I saw it smoking, I knew I had to go up there and get a good look. Once that happened, I was hooked."

With his adventurous spirit, she wasn't surprised but knew there was a lot more to his decision than that. "I confess it would be fantastic to see it up close the way you do. Have you been to other volcanoes?"

"Many of them."

"You lucky man! On the way down here I watched a Hollywood movie with Louis Jourdan about a volcano erupting in Polynesia."

"You must mean *Bird of Paradise*."

"Yes. It was really something. Your line of work has to be very dangerous."

For a second she thought she saw a flicker of some emotion in his eyes, but it passed. "Not so much nowadays. The main goal is to learn how to predict trouble so that timely warnings can be issued for cautioning and evacuating people in the area. We've devised many safe ways to spy on active volcanoes over the decades."

"How did your parents feel about you becoming a volcanologist?"

A smile broke the corner of his mouth, as if her question had amused him. "When I explained the reasons for my interest, they approved."

That was too pat an answer. He sounded as if he wanted to get off the subject, but she couldn't let it go. "What argument did you give them?"

His brows lifted. "Did you think I needed one?"

She took a quick breath. "If they were anything like my grandmother, who was the soul of caution, then yes!"

He stopped outside the entrance to her wing of the palace. Moonlight bathed his striking male features, making them stand out like those of the Roman-god statues supporting the fountain in the distance. His sudden serious demeanor gave her more insight into his complex personality.

"A king's first allegiance is to the welfare of his people. I explained to my parents that when Etna erupts again, and she will, I don't want to see a repeat of what happened in 1669."

Carolena was transfixed. "What *did* happen?"

"That eruption turned into a disaster that killed over twenty-nine thousand people."

She shuddered, remembering the film. "I can't even imagine it."

He wore a grim expression. "Though it couldn't happen today, considering the sophisticated warning systems in place, people still need to be educated about the necessity of listening and heeding those warnings of evacuation."

"In the film, there'd been no warning."

"Certainly not a hundred years ago. That's been my

greatest concern. Gemelli has a population of two hundred thousand, so it can't absorb everyone fleeing the mainland around Catania, but I want us to be prepared as much as possible."

"How do you get your people prepared?"

"I've been working with our government to do mock drills to accommodate refugees from the mainland, should a disaster occur. Every ship, boat, barge, fishing boat would have to be available, not to mention housing and food and airlifts to other islands."

"That would be an enormous undertaking."

"You're right. For protection against volcanic ash and toxic gas, I've ordered every family outfitted with lightweight, disposable, filtering face-piece mask/respirators. This year's sightings have convinced me I've only scratched the surface of what's needed to be done to feel at all ready."

"Your country is very fortunate to have you for the watchman."

"The watchman? That makes me sound like an old sage."

"You're hardly old yet," she quipped.

"I'm glad you noticed." His remark caused her heart to thud for no good reason.

"I'm very impressed over what you do."

"It's only part of what I do."

"Oh, I know what a prince does." She half laughed. "Abby once read me Vincenzo's itinerary for the day and I almost passed out. But she never told me about *your* scientific background."

"It isn't something I talk about."

"Well, I think it's fascinating! You're likean astronaut or a test pilot, but the general population doesn't know what you go through or how you put your life on the line."

"That's a big exaggeration."

"Not at all," she argued. "It's almost as if you're leading a double life. What a mystery you are!"

She wouldn't have put it past Abby to have chosen that particular film because she knew about Valentino's profession and figured Carolena would get a kick out of it once she learned about his secret profession.

After a low chuckle, he opened the doors so they could walk down the hallway and around the corner to her room. She opened her door. Though she was dying to ask him a lot more questions about his work in volcanology, she didn't want him to think she expected his company any longer. She was also aware the queen was waiting for him.

"It's been a lovely evening. Thank you for everything."

His eyes gleamed in the semidarkness. "What else do you do besides give unsuspecting males a heart attack while you're diving?"

Heat scorched her cheeks. "I thought I was alone."

"Because I was late getting back, I cut through that part of the grounds and happened to see you. It looks like I'm going to have to do it more often."

He was a huge flirt. The tabloids hadn't been wrong about him. "I won't be here long enough to get caught again. I have a law practice waiting for me back in Arancia."

He studied her for a moment. "I heard you're in the same firm with Abby."

"We were until her marriage. Now she's a full-time mother to your nephew."

A heart-stopping smile appeared. "It must be tough on your male colleagues working around so much beauty and brains."

"They're all married."

"That makes it so much worse."

She laughed. "You're outrageous."

"Then we understand each other. Tomorrow we'll be eating breakfast on the terrace off the morning room. I'll send a maid for you at eight-thirty. *Buona notte,* Carolena."

"Buona notte."

"Val," he said again.

"Val," she whispered before shutting the door. She lay against it, surprised he was so insistent on her using his nickname, surprised he'd made such an impact on her.

After their delicious meal, she wasn't ready for bed yet. Once she'd slipped on her small garden-print capri pajamas, she set up her laptop on the table and started to look up Mount Etna. The amount of information she found staggered her. There were dozens of videos and video clips she watched until after one in the morning.

But by the time she'd seen a video about six volcanologists killed on the Galeras volcano in the Colombian Andes in 1993, she turned off her computer. The scientists had been standing on the ground when it began to heave and then there was a deafening roar. The vol-

cano exploded, throwing boulders and ash miles high
and they'd lost their lives.

The idea of that happening to the prince made her ill.
She knew he took precautions, but as he'd pointed out,
there was always a certain amount of risk. The desire to
see a vent up close would be hard to resist. That's what
he did in his work. He crept up close to view the activity and send back information. But there might come a
day when he'd be caught. She couldn't bear the thought
of it, but she admired him terribly.

The playboy prince who'd had dozens of girlfriends
didn't mesh with the volcanologist whose name was Val.
She didn't want to care about either image of the sensa-
tional-looking flesh-and-blood man. When Carolena finally pulled the covers over her, she fell asleep wishing
she'd never met him. He was too intriguing for words.

At seven-thirty the next morning her cell phone rang,
causing her to wonder if it was the prince. She got a
fluttery feeling in her chest as she raised up on one
elbow to reach for it. To her surprise it was Abby and
she clicked on. "Abby? Are you all right? How's Max?"

"He's still running a temperature and fussing. I think
he's cutting another tooth. The reason I'm calling is
because I'm going to miss breakfast with you and stay
in the apartment with him. It will give Vincenzo and
Valentino time to get some work done this morning."

"Understood. I'm so sorry Max is sick."

"It'll pass, but under the circumstances, why don't
you order breakfast in your room or out by the pool.
I'll get in touch with you later in the day. If you want

a limo, just dial zero and ask for one to drive you into town, and do a little shopping or something."

"Don't worry about me. I'll love relaxing by the pool. This is heaven after the hectic schedule at the law firm."

"Okay, then. Talk to you soon."

This was a good turn of events. The less she saw of Valentino, the better.

CHAPTER TWO

BY TEN-THIRTY A.M., Valentino could see that Vincenzo wasn't able to concentrate. "Let's call it a day. I can see you want to be with Abby and Max. When I've finished with some other business, we'll meet for dinner."

Vincenzo nodded. "Sorry, Valentino."

"You can't help this. Family has to come first." He walked his brother-in-law out of his suite where they'd had breakfast while they talked. When they'd said good-bye, he closed the door, realizing he had a free day on his hands if he wanted it.

In truth, he'd never wanted anything more and walked over to the house phone to call Carolena Baretti's room, but there was no answer. He buzzed his assistant. "Paolo? Did Signorina Baretti go into town?"

"No. She had breakfast at the pool and is still there."

"I see. Thank you."

Within minutes he'd changed into trunks and made his way to the pool with a beach towel and his phone. He spotted her sitting alone reading a book under the shade of the table's umbrella. She'd put her hair in a braid and was wearing a lacy cover-up, but he could see a spring-green bikini beneath it.

"I guess it was too much to hope you were wearing that purple swimsuit I found you in last evening."

She looked up. Maybe it was a trick of light, but he thought she looked nervous to see him. Why?

Carolena put her book down. "You've finished your work with Vincenzo already?"

He tossed the towel on one of the other chairs. "Between you and me, I think he wanted to take a nap with his wife."

A smile appeared. "They deserve some vacation time away from deadlines."

"Amen. We'll do more work tomorrow when Max is feeling better. Come swim with me."

She shook her head. "I've already been in."

"There's no law that says you can't swim again, is there?" He put his phone on the table.

"No. Please—just forget I'm here."

"I'm afraid that would be impossible," he said over his shoulder before plunging in at the deep end to do some laps. When he eventually lifted his head, he was shocked to discover she'd left the patio and was walking back to her wing of the palace on those long shapely legs.

Nothing like this had ever happened to him before. Propelled into action, he grabbed his things and caught up to her as she was entering the door of her apartment. Valentino stood in the aperture so she couldn't close it on him.

"Did you go away because I'd disturbed you with

my presence? Or was it because you have an aversion to me, *signorina?*"

Color swept into her cheeks. "Neither one."

His adrenaline surged. "Why didn't you tell me you preferred to be alone?"

"I'm just a guest. You're the prince doing your own thing. This is your home. But I had no intention of offending you by leaving the pool."

He frowned. "Yesterday I asked if you were afraid of me. You said no, but I think you are and I want to know why. It's true that though I've been betrothed to Princess Alexandra for years, I've had a love life of sorts. In that way I'm no different than Vincenzo before he married Michelina. But I've the feeling Abby has painted me as such a bad boy to you, you're half terrified to be alone with me."

"Nothing of the sort, Your Highness!" She'd backed away from him. "Don't ever blame her for anything. She thinks the world of you!"

That sounded heartfelt. "Then invite me in so we can talk without the staff hearing every word of our conversation."

She bit her lip before standing aside so he could enter. "I'll get you a dry towel so you can sit down." He closed the door and watched her race through the suite. She soon came hurrying back with a towel and folded it on one of the chairs placed around the coffee table.

"Thank you," he said as she took a seat at the end of the couch.

He sat down with his hands clasped between his legs and stared at her. "What's wrong with you? Though

I've told you I find you attractive, it doesn't mean I'm ready to pounce on you." She averted her eyes. "Don't tell me you don't know what I'm talking about."

"I wasn't going to, and I didn't mean to be rude. You have to believe me."

She sounded sincere enough, but Valentino wasn't about to let her off the hook. "What else am I to think? Last night I thought we were enjoying each other's company while we talked, but today you act like a frightened schoolgirl. Has some man attacked you before? Is that the reason you like to be alone and ran the minute I dived into the water?"

Her head lifted. "No! You don't understand."

"Since you're a special guest, help me so I don't feel like some pariah."

"Forgive me if I made you feel that way." Her green orbs pleaded with him. "This has to do with me, not you."

"Are you this way on principle with every man you meet? Or am I the only one to receive that honor?"

She stood up. "I—I'm going through a difficult time right now." Her voice faltered. "It's something I really can't talk about. Could we start over again, as if this never happened?"

Much as he'd like to explore her problem further, he decided to let it rest for now. "That all depends." On impulse he said, "Do you like to ride horses?"

"I love it. I used to ride all the time on my grandparents' farm."

Good. "Then I'll have lunch sent to your room, and I'll collect you in an hour. We'll ride around the grounds. It's someplace safe and close to Abby, who's hoping you're having a good time. But if you're afraid of what happened to my sister while she was riding, we could play tennis."

"I'm not afraid, but to go riding must be a painful reminder to you."

"I've worked my way through it. Accidents can happen anytime. To worry about it unnecessarily takes away from the quality of life. Don't you think?"

Her eyes suddenly glistened. "Yes," she whispered with such deep emotion he was more curious than ever to know what was going on inside her, and found himself wanting to comfort her. Instead he had to tear himself away.

"I'll be back in an hour." Reaching for his towel and phone, he left the apartment and hurried through the palace to his suite. Maybe by the end of their ride today, he'd have answers…

Carolena stood in the living room surprised and touched by his decency. He'd thought she'd been assaulted by a man and wanted to show her she didn't need to be afraid of him while he entertained her. No doubt he felt an obligation to her with Vincenzo and Abby indisposed.

He was sensitive, too. How many men would have worried she might be afraid to ride after what had happened to his sister? She'd gotten killed out riding, but he didn't let that stop him from living his normal life. His concern for Carolena's feelings increased her admiration for him.

So far she'd been a perfectly horrid guest, while he

was going out of his way to make this trip eventful for her when he didn't have to. This wasn't the behavior of a playboy. The crown prince was proving to be the perfect host, increasing her guilt for having offended him.

Within the hour he came for her in a limo and they drove to the stables across the vast estate. Once he'd picked the right mare for her, they headed out to enjoy the scenery. In time, he led them through a heavily wooded area to a lake. They dismounted and walked down to the water's edge.

"What a beautiful setting."

"We open it to the public on certain days of the month."

"Abby used to tell me she felt like a princess in a fairy tale growing up on the palace grounds in Arancia. If I lived here, I'd feel exactly the same way. You and your siblings must have spent hours here when you were young." On impulse she asked, "Were they interested in volcanology, too?"

His eyes swerved to hers. She had the feeling she'd surprised him by her question. "Quite the opposite."

That sounded cryptic. "What's the real reason you developed such a keen interest? It isn't just because Etna is there."

"It's a long story." There was that nuance of sadness in his voice again.

"We've got the rest of the afternoon." She sank onto her knees in the lush grass facing the water where an abundance of waterfowl bobbed around. "Humor me. Last night I was up until one o'clock looking at video clips of Etna and other volcanoes. They were incredible. I really want to know what drove you to become so interested."

He got down on the grass next to her. "My father had a sibling, my uncle Stefano. He was the elder son and the crown prince, but he never wanted to be king. He fought with my grandfather who was then King of Gemelli.

"Uncle Stefano hated the idea of being betrothed and having to marry a woman picked out for him. Our country has never had a sovereign who wasn't married by the time he ascended the throne. It's the law. But Stefano didn't ever want to be king and left home at eighteen to travel the world. I knew he had various girlfriends, so he didn't lead a celibate life, but he never married.

"In time, volcanoes fascinated him and he decided he wanted to study them. To appease my grandparents, he came home occasionally to touch base. I was young and loved him because he was so intelligent and a wonderful teacher. He used to take me up on Etna.

"The day came when I decided I wanted to follow in his footsteps and announced I was going to attend the university to become a geologist. My parents could see my mind was made up.

"While I was at school, the family got word he'd been killed on the Galeras volcano in the Colombian Andes."

"Valentino—" she gasped. "I read about it on the website last night. One of the people killed was your uncle?"

Pain marred his striking male features. "He got too close. The ash and gas overpowered him and he died."

She shuddered. "That's horrible. I should have thought

it would have put you off wanting anything more to do with your studies."

"You might think it, but I loved what I was doing. Statistics prove that on average only one volcanologist dies on the job each year or so."

"That's one too many!"

"For our family it was traumatic because of the consequences that followed. His body was shipped home for the funeral. A few weeks later my grandfather suffered a fatal heart attack, no doubt from the shock. His death meant my father took over as king with my mother at his side.

"While we were still grieving, they called me into their bedroom and told me they were all right with my desire to be a volcanologist. But they prayed I wouldn't disappoint them the way my uncle had disappointed my grandfather. They said my uncle Stefano had disgraced the family by not taking up his royal duties and marrying.

"I was torn apart because I'd loved him and knew he'd suffered because he'd turned his back on his royal heritage. But when I heard my parents' sorrow, I promised I would fulfill my princely obligation to the crown and marry when the time was right. They wouldn't have to worry about me. Michelina and I made a pact that we'd always do our duty."

"You mean that if she'd wanted to marry someone else other than Vincenzo, she would still have done her duty."

He nodded. "I asked her about that, knowing Vincenzo didn't love her in the way she loved him. She said it didn't matter. She was committed and was hoping he'd fall in love with her one day."

"Did you resent him for not being able to love your sister?"

"How could I do that when I don't love Alexandra? When I saw how hard he tried to make Michelina happy by agreeing to go through the surrogacy process, my affection for him grew. He was willing to do anything to make their marriage better. Vincenzo is one of the finest men I've ever known. When he ended up marrying Abby, I was happy for him."

"You're a remarkable person. So was your sister."

"I loved her. She could have told our parents she refused to enter into a loveless marriage, but she didn't. Uncle Stefano's death had affected all of us, including our brother, Vito. One day after his military service is over, he, too, will have to marry royalty because he's second in line to the throne."

"The public has no idea of the anguish that goes on behind locked royal doors."

"We're just people who've been born to a strange destiny. I didn't want to disappoint my parents or be haunted with regrets like my uncle. Fortunately, Mother is still capable of ruling, and my time to fulfill my obligation hasn't come yet."

"But it will one day."

"Yes."

"It's hard to comprehend a life like yours. May I be blunt and ask you if you have a girlfriend right now?"

"I've been seeing someone in town."

She had to suppress a moan. *Did you hear that, Carolena?* "And she's all right with the situation?"

"Probably not, but from the beginning she's known we couldn't possibly have a future. In case you're wondering, I haven't slept with her."

Carolena shook her head. "You don't owe me any explanation."

"Nevertheless, I can see the next question in your eyes and so I'll answer it. Contrary to what the media says about me, there have been only a few women with whom I've had an intimate relationship, but they live outside the country."

"Yet knowing you are betrothed has never stopped any of them from wanting to spend time with you?"

"No. The women I've known haven't been looking for permanency, either." He smiled. "We're like those ships passing in the night."

It sounded awful. Yet, since Berto, she hadn't been looking for permanency, either, and could relate more than he knew.

"I've warned my latest girlfriend our relationship could end at any time. You're within your rights to condemn me, Carolena."

"I could never condemn you," she whispered, too consumed by guilt over how she'd accidentally brought out Berto's death to find fault with anyone. "You've had every right to live your life like any ordinary man. But like your uncle, it must have been brutal for you to have grown up knowing your bride was already chosen for you."

"I've tried not to think about it."

Her mind reeled from the revelations. "Does your betrothed know and understand?"

"I'm quite sure Princess Alexandra has had relationships, too. It's possible she's involved with someone she cares about right now. Her parents' expectations for her haven't spared her anguish, either."

"No," she murmured, but it was hard to understand. How could any man measure up to Valentino? If Princess Alexandra was like his sister, she'd been in love with Valentino for years. "Does she support your work as a volcanologist?"

"I haven't asked her."

"Why not?"

"Up to now we've been living our own lives apart as much as possible."

"But this is an integral part of your life!"

He sat up, chewing on the end of a blade of grass. "Our two families have spent occasional time together over the years. But the last time my brother was home on leave and went to Cyprus with me and my mother, he told me that Alexandra admitted she never liked the idea that I was a volcanologist."

"And that doesn't worry you?"

He studied her for a long moment. "It's an issue we'll have to deal with one day after we're married."

"By then it will be too late to work things out between you," she cried. "How often do you fly to Catania?"

"Four times a week."

"She's not going to like that, not if she hates the idea of it."

He gave her a compassionate smile. "Our marriage won't be taking place for a long time, so I choose not to worry about it."

"I don't see how you can stand it."

"You learn to stand it when you've been born into a royal family. Why fate put me in line for the throne instead of you, for example, I don't know."

"You mean a woman can rule?"

"If there are no other males. Under those circumstances, she must marry another royal so she can reign. But my grandparents didn't have a daughter. Uncle Stefano should have been king, but he rebelled, so it fell to my father to rule."

Tears trickled down her cheeks. "How sad for your uncle."

"A double sadness, because though he'd abdicated in order to choose his own life, he was burdened with the pain of disappointing his parents."

"There's been so much pain for all of you. And now your own sister and father have passed on."

He nodded. "It's life."

"But it's so much to handle." Her voice trembled. Carolena wanted to comfort him but realized no one could erase all that sadness. She wiped the moisture off her cheeks. "You didn't have to tell me anything. I feel honored that you did."

His gaze roved over her. "Your flattering interest in what I do prompted me to talk about something I've kept to myself for a long time. It felt good to talk about it. Why don't you try it out on me by telling me what's bothering you."

Her eyes closed tightly for a moment. "Let's just say someone that I loved died and it was my fault. Unlike you, I can't seem to move on from the past."

"Maybe you haven't had enough time to grieve."

Carolena could tell him seven years had been more than enough time to grieve. At this point, grief wasn't her problem. Guilt was the culprit. But all she said to him was, "Maybe."

"It might be therapeutic to confide in someone. Even me."

His sincerity warmed her heart, but confiding in him would be the worst thing she could do. To remain objective around him, she needed to keep some barriers between them. "You have enough problems."

"None right this minute."

He stared hard at her. "Was his death intentional?"

"No."

"I didn't think it was. Have you gone for counseling?"

"No. It wouldn't help."

"You don't know that."

"Yes, I do." In a panic, she started to get up. He helped her the rest of the way. "Thank you for being willing to listen." It was time to change the subject. "Your uncle would be so happy to see how he guided you on your particular path, and more especially on how you're putting that knowledge to exceptional use. If I'd had such an uncle, I would have made him take me with him, too. What you do can be dangerous, but it *is* thrilling."

"You're right about that," he said, still eyeing her

speculatively. "Shall we head out? By the time we reach the palace, hopefully Vincenzo will have good news for us about Max and we can all eat dinner together."

"I hope so."

They mounted their horses and took a different route to the stable. A limo was waiting to take them back to her wing of the palace. When they arrived, she opened the car door before he could. "You don't need to see me inside. Thank you for a wonderful day."

He studied her through veiled eyes. "It was my pleasure. I'll call you when I've spoken with Vincenzo."

She nodded before getting out of the limo. After hurrying inside, she took a quick shower, applied her makeup and arranged her hair in a loose knot on top of her head. For the first time in years her thoughts hadn't been on Berto. They'd been full of the prince, who'd brought her alive from the moment he'd appeared at the side of the pool.

No matter that he had a girlfriend at the moment, it was hard to breathe every time Carolena thought of the way he'd looked at her. She could understand why any woman lucky enough to catch his eye would be willing to stay in a relationship as long as possible to be with him. There was no one like him.

Needing to do something with all this energy he'd generated through no fault of his own, she got dressed, deciding to wear a short-sleeved crocheted lace top in the same egg shell color as her linen pants. The outfit was light and airy. She toned it with beige ankle-strap crisscross espadrilles.

While she was waiting for a phone call, she heard

a knock on the door and wondered if it might be the prince. With a pounding heart she reached for her straw bag and opened it, but it was the maid, and Carolena was furious at herself for being disappointed.

"*Signorina?* His Highness has asked me to accompany you to dinner. He's waiting on the terrace."

What about Abby and Vincenzo? "Thank you for coming to get me."

No shortcuts through the grounds this time, but it gave Carolena the opportunity to see more of the ornate palace. By the time she arrived at the terrace, Vincenzo had already joined the prince, but there was no sign of Abby or Max. The two men stood together chatting quietly.

She had the impression this terrace was a recent addition. It was a masterpiece of black-and-white marble checkerboard flooring, Moorish elements and cream-colored lattice furniture in Italian provincial. A collection of exotic trees and flowering plants gave the impression they were in a garden.

Valentino's dark blue gaze saw her first. He broke from Vincenzo and moved toward her wearing jeans and a sand-colored polo shirt. "*Buonasera,* Carolena. You look beautiful."

Don't say that. "Thank you."

His quick smile was a killer. "I hope you're hungry. I told the kitchen to prepare chicken the way Abby tells me you like it."

"You're very kind." Too kind. She flashed him a smile as he helped her get seated. Valentino had no equal as a host. She decided he had no equal, period.

Vincenzo walked over and kissed her cheek before sitting down at the round table opposite her. A sumptuous-looking meal had been laid out for them. A maid came out on the terrace just then and told Valentino his mother wanted to speak to him when he had a minute. He nodded before she left.

"Where's Abby, Vincenzo?"

"Max fussed all day and is still feverish, so we're taking turns."

"The poor little thing. Do you think it's serious?"

"We don't know. Our doctor said it could be a virus, but Max isn't holding down his food. That has me worried."

"I don't blame you. Is there something I can do to help?"

"Yes," Valentino inserted. "If Max is still sick tomorrow, you can keep me company, since Vincenzo will be tied up taking care of his family."

He actually sounded happy about it, but the news filled Carolena with consternation. She'd been with him too much already and her attraction to him was growing. She flicked him a glance. "You don't have to worry about entertaining me. I brought my laptop and always have work to do."

"Not while you're here." Valentino's underlying tone of authority quieted any more of her excuses. "No doubt you and Abby had intended to visit some of the shops and museums in Gemelli while on holiday, but I can think of something more exciting for tomorrow *if* you're up to it."

Vincenzo shot her a glance she couldn't decipher. "Be careful."

She chuckled. "Is that a warning?"

After finishing his coffee, a glimmer of a smile appeared. "On my first business visit here years ago, Valentino dangled the same option in front of me."

"What happened?"

He studied her for a moment. "That's for you to find out."

"Now you've made me nervous."

"Maybe you should be." She couldn't tell if Vincenzo's cryptic response was made in jest or not.

"You've frightened her," Valentino muttered. Again, Carolena was confused by the more serious undertone of their conversation.

"Then I'm sorry and I apologize." Vincenzo put down his napkin and got to his feet. "Enjoy your evening. We'll talk again in the morning. Please don't get up."

"Kiss that baby for me and give Abby my love."

"I will."

She'd never seen Vincenzo so preoccupied. Being a new father wasn't easy, but she sensed something else was on his mind, as well.

"What went on just now?" she asked as soon as he left the terrace.

Valentino had been watching her through narrowed eyes. "I'm afraid he thinks my idea of a good time could backfire." Carolena believed there was more to it than that, but she let it go for now.

"You mean it might be one of those surprises that's the wrong kind for me?"

"Possibly."

"Well, if you don't tell me pretty soon, I might expire on the spot from curiosity."

She thought he'd laugh, but for once he didn't. "I'd like to take you sailing to Taormina. It's an island Goethe called 'a part of paradise.' The medieval streets have tiny passages with secrets I can guarantee you'll love."

"It sounds wonderful, but that wasn't the place you had in mind when you were talking with Vincenzo."

"I've had time to think the better of it."

A rare flare of temper brought blood to her cheeks. "Vincenzo is Abby's husband, not mine."

"And he enjoys her confidence."

"In other words, he's trying to protect me from something he thinks wouldn't be good for me."

"Maybe."

Carolena's grandmother used to try to protect her the same way. But if she got into it with the prince, she'd be acting like the willful child her grandparent used to accuse her of being. Averting her eyes, she forced herself to calm down and said, "It's possible Max will be better, but in case he isn't, I'd love a chance to go sailing. It's very kind of you."

She heard his sharp intake of breath. "Now you're patronizing me."

"What do you expect me to do? Have a tantrum?" The question was out of her mouth before she could stop it. She was mortified to realize she was out of control. Something had gotten into her. She didn't feel at all herself.

"At least it would be better than your pretense to mollify me," came the benign response.

What? "If you weren't the prince—"

"I asked you to forget my title."

"That's kind of hard to do."

"Why don't you finish what you were about to say. If I weren't the prince…"

"Bene." She sucked in her breath. "If neither of you were princes, I'd tell you I've been taking care of myself for twenty-seven years and don't need a couple of guys I hardly know to decide what's best for me. If that sounds ungracious, I didn't mean for it to offend you, but you did ask."

A look of satisfaction entered his eyes. "I was hoping you would say that. How would you like to fly up on Etna with me in a helicopter? We'll put down in one spot and I'll show you some sights no visitor gets to see otherwise."

Gulp. She clung to the edge of the table from sheer unadulterated excitement. Valentino intended to show her that ten-thousand-foot volcano up close? After seeing that movie, what person in the world wouldn't want the opportunity? She couldn't understand why Vincenzo thought it might not be a good experience for her.

"You love your work so much you'd go up there on your day off?"

"You can ask that after what I revealed to you today? Didn't you tell me you thought it sounded thrilling?"

"Yes." She stood up and gazed into those intelligent,

dark blue eyes. Ignoring the warning flags telling her to be prudent, she said, "I'd absolutely love it."

A stillness surrounded them. "Never let it be said I didn't give you an out."

"I don't want one, even if Vincenzo thought I did."

A tiny nerve throbbed at the side of his hard jaw. "If Max is still sick in the morning, we'll leave around eight-thirty. You'll need to wear jeans and a T-shirt if you brought one. If not, you can wear one of mine."

"I have one."

"Good, but you can't go in sandals."

"I brought my walking boots."

"Perfect."

"I'll see you in the morning then."

As she started to leave, he said, "Don't go yet."

Valentino—I can't spend any more time with you to-night. I just can't! "Your mother is waiting for you and I have things to do. I know the way back to my room."

"Carolena?"

With a pounding heart, she paused at the entrance. "Yes?"

"I enjoyed today more than you know."

Oh, but I do, her heart cried.

"The horseback ride was wonderful. Thank you again." In the next breath she took off for the other wing of the palace. Her efforts to stay away from him weren't working. To see where he spent his time and share it with him was too great a temptation to turn down, but she recognized that the thing she'd prayed would never happen was happening!

She was starting to care about him, way too much.

Forget the guilt over Berto's death that had prevented her from getting close to another man. Her feelings were way too strong for Valentino. Already she was terrified at the thought of handling another loss when she had to fly back to Arancia with Abby and Vincenzo.

But if she said she wasn't feeling well now and begged off going with him tomorrow, he'd never believe her. Though she knew she was walking into emotional danger by getting more involved, she didn't have the strength to say no to him. *Help*.

CHAPTER THREE

LETTING CAROLENA GO when it was the last thing he wanted, Valentino walked through the palace to his mother's suite. The second he entered her sitting room he was met with the news he'd been dreading all his adult life.

While he'd been riding horses with Carolena, his mother had worked out the details of his coming marriage to Princess Alexandra of Cyprus. Both royal families had wanted a June wedding, but he'd asked for more time, hoping for another year of freedom. Unfortunately they'd forced him to settle on August tenth and now there was no possibility of him changing his mind.

Tonight his mother had pinned him down, gaining his promise there'd be no more women. By giving his word, it was as good as writing it in cement.

Ages ago he and Michelina had talked about their arranged marriages. Valentino had intended to be true to Alexandra once their marriage date was set, but he'd told Michelina he planned to live a full life with other women until his time came.

She, on the other hand, never did have the same problem because she'd fallen in love with Vincenzo long before they were married and would never have been unfaithful to him. Vincenzo was a good man who'd kept his marriage vows despite the fact that he didn't feel the same way about her. Valentino admired him more than any man he knew for being the best husband he could under the circumstances.

But after seeing Abby and Vincenzo together while they'd been here, he longed for that kind of love. A huge change had come over Vincenzo once he and Abby had fallen for each other. He was no longer the same man. Valentino could see the passion that leaped between them. Last night he'd witnessed it and knew such a deep envy, he could hardly bear it.

After eight months of marriage their love had grown stronger and deeper. Everyone could see it, his mother most of all. Both she and Valentino had suffered for Michelina. She'd had the misfortune of loving Vincenzo who couldn't love her back in the same way. It would have been better if she hadn't fallen for him, but he couldn't handle thinking about that right now.

The only thing to do where Alexandra was concerned was try to get pregnant soon and build a family the way his own parents had done. Even if the most important element was missing, children would fill a big hole. That's what Michelina had tried to do by going ahead with the surrogacy procedure.

Unfortunately, he hadn't counted on the existence of Carolena Baretti. Her unexpected arrival in Gemelli had knocked him sideways for reasons he hadn't been able to identify yet. Instead of imagining his future life, his thoughts kept running to the gorgeous brunette who was a guest in the other wing of the palace.

Something had happened to him since he'd come upon Abby's friend in the swimming pool that first evening. He'd promised his mother no more women and he'd meant it. But like a lodestone he'd once found on an ancient volcano crater attracting his tools, her unique personality and stunning physical traits had drawn him in.

He'd met many beautiful women in his life, but never one like her. For one thing, she hadn't thrown herself at him. Quite the opposite. That in itself was so rare he found himself attracted on several levels.

Because she was Abby's best friend, she was already in the untouchable category, even if he hadn't promised his mother. Yet this evening, the last thing he'd wanted to do was say good-night to her.

They'd shared a lot today. Intimate things. Her concern for him, the tears she'd shed for his uncle, touched him on a profound level. He'd never met a woman so completely genuine. To his chagrin she made him feel close to her. To his further disgust, he couldn't think beyond having breakfast with her in the morning.

With his blood effectively chilled now that the conversation with his mother was over, he excused himself and called for his car to come around to his private entrance. He told his driver to head for Tancredi's Restaurant on the east end of the island, a twenty-minute drive.

Once on his way, he phoned his best friend from his university days to alert him he was coming. Matteo owned the place since his father had died. He would be partying in the bar with a few of their mutual friends now that there were no more customers.

After the limo turned down the alley behind the restaurant, Matteo emerged from the backdoor and climbed inside.

"Ehi, Valentino—"

"Sorry I'm late, but tonight certain things were unavoidable."

"Non c'è problema! It's still early for us. Come on. We've been waiting for you."

"I'm afraid I can't."

"Ooh. Adriana's not going to like hearing that."

"She's the reason I asked you to come out to the limo. Can I depend on you to put it to her gently that I won't be seeing her again?"

He frowned. "Why not?"

They stared at each other before Matteo let out an epithet. "Does this mean you're finally getting married?" He knew the union had been arranged years ago.

Valentino grimaced. "Afraid so." Once he'd gone to his mother's apartment, she'd forced him to come to a final decision after talking with his betrothed's parents. "They're insisting on an August wedding and coronation. The president of the parliament will announce our formal engagement next week."

He realized it was long past time to end his brief, shallow relationship with Adriana. For her best interest he should have done it a month ago. Instinct told him she would be a willing mistress after his marriage, but Valentino didn't feel that way about her or any woman. In any case, he would never go down that path.

Matteo's features hardened. "I can't believe this day has finally come. It's like a bad dream."

A groan escaped Valentino's throat. "But one I'm committed to. I've told you before, but I'll say it again. You've been a great friend, Matteo. I'll never forget."

"Are you saying goodbye to me, too?" he asked quietly.

His friend's question hurt him. "How can you even ask me that?"

"I don't know." Matteo drove his fist into his other palm. "I knew one day there was going to be a wedding and coronation and I know of your loyalty. Now everything's going to change."

"Not my friendship with you."

"I hope not. It's meant everything to me."

"My father told me a king has no friends, but I'm not the king yet. Even when I am, you'll always be my friend. I'll call you soon." He clapped him on the shoulder before Matteo got out of the limo. Once he'd disappeared inside the restaurant, Valentino told his driver to head back to the palace. But his mood was black.

After a sleepless night he learned that Max wasn't any better, so he followed through on his plans to pick up Carolena at her apartment. He found her outside her door waiting for him. The sight of her in jeans and a T-shirt caused another adrenaline rush.

Her eyes lifted to his. "Is there anything else you can think of I might need before we leave?"

He'd already taken inventory of her gorgeous figure and still hadn't recovered. "We'll be flying to the center in my helicopter. Whatever is missing we will find there."

"Then I'm ready." Carolena shut the suite and followed him down the hallway and out the doors. They crossed the grounds to the pad where his helicopter was waiting. "I hope this isn't a dream and I'm going to wake up in a few minutes. To see where you spend your time kept me awake all night."

Nothing could have pleased Valentino more than to know she was an adventurous woman who'd taken an interest in his research. But he knew in his gut her interest in him went deeper than that. "Perhaps now you'll understand that after a day's work on the volcano, I have trouble getting to sleep, too."

Besides his family and bodyguards, plus close friends like Matteo, he rarely shared his love for his work with anyone outside of his colleagues at the center. For his own protection, the women he'd had relationships with knew nothing about his life.

He'd called ahead to one of the center's pilots who would be taking them up. The helicopter was waiting for them when they touched down.

"Dante Serrano, meet Signorina Carolena Baretti from Arancia. She's the best friend of my brother-in-law's wife. They're staying at the palace with me for a few days. I thought she might like to see Etna at closer range."

The pilot's eyes flared in male admiration and surprise before he shook Carolena's hand and welcomed her aboard. This was a first for Valentino, let alone for Dante, who'd never known Valentino to fly a female with him unless she happened to be a geologist doing work.

He helped her into the seat behind the pilot, then took the copilot's seat. While the rotors whined, he turned to her. "Your first volcano experience should be from the air."

"I'm so excited to be seeing this up close, I can hardly stand it." Her enthusiasm was contagious. "Why does it constantly smoke?"

"That's because it's continually being reshaped by seismic activity. There are four distinct craters at the summit and more than three hundred vents on the flanks. Some are small holes, others are large craters. You'll see things that are invisible or look completely different from the surface."

"You're so right!" she cried after they took off. Once they left Catania, they passed over the fertile hillsides and lush pines. "The vistas are breathtaking, Val. With the Mediterranean for a background, these snow-topped mountains are fabulous. I didn't expect to see so much green and blue."

Her reaction, on top of her beautiful face, made it impossible for Valentino to look anywhere else. "It's a universe all its own."

'I can't believe what I'm seeing.'

The landscape changed as they flew higher and higher. "We're coming up on some black lava deserts. Take a good look. Mount Etna is spitting lava more violently than it has in years, baffling us. Not only is it unpredictable, the volcano is raging, erupting in rapid succession."

He loved her awestruck squeals of delight. "I suppose you've walked across those deserts."

"I've climbed all over this volcano with Uncle Stefano."

"No wonder you love your work so much! I would, too!"

"The range of ash fall is much wider than usual. That's why I always come home dirty."

"Now I understand. Come to think of it, you did look like you'd been putting out a fire."

Dante shared a grin with Valentino. "Signorina Baretti," He spoke over his shoulder. "Even in ancient times, the locals marveled at the forces capable of shooting fountains of lava into the sky. In Greek and Roman mythology, the volcano is represented by a limping blacksmith swinging his hammer as sparks fly.

"Legend has it that the natural philosopher Empedocles jumped into the crater two thousand five hundred years ago. What he found there remained his secret because he never returned. All that remained of him were his iron shoes, which the mountain later spat out."

"That's a wonderful story, if not frightening."

All three of them laughed.

"The really fascinating part is coming up. We're headed for the Bove Valley, Etna's huge caldera. You're going to get a bird's-eye view of the eastern slope." They flew on with Dante giving her the full treatment of the famous volcano that produced more stunned cries from Carolena.

"How big is it?"

"Seven kilometers from east to west, six kilometers from north to south."

She was glued to the window, mesmerized. Valentino knew how she felt. He signaled Dante to fly them to Bocca Nuova.

"When we set down on the side of the pit, you'll see a new fumarole in the saddle between the old and new southeast crater. I want you to stay by me. This is where I was working the other day. You won't need a gas mask at this distance, but you can understand why I want every citizen of Gemelli to be equipped with one."

"After seeing this and hearing about your uncle Stefano, I understand your concern, believe me."

Before long, he helped her out and they walked fifty yards to a vantage point. "This is a place no one is allowed except our teams. The organized tours of the thousands of people who came to Etna are much farther below."

Soon they saw the vent releasing the same bluish gas and ash he'd recorded the other day.

"This fumarole was formed by that long fissure you can see."

While they stood there gazing, the noise of explosions coming from deep within the volcano shook the ground. When she cried out, he automatically put his arm around her shoulders and pulled her tight against his side. He liked the feel of her womanly body this close.

"Don't be alarmed," he murmured into her fragrant hair. "We're safe or I wouldn't have brought you up here."

She clung to him. "I know that, but I have to tell you a secret. I never felt insignificant until now." Those were his very thoughts the first time he'd come up on Etna. After a long silence, she lifted her eyes to him. In them he saw a longing for him that she couldn't hide when she said, "It's awesome and mind blowing all at the same time."

Those dazzling, dark-fringed green eyes blew him away, but not for the reasons she'd been alluding to. He was terrified over the feelings he'd developed for her. "You've taken the words right out of my mouth."

The desire to kiss her was so powerful, it took all the self-control he possessed not to crush her against him. He was in serious trouble and knew it.

Fighting his desire, he said, "I think you've seen enough for today. We've been gone a long time and need to eat. Another day and I'll take you on a hike through some lava fields and tunnels you'll find captivating." *Almost as captivating as I'm finding you.*

"I doubt I'll ever be in Gemelli again, but if I am, I'll certainly take you up on your offer. Thank you for a day I'll never *ever* forget." He felt her tremulous voice shake his insides.

"Nor will I." The fact that she was off-limits had no meaning to him right now.

On their way back to the center, he checked his phone messages. One from Vincenzo and two from his mother. He checked Vincenzo's first.

I'm just giving you a heads-up. Max isn't doing well, so we're flying back to Arancia at nine in the morning. Sorry about this, but the doctor thinks he may have gas-

troenteritis and wants to check him out at the hospital.
Give me a call when you're available.

Valentino's lips thinned. He was sorry about the
baby, but it meant Carolena would be leaving in the
morning.

The queen's first message told him she was upset
they were going to have to leave with her grandson.
She was crazy about Max and her reaction was under-
standable. Her second message had to do with wedding
preparations. Since he couldn't do anything about either situation at the moment, he decided to concentrate
on Carolena, who would be slipping away from his life
much sooner than he'd anticipated.

Once they touched down at the center and had
thanked Dante for the wonderful trip, they climbed on
board Valentino's helicopter. But instead of flying back
to the palace where his mother expected him to join her
the second he got back, he instructed his pilot to land
on the royal yacht anchored in the bay. They could have
dinner on board away from the public eye.

Carolena was a very special VIP and the crew would
think nothing of his entertaining the close friend of his
new sister-in-law who was here with the prince of Arancia visiting the queen.

He called ahead to arrange for their meal to be served
on deck. After they arrived on board and freshened
up, they sat down to dinner accompanied by soft rock
music as the sun disappeared below the horizon. Both
of them had developed an appetite. Valentino loved it
that she ate with enjoyment.

"Try the Insolia wine. It has a slightly nutty flavor

with a finish that is a combination of sweet fruit and sour citrus. I think it goes well with swordfish."

"It definitely does, and the steak is out of this world, Val. Everything here in Gemelli is out of this world."

From the deck they could see Etna smoking in the far distance. She kept looking at it. "To think I flew over that volcano today and saw a fumarole up close." Her gaze swerved to his. "Nothing I'll ever do in life will match the wonder of this day, and it's all because of you."

He sipped his wine. "So the surprise didn't turn out to be so bad, after all."

"You know it didn't." Her voice throbbed, revealing her emotion. "I can't think why Vincenzo warned me against it. Unless—"

When she didn't finish, he said, "Unless what?"

"Maybe watching Michelina when she had her riding accident has made him more cautious than usual over the people he loves and cares about. Last night I could tell how worried he was about Max."

Valentino hadn't thought of that, but he couldn't rule it out as a possibility, though he didn't think it was Vincenzo's major concern. Now that they were talking about it, his conversation at dinner with Vincenzo in front of her came back to haunt him.

He'd been warning Valentino, but maybe not about the volcano. Unfortunately, Vincenzo had always been a quick study. Possibly he'd picked up on Valentino's interest in Carolena. Whatever had gone on in Vincenzo's mind, now was the time to tell her about the change in their plans to fly back to Arancia.

"I checked my voice mail on the way to the yacht. You can listen." He pulled his cell phone from his pocket and let her hear Vincenzo's message.

In an instant everything changed, as he knew it would. "The poor darling. It's a good thing we're going home in the morning. I'm sure Max will be all right, but after no sleep, all three of them have to be absolutely miserable."

Make that an even four.

The idea of Carolena leaving Gemelli filled him with a sense of loss he'd never experienced before. The deaths of his father and sister were different. It didn't matter that he'd only known her twenty-four hours. To never be with her again was anathema to him.

He could have predicted what she'd say next. "We'd better get back to the palace. I need to pack."

"Let's have our dessert first. You have to try *cassata alla sicilana*." Anything to prolong their time together.

"Isn't that a form of cheesecake?"

"Cake like you've never tasted anywhere else."

An impish smile broke one corner of her voluptuous mouth. "Something tells me you're a man who loves his sweets."

"Why do you think that?"

"I don't know. Maybe it's because of the way you embrace life to the fullest and enjoy its richness while at the same time reverencing it. When the gods handed out gifts, you received more than your fair share."

He frowned. "What do you mean?"

"There aren't many men who could measure up to

you. Your sister used to sing your praises to Abby, who said she worshipped you."

"The feeling was mutual, believe me."

"According to Abby, Michelina admitted that the only man who came close to you was Prince Vincenzo. That's high praise indeed. Luckily for your country, you're going to be in charge one day."

One day? That day was almost upon him!

For the wedding date to have been fixed at the same time he'd met Signorina Baretti, the pit in Valentino's stomach had already grown into a caldera bigger than the one he'd shown her today.

He'd spun out every bit of time with her he could squeeze and had no legitimate choice but to take her back to the palace.

"It's getting late. I'm sure Vincenzo will want to talk to you tonight."

Valentino shook his head. "With the baby sick, that won't be happening." In truth, he wasn't up to conversation with Vincenzo or his mother. For the first time in his life he had the wicked instinct to do what he wanted and kidnap this woman who'd beguiled him.

"I have a better idea. It's been a long day. We'll stay on the yacht and fly you back on time in the morning. I'll instruct the maid to pack your things. As for tonight, anything you need we have on board."

Carolena's breath caught. "What about your girlfriend? Won't she be expecting you?"

His dark blue eyes narrowed on her face. "Not when I'm entertaining family and friends. As for the other question you don't dare ask, I've never brought a woman on board the yacht or taken one up on the volcano."

He'd been so frank and honest with her today, she believed him now. His admission shook her to her core. "If I didn't know better, I would think you were propositioning me," she teased to cover her chaotic emotions. There she went again. Saying something she shouldn't have allowed to escape her lips.

His jaw hardened. "I'm a man before being a prince and I *am* propositioning you, but I can see I've shocked you as much as myself."

She could swear that was truth she'd heard come out of him. Carolena was Abby's friend, yet that hadn't stopped him, and obviously that fact wasn't stopping her. It was as if they were both caught in a snare of such intense attraction, they knew no boundaries.

"Do you want to know something else?" he murmured. "I can see in those glorious green eyes of yours that you'd like to stay on board with me tonight. True desire is something you can't hide. We've both felt it since we met, so there's no use denying it."

"I'm not," she confessed in a tremulous voice. Carolena could feel her defenses crumbling and started to tremble. Never had she been around a man who'd made her feel so completely alive.

"My kingdom for an honest woman, and here you are."

"Only you and Vincenzo could say such a thing and get away with it."

Her humor didn't seem to touch him. "Tell me about

the man who died. You *were* speaking about a man. Are you still terribly in love with him?"

His question reached the core of her being. "I'll always love him," she answered honestly.

He reached across the table and grasped her hand. "How long has he been gone?"

She couldn't lie to him. "Seven years."

After a moment of quiet, he said, "That's a long time to be in love with a memory. How did he die?"

"It doesn't matter. I don't want to talk about it."

Those all-seeing eyes of his gazed through to her soul. "Yet somehow you still feel responsible for his death?"

"Yes."

"Has it prevented you from getting close to another man?"

"I've been with other men since he died, if that's what you mean."

"Carolena—tell me the truth. Is there one man who's vitally important to you now?"

Yes. But he's not in Arancia.

"No one man more than another," she dissembled.

She heard his sharp intake of breath. "Then do you dare stay with me the way you dared to get close to Etna's furnace today? I'm curious to see how brave a woman you really are."

His thumb massaged her palm, sending warmth through her sensitized body until her toes curled. "You already know the answer to that."

"Dance with me, *bellissima,*" he begged in a husky

whisper. "I don't give a damn that the crew can see us. You've entranced me and I need to feel you in my arms."

It was what she wanted, too. When she'd heard Vincenzo say that they were leaving in the morning, she'd wanted to cry out in protest that she'd only gotten here. She hadn't had enough time with Valentino. *Not nearly enough.*

He got up from the table and drew her into his arms. She went into them eagerly, aching for this since the time he'd put his arm around her up on the volcano. It felt as if their bodies were meant for each other. She slid her arms around his neck until there was no air between them. They clung out of need in the balmy night air that enveloped them like velvet.

His hands roved over her back and hips as they got a new sense of each other only touch could satisfy. They slow danced until she lost track of time. To hold and be held by this amazing man was a kind of heaven.

She knew he was unattainable. Abby had told her he'd been betrothed to Princess Alexandra in his teens, just like Vincenzo's betrothal to Princess Michelina. One day Valentino would have to marry. He'd explained all that yesterday.

Carolena understood that. It didn't bother her since she shunned the idea of commitment that would lead to her own marriage. Marriage meant being responsible for another person's happiness. She couldn't handle that, but selfishly she did desire this one night with Valentino before she flew back to Arancia and never saw him again.

Tonight he'd made her thankful she'd been born a

woman. Knowing he wanted her as much as she wanted him brought indescribable joy. One night with him would have to be enough, except that he still hadn't kissed her yet and she was dying for it. When he suddenly stopped moving, she moaned in disappointment.

His hands squeezed her upper arms. "The steward will show you downstairs to your cabin," he whispered before pulling the phone from his pocket. "I'll join you shortly."

Carolena was so far gone she'd forgotten about the prying eyes of the crew, but Valentino was used to the whole world watching him and did what was necessary to keep gossip to a minimum. Without words she eased away from him and walked over to the table for her purse before following the steward across the deck to the stairs.

The luxury yacht was a marvel, but Carolena was too filled with desire for Valentino to notice much of anything. Once she reached the cabin and the steward left, she took a quick shower and slipped into one of the white toweling bathrobes hanging on a hook. The dressing room provided every cosmetic and convenience a man or woman could need.

She sat in front of the mirror and brushed her hair. *Entranced* was the right word. Though she knew she'd remain single all her life, she felt as if this was her wedding night while she waited for him to come. The second he entered the room he would hear the fierce pounding of her heart.

Soon she heard his rap on the door. "Come in," she called quietly. He walked in and shut the door behind him, still dressed in the clothes he'd worn during their trip.

Without saying anything, he reached for her hand and drew her over to the bed where he sat down and pulled her between his legs. His gaze glowed like hot blue embers. Everywhere it touched, she was set on fire. Her ears picked up the ragged sound of his breathing.

"You look like a bride."

But, of course, she wasn't a bride, and she sensed something was wrong. She could feel it. "Is that good or bad?"

He ran his hands up and down her arms beneath the loose sleeves of her robe as if even his fingers were hungry for her. "Carolena—" There was an unmistakable plea for understanding in his tone.

"Yes?" Whatever was coming, she knew she wasn't going to like it.

"I talked frankly with you yesterday about my personal life. But what you couldn't know was that last night after you went back to your room, I met with my mother." His chest rose and fell visibly. "While you and I were out riding, my wedding date to Princess Alexandra was finally set in stone. We're being married on August tenth, the day of my coronation."

Carolena stood stock-still while the news sank in. That was only two months from now...

"Though I made the promise to my mother that I'd be faithful to Alexandra from here on out, I really made it to myself and have already gotten word to my latest girlfriend that it's over for good."

She could hardly credit what she was hearing.

"But little did I know I was already being tested by none other than Abby's best friend."

A small cry escaped her throat. "I shouldn't have come, but Abby kept insisting." She shivered. "This is all my fault, Val."

"There you go again, taking on blame for something that's no one's fault. If we were to follow that line of thinking, shall I blame myself for inviting Vincenzo to come on this trip? Shall we blame him for bringing his wife and her best friend?"

His logic made Carolena feel like a fool. "Of course not."

"At least you admit that much. In my whole life I've never wanted a woman more than I've wanted you, since the moment we met at the swimming pool. But it's more than that now. Much more."

"I know. I feel it, too." But she remained dry eyed and smiled at him. "The gods are jealous of you. They're waiting for you to make a mistake. Didn't you know that?"

He squeezed her hands gently. "When I dared you to stay with me tonight, I crossed a line I swore I would never do."

"I believe you. But the fact is, it takes two, Val. I didn't know your wedding date had been set, of course. Yet even knowing you were betrothed, I crossed it, too, because I've never known desire like this before, either. I've never had an affair before."

"Carolena..."

He said her name with such longing, she couldn't stand it. "Let's not make this situation any more impossible. Go back to the palace tonight knowing you've passed your test."

"And leave you like this?" he cried urgently, pulling her closer to him. "You don't really mean that!"

"Yes. I do. You have Vincenzo to think about, and a mother who's waiting for your return. Your wedding's going to take place soon. You need to concentrate on Alexandra now."

But she knew he wasn't listening. He got to his feet, cupping her face in his hands. "I don't want to leave you." He sounded as if he was in agony. "Say the word and I won't."

Abby could hear her grandmother's voice. *You go where angels fear to tread without worrying about anyone else but yourself.*

Not this time, *nonnina.*

"Thank you for your honesty. It's one of your most sterling qualities. You truly are the honorable man your sister idolized. But I have enough sins on my conscience without helping you add one to yours."

His brows formed a bar above his eyes. "You told me you caused the death of the man you loved, but you also said it wasn't intentional."

She averted her eyes. "It wasn't."

"Then no sin has been committed."

"Not if we part now. I don't want you going through life despising yourself for breaking the rule you've set. Believe it or not, I *want* you to go, Val," she told him. "After the promise you made to your parents when your uncle died, I couldn't handle it otherwise."

"Handle what? You're still holding back on me. Tell me what it is."

"It's no longer of any importance."

"Carolena—"

He was willing to break his vow for her because he wanted her that much. Just knowing that helped her to stay strong. But he didn't realize all this had to do with her self-preservation.

"Val, if it's all right with you, I'd like to remain on board until tomorrow morning and then fly back to the palace. But please know that when I leave Gemelli, I'll take home the memory of a man who for a moment out of time made me feel immortal. I'll treasure the memory of you all my life."

She pulled away from him and walked over to the door to open it. *"Addio,* sweet prince."

CHAPTER FOUR

THE MOMENT VALENTINO walked into the palace at eleven that night, he texted Vincenzo, who was still up. They met in Valentino's suite.

"How did your day go?" his brother-in-law asked after he'd walked into the sitting room.

Valentino was still on fire for the woman who'd looked like a vision when he'd walked into her cabin.

"After we left Etna, I thought Carolena would like dinner on the yacht where there's a wonderful view of the island. She's staying there overnight. My pilot will fly her back in the morning. You should have seen her when we got out of the helicopter and walked over to view one of the fumaroles. She was one person who really appreciated the experience."

"Michelina would never step foot on Etna and was always afraid for you. Sorry about this morning. I guess I thought it might frighten Carolena."

Valentino had forgotten about his sister's fear. It showed how totally concentrated he'd been on Carolena. "If she was, she hid it well. Now I want to hear about Max. How is he?"

"For the moment both he and Abby are asleep. It'll be a relief to get him home. After the doctor tells us what's wrong and we can relax, I'd like it if you could arrange to fly to Arancia so we can talk business."

He nodded. "I'm as anxious as you to get started on the idea we've discussed. I'll clear my calendar." It would mean seeing Carolena again. He was going to get the truth out of her one way or another.

"Abby thinks Carolena would be a good person to consult over the legalities of the plans we have in mind. Did I mention her expertise is patent law? It's exactly what we need."

She was a patent attorney? Valentino's heart leaped to think he didn't need to find an excuse to see her again when he had a legitimate reason to be with her before long. On his way to the palace, he'd come close to telling the pilot he'd changed his mind and wanted to go back to the yacht.

"Valentino? Did you hear what I said?"

"Sorry. The news about her work in patent law took me by surprise. Abby and Carolena are both intelligent women. With them being such close friends and attorneys, it will be a pleasure to have them consult with us. I've worried about finding someone we could really trust."

"Amen to that. We don't want anyone else to get wind of this until it's a fait accompli," Vincenzo muttered. "Abby asked me to thank you for taking such good care of Carolena today."

If he only knew how dangerously close Valentino had come to making love to her. Once that happened, there'd be no going back because he knew in his gut he'd want her over and over again. That would jeopardize both their lives and put them in a different kind of hell.

"It's always a rush to go up on Etna with someone who finds it as fascinating as I do."

"She really liked it?"

"I wish I had a recording while we were in the air."

Vincenzo smiled. "That'll make Abby happy. She brought Carolena along because seven years ago yesterday her fiancé was killed days before she became a bride. Apparently this date in June is always hard for her. They were very much in love."

Fiancé?

Valentino's gut twisted in deepest turmoil when he remembered telling her she looked like a bride. More than ever he was determined to find out what kind of guilt she'd been carrying around all this time.

"Abby says she dates one man after another, but it's only once or twice, never really getting to know anyone well. She believes she's depressed and is pretty worried about her. Abby was hoping this trip would help her get out of herself. Sounds like your day on the volcano may have done just that."

The revelations coming one after the other hit Valentino like a volcanic bomb during an eruption.

"I hope so."

"I'd better get back to our suite. It'll be my turn to walk the floor with Max when he wakes up again. My poor wife is worn out."

"From the looks of it, so are you." He patted Vincenzo on the shoulder before walking him to the door.

"I'll have breakfast sent to your suite at eight. Carolena will be waiting for you on the helicopter."

"Thanks for everything, Valentino."

"The queen says this will pass. She ought to know after raising me and my siblings. See you in the morning."

After his brother-in-law left, Valentino raced out of the palace to the swimming pool. He did laps until he was so exhausted he figured he might be able to sleep for what was left of the rest of the night. But that turned out to be a joke. There were certain fires you couldn't put out.

The next morning when he walked out to the landing pad with Vincenzo and his family, Carolena was still strapped in her seat. One of his security men put the luggage from her room on board as he climbed in.

Other than a smile and another thank-you for the tour of the volcano, she displayed no evidence of having missed Valentino or passing a tormented night. They were both accomplished actors playing roles with such expertise they might even have deceived each other. Except for the slight break he heard in her voice that caused his heart to skip several beats.

Four days later Carolena had just finished taking a deposition in her office and had said goodbye to her client when her new secretary, Tomaso, told her Abby was on the line. She hoped it was good news about the baby and picked up.

"Abby? How are you? How's Max?"

"He's doing great. The gastroenteritis is finally gone."

"Thank heaven!"

"I feel so terrible about what happened on our trip."

"Why do you say that? I was sorry for you, of course, but I had a wonderful time!"

"You're always such a good sport. I know it made Valentino's day for someone to be excited about his work."

"He's an incredible man, Abby." Carolena tried to keep the tremor out of her voice.

"He was impressed with you, too. That's one of the reasons I'm calling. He flew into Arancia this morning so he and Vincenzo can talk business."

She almost had heart failure. It was a good thing she was sitting down. Valentino was here?

"Since you're a patent law attorney, both men want you to meet with them. They need your legal counsel along with mine."

Her pulse raced off the chart. "Why?" She'd thought she'd never see him again and had been in such a depression, she'd decided that if she didn't get over it, she would have to go for professional help.

"They're putting together a monumental idea to benefit both our countries. I'll tell you all about it when you get here. Can you come to the palace after work? The four of us will talk and have dinner together."

Carolena jumped up from her leather chair. No, no, no. She didn't dare put herself into a position like that again. Legitimate or not, Valentino had to know how hard this was going to be for her. She didn't have his self-control.

If for any reason she happened to end up alone with him tonight, she might beg him to let her spend the night because she couldn't help herself. How wicked would that be? She'd spend the rest of her life mourning another loss because there could never be another time with him. This was one time Carolena couldn't do what Abby was asking.

"I'm afraid I can't."

"Why not?"

"I have a date for the symphony."

"Then cancel it. I just found out this morning that Valentino is rushed for time. Did I tell you his wedding and coronation are coming up in August?"

She bit her lip. "No. I don't believe you mentioned it."

"He'd hoped to get this business settled before flying back to Gemelli tomorrow."

Here today, gone tomorrow? She couldn't bear it. This request had put her in an untenable position. What to do so she wouldn't offend her friend? After racking her brain, she came up with one solution that might work. It would *have* to work since Carolena didn't dare make a wrong move now.

She gripped the phone tighter. "I have an idea that won't waste Valentino's time. Would it be possible if you three came to the office this afternoon?" Neutral ground rather than the palace was the only way for her to stay out of temptation's way.

"I'm afraid not. It would require too much security for the two of them to meet anywhere else. The security risk is higher than usual with Valentino's coronation coming up soon. How would it be if you cleared your slate for this afternoon and came to the palace? Say two o'clock?"

By now Carolena was trembling.

"We'll talk and eat out by the pool. If you leave the palace by six-thirty, you'll be in time for your date."

Carolena panicked. "I'd have to juggle some appointments." That was another lie. "I don't know if Signor Faustino will let me. I'm working on a big case."

"Bigger than the one for the princes of two countries?" Abby teased.

Her friend had put her on the royal spot. The writing was on the wall. "I—I'll arrange it." Her voice faltered.

"Perfect. The limo will pick you up at the office at one forty-five. Come right out to the terrace by the pool after you arrive."

"All right," she whispered before hanging up.

In an hour and a half Carolena would be seeing Valentino again. Already she had this suffocating feeling in her chest. It was a good thing she had another client to take up her time before the limo came for her. When she left the office she'd tell Tomaso she was going out for a business lunch with a client, which was only the truth.

Luckily she'd worn her sleeveless black designer shift dress with the crew neck and black belt to work. She'd matched the outfit with black heels. There was no need to do anything about her hair. All she had to do was touch up her makeup. When she showed up at the palace, it would carry out the lie that she'd be going to the symphony later.

Valentino had just finished some laps in the pool when he saw Carolena walk past the garden toward them in a stunning, formfitting black dress. Only a woman with her figure could wear it. Abby had told him she was going to the symphony later with a man.

She'd parted her hair in the middle above her forehead and had swept a small braid from each side around to the back, leaving her dark hair long. Two-tiered silvery earrings dangled between the strands. He did a somersault off the wall of the pool to smother his gasp.

If he'd hoped that she wouldn't look as good to him after four days, he could forget that! The trick would be to keep his eyes off her while they tried to do business. While Abby laid out their lunch beneath the overhang, Vincenzo sat at one of the tables working on his laptop. Both of them wore beach robes over their swimsuits. Max was down for a nap in the nursery.

She headed for Abby. A low whistle came out of Vincenzo and he got up to greet her. "I've never seen you looking lovelier, Carolena."

"Thank you," she said as the two women hugged.

Valentino climbed out of the shallow end of the pool and threw on a beach cover-up. "We're grateful you could come this afternoon."

Carolena shot him a brief glance. "It's very nice to see you again, Val. Signor Faustino was thrilled when he found out where I was going. Needless to say, he considers it the coup of the century that I've been summoned to help the princes of Gemelli and Arancia with a legal problem."

Abby was all smiles. "Knowing him, he'll probably make you senior partner at their next meeting."

"Don't wish that on me!" That sounded final.

Valentino moved closer. "You mean, it isn't your dream?"

"Definitely not." She seemed so composed, but it was deceiving, because he saw a nerve throbbing frantically at the base of her throat where he longed to kiss her.

He smiled. "Our conversation on the deck of the yacht was cut short and didn't give us time to cover your dreams before I had to leave."

Being out of the sun, she couldn't blame it for the rose blush that crept into her face. "As I recall, we were discussing *your* dreams for Gemelli, Val."

Touché. But his unrealized personal dream that had lain dormant deep in his soul since his cognizance of life was another matter altogether.

"In truth, I hope to make enough money from the law practice that one day in the future I can buy back my grandparents' small farm and work it." Her green eyes clouded for a moment. "I'm a farmer's daughter at heart."

"I understand your parents are not alive."

"No, nor are my grandparents. Their farm was sold. There have been Barettis in Arancia for almost a hundred years. I'm the only Baretti left and want to keep up the tradition by buying the place back."

Had her fiancé been a farmer, too? Valentino knew a moment of jealousy that she'd loved someone else enough to create such a powerful emotion in her.

"I had no idea," he murmured, "but since it's in your blood, that makes you doubly valuable for the task at hand." His mind was teeming with new ideas to keep her close to him.

"Abby said you and Vincenzo were planning something monumental for both your countries. I confess I'm intrigued."

"Hey, you two," Abby called to them. "Come and help yourselves to lunch first, then we'll get down to business."

He followed Carolena to the serving table. After they'd filled their plates, they sat down at one of the round tables where the maid poured them iced tea. Once they'd started eating, he said, "Vincenzo? Why don't you lay the groundwork for the women and we'll go from there."

"Our two countries have a growing problem because of the way they are situated on coastal waters. We all know the land around the Mediterranean is one of the most coveted terrains on earth. Over the years, our prime properties of orange and lemon groves that have sustained our economies for centuries have been shrinking due to man's progress. Our farmers are being inundated with huge sums of money to sell their land so it can be developed for commercial tourism."

"I know that's true," Carolena commented. "My grandfather was approached many times to sell, but he wouldn't do it."

Vincenzo nodded. "He's the type of traditional farmer fighting a battle to hold on to his heritage. Farmers are losing their workers, who want to go to the city. In the process, we're losing a vital and precious resource that has caused Valentino and me to lose sleep. Something has to be done to stop the trend and rebuild the greatness of what we've always stood for. We've come up with an idea to help our farmers by giving them a new incentive. You tell them, Valentino."

Carolena's gaze swerved to him. He could tell Vincenzo had grabbed the women's attention.

"We need to compete with other countries to increase our exports to fill the needs of a growing world market and build our economies here at home. The lemons of Arancia are highly valued because of their low acidity and delicate flavor.

"Likewise the blood oranges of Gemelli are sought after for their red flesh and deep red juice. The juice is exceptionally healthy, being rich in antioxidants. What we're proposing is to patent our fruit in a joint venture so we can grow an enviable exporting business.

"With a unique logo and marketing strategy, we can put our citrus fruits front and center in the world market. When the buyer sees it, they'll know they're getting authentic fruit from our regions alone and clamor for it."

"That's a wonderful idea," Carolena exclaimed. "You would need to be filed as a Consortium for the Promotion of the Arancian Lemon and the Gemellian Blood Orange. The IGP logo will be the official acknowledgment that the lemons and oranges were grown in your territories according to the traditional rules."

Vincenzo leaned forward. "That's exactly what we're striving for. With the right marketing techniques, the citrus business should start to flourish again. We'll come up with a name for the logo."

"That's easy," Abby volunteered. "AG. Two tiny letters stamped on each fruit. You'll have to make a video that could be distributed to every country where you want to introduce your brand."

Bless you, Abby. She was reading Valentino's mind. He needed more time alone with Carolena to talk about their lives. Abby had just given him the perfect excuse. He exchanged glances with Vincenzo before he looked at Carolena.

"The right video would sell the idea quickly, but we need a spokesperson doing the video to put it across. You'd be the perfect person for several reasons, Carolena."

"Oh, no." He saw the fear in her eyes and knew exactly what put it there, but he couldn't help himself. What he felt for Carolena was stronger than anything he'd ever known.

"You have the looks and education to sell our idea," Valentino persisted. "We'll start in Gemelli with you traveling around to some of the orange groves. With a farming background that dates back close to a century, you'll be the perfect person to talk to the owners."

Valentino could tell by the way Vincenzo smiled at Carolena that he loved the idea. His friend said, "After you've finished there, we'll have you do the same thing here in Arancia with our lemon farmers. We'll put the video on television in both countries. People will say, 'That's the beautiful Signorina Baretti advertising the AG logo.' You'll be famous."

She shook her head. "I don't want to be famous."

"You get used to it," Valentino quipped. "While you're in Gemelli, you'll stay at the palace and have full security when you travel around with the film crew.

I'll clear my calendar while you're there so I can be on hand. The sooner we get started, the better. How long will it take you to put your affairs in order and fly down?"

"But—"

"It'll be fun," Abby spoke up with enthusiasm. "I can't think of another person who could do this."

"Naturally you'll be compensated, Carolena," Vincenzo added. "After coming to the aid of our two countries, you'll make enough money to buy back your grandparents' farm, if that's what you want."

She got up from the chair on the pretense of getting herself another helping of food. "You're all very flattering and generous, but I need time to think about it."

Valentino stared up at her. "Do that while you're at the symphony tonight with your date, and we'll contact you in the morning for your answer." He could swear she didn't really have plans. She proved it when she looked away from him.

Forcing himself to calm down, he checked his watch. "Since we have several hours before you have to leave in the limo, I suggest we get to work on a script. Perhaps the video could start with you showing us your old farm. It will capture everyone's interest immediately. We'll shoot that segment later."

"It's a beautiful place!" Abby cried. "You'll do it, right?" she pleaded with her friend. "You've worked nonstop since law school. It's time you had some fun along with your work. Your boss, Signor Faustino, will get down on his knees to you."

Vincenzo joined in. "I'll have you flown down on the jet."

Valentino found himself holding his breath.

You go where angels fear to tread, Carolena.

The words pummeled her as the royal jet started its descent to Gemelli's airport. As she saw the smoke of Etna out of the window, memories of that glorious day and evening with Valentino clutched at her heart.

She'd be seeing him in a few minutes. If this offer to do the video had been Valentino's wish alone, she would have turned him down. But the excitement and pleading coming from both Abby and Vincenzo two days ago had caused her to cave. Deep down she knew a great deal was riding on this project for their two countries.

After another sleepless night because of Valentino, she'd phoned Abby the next morning to tell her she'd do it. But her friend had no idea of her fatal attraction to him.

It *was* fatal and Valentino knew it. But he was bound by a code of honor and so was she. If she worked hard, the taping could be done in a couple of days and she could go back to Arancia for good.

One of Valentino's staff greeted the plane and walked her to her old room, where she was once again installed. He lowered her suitcase to the parquet floor. "In forty five minutes His Highness will be outside in the limo waiting to take you for a tour of some orange groves. In the meantime, a lunch tray has been provided for you."

"Thank you."

After quickly getting settled, she ate and changed

into jeans and a blouson, the kind of outfit she used to wear on her grandparents' farm. Earlier that morning she'd put her hair in a braid to keep it out of her way. On her feet she wore sensible walking boots. Inside her tote bag she carried a copy of the script, which she'd read over many times.

Before walking out the door, she reached for it and for her grandmother's broad-brimmed straw hat she'd always worn to keep out the sun. Armed with what she'd need, she left the room for the limo waiting out at the side entrance of the palace.

When she walked through the doors, Valentino broke away from the driver he'd been talking to and helped her into the limo. The sun shone from a blue sky. It was an incredible summer day. Once inside, he shut the door and sat across from her wearing a navy polo shirt and jeans. He looked and smelled too marvelous for words.

Within a minute they left the palace grounds and headed for the outskirts of the city. "I've been living for you to arrive," he confessed in his deep voice. "How was the symphony?"

His unexpected question threw her. "Wonderful."

"That's interesting. I found out it wasn't playing that night, nor did you go to dinner with your boyfriend. In case you were wondering, the limo driver informed Vincenzo you told him to take you back to your apartment. Why manufacture an excuse?"

Heat rushed to her face. "I'm sure you know the reason."

"You mean that you were afraid you might end up alone with me that evening?"

"I thought it could be a possibility and decided to err on the side of caution."

"Once I overheard Vincenzo tell Abby about your fictional evening out, you don't know how close I came to showing up at your apartment that night."

This wasn't going to work. The longing for him made her physically weak. "Does your mother know you flew me up on Etna?" she blurted.

"She has her spies. It's part of the game. That's why I didn't attack you on the deck of the yacht."

"But we danced for a long time."

He leaned forward. "Dancing is one thing, but the steward would have told her I didn't spend the night with you. In fact, I wasn't in your room more than a few minutes."

"She's no one's fool, Val."

"What can I say?" He flashed her a brief smile. "She's my mother. When she thought you'd gone out of my life by flying back to Arancia with Abby and Vincenzo, no doubt she was relieved. But now that you're here again so soon, she knows my interest in you goes deeper than mere physical attraction."

"With your marriage looming on the horizon, she has every right to be upset."

"That's a mother's prerogative. For that, I apologize."

Valentino's life truly wasn't his own. Every move he made was monitored. Only now was she beginning to appreciate how difficult it must have been for him growing up, but she couldn't worry about that right now. She had a job to do. The sooner she got to it, the sooner she could fly back to Arancia. *Away from him.*

The surrounding countryside basked under a heavenly sun. They came to the first grove where the trees were planted in rows, making up football-pitch-length orchards. She watched men and women in blue overalls go from tree to tree, quickly working their way up and down ladders to fill plastic crates with the brightly colored produce. It brought back memories from her past.

The limo pulled to a stop. "We'll get out and walk from here."

He opened the door to help her. With a shaky hand she reached for her hat. The moment she climbed out, the citrus smell from the many hectares of orange groves filled her senses.

Valentino's dark blue eyes played over her face and figure with a hunger that brought the blood to her cheeks. When she put the hat on her head, he felt the rim of it. "I like that touch of authenticity."

"It was my grandmother's. I thought I'd wear it to bring me luck." Maybe it would help her to keep her wits. But already she was suffering from euphoria she shouldn't be feeling. It was because they were together again. For a while, happiness drove away her fears as they began walking toward the *masseria,* the typical farmhouse in the area.

"As you can see, the groves here have a unique microclimate provided by the brooding volcano of Etna. Warm days and cool nights allow us to produce what we feel are the best blood oranges in the world."

"You ought to be the one on the video, Val. I can hear your love of this island in your voice."

"Yet anyone will tell you a beautiful woman is much more exciting to look at."

Not from her vantage point. Valentino was drop-dead gorgeous. Abby had said as much about Michelina's older brother before Carolena had ever even seen a picture of him.

Several of the security men went on ahead to bring the grove owner to her and Valentino. The man and his son were delighted to be interviewed and would have talked for hours. No problem for them to be part of the video.

After saying goodbye, they drove on to the next orange grove, then the next, stopping for a midafternoon lunch brought from the palace kitchen. Six stops later they'd reached the eastern end of the island. Already it was evening. They'd been so busy, she hadn't realized how much time had passed.

Carolena gave him a covert glance. "There wasn't one farmer who didn't want to be a part of your plan to keep people on the farms and grow more profits."

He sat back in the seat looking relaxed, with his arms stretched out on either side of him. "You charmed everyone. Being a farmer's daughter and granddaughter got them to open right up and express their concerns. I marveled at the way you were able to answer their questions and give them the vision of what we're trying to do."

"I had a script. You didn't. Give yourself the credit you deserve, Val. They fell over themselves with joy to think their prince cares enough about the farmers to honor them with a personal visit. Securing their future secures the entire country and they know it."

"I believe Vincenzo and I are onto something, Carolena, and you're going to be the person who puts this marketing strategy over. After a hard day's work, this calls for a relaxing dinner. I've told the driver to take us to a restaurant here on the water where we can be private and enjoy ourselves. I called ahead to place our order."

This was the part she was worried about. "I think we should go back to the palace."

"You're worrying about my mother, but since she's been worrying about me since I turned sixteen, it's nothing new. I hope you're hungry. We're going to a spot where the *tunnacchiu 'nfurnatu* is out of this world. The tuna will have been caught within the last hour."

It was impossible to have a serious talk with Valentino right now. After they'd eaten, then she'd speak her mind.

The limo pulled down a narrow alley that led to the back entrance of the restaurant he'd been talking about. Valentino got out first and reached for her hand. He squeezed it and didn't let go as he led them to a door one of the security men opened for them.

Cupping her elbow, he walked her down a hallway to another door that opened on to a small terrace with round candlelit tables for two overlooking the water. But they were the only occupants. She shouldn't have come to this romantic place with him, but what could she do?

The air felt like velvet, bringing back memories of their night on the yacht. A profusion of yellow-and-orange bougainvillea provided an overhang Carolena found utterly enchanting.

He helped her to be seated, then caressed her shoulders. She gasped as his touch sent a white-hot message through her. "I've been wanting to feel you all day." Between the heat from his body, plus the twinkling lights on the water from the other boats, she sensed the fire building inside her.

"Benvenuto, Valentino!" An unfamiliar male voice broke the silence, surprising Carolena.

Valentino seemed reluctant to remove his hands. "Matteo Tancredi, meet my sister-in-law's best friend, Carolena Baretti. Carolena, Matteo is one of my best friends and the owner of this establishment."

"How do you do, *signor*." She extended her hand, hoping his friend with the broad smile and overly long brown hair didn't notice the blush on her face.

"I'm doing very well now that Valentino is here. He told me he was coming with the new star of a video that is going to make Gemelli famous."

She shook her head. "Hardly, but we're all hoping this venture will be a success."

"Anything Valentino puts his mind to is certain to produce excellent results." She heard a nuance of deeper emotion in his response. Still staring at her, he said, "I'll bring some white wine that is perfect with the fish. Anything you want, just ask."

"Thank you."

The two men exchanged a private glance before Matteo disappeared from the terrace. Valentino sat down opposite her. A slight breeze caused the candle to flicker, drawing her attention to his striking features. She averted her eyes to stop making a feast of him.

"Where did you meet Matteo?"

"At the college in Catania."

"Is he married?"

"Not yet. He was studying geology when his father took ill and died. The family needed Matteo to keep this place running, so he had to leave school."

"Wasn't there anyone else to help?"

"His mother and his siblings, but his father always relied on Matteo and didn't like the idea of him going to college."

"Matteo's the eldest?"

"Yes."

"Like the way your father relied on you rather than your younger brother?"

He stared at her through shuttered eyes. "Yes, when you put it that way."

"I can see why. After watching you as you talked with the farmers today, I think you should be the one featured on the film, Val. You're a natural leader."

Before she could hear his response, Matteo brought them their dinner and poured the wine. "Enjoy your meal."

"I'm sure it's going to taste as good as it smells. I think I'm in heaven already," she told him.

"Put it in writing that you were in heaven after eating the meal, and I'll frame it to hang on the wall with the testimonials of other celebrities who've eaten here. But none of them will be as famous as you."

Gentle laughter fell from her lips. "Except for the prince, who is in a category by himself."

"Agreed."

"What category is that?" Valentino asked after Matteo had left them alone.

"Isn't it obvious?" She started eating, then drank some wine.

He picked at his food, which wasn't at all like him. "For one night can't you forget who I am?" Suddenly his mood had turned darker and she felt his tension.

Over the glass, she said, "No more than you can. We all have a destiny. I saw you in action today and am so impressed with your knowledge and caring, I can't put it into words. All I know is that you should be the one featured on the video, not me.

"There's an intelligence in you that would convince anyone of anything. First thing tomorrow, I'm flying back to Arancia while you get this video done on your own. Then your mother will have no more reason to be worried."

His brows furrowed in displeasure. "Much as she would like you to be gone, you can't do that."

"Why not?"

"Because you're under contract to Vincenzo and me." As if she could forget. "The economic future of our two countries is resting on our new plan of which you are now an integral part."

She fought for breath. "But once I've finished the other video session in Arancia, then my work will be done. Just so you understand, I'm leaving Gemelli tomorrow after the filming and won't be seeing you again."

"Which presents a problem for me since I never want you out of my sight. Not *ever*," he added in a husky whisper.

She couldn't stop her trembling. "Please don't say things like that to me. A relationship outside a royal engagement or marriage could only be a tawdry, scandalous affair, so why are you talking like this?"

"Because I'm obsessed with you," he claimed with primitive force. "If it's not love, then it's better than love. I've never been in love, but whatever this feeling is, it's not going away. In fact, it's getting worse, much worse. I'm already a changed man. Believe me, this is an entirely new experience for me."

Incredulous, she shook her head. "We hardly know each other."

"How long did it take you to fall in love with your fiancé?"

She let out a small cry. "How did you find out I had a fiancé?"

"Who else but Abby."

"I wish she hadn't said anything."

"You still haven't answered my question."

"Berto and I were friends on neighboring farms before we fell in love. It's not the same thing at all."

"Obviously not. At the swimming pool last week you and I experienced a phenomenon as strong as a pyroclastic eruption. It not only shook the ground beneath us *before* we were up on the volcano, it shook my entire world so much I don't know myself anymore."

"Please don't say that!" She half moaned the words in panic.

"Because you know it's true?" he retorted. "Even if you weren't the perfect person to do this video for us, I would have found another means to be with you. I've given you all the honesty in me. Now I want all your honesty back. Did you agree to do this video because you wanted to help and felt it was your duty because of your friendship with Abby? Or are you here because you couldn't stay away from me?"

She buried her face in her hands. "Don't ask me that."

"I have to. You and I met. It's a fact of life. Your answer is of vital importance to me because I don't want to make a mistake."

"What mistake? What on earth do you mean?"

"We'll discuss it on the way back to the palace. Would you care for dessert?"

"I—I couldn't." Her voice faltered.

"That makes two of us."

When Matteo appeared, they both thanked him for the delicious food. He followed them out to the limo where they said their goodbyes.

Once inside, Valentino sat across from her as they left the restaurant and headed back to the city. He leaned forward. "Tell me about your fiancé. How did he die?"

She swallowed hard. "I'd rather not get into it."

"We're going to have to." He wasn't about to let this go until he had answers.

"Th-there was an accident."

"Were you with him when it happened?"

Tears scalded her eyelids. "Yes."

"Is it still so painful you can't talk about it?"

"Yes."

"Because you made it happen."

"Yes," she whispered.

"In what way?"

Just remembering that awful day caused her lungs to freeze. "I was helping him with his farm chores and told him I would drive the almond harvester while he sat up by the yellow contraption. You know, the kind that opens into a big upside-down umbrella to catch all the almonds at once?"

"I do. More almonds can be harvested with fewer helpers."

She nodded. "He said for me to stay back at the house, but I insisted on driving because I wanted to help him. I'd driven our family's tractor and knew what to do. We'd get the work done a lot faster. Berto finally agreed. As we were crossing over a narrow bridge, I got too close to the wall and the tractor tipped. Though I jumped out in time, he was thrown into the stream below.

"The umbrella was so heavy, it trapped his face in six inches of water. He couldn't breathe—I couldn't get to him or move it and had to run for help. By the time his family came, it was too late. He'd…drowned."

In the next second Valentino joined her on the seat and pulled her into his arms.

"I'm so sorry, Carolena."

"It was my fault, Val. I killed him." She couldn't stop sobbing.

He rocked her for a long time. "Of course you didn't. It was an accident."

"But I shouldn't have insisted on driving him."

"Couldn't he have told you no?"

She finally lifted her head. Only then did he realize she'd soaked his polo shirt. "I made it too difficult for him. My grandmother told me I could be an impossible child at times."

Valentino chuckled and hugged her against his side. "It was a tragic accident, but never forget he wanted you with him because he loved you. Do you truly believe he would have expected you to go on suffering over it for years and years?"

"No," she whispered, "not when you put it that way."

"It's the only way to put it." His arms tightened around her. "Abby told me he was the great love of your life."

No. Abby was wrong. Berto had been her *first* love. Until his death she'd thought he'd be her only love. But the *great* love of her life, the one man forbidden to her, was holding her right now. She needed to keep that truth from him.

"As I told you before, I'll always love Berto. Forgive me for having broken down like that."

CHAPTER FIVE

VALENTINO KISSED HER hair. "I'm glad you did. Now there are no more secrets between us." Before Carolena could stop him, he rained kisses all the way to her mouth, dying for his first taste of her. She turned her head away, but he chased her around until he found the voluptuous mouth he'd been aching for.

At first she resisted, but he increased the pressure until her lips opened, as if she couldn't help herself. He felt the ground shake beneath him as she began to respond with a growing passion he'd known was there once she allowed herself to let go.

Because they were outside the entrance and would need to go in shortly, he couldn't do more than feast on her luscious mouth. His lips roved over each feature, her eyelids, the satin skin of her throat, then came back to that mouth, giving him a kind of pleasure he'd never known before.

They kept finding new ways to satisfy their burning longing for each other until he didn't know if it was his moan or hers resounding in the limo. *"Carolena—"* he cried in a husky voice. "I want you so badly I'm in pain."

"So am I." She pulled as far away from him as she could. "But this can't go on. It should never have happened. Have you told Vincenzo about me?"

"No."

"I'm thankful for that. After being on the yacht with you, I suppose this was inevitable. Maybe it's just as well we've gotten this out of our system now."

He buried his face in her neck. "I have news for you, *bellissima*. You don't get this kind of fire out of your system. It burns hotter and hotter without cessation. Now that I know how you feel about me, we need to have a serious talk about whether I get married or not."

Her body started to tremble. *"What did you say?"*

"You heard me. I made a vow to myself and my mother there'd be no more women, and I meant it. So what just happened between us means an earthshaking development has taken place we have to dea—"

"Your Highness?" a voice spoke over the mic, interrupting him. "We've arrived."

Carolena let out a gasp. "I can't get out yet. I can't let the staff see me like this—"

He smiled. "There's no way to hide the fact that you've been thoroughly kissed. How can I help?"

"Hand me my bag so I can at least put on some lipstick."

"You have a becoming rash, all my fault."

She groaned. "I can feel it. I'll have to put on some powder."

"Your bag and your hat, *signorina*. Anything else?"

"Don't come near me again."

"I'm accompanying you to your apartment. Are you ready?"

"No." She sounded frantic. "You get out first. I'll follow in a minute."

"Take your time. We're not in a hurry." He pressed another hot kiss to her swollen lips before exiting the limo a man reborn. This had to be the way the captive slave felt emerging from his prison as Michelangelo chipped away the marble to free him.

In a minute she emerged and hurried inside the palace. Valentino trailed in her wake. He followed her into her apartment and shut the door. But he rested against it and folded his arms.

"Now we can talk about us in total privacy."

She whirled around to face him. "There *is* no us, Val. If you were a mere man engaged to a woman you didn't love, you could always break your engagement in order to be with a person you truly care about. In fact, it would be the moral thing to do for both your sakes."

"I hear a but," he interjected. "You were about to say that since I'm a prince, I can't break an engagement because it would be immoral. Is that what you're saying?"

A gasp escaped her lips. "A royal engagement following a royal betrothal between two families who've been involved for years is hardly the same thing."

"Royal or not, an engagement is an engagement. It's a time to make certain that the impending marriage will bring fulfillment. My sister hoped with all her heart the marriage to Vincenzo would bring about that magic because she loved him, but he wasn't in love with her and it never happened."

"I know. We've been over this before," Carolena said in a quiet voice. "But you made a vow to yourself and your family after your uncle Stefano's death. I agreed to come to Gemelli in order to help you and Vincenzo. I—I rationalized to myself that our intense attraction couldn't go anywhere. Not with your wedding dawning.

"But now for you to be willing to break your engagement to be with me is absolutely terrifying. You've helped me to get over my guilt for Berto's death, but I refuse to be responsible for your breakup with Princess Alexandra. You made a promise—"

"That's true. I promised to fulfill my royal duty. But that doesn't mean I have to marry Alexandra. After what you and I shared a few minutes ago, I need more time. Day after tomorrow parliament convenes. You and I have forty-eight hours before my wedding is officially announced to the media. *Or not.*"

If he was saying what she thought he was saying…

"You're scaring me, Val!"

"That's good. On the yacht you had the power to keep me from your bed, which you ultimately did. Your decision stopped us from taking the next step. But tonight everything changed.

"Whatever your answer is now, it will have eternal consequences for both of us because you know we're on fire for each other in every sense of the word. Otherwise you would never have met with me and Vincenzo to discuss our project in the first place. Admit it."

She couldn't take any more. "You're putting an enormous burden on me—"

"Now you know how *I* feel."

"I can't give you an answer. You're going to be king in seven weeks!"

"That's the whole point of this conversation. There'll be no coronation without a marriage. I'll need your answer by tomorrow night after the taping here is finished. Once parliament opens its session the next morning and the date for my wedding is announced, it will be too late for us."

Carolena was in agony. "That's not fair!"

His features hardened. "Since when was love ever fair? I thought you found that out when your fiancé died. I learned it when my sister died before she could hold her own baby."

Tears ran down her cheeks once more. "I can't think right now."

"By tomorrow evening you're going to have to! Until then we'll set this aside and concentrate on our mission to put Gemelli and Arancia on the world map agriculturally."

"How can we possibly do that? You've done a lot more than proposition me. I can hardly take it in."

"That's why I'm giving you all night to think about it. I want a relationship with you, Carolena. I'm willing to break my long-standing engagement to Princess Alexandra in order to be with you. In the end she'll thank me for it. Gemelli doesn't need a king yet."

"You can't mean it!"

"Had I not told you of my engagement, we would have spent that night on the yacht together. But the fact that I *did* tell you proved how important you were to me. I realized I wanted much more from you than one night of passion beneath the stars. Sleeping together to slake our desire could never be the same thing as having a full relationship."

His logic made so much sense she was in utter turmoil.

"However, there is one thing I need to know up front. If your love for Berto is too all consuming and he's the one standing in the way of letting me into your life, just tell me the truth right now. If the answer is yes, then I swear that once this video is made, I'll see you off on the jet tomorrow night and our paths will never cross again."

She knew Valentino meant what he said with every fiber of his being. He'd been so honest with her, it hurt. If she told him anything less she'd be a hypocrite.

"I would never have wanted to sleep with you if I hadn't already put Berto away in my heart."

"That's what I thought," he murmured in satisfaction.

"But when you speak of a relationship, we're talking long-distance. With you up on the volcano while I'm in court in a different country... How long could it last before you're forced to give me up and find a royal bride in order to be king? Your mother would despise me. Abby would never approve, nor would Vincenzo. The pressure would build until I couldn't stand the shame of it."

His eyes became slits. "Do you love me? That's all I want to know."

Carolena loved him, all right. But when he ended it—and he'd be the one to do it—she'd want to die. "Love isn't everything, Val."

"That's not what I wanted to hear, Carolena."

"I thought you gave me until tomorrow evening for my answer."

"I made you a promise and I'll keep it. Now it's getting late. I'll say good-night here and see you at eight in the morning in this very spot. *Buona notte,* Carolena."

Valentino was headed for his suite in the palace when his brother came out of the shadows at the top of the stairs wearing jeans and a sport shirt instead of his uniform. "Vito? What are you doing here? I didn't know you were coming!"

They gave each other a hug. "I've been waiting for you."

Together they entered his apartment. "I take it you've been with mother."

"*Sí.* She phoned me last week and asked me to come ASAP." Valentino had a strong hunch why she'd sent for her second son. "I arranged for my furlough early and got here this afternoon."

"It's good to see you." They sat down in the chairs placed around the coffee table. "How long will you be here?"

"Long enough for me to find out why our mother is so worried about you. Why don't you tell me about the woman you took up on the volcano last week before you spent part of the night dancing with her on the yacht. And all this happening *after* you'd set the date for your marriage to Alexandra."

Valentino couldn't stay seated and got out of the chair. "Do you want a beer?"

"Sure."

He went in the kitchen and pulled two bottles out of the fridge. After they'd both taken a few swallows, Vito said, "I'm waiting."

"I'm aware of that. My problem is finding a way to tell you something that's going to shock the daylights out of you."

With a teasing smile, Vito sat back in the chair and put his feet up on the coffee table. "You mean that at the midnight hour, you suddenly came upon the woman of your dreams."

Valentino couldn't laugh about this. "It was evening, actually. I'd just come from the helicopter. Carolena was in the swimming pool ready to take a dive."

"Aphrodite in the flesh."

"Better. Much better." The vision of her in that bathing suit never left him. He finished off the rest of his beer and put the empty bottle on the table.

"Abby's best friend, I understand. Did I hear mother right? She's helping you and Vincenzo with a marketing video?"

He took a deep breath. "Correct." Valentino explained the project to his brother.

"I'm impressed with your idea, but you still haven't answered my question." Vito sat forward. "What is this woman to you? If word gets back to Alexandra about your dining and dancing with her on the yacht, you could hurt her a great deal."

Valentino stared hard at his brother, surprised at the extent of the caring he heard in his voice. "For the first time in my life I'm in love, Vito."

"You?"

He nodded solemnly. "I mean irrevocably in love."

The news robbed his brother of speech.

"I can't marry Alexandra. There'll be no wedding or coronation in August, no announcement to Parliament."

Color left Vito's face before he put his bottle down and got to his feet. He was visibly shaken by the news.

"Until I met Carolena, I deluded myself into thinking Alexandra and I could make our marriage work by having children. Now I realize our wedding will only doom us both to a life of sheer unhappiness. I don't love her and she doesn't love me the way Michelina loved Vincenzo.

"Despite what our parents wanted and planned for, *I* don't want that kind of marriage for either of us. Tomorrow evening I'm planning to fly to Cyprus and break our engagement. The news will set her free. Hopefully she'll find a man she can really love, even if it causes a convulsion within our families."

Somehow he expected to see and hear outrage from his brother, but Vito did neither. He simply eyed him with an enigmatic expression. "You won't have to fly there. Mother has invited her here for dinner tomorrow evening."

His brows lifted. "That doesn't surprise me. Under the circumstances, I'm glad she'll be here. After I see Carolena off on her flight back to Arancia, I'll be able to concentrate on Alexandra."

"What are you planning to do with Carolena? You can't marry her, and Mother doesn't want to rule any longer."

Valentino cocked his head. "I'm not the only son.

You're second in line. All you'd have to do is resign your commission in the military and get married to Princess Regina. Mother would step down so you could rule. As long as one of us is willing, she'll be happy."

"Be serious," he snapped. "I'm not in love with Regina."

His quick-fire response led Valentino to believe his brother was in love with someone else. "Who is she, Vito?"

"What do you mean?"

"The woman you *do* love." His brother averted his eyes, telling Valentino he'd been right about him.

"Falling in love has totally changed you, Val."

"It has awakened me to what's really important. Carolena makes me feel truly alive for the first time in my life!"

Vito shook his head in disbelief. "When am I going to meet her?"

"The next time I can arrange it."

"When will you tell Mother you're breaking your engagement?"

"After I've talked to Alexandra and we've spoken to her parents. Will you meet the princes at the plane for me? Carolena and I will be finishing up the filming about that time. You'd be doing me a huge favor."

His brother blinked like someone in a state of shock. "If that's what you want." When he reached the door to leave, he glanced around. "Val? Once you've broken with Alexandra, you can't go back."

"I never wanted the marriage and have been putting it off for years. She hasn't pushed for it, either. We're both aware it was the dream of both sets of parents. I've always liked her. She's a lovely, charming woman who deserves to be loved by the right man. But I'm not that man."

After a silence, "I believe you," he said with puzzling soberness.

"A domani, Vito."

The film crew followed behind the limo as they came to the last orange grove. Carolena looked at the script one more time as the car pulled to a stop, but the words swam before her eyes. The hourglass was emptying. Once this segment of the taping was over, Valentino expected an answer from her.

Though he hadn't spoken of it all day, the tension had been building until she felt at the breaking point. She couldn't blame the hot sun for her body temperature. Since last night she'd been feverish and it was growing worse.

After reaching for her grandmother's sun hat, she got out of the limo and started walking down a row of orange trees where the photographer had set up this scene with the owner of the farm and his wife.

Her braid swung with every step in her walking boots. She felt Valentino's eyes following her. He watched as one of the crew touched up her makeup one more time before putting the hat on her head at just the right angle. She'd worn jeans and a khaki blouse with pockets. Casual yet professional.

Once ready, the filming began. Toward the end of the final segment, she held up a fresh orange to the camera. "Eating or drinking, the blood orange with the AG stamp brings the world its benefits from nature's hallowed spot found nowhere else on earth." She let go with a full-bodied smile. "*Salute* from divine Gemelli."

Valentino's intense gaze locked onto hers. "*Salute*," he murmured after the tape stopped rolling and they started walking toward the limo. "The part you added at the end wasn't in the script."

Her heart thudded unmercifully. "Do you want to redo it?"

"Anything but. I've always considered Gemelli to be 'nature's hallowed spot.' You could have been reading my mind."

"It's hard not to. As I've told you before, you show a rare reverence for the island and its people."

As he opened the limo door for her, the rays of the late-afternoon sun glinted in his dark blond hair. "Your performance today was even more superb than I had hoped for. If this video doesn't put our message across, then nothing else possibly could. I'm indebted to you, Carolena. When Vincenzo sees the tape, he'll be elated and anxious for the filming to start in the lemon groves of Arancia."

"Thank you." She looked away from him and got in the limo, taking pains not to brush against him. Once he climbed inside and sat down opposite her, she said, "If we're through here, I need to get back to the palace."

"All in good time. We need dinner first. Matteo has not only lent us his boat, he has prepared a picnic for us to eat on board. We'll talk and eat while I drive us back." Despite having dinner plans that night, Val decided spending time with Carolena on her last night was too important to miss. He would make arrangements to see Princess Alexandra at the palace afterward.

Carolena had this fluttery feeling in her chest all the way to the shore, where they got out and walked along the dock to a small cruiser tied up outside the restaurant. There would be no crew spying on them here. His security people would be watching them from other boats so they could be strictly alone.

Throughout the night Carolena had gone back and forth fighting the battle waging inside her. By morning she knew what her answer would be. But right now she was scared to death because he had a power over her that made her mindless and witless.

While Valentino helped her on board and handed her a life jacket to put on, Matteo appeared and greeted them. The two men chatted for a minute before Val's friend untied the ropes and gave them a push off. Carolena sat on a bench while Valentino stood at the wheel in cargo pants and a pale green sport shirt.

After they idled out beyond the buoys, he headed into open calm water. Having grown up on an island, he handled the boat with the same expertise he exhibited in anything he did.

She saw a dozen sailboats and a ferry in the far distance. High summer in the Mediterranean brought the tourists in droves. Closer to them she glimpsed a few small fishing boats. Most likely they were manned by Valentino's security people.

When they'd traveled a few miles, he turned to her.

"If you'll open that cooler, I'll stop the engine while we eat."

Carolena did his bidding. "Your friend has made us a fabulous meal!" Sandwiches, salad, fruit and drinks. Everything they needed had been provided. Because of nerves, she hadn't been hungrier earlier, but now she was starving. By the way his food disappeared, Valentino was famished, too.

When they couldn't eat another bite, she cleaned things up and closed the lid. "Please tell Matteo the food was wonderful!" She planned to send him a letter and thank him.

Valentino took his seat at the wheel, but he didn't start the engine or acknowledge what she'd said. "Before we get back, I want an answer. Do I call off the engagement so you and I can be together without hurting anyone else? I haven't touched you on purpose because once I do, I won't be able to stop."

The blood pounded in her ears. She jumped to her feet and clung to the side of the boat. The sun had dropped below the horizon, yet it was still light enough to see the smoke from Etna. Everywhere she looked, the very air she breathed reminded her of Valentino. He'd changed her life and she would never be the same again.

But her fear of being responsible for someone else wasn't the only thing preventing her being able to answer him the way he wanted. Already she recognized that if she got too close to him, the loss she would feel when she had to give him up would be unbearable. To be intimate with him would mean letting him into her heart. She couldn't risk that kind of pain when their affair ended. An affair was all there could ever be for them.

If she left Gemelli first thing in the morning and never saw him again, she'd never forget him, but she'd convinced herself that by not making love with him, she could go on living.

"It's apparent the answer is no."

His voice sounded wooden, devoid of life. It cut her to the quick because she knew that by her silence she'd just written her own death sentence.

Slowly she turned around to face him. His features looked chiseled in the semidarkness. "I saw the light in every farmer's eyes when they talked with you. They were seeing their future king. Putting off your wedding and coronation to be with me won't change your ultimate destiny.

"But you were right about us. What we felt at the pool was like a pyroclastic eruption. They don't come along very often. I read that there are about five hundred active volcanoes on earth, and fifteen hundred over the last ten thousand years. That's not very many when you consider the span of time and the size of our planet. You and I experienced a rare phenomenon and it was wonderful while it lasted, but thank heaven it blew itself out before we were consumed by its fire. No one has been hurt."

"No one?" The grating question fell from the white line of his lips. She watched his chest rise and fall visibly before he made a move to start the engine.

In agony, Carolena turned and clung to the side of

the boat until he pulled into a dock on palatial property some time later.

A few of his staff were there to tie it up. After she removed her life jacket, Valentino helped her off the boat and walked her across the grounds to her apartment. By the time they reached her door, her heart was stuck in her throat, making her feel faint.

"I'm indebted to you for your service, Carolena. Tomorrow my assistant will accompany you to the helicopter at seven-thirty. He'll bring your grandmother's hat with him. Your jet will leave at eight-fifteen from the airport."

Talk about pain…

"Thank you for everything." She could hardly get the words out.

His hooded blue eyes traveled over her, but he didn't touch her. *"Buon viaggio, bellissima."*

When he strode away on those long, powerful legs, she wanted to run after him and tell him she'd do anything to be with him for as long as time allowed them. But it was already too late. He'd disappeared around a corner and could be anywhere in the palace by now.

You had your chance, Carolena. Now it's gone forever.

CHAPTER SIX

"Abby?"

"Carolena—thank heaven you called! Where are you?"

"I'm back at the office."

"You're kidding—"

"No." Carolena frowned in puzzlement.

"I thought you'd be in Gemelli longer."

"There was no need. I finished up the video taping last evening. I'm pleased to say it went very well. This morning I left the country at eight-fifteen. When the jet landed in Arancia, I took a taxi to my apartment and changed clothes before coming to the firm. It's amazing how much work can pile up in a—"

"Carolena—" Abby interrupted her, which wasn't like her.

She blinked. "What's wrong?"

"You don't know?" Her friend sounded anxious.

"Know what?" She got a strange feeling in the pit of her stomach.

"Vincenzo's source from Gemelli told him that the queen opened parliament this morning without Valentino being there and no announcement was made about his forthcoming marriage. Parliament only convenes four times a year for a week, so the opportunity has been missed."

Carolena came close to dropping her cell phone.

"When you were with him, did he tell you anything? Do you have any idea what has happened?"

"None at all." It was the truth. Carolena could say that with a clear conscience. "When the taping was over last evening, we returned to the palace with the camera crew and I went straight to bed once I got back to my apartment."

She had no clue where Valentino had gone or what he'd done after he'd disappeared down the hall. But if he had been in as much turmoil as Carolena... She started to feel sick inside. "This morning I had breakfast in my room, then his assistant took me to the helicopter at seven-thirty and wished me a good flight. I know nothing."

"It's so strange. Vincenzo has tried to get through to him on his cell phone, but he's not taking calls. Something is wrong."

"Maybe he decided to announce it at the closing."

"I said the same thing to my husband, but he explained it didn't work that way. Any important news affecting the country is fed to the media early on the first day for dissemination."

"Maybe Valentino and the princess decided to postpone their wedding for reasons no one knows about. From what I've seen of him, he's a very private person."

"You're right, but over the last year he and Vincenzo

have grown close. My husband is worried about him. Frankly, so am I."

That made three of them.

Carolena gripped the phone tighter. She'd told Valentino a relationship with him wouldn't work, so if he'd decided to call off the wedding, then he did it for reasons that had nothing to do with her. She refused to feel guilty about it, but she'd grown weak as a kitten and was glad she was sitting down.

"I'm sure he'll get back to Vincenzo as soon as he can. Do you think it's possible there was some kind of emergency that required his presence at the volcanology lab in Catania?"

"I hadn't even thought of that. I'll ask Vincenzo what he thinks."

For all Carolena knew, Val had returned the boat to Matteo where he could confide in his friend in private before parliament opened. But like Vincenzo, she was getting more anxious by the minute.

"Did I tell you Valentino had a copy made of the video? His assistant brought it to me. I've got it right here and will courier it to the palace so you and Vincenzo can see what you think."

"I have a better idea. Come to the palace when you're through with work. We'll have a light supper and watch it. Maybe by then Vincenzo will have heard from him. I take it you haven't seen the video yet."

"No, and I have to tell you I'm nervous."

"Nonsense. I'll send the limo for you at five o'clock. Max will be excited to see you."

"That little darling. I can't wait to hold him." The

baby would be the distraction she needed. But until quitting time, she had a stack of files to work through.

"*Ciao,* Abby."

Three hours later Abby greeted her at the door of their living room, carrying Max in her arms. His blue sunsuit with a dolphin on the front looked adorable on him. "If you'll take the video, I'll tend him for a while." Then, to the little boy, "You remember me, don't you?"

She kissed one cheek then the other, back and forth until he was laughing without taking a breath. "Oh, you precious little thing. I can tell you're all better."

In a few minutes Vincenzo joined them. The second Max saw him, he lunged for his daddy. Their son was hilarious as he tried to climb on everything and clutched at anything he could get his hands on.

After they ate dinner in the dining room, Abby put the baby to bed and then they went back to the living room to watch the video. The whole time her hosts praised the film, Carolena's thoughts were on Valentino, who'd been standing next to the cameraman watching her.

Where was he right now? Enough time had gone by for her anxiety level to be off the charts.

When the film was over, Vincenzo got to his feet and smiled at her. "It's outstanding from every aspect, but *you* made it come alive, Carolena."

"It's true!" Abby chimed in.

"Thank you. I enjoyed doing it. The farmers were so thrilled to meet Valentino in person and listen to his ideas, it was really something to watch."

"Tomorrow we'll drive to the lemon groves to set up appointments."

Abby hugged her. "You were fabulous, Carolena! That hat of your grandmother's was perfect on you. I'm sorry she's not alive to see you wearing it."

Carolena would have responded, but Vincenzo's cell phone rang, putting a stop to their conversation. He checked the caller ID, then glanced at them. "It's Valentino. I'll take it in the bedroom." With those words Carolena's heart fluttered like a hummingbird's wings.

Abby let out a relieved sigh. "Finally we'll learn what's going on. If he hadn't called, I was afraid my husband would end up pacing the floor all night. He worries about Queen Bianca, who's had her heart set on this marriage. She really likes Alexandra."

Every time Abby said something, it was like another painful jab of a needle, reminding Carolena of the grave mistake she could have made if she'd said yes to Valentino. Last night had been excruciating. Several times she'd let down her resolve and had been tempted to reach for the phone. The palace operator would put her call through to Valentino. And then what? She shivered. Beg him to come to her room so they could talk?

When she thought she couldn't stand the suspense a second longer, Vincenzo walked into the living room. For want of a better word, he looked stunned. Abby jumped up from the couch and ran over to him. "What's happened, darling?"

He put his arm around her shoulders. "He and Alexandra have called off their marriage."

Valentino had actually done it?

"Oh, no—" Abby cried softly.

"Valentino has spoken with the queen and Alexandra's parents. It's final. He told me he doesn't want to be married unless it's to a woman he's in love with." Carolena felt Vincenzo's searching gaze on her, causing her knees to go weak. Had Valentino confided in him about her?

"Michelina always worried about him," Abby whispered.

Vincenzo looked at his wife. "Evidently, Alexandra feels the same way, so in that regard they're both in better shape than their parents, who've wanted this match for years. He says that after sixteen years of being betrothed, he feels like he's let out of prison. I'm one person who can relate to everything he said."

Abby hugged him tightly.

"But there's a big problem. Bianca doesn't want to continue ruling, so it will be up to parliament if they'll allow Valentino to become king without a wife. It's never been done, so I doubt it will happen."

"Where's Valentino now?"

"Since Vito is home on leave from the military and wants to spend time with their mother, Valentino is planning to fly here in the morning and finish up our project with Carolena."

The news was too much. Carolena sank into the nearest chair while she tried to take it all in.

"I told him we watched the video and have a few ideas. Apparently he's seen it several times, too, and has some suggestions of his own. We'll ask the nurse to tend Max so the four of us can make a day of it."

By now Carolena's stomach was in such upheaval, she was afraid she was going to be sick. "In that case, I need to leave and study the script we wrote for the filming here before I go to bed. Thanks for dinner. I'll see you tomorrow."

Abby walked her to the door. "I'll phone you in the morning to let you know what time the limo will come for you. It all depends on Valentino." She stared at Carolena. "He's fortunate that Alexandra wasn't in love with him. If Michelina hadn't loved Vincenzo so much, he—"

"I know," Carolena broke in. "But their two situations weren't the same and your husband is an honorable man." What had happened to Valentino's promise to not fail his parents like his uncle Stefano had done?

Abby's eyes misted over. "So is Valentino. Rather than put himself and Alexandra through purgatory, he had the courage to go with his heart. I admire him for that. The volcanologist in him must be responsible for going where others fear to tread. With that quality he'll make an extraordinary king one day when the time is right."

But he wouldn't, not if he followed in his uncle's footsteps.

With those words, Carolena felt her grandmother's warning settle on her like the ash from Mount Etna.

"See you tomorrow, Abby." They hugged.

"There's a limo waiting for you at the front entrance, but before you go, I have to tell you I've never seen you looking more beautiful than you did in that video. There was an aura about you the camera captured, as if you were filled with happiness. Do you know you literally glowed? The sadness you've carried for years seems to have vanished."

It was truth time. "If you're talking about Berto, then you're right. The trip to Gemelli has helped me put the past into perspective. I thank you for that. *Buona notte,* dear friend."

Valentino's jet landed at the Arancia airport the next morning at 7:00 a.m. He told the limo driver waiting for him to drive straight to Carolena's condo building.

At quarter to eight they pulled around the back. He'd arrived here fifteen minutes early on purpose and would get inside through the freight entrance. Abby had told her they'd come for her at 8:00 a.m., but Valentino told Abby he'd pick up Carolena on the way from the airport to save time. They could all meet at the first lemon grove on the outskirts of Arancia at nine.

One of his security people went ahead to show him the way. Though she planned to be outside waiting, he wanted the element of surprise on his side by showing up at her door ahead of time.

The knowledge that he was free to be with her set off an adrenaline rush like nothing he'd ever known. He rounded the corner on the second floor and rapped on the door. A few seconds later he heard her voice. "Who's there?"

Valentino sucked in his breath. "Open the door and find out."

After a silence, *"Your Highness?"* It came out more like a squeak.

"No. My name is Val."

Another silence. "It *is* you."

The shock in her voice made him smile. "I'm glad you remembered."

"Of course I remembered!" she snapped. That sounded like the woman he'd first met. "You shouldn't have come to my condo."

"Why not? Circumstances have changed."

"They haven't where I'm concerned." Her voice shook.

"That's too bad because the pyroclastic eruption you thought had blown itself out was merely a hiccup compared to what's happening now."

"I can't do this."

"Neither of us has a choice."

"Don't say that—"

"Are you going to let me in, or do I have to beg?"

"I—I'm not ready yet," she stammered.

"I've seen you in a bathrobe before." The sight of her had taken his breath.

"Not this time!"

The door opened, revealing a fully dressed woman in a peasant-style white blouse and jeans. Her long sable hair, freshly shampooed, framed a beautiful face filled with color. With those green eyes, she was a glorious sight anytime. "Please come in. I need to braid my hair, but it will only take me a minute." She darted away.

He shut the door. "I'd rather you left it long for me," he called after her before moving through the small entrance hall to her living room. It had a cozy, comfortable feel with furnishings that must have belonged to her family. Lots of color in the fabric. Through the French doors he glimpsed a book-lined study with a desk and computer.

"I'm afraid it will get too messy."

Valentino had expected that response and wandered around the room. There was a statue on an end table that caught his eye. On close examination it turned out to be a reproduction of Rodin's *The Secret*. The sculpture of two white marble hands embracing could have described both the evocative and emotive nature of his experience with Carolena.

He found it fascinating she would have chosen this particular piece. There was an intimacy about it that spoke to the male in him. She was a woman of fire. He'd sensed it from the beginning and wanted to feel it surround him.

Next, he saw some photographs of her with a man in his early twenties, their arms around each other. This had to be Berto. They looked happy. The loss would have been horrendous in the beginning.

On one of the walls was a large framed photograph of a farmhouse. No doubt it was the one she wanted to buy back one day. His gaze dropped to the table below it, where he was able to look at her pictures comprising several generations.

"I'm ready."

He picked up one of them. "Your parents?" He showed the photo to her.

"Yes."

"There's a strong resemblance to your mother. She was beautiful."

"I agree," she said in a thick-toned voice.

"What happened to them?"

Her eyes filmed over. "Mother could never have another child after me and died of cervical cancer. A few years later my father got an infection that turned septic and he passed away, so my grandparents took over raising me. Later on, my grandfather died of pneumonia. He worked so hard, he just wore out. Then it was just my grandmother and me."

He put the picture down and slid his hands to her shoulders. "You've had too much tragedy in your young life."

Her eyes, a solemn green, lifted to his. "So have you. Grandparents, an uncle, a sister and a father gone, plus a kingdom that needs you and will drain everything out of you…"

Valentino kissed her moist eyelids. "You're a survivor, Carolena, with many gifts. I can't tell you how much I admire you."

"Thank you. The feeling is mutual, but you already know that." She'd confined her hair in a braid, which brought out the classic mold of her features.

"I came early so we could talk before we meet Vincenzo and Abby."

He could feel her tension as she shook her head and eased away from him. "Even though you've broken your engagement to Princess Alexandra, which is a good thing considering you don't love her, what you've done changes nothing for me. I don't want an affair with you,

Val. That's all it would be until you have to marry. After your uncle's death, you made that promise to yourself and your parents, remember?"

"Of course." He put his hands on his hips. "But I want to know about you. What do *you* want?"

The grandfather clock chimed on the quarter past. "It's getting late." She walked to the entrance hall.

Valentino followed her. "I asked you a question."

She reached for her straw bag on the credenza. "I want to finish this taping and get back to my law practice."

He planted himself in front of the door so she couldn't open it. "Forget I'm a prince."

Her jaw hardened. "That's the third time you've said that to me."

"What would you want if I weren't a prince? Humor me, Carolena."

He heard her take a struggling breath. "The guarantee of joy in an everlasting marriage with no losses, no pain."

That was her past grief talking. "As your life has already proved to you, there is no such guarantee."

Her eyes narrowed on him. "You *did* ask."

"Then let me add that you have to grab at happiness where you find it and pray to hold on to it for as long as possible."

"We can't. You're a prince, which excludes us from taking what we want. Even if you weren't a prince, I wouldn't grab at it."

His face looked like thunder. "Why not?"

"It—it's not important."

"The hell it isn't."

"Val—we need to get going or Abby and Vincenzo will start to worry."

"The limo is out in the back, but this conversation isn't over yet." He turned and opened the door. After their stops at the various farms, they would have all night tonight and tomorrow night to be together, not to mention the rest of their lives. "I brought your hat with me, by the way."

"Thank you. I would hate to have lost it."

He escorted her out to the limo. With the picture of the marble statue still fresh in his mind, he reached for her hand when they climbed into the car. He held on to it even though he sat across from her. The pulse at her wrist was throbbing.

"Was the Rodin statue a gift from Berto?"

"No. I found it in a little shop near the Chapelle Matisse in Vence, France, with my grandmother. I was just a teenager and we'd gone to France for the weekend. She didn't care for the sculpture, but I loved it and bought it with my spending money. I don't quite know why I was so taken with it."

"I found it extraordinary myself. It reminded me of us. Two would-be lovers with a secret. With only their hands, Rodin's genius brought out their passion." He pressed a kiss to the palm of hers before letting it go.

"I don't like secrets."

"Nor I, but you're being secretive right now."

"Now isn't the time for serious conversation."

"There'll be time later. Vincenzo has planned our itinerary. The farmer at the first grove speaks Mentonasc, so Abby is going to be our translator. She won't want to be in the video, but when we start taping tomorrow, Vincenzo and I are depending on you to get her in it. A blonde and a brunette, both beauties, will provide invaluable appeal."

"You're terrible," she said, but he heard her chuckle. Some genuine emotion at last.

"Matteo told me about the special bottle of Limoncello you express mailed to him from Arancia to thank him for the picnic. The man was very touched, especially by your signature on the label with the five stars next to it."

"You have a wonderful friend in him."

"He has put it up on the shelf behind the counter where all the customers will see it. When your video is famous, he will brag about it. Before we got off the phone he asked me to thank you."

"That was very nice of him." Before long they arrived at the first lemon grove. "It looks like we've arrived."

"Saved by the bell," he murmured.

Praying the others wouldn't look too closely at her, Carolena got out of the limo. It was a good thing the filming wouldn't be until tomorrow. If she'd had to deal with the crew's makeup man, he would know she felt ill after making her exit speech to Valentino.

To her relief, Abby was already talking to the farmer and his two sons. Being fluent in four languages made her a tremendous asset anytime, but Carolena could tell this farming family was impressed that Prince Vincenzo's wife could speak Mentonasc.

He introduced everyone. She could tell the family was almost overcome in the presence of two princes, but Abby had a way of making them feel comfortable while she put her points across. Before long, the four of them left to move on to the next grove. Carolena would have stayed with Abby, but Valentino cupped her elbow and guided her to their limo.

"We all need our privacy," he murmured against her ear after they got back in the car. He acted as though they'd never had that earlier conversation. Even though he sat across from her, being this close to him caused her to be a nervous wreck. His half smile made him so appealing, it was sinful.

"It's a good thing I'll be along tomorrow, too. The younger men couldn't take their eyes off of you. I'm going to have to guard you like a hawk."

In spite of how difficult it was to be alone with him, she said, "You're very good on a woman's ego."

"Then you can imagine the condition my ego is in to be the man in your life. In feudal times they'd have fought me for you, but they'd have ended up dying at the end of a sword."

"Stop—"

He leaned forward, mesmerizing her with those dark blue eyes. "I *am* the man in your life. The only man."

A shudder passed through her body. "I won't let you be in my life, and I can't be the woman in yours. When the taping is over, we won't be seeing each other again."

"Then you haven't read your contract carefully."

Her pulse raced in alarm. "I didn't sign a contract."

"You did better than that. You gave me and Vincenzo

your word. That's as good as an oath. Implicit in the contract is your agreement to deliver the videos and flyers with the AG logo to the fruit distributors around the country. We'll go together. It'll take at least a week. Fortunately my brother will be around to help my mother."

Aghast, she cried, "I can't be gone from the firm that long."

"Vincenzo already cleared it with Signor Faustino. Day after tomorrow we'll fly back to Gemelli to begin our tour. By then the tapes and flyers will be ready. I haven't had a vacation in two years and am looking forward to it."

She could see there was no stopping Valentino. Fear and exhilaration swept over her in alternating waves. "What about your work at the geophysics center?"

"I'm long overdue the time off. You're stuck with me. For security's sake, we'll sleep on the yacht at night and ferry across to the island by helicopter during the day. Don't worry. I won't come near you, not after you made your thoughts clear to me."

"You promise?"

He sat back. "I promise not to do anything you don't want me to do. It'll be all business until this is over."

"Thank you." She knew he would keep his promise. The only problem was keeping the promise to herself to keep distance between them.

"Our last stop tomorrow will be the Baretti farm. Judging from the photograph in your living room, the house has a lot of character."

"I loved it, but I don't want us to bother the new owners."

"We won't. You let us know when to stop and the cameraman will take some long shots while you talk about life on the farm growing up. When the film is spliced, we'll start the video with your visit. Will it be hard to see it again?"

Her heartbeat sped up. "I don't know."

"We don't have to do that segment if you decide against it."

"No. I'd like to do it as a tribute to my family." Emotion had clogged her throat.

"I'm glad you said that because I long to see the place where you grew up. I want to learn all about you. The first tree you fell out of, your first bee sting."

Valentino was so wonderful she could feel herself falling deeper and deeper under his spell. "I know about the putti but have yet to learn which staircase at the palace was your first slide. No doubt you spent hours in the Hall of Arms. A boy's paradise."

"Vito and I had our favorite suits of armor, but we put so many dents in them, they're hardly recognizable."

"I can't imagine anything so fun. My friends and I fought our wars in the tops of the trees throwing fruit at each other. The trouble we got into would fill a book. My grandmother would tell you I was the ringleader. And you were right. I did fall out of a tree several times."

His low chuckle warmed her all the way through and set the tone for the day. She had to admit it was heaven to be with him like this. Carolena needed to cherish every moment because the time they spent together would be coming to an end too soon.

Eight hours later when she was alone back at her condo, she called Abby's cell phone, desperate to talk about what was happening to her.

"Carolena?"

"Sorry to bother you." She took a deep breath. "Are you free?"

"Yes. The baby's asleep and I'm in the bedroom getting ready for bed. Vincenzo and Valentino are in the study talking business. Everything went so well today, they're both elated and will probably be up for another couple of hours. What's wrong?"

She bit her lip. "I'm in trouble."

"I *knew* it."

"What do you mean?"

"You and Valentino. Vincenzo and I watched you two that first night while we were having dinner when he couldn't take his eyes off you. You're in love."

No—

"My husband was certain of it when Valentino took you up on Mount Etna. You're the reason he called off his wedding."

"Don't say that, Abby! We haven't fallen in love. He's just infatuated. You know… forbidden fruit. It'll pass."

"He's enjoyed a lot of forbidden fruit over the years, but he never ended it with Alexandra until he met you."

"That's because he was with me the night his mother insisted on setting the wedding date. When confronted with the reality, it made him realize he can't marry a woman he doesn't love. *That* I understand. But it wasn't because of me. All I did was serve as the catalyst."

"Are you only infatuated, too?"

"What woman wouldn't be?" she cried in self-defense. "Unfortunately he's the first man since Berto to attract me, but I'll get over it."

After a pause. "Have you—"

"No!" she defended.

"Carolena, I was only going to ask if you two had talked over your feelings in any depth."

"Sorry I snapped. We've talked a little, but I'm afraid of getting too familiar with him." She'd come so close to making love with him.

"I've been there and know what you're going through. Let's face it. No woman could resist Valentino except a strong woman like you. He's temptation itself. So was Vincenzo. You'll never know how hard it was to stay away from him."

"Yes, I do. I lived through that entire experience with you. But my case is different. Please try to understand what I'm saying. Everything came together to lay the groundwork for the perfect storm because that's all it is. A perfect storm."

"Then what's the problem?"

"He wants me to fly down to Gemelli the day after tomorrow and spend a week distributing all the marketing materials with him. I—I can't do it, Abby."

"If you're not in love with him, then why can't you go? He has employed you to do a job for him."

"How can you of all people ask me that? Don't you remember after the baby was born? Your father hid you and was ready to fly you back to the States to get you away permanently from Vincenzo so there'd be no hint of scandal."

"But Vincenzo found me and proposed."

"Exactly. Your situation was unique from day one. Vincenzo was married to a princess before he married you. You carried his baby and the king made an exception in your case because he could see his son was in love with you. It's not the same thing at all with Valentino and me. He only *thinks* he's in love."

"So he's already gone so far as to tell you how he feels?"

She swallowed hard. "Like I said, I'm a new face, but certainly not the last one. Be honest, Abby. Though he never loved Alexandra, he'll have to find another royal to marry. In the meantime, if people see me with him, they'll link me with his broken betrothal and there really will be a scandal. I don't want to be known as the secret girlfriend who caused all the trouble."

Her statue of *The Secret* had taken on a whole new meaning since morning. She'd never look at it again without remembering the way he'd kissed her in the limo.

"What trouble? No one knows about you."

"No one except the entire palace staff, his best friend on the island, his colleagues at the volcanology institute in Catania *and* his mother. By the time we've traveled all around the island, the whole country will have seen us together. The queen doesn't want me back in Gemelli."

"Valentino loves her, but he makes his own decisions. If he wants you there, she can't stop him except to bring pressure to bear on you."

"What should I do?"

"I'm the last person to ask for advice."

"Do it anyway. I trust your judgment."

"Well, if I were in your shoes, I believe I'd give myself the week to honor my commitment to him. In that amount of time you'll either lose interest in each other or not. No one can predict the future, but while you're still under contract, do your part. Maybe it will help if you treat him like the brother you and I always wished we'd had."

A brother…

CHAPTER SEVEN

"VAL? SINCE WE'RE already on the eastern side of the island, why don't we stop for dinner at Matteo's restaurant before we fly back to the yacht." She wanted people around them and thought the suggestion pleased him.

"I'll call ahead and see what can be arranged."

Matteo looked happy to see them, but the place was busy and they could only chat for a moment with him. After another delicious dinner, she hurried out to the limo with Valentino, anxious to leave. They headed for the heliport on the eastern end of the island. Within a few minutes they were flying back to the yacht.

In three days they'd covered a lot of territory. He'd stuck to business while they'd dispensed the videos and flyers. When they were in the limo, he sat across from her and there was no touching beyond his helping her in and out of the car.

Each night she'd pleaded fatigue to keep her distance from him. To her surprise, he'd told her he, too, was tired and didn't try to detain her before she went to her cabin. Instead, he'd thanked her for a wonderful job and wished her a good night's sleep. She was a fool to wish that he wasn't quite so happy to see her go to bed.

The queen's spies would find no fault in him. His behavior abated Carolena's fears that the time they were forced to spend together on this project would make her too uncomfortable. In truth, she discovered she was having fun doing business with him. He knew so much about the economics that ran his country, she marveled. With others or alone, they had fascinating conversations that covered everything including the political climate.

Valentino remained silent until they'd climbed out of the helicopter. "We need to talk. Let's do it in the lounge before you go to bed."

She walked across the deck with him. When they entered it, she sat down on one of the leather chairs surrounding a small table.

"Would you like a drink?"

"Nothing for me, thank you."

He stood near her, eyeing her with a sober expression. "What were you and Matteo talking about while I took that phone call from Vito?"

Carolena had known he'd ask that question. "He... wanted to know if you'd broken your engagement. I told him yes."

"What else did he say?"

She couldn't handle this inquisition any longer. "Nothing for you to worry about. He's not only a good friend to you, he's incredibly discreet." She looked away to avoid his piercing gaze. "He reminds me of Abby in the sense that I'd trust her with my life."

Valentino studied her until she felt like squirming.

"Do you feel the same about me? Would you trust me with your life?"

The question threw her. She got up from the chair. "I'm surprised you would ask that when you consider I went up on the volcano with you. I'll say good-night now." It was time to go to bed.

"I'd still like a more in-depth answer." The retort came back with enviable calm. "Tell me what you meant earlier when you said you wouldn't grab at happiness even if I weren't a prince?"

"Do I really have to spell it out for you?"

"I'm afraid you do." His voice grated.

She eyed him soberly. "I don't want to be in love again and then lose that person. I've been through it once and can't bear the thought of it. Call me a coward, but it's the way I'm made.

"Whatever you do with the rest of your life, I don't want to be a part of it. As I told you on the yacht the night I thought I would be sleeping with you, I'll never forget how you made me feel, but that's a happy memory I can live with and pull out on a rainy day.

"To have an affair now is something else again. I couldn't do it with you or any man because it would mean giving up part of myself. And when the affair was over, I wouldn't be able to stand the pain of loss because I know myself too well."

He rubbed the back of his neck. "Thank you for your answer. It's all making sense now. Just so you know, I'll be flying to the palace early in the morning."

She was afraid to ask him why, in case he felt she was prying.

"You can sleep in, though I don't know another female who needed her beauty sleep less than you. The steward will serve you breakfast whenever you want it."

"Thank you."

"After I return at ten, we'll do our tour of the south end of the island."

His comment relieved her of the worry that he wouldn't be gone long. Already she missed him, which was perfectly ridiculous.

"After work we'll take the cruiser to a nearby deserted island where we'll swim and watch the wildlife. It's a place where we ought to be able to see some nesting turtles. If it were fall we'd see the flamingos that migrate there on their way to and from Africa. You should see it before you fly back to Arancia."

"I can't wait."

"Neither can I. You'll love it. *A domani.*"

Valentino knocked on Vito's bedroom door early the next morning. His brother was quick to open it wearing a robe. He needed a shave and looked as if he hadn't had any sleep. "What was so urgent I needed to fly here this early?"

Dark shadows below Vito's eyes testified that his younger brother was in pain. "Thanks for getting here so fast. Come on in."

He'd never seen Vito this torn up, not even after Michelina's death. "I take it this isn't about Mother. What's wrong?" He moved inside and followed him into the living room.

Vito spun around, his face full of too many lines for

a thirty-year-old. "I have a confession to make. After you hear me out, I'll understand if you tell me to get the hell out of your life."

Valentino's brows furrowed. "I'd never do that."

"Oh, yes, you would. You will." He laughed angrily. "But I can't keep this to myself any longer." His dark brown eyes filled with tears. "Do you want to know the real reason I went into the military five years ago?"

"I thought it was because you wanted to, and because our father said you were free to do what you wanted."

He shook his dark head. Vito resembled their mother. "What I wanted was Alexandra."

A gasp came out of Valentino. Those words shook him to the foundations.

"I fell in love with her. I don't know how it happened. It just did."

Valentino knew exactly how it happened. He knew it line and verse.

"All the years you were betrothed, you were hardly ever around, and when you were, it was only for a day. Whereas I spent a lot of time with her. One night things got out of control and I told her how I felt about her. We went riding and she told me she was in love with me, too. We ended up spending the weekend together knowing we could never be together again."

"Vito—"

"You were betrothed to her, and the parents had another woman picked out for me, so I left to join the military with the intention of making it my career for as long as possible. I was a coward and couldn't face you, but I should have."

Pure unadulterated joy seized Valentino. He didn't need to hear another word. It suddenly made sense when he remembered his brother occasionally telling him things about Alexandra that surprised Valentino. It explained the huge relief he saw in Alexandra's eyes when he'd called off the marriage. But what he'd thought was relief was joy.

In the next breath he gave his brother the biggest bear hug of his life, lifting him off the ground. "You're more in love with her than ever, right?"

Vito staggered backward with a look of disbelief in his eyes. "Yes, but how come you're acting like this? You have every right to despise me."

He shook his head. "Nothing could be further from the truth. If anything, I've been the despicable one for not ending it with Alexandra years ago. I knew something earthshaking had happened to make you go away. I was afraid I'd offended you in some way. Now that you've told me, I'm so incredibly happy for you and Alexandra, you could have no idea.

"Don't waste another moment, Vito. All this time you two have been in pain… Give up your commission and marry her. Grab at your happiness! Mother loves her, and her parents want to join our two families together. When they find out you're going to be king instead of me, they'll be overjoyed."

"I don't want to be king."

"Yes, you do. You told me years ago. The point is, *I* don't. I never wanted it."

"But—"

"But nothing," Valentino silenced him. "Mother is

perfectly healthy. Maybe she's going to have to rule for a lot longer than she'd planned."

His brother rubbed the back of his neck in confusion. "What's going on with you? Do I even know you?"

He grinned. "We're brothers, and I've got my own confession to make, but you'll have to hear it later. In the meantime, don't worry about me. And don't tell Mother I've been to the palace this morning. I'll be back in a few days." He headed for the door and turned to him. "When I see you again, I'd better hear that you and Alexandra have made your wedding plans or there *will* be hell to pay."

Valentino flew out the door and raced across the grounds to the helicopter. The knowledge that Vito and Alexandra had been lovers had transformed him, removing every trace of pain and guilt.

"Carolena?"

She peered around the deck chair where she'd been reading a magazine in her sunglasses. "Hi!"

This morning she'd put her vibrant hair back in a chignon and was wearing pleated beige pants with a peach-colored top her figure did wonders for. Between her sensational looks and brilliant mind, she was his total fantasy come to life.

"If you're ready, we'll get business out of the way, then come back and take off for the island." He'd told one of the crew to pack the cruiser with everything they'd need if they wanted to spend the night there.

Throughout the rest of the day they'd gotten things down to a routine and touched base with the many heads of fruit consortiums in the district. The plan to market the island's blood oranges under the AG logo had already reached the ears of many of them with rave results.

Valentino had demands for more of the videos made in Gemelli than he'd anticipated. He gave orders to step up production of the flyers, too. Two more days and he and Carolena would have covered the whole country. By this time next year he'd know if their efforts had helped increase their exports around the world and produced financial gains.

As he'd told Carolena, there were no guarantees in life. This plan of his and Vincenzo's to help their countries' economies was only one of many. It was far too early to predict the outcome, but since she'd come into his life, he had this feeling something remarkable was going to happen.

With their marketing work done, Valentino drove the cruiser under a late-afternoon sun along a string of tiny deserted islands with rocky coastlines.

Carolena had been waiting for this all day. "What's that wonderful smell in the breeze?"

"Rosemary and thyme. It grows wild here among the sand dunes and beaches. Vito and I spent a lot of our teenage years exploring this area. In the fall this place is covered with pink flamingos, herons and storks. We used to camp out here to watch them and take movies."

"I envy you having a brother to go on adventures with. No one's childhood is idyllic, but I think yours must have come close."

"We tried to forget that we were princes put into

a special kind of gilded cage. However, I would have liked your freedom."

"But it wouldn't have exposed you to the world you're going to rule one day. Someone has to do it."

He lifted one eyebrow. "That's one way of looking at it. Ten years ago we worked on our father to get legislation passed in parliament to declare this a natural preserve so the tourists wouldn't ruin it. Since that time, our Gemellian bird-watching society has seen continual growth of the different species, and I've had this place virtually to myself."

She laughed. "Seriously, that has to be very gratifying to you." His dedication to the country's welfare continued to astound Carolena. "This is paradise, Val. The sand is so white!"

He nodded. "It feels like the most refined granulated sugar under your feet. We'll pull in to that lagoon, one of my favorite spots."

The water was as blue as the sky. They were alone. It was as if they were the only people left on earth. After he cut the engine, she darted below to put on her flowered one-piece swimsuit. It was backless, but the front fastened up around the neck like a choker, providing the modesty she needed to be around Val.

When she came back up on deck, she discovered he'd already changed into black trunks. The hard-muscled physique of his bronzed body took her breath. His gaze scrutinized her so thoroughly, he ignited a new fire that traveled through hers.

"Not that the suit you're wearing isn't delectable, but what happened to that gorgeous purple concoction you were wearing when we first met? I've been living to see you in it again."

A gentle laugh broke from her. "You mean that piece of nothing?" she teased. "I've never owned anything indecent before. When I saw it in the shop before I flew down here with Abby, I decided to be daring and buy it. I was a fool to think I'd be alone."

"The sight of you almost in it put an exclamation point on the end of my grueling workday."

She blushed. "*Almost* being the operative word. You're a terrible man to remind me."

"You're a terrible woman to deprive me of seeing you in it again."

Carolena had been trying to treat him like a brother, but that was a joke with the heat building between them. She needed to cool off and there was only one way to do it. She walked to the end of the cruiser and without hesitation jumped into the water.

"Oh—" she cried when she emerged. "This feels like a bathtub! Heaven!"

"Isn't it?"

She squealed again because he'd come right up next to her. They swam around the boat, diving and bobbing like porpoises for at least half an hour. "I've never had so much fun in my life!"

He smiled at her with a pirate's grin that sent a thrill through her. "I'll race you to shore, but I'll give you a head start."

"You're on!" She struck out for the beach, putting everything into it. But when she would have been able to stand, he grabbed hold of her ankles and she landed in the sand. Laughter burst out of her. "That wasn't fair!"

He'd come up beside her and turned her over. "I know," he whispered against her lips. "But as you've found out, I play by a different set of rules. Right now I'm going to kiss the daylights out of you."

"No, Val—" she cried, but the second she felt his hungry mouth cover hers, she couldn't hold off any longer. This time they weren't in the back of the limo while the driver was waiting for them to get out.

There was nothing to impede their full pleasure as they wrapped their arms around each other. Slowly they began giving and taking one kiss after another, relishing the taste and feel of each other. While their legs entwined, the warm water lapped around them in a silky wet blanket.

"You're so beautiful I could eat you alive. I'm in love with you, *adorata*. I've never said it to another woman in my life, so don't tell me it isn't love."

She looked into his eyes blazing with blue fire. "I wasn't going to," she cried in a tremulous whisper before their mouths met in another explosion of desire. Carried away by her feelings, she quit fighting her reservations for the moment and gave in to her longings. She embraced him with almost primitive need, unaware of twilight turning into night.

"I'm in love with you, too, Val," she confessed when he allowed her to draw breath. "I've been denying it to myself, but it's no use. Like I told you on the yacht that first night, you make me feel immortal. Only a man who had hold of my heart could make me thankful I've been born a woman."

He buried his face in her throat. "You bring out feelings in me I didn't know were there. I need you with me, Carolena. Not just for an hour or a day." He kissed her again, long and deep, while they moved and breathed as one flesh.

"I feel the same way," she whispered at last, kissing his jaw where she could feel the beginnings of a beard. No man had ever been as gorgeous.

"Another time we'll come out here in the middle of the night to watch the turtle fledglings hatch and make their trek to the water. Tonight I want to spend all the time we have on the cruiser with you. It's getting cooler. Come on before you catch a chill."

He got up first and pulled her against him. Dizzy from the sensations he'd aroused, she clung to him, not wanting to be separated from him for an instant, but they had to swim back to the boat. Valentino grasped her hand and drew her into the water. "Ready?"

"Yes."

Together they swam side by side until they reached the back of the cruiser. He levered himself in first so he could help her aboard. "You take a shower while I get the cruiser ready for bed. We'll eat in the galley. But I need this first." He planted another passionate kiss on her mouth, exploring her back with his hands before she hurried across the deck and down the steps.

She'd packed a bag with the essentials she'd need. After carrying it into the shower, she turned on the water and undid her hair. It felt marvelous to wash out the sand and have a good scrub. Aware Valentino would want a shower, too, she didn't linger.

Once she'd wrapped her hair in a towel and had dried herself, she pulled out her toweling robe. But when she started to put it on, it was like déjà vu and stopped her cold. What was she doing?

Yes she'd broken down and admitted that she loved him, but nothing else had changed. Though he'd spoken of his love and need to be with her all the time, he was still a prince with responsibilities and commitments she could never be a part of.

Abby had suggested she treat Valentino like a brother in order to make it through the rest of the week, but that tactic had been a total and utter failure. Carolena was painfully, desperately in love with him.

If they made love tonight, her entire world would change. She'd be a slave to her need for him and act like all the poor lovesick wretches throughout time who'd made themselves available to the king when he called for them.

It was sick and wrong! No matter how much she loved Valentino, she couldn't do that to herself. Carolena couldn't imagine anything worse than living each minute of her life waiting for him to reach out to her when he had the time. Once he married and had children, that really would be the end for her.

If she couldn't have him all to herself, she didn't want any part of him. There was no way to make it work. None. She'd rather be single for the rest of her life.

On the yacht that first night she'd told him he'd passed his test and could leave her cabin with a clear conscience. Now it was time for her to pass her test and go away forever.

She quickly put on clean underwear and a new pair of lightweight sweats with short sleeves. The robe she buried in the bottom of the bag. After removing the towel, she brushed her hair back and fastened it at the nape with an elastic.

After putting her bag outside the door, she headed straight into the galley and opened the fridge to get the food set out for them. When she'd put everything on the table, she called to him. A minute later he showed up in a striped robe. He'd just come out of the shower and his dark blond hair was still damp. Talk about looking good enough to eat!

She flashed him a smile. "Is everything fine topside?"

"We're set for the night." His eyes took in her sweats. Carolena knew her friendly air didn't fool him, but he went along with her. "I like your sleepwear. Reminds me of Vito's military fatigues."

"This is as close as I ever hope to get to war," she quipped. "Why don't you sit down and eat this delicious food someone has prepared for us." He did her bidding. She poured coffee for them. "How is your brother, by the way? Will he be in Gemelli long before he has to go back on duty?"

"I don't know." His vague answer wasn't very reassuring. "He wants to meet you when we get back to the palace."

She bit into a plum. "I'm afraid that won't be possible."

Lines marred his handsome features. "Why would you say something like that? He's my only sibling still alive. Naturally I want him to meet you and get to know you."

"Under normal circumstances there's nothing I'd like more, but nothing about you and me is normal."

His head reared back. "What are you trying to tell me now?"

Carolena eyed him with a frank gaze. "I've already admitted that I'm in love with you, but I've come to my senses since we came back on board and I don't intend to sleep with you tonight or any other night. I want a clean break from you after I've finished out my contract, so there's no need to be involved with any members of your family."

He got that authoritative look. It was something that came over him even if he wasn't aware of it. "There isn't going to be a break."

"So speaks the prince. But this commoner has another destiny. Don't ask me again to forget that you're royalty. It would be pointless. Do you honestly believe I could stand to be your lover in your secret life and watch you play out your public life with a royal wife and children? Other foolish women have done it for centuries, but not me."

Valentino tucked into his pasta salad, seemingly not in the least bothered by anything she'd said.

"Did you hear me?"

"Loud and clear." He kept on eating.

Her anger was kindled. "Stop acting like a husband who's tired of listening to his nag of a wife. Have you ever considered why she nags him?"

"The usual reasons. I had parents, too, remember."

"You're impossible!"

Quiet reigned until he'd finished his coffee. After he put down the mug, he looked at her with those intelligent dark blue eyes. "How would *you* like to be my wife? I already know you have a temper, so I'm not shaking in my boots."

Her lungs froze. "That was a cruel thing to say to me."

His sinuous smile stung her. "Cruel? I just proposed marriage to you and that's the answer you give me?"

Carolena shook her head. "Stop teasing me, Val. Why are you being like this? I thought I knew you, but it's obvious I don't. The only time I see you serious is when you're wearing your princely mantle."

He sat back in the chair. "For the first time in my life, I've taken it off."

She started to get nervous. "Just because you broke your engagement, it doesn't mean you've changed into someone else."

"Oh, but I have!"

"Now you're scaring me again."

"Good. I like it when you're thrown off base. First, let me tell you about my talk with Vito this morning."

Carolena blinked. "That's where you were?"

"He sent me an urgent message telling me he needed to see me as soon as possible. Otherwise I would never have left you."

This had to do with their mother. Guilt attacked her. "Is your mother ill?" she asked.

"No. Last week I told Vito I was breaking my engagement to Alexandra. Since I had business with you,

I asked him to meet the princess's plane when she flew in to Gemelli."

"She came to the palace?"

"That's right. What I didn't know until this morning was that Vito and Alexandra were lovers before he went into the military."

The blood hammered in her ears.

"He signed up intending to make a career of it in order to stay away from her permanently. Neither my parents nor I knew why."

"Those poor things," she whispered.

Valentino nodded. "But after hearing that I'd broken our engagement, he found the courage to face me this morning. To my surprise, I learned she was on the verge of breaking it off with me, but Vito wanted to be the one to tell me. That was why she was so happy that I got there first."

Carolena could hardly take it in. "You mean, they've been in love all these years?"

"Yes. It's the forever kind."

She was dumbstruck.

"When I left Vito, I told him there'd better be a marriage between the two of them soon or he'd have to answer to me. Mother will have no choice but to see him crowned king. The promise that one of her sons will reign makes everything all right. He'll rule instead of me. No one will have to be disappointed, after all."

By now Carolena's whole body was shaking. "Are you saying you'd give up your dream in order to marry me?"

"It was never my dream. My parents thrust the idea upon me as soon as I was old enough to understand."

Dying inside, she got to her feet. "Does your mother know any of this?"

"Maybe by now, which brings me to what I have to say to you. I meant what I said earlier tonight. I want you with me all the time, day and night. Forever." He cocked his head. "Did you mean what you said the other day at your condo when I asked you what *you* wanted?"

Hot tears stung her eyelids. "Yes. But we both concluded it wasn't possible."

"Not both——" He leaned forward and grasped her hand. "I told you that true love had to be grabbed and enjoyed for the time given every mortal. When I asked you to fly up on Etna with me even though you knew there was a risk, you went with me because you couldn't bear to miss the experience."

"That was a helicopter ride. Not a marriage. There can't be one between you and me. You're supposed to be the King!"

"Am I not supposed to have any say in the matter, *bellissima?*"

"Val… You're not thinking clearly."

"I'm a free man, Carolena, and have never known my path better than I do now. When Michelina passed away, Vincenzo was free to marry Abby and he did so in the face of every argument. Lo and behold he's still the prince.

"Whether the government makes him king after his father dies, no one can say. As for me, I'll still be a prince when I marry you. The only difference is, I'll work for Vito after he's crowned."

"You mean *if* he's crowned. Your mother will forbid it."

"You don't know Vito. He wanted Alexandra enough to go after her. It looks like he's got the stuff to make a remarkable king. Once Mother realizes their marriage will save her relationship with Alexandra's parents, she'll come around."

"Does Vito want to be king?"

"I don't think he's given it much thought since everyone thought I'd be the one to assume the throne. But when we were younger and I told him I wanted to be a full-time volcanologist, he said it was too bad I hadn't been born the second son so I could do exactly what I wanted.

"When I asked him what he wanted, he said it might be fun to be king and bring our country into the age of enlightenment. Then he laughed, but I knew he wasn't kidding."

"Oh, Val…"

"Interesting, isn't it? At times, Michelina made the odd remark that he should have been born first. She and I were close and she worried for me always having to do my duty. I worried about her, too. She was too much under the thumb of our parents who wanted her marriage to Vincenzo no matter what."

"If people could hear you talk, they'd never want to trade places with you." She had a tragic look on her beautiful face. "As for your poor mother…"

"She's had to endure a lot of sorrow and disappointment and I'm sorry for that. Naturally I love her very much, but she doesn't rule my life even if she is the queen. I'm not a martyr, Carolena. It turns out Vito isn't, either. To have to marry another royal is archaic to both of us, but in his case he happened to fall in love with one."

"Your mother will think you've both lost your minds."

"At first, maybe. But just because she was pressured into marriage with my father doesn't mean Vito or I have to follow suit. The times have changed and she's being forced to accept the modern age whether she likes it or not. Michelina went through a surrogate to have a baby with Vincenzo. That prepared the ground and has made her less rigid because she loves her grandson."

"But you're her firstborn. She's pinned her hopes on you."

"Haven't I gotten through to you yet? Her hopes aren't mine. When I decided to get my geology degree, she knew I was going to go my own way even if I ended up ruling. After she finds out that Vito wanted to be betrothed to Alexandra years ago instead of me, she's going to see that you can't orchestrate your children's lives without serious repercussions."

"I'm too bewildered by all this. I—I don't know what to say."

"I want you for my wife. All you have to say is yes."

She sank back down in her chair. "No, that isn't all."

"Then talk to me. We've got the whole night. Ask me anything you want."

"Val—it isn't that simple."

"Why not?"

"I—I don't know if I want to be married."

"Because there are no guarantees? We've already had this conversation."

"But that was when we were talking hypothetically."

"Whereas now this is for real?"

She lowered her head. "Yes. For one thing, I don't think I'd make a good wife."

"I've never been a husband. We'll learn together."

"Where would we live?"

"Shall we buy your family's farm and live there?"

Carolena's head flew back. "I would never expect you to move to a different country and do that—your work for the institute is far too important!"

Valentino was trying to read between the lines, but she made it difficult. "I can tell the thought of living at the palace holds little appeal. We'll get our own place."

Her body moved restlessly. "You'd hate it. After a while you'd want to move back."

"There's nothing I'd love more after a hard day's work than to come home to my own house and my own bride. Would you like us to buy a farm here? Or would you prefer working for a law firm in Gemelli?"

She looked tortured. "I don't know." She got up from the chair again. "I can't answer those questions. You haven't even talked to your mother yet. It would be pointless to discuss all this when she doesn't know anything that's gone on with you."

"When we get back to the palace day after tomorrow, we'll go to her and tell her our plans."

"But we don't have any plans!"

He got to his feet. "We love each other and don't want to be separated. That forms the foundation of our plans. Come to bed with me and we'll work out the logistics of when and where we want to be married, how many children we want to have. Do we want a dog?"

"I'm not going to sleep with you."

"Yes, you are. There's only one bed on the cruiser, but if you ask me not to make love to you, I won't."

After a minute, she said, "You go on ahead. I'll be there once I've cleaned up the kitchen."

"I'll help. This will get me into practice for when we're married."

They made short work of it.

"I'll just get ready for bed," Carolena said.

"You do that while I turn out the lights."

She hurried out of the galley. He could tell she was frightened. Valentino was, too, but his fears were different. If he couldn't get her to marry him, then his life really wouldn't have any meaning.

Once he'd locked the door at the bottom of the stairs, he made a trip to the bathroom to brush his teeth. The cabin was cloaked in darkness when he joined her in bed still wearing his robe. She'd turned on her side away from his part of the bed. He got in and stretched out on his back.

"Val?"

"Yes?"

"Berto and I never spent a night together alone."

His thoughts reeled. "Not even after you were engaged?"

"No. Our families were old-fashioned."

He sat up in bed. "Are you telling me you two never made love?"

"It was because we didn't want to lie to the priest who'd asked us to wait."

"So you've never been intimate with a man."

"No. After he was killed, I kept asking myself what we'd been waiting for. I know now that a lot of my grief had to do with my sense of feeling cheated. I was so sure another man would never come along and I'd never know fulfillment. It made me angry. I was angry for a long time."

He squeezed her shoulder. "Carolena…"

"Once I started dating, I went through guy after guy the way the tabloids say you've gone through women. But after knowing you for the last week, it all had to have been made up because you don't have that kind of time."

A smile broke the corners of his mouth.

"The fact is, I don't have your experience, but that part doesn't bother me. I just wanted you to know the truth about me. I have no idea if I'd be a satisfying lover or not."

She was so sweet, it touched his heart. "That could work both ways."

"No, it couldn't. When you were kissing me out in the lagoon, I thought I might die on the spot from too much ecstasy." That made two of them. "I'm frightened by your power over me."

His brows knit together. "Why frightened?"

"Because I'm afraid it's all going to be taken away from me."

She'd had too many losses.

"Don't you know I have the same fear? I lost hope

of ever finding a woman I could love body and soul. Yet the moment I was resigned to my fate, I discovered this exquisite creature standing on the diving board of my swimming pool. You've changed my life, Carolena Baretti."

He rolled her into his arms and held her against his body. "I want to be your husband."

She sobbed quietly against his shoulder. "I need more time before I can tell you yes or no. I have too many issues welling up inside of me.

"When I get back to Arancia, I'm going to make an appointment with a professional. I hope someone can help me sort all this out. I should have gone to counseling after Berto died, but I was too wild with pain to even think about it. Instead, I started law school and poured all my energy into my studies."

"How did you end up becoming an attorney?"

"My grandmother insisted I go to college. She said I needed to do something else besides farming in case I had to take care of myself one day. For an old-fashioned woman, she was actually very forward thinking.

"While I was at school studying business, we met with some professors for career day. One of them encouraged me to try for the law entrance exam. I thought why not. When I succeeded in making a high score, the rest was history. Eventually I met Abby and for some reason we just clicked. The poor thing had to listen while I poured out my heart about Berto, but school did help me."

He had to clear the lump in his throat. "Work's a great panacea."

"Yes, but in my case it made me put off dealing with the things that were really wrong with me. Meeting you has brought it all to the surface. I don't want to burden you with my problems, Val. I can't be with you right now. You have to understand that if I can't come to you having worked things out, then it's no good talking about marriage. Please tell me you understand that."

She was breaking his heart. Abby had told him she'd been in a depression for a long time. Carolena reminded him of Matteo, who had certain issues that wouldn't allow him to marry yet.

He clutched her tighter, terrified he was going to lose her. "I do," he whispered into her hair. *I do.* "Go to sleep now and don't worry about anything."

"Please don't say anything to your mother about me. Please," she begged.

"I promise I won't."

"You always keep your promises. I love you, Val. You have no idea how much. But I can't promise you how long it's going to take me before I can give you an answer."

CHAPTER EIGHT

FOUR DAYS LATER the receptionist at the hospital showed
Carolena into the doctor's office in Arancia for her appointment.

"*Buongiorno,* Signorina Baretti." The silver-haired
psychologist got to his feet and shook her hand before
asking her to sit down.

"Thank you for letting me in to see you on such short
notice, Dr. Greco. Abby has spoken so highly of you, I
was hoping you could fit me in."

"I'm happy to do it. Why don't you tell me what's
on your mind."

"I should have come to someone like you years ago."

"Let's not worry about that. You're here now. Give
me a little background."

He made a few notes as she started to speak. Pretty
soon it all came gushing out and tears rolled down her
cheeks. "I'm sorry."

"It's all right. Take your time."

He handed her some tissues, which she used. Finally she got hold of herself. "I don't know what more
to tell you."

"I don't need to hear any more. What I've gleaned from everything you've told me is that you have two problems. The biggest one is an overriding expectation of the prince. Because he isn't meeting that expectation, it's preventing you from taking the next step in your life with him."

"Expectation?" That surprised her. She thought she was going to hear that she was losing her mind.

"I find you've dealt amazingly well with everything that's gone on in your past life. But you've got a big problem to overcome, and unless you face it head-on, you'll remain conflicted and depressed."

It was hard to swallow. "What is it?"

"You've just found out the prince wants to marry you. But it means that for your sake he plans to give up his right to sit on the throne one day as king and you don't like that because you've never imagined he could do such a thing. It hasn't been your perception. To some degree it has shocked and maybe even disappointed you, like glitter that comes off a shiny pair of shoes."

Whoa.

"When you were telling me about all the farmers you met who held him in such high esteem, your eyes shone with a bright light. I watched your eyes light up again when you told me how he's preparing the country in case of an eruption on Mount Etna. Your admiration for him has taken a hit to learn he's willing to be an ordinary man in order to be your husband."

"But his whole life has been a preparation for being king."

"Let me put this another way. Think of a knight

going into battle. In his armor astride his horse, he looks splendid and triumphant. But when he takes it off, you see a mere man.

"Your prince is a man first. What you need to do is focus on that."

She kneaded her hands. "Valentino's always telling me to forget he's a prince."

"That's right. The man has to be true to himself. If he had nothing to bring you but himself, would you take him?"

"Yes—" she cried. "He's so wonderful you can't imagine. But what if he marries me and then wishes he hadn't and wants to be king?"

"How old did you say he was?"

"Thirty-two."

"And he called off his wedding to a princess he doesn't love?"

"Yes."

"Then I'd say the man is more than old enough to know his own mind."

"It's just that he already makes a marvelous ruler."

"I thought you said his mother is the ruler."

"Well, she is."

"And he's not the king, so what you're telling me is that he's still marvelous just being a man, right?"

His logic was beginning to make all kinds of sense. "Yes."

"Your other problem is guilt that could be solved by a simple conversation with the queen."

Carolena gulped. "I don't think I could."

"You're going to have to because you're afraid she'll

never forgive you if you marry her son, thus depriving him of his birthright."

Dr. Greco figured all that out in one session? "What if she won't?"

"She might not, but you're not marrying her, and the prince isn't letting her feelings stand in the way of what he wants. It would be nice to have her approval, of course, but not necessary. There's no harm in approaching her and baring your soul to her. She'll either say yes or no, but by confronting her, you'll get rid of that guilt weighing you down."

Valentino had promised he wouldn't talk to his mother about her yet...

"My advice to you is to go home and let this percolate. When you've worked it all out, let me know."

It was scary how fast he'd untangled her fears so she could understand herself. The doctor was brilliant. She jumped to her feet, knowing what she had to do. "I will, Doctor. Thank you. Thank you so very much."

Valentino hunkered down next to Razzi. Both wore gas masks. "Those strombolian explosions are building in intensity."

"You're not kidding. Something big is going on."

He and Razzi had been camped up there for three days taking readings, getting any activity on film. His work kept him from losing his mind. He had no idea how long it would be before he heard from Carolena.

Valentino wasn't surprised to see that a new lava flow had started from the saddle area between the two Southeast Crater cones.

"Look, Razzi. More vents have opened up on the northeast side of the cone."

"There's the lava fountain. It's getting ready to blow."

He gazed in wonder as a tall ash plume shot skyward. Though it was morning, it felt like midnight. Suddenly there were powerful, continuous explosions. The loud detonations that had continued throughout the night and morning sent tremors through the earth.

"We're too close!" The ground was getting too unstable to stand up. "More lava fountains have started. This is it. Come on, Razzi. We need to move back to the other camp farther down."

They recognized the danger and worked as a team as they gathered their equipment and started their retreat. He'd witnessed nature at work many times, but never from this close a vantage point.

The continual shaking made it more difficult to move as fast as they needed to. Halfway to the other camp a deafening explosion reached his ears before he was thrust against the ground so hard the impact knocked off his gas mask.

Everything had gone dark. He struggled to find it and put it back on. In frustration he cried to Razzi, but the poisonous fumes filled his lungs. For the first time since coming up on Etna, Valentino had the presentiment that he might not make it off the volcano alive.

His last thought was for Carolena, whose fear of another loss might have come to pass.

Once Carolena had taken a taxi back to her condo, she made a reservation to fly to Gemelli later in the day.

This was one time she didn't want to burden Abby with her problems.

Officially, Carolena was still out of the office for another week, so she didn't need to make a stop there to talk to Signor Faustino. All she needed to do was pack another bag and take care of some bills before she called for a taxi to drive her to the airport.

The necessity of making all her own arrangements caused her to see how spoiled she'd become after having the royal jets at her disposal. It seemed strange to be taking a commercial jet and traveling in a taxi rather than a limo. Everything took longer. She was tired when she arrived in Gemelli at five-thirty that evening and checked herself into a hotel.

Because she hadn't seen or heard from Valentino for the past four days, she was practically jumping out of her skin with excitement at the thought of being with him again. Her first order of business was to phone the palace. She wanted to surprise him.

After introducing herself to the operator, she asked to speak to Valentino, but was told he was unavailable. The news crushed her. Attempting to recover, she asked if she could speak to Vito Cavelli. Through his brother she could learn Valentino's whereabouts, and possibly he would help her to meet with the queen.

Before long she heard a male voice come on the line. "Signorina Baretti? It's really you?"

"Yes, Your Highness."

"Please call me Vito. You're the famous video star."

"I don't know about famous."

"You are to me. Mother and I have seen the video. It's superb."

"Thank you. I was just going to say that if anyone is renowned, it's you for drawing all those interesting mustaches on the putti around the outside of the palace."

He broke into rich laughter that reminded her so much of Val, she joined in. "Are you calling from Arancia?"

She gripped her phone tighter. "No. I just flew in to Gemelli and am staying at the Regency Hotel."

"*Grazie a Dio* you're here," he said under his breath. His sudden change of mood alarmed her.

"What's wrong?"

"I was hoping you could tell me. Four days ago Valentino left for Catania, but I haven't talked to him since. I've left message after message."

That meant he was working on Etna.

"*Signorina?* Does my brother know you're here?"

"Not yet. I wanted to come to the palace and surprise him."

"Do you have his private cell phone number?"

"Yes. As soon as we hang up, I'll call him."

"Once you've reached him, will you ask him to return my call? I have something important to tell him."

Her brows furrowed. It wasn't like Valentino to remain out of reach. He was too responsible a person to do that. "Vito?"

"*Si?*"

"There's a favor I'd like to ask of you."

"Name it."

"Would it be possible for me to talk to your mother

either tonight or in the morning? It's of extreme importance to me."

"I'm afraid she's not in the country, but she should be back tomorrow afternoon and then we'll arrange for you to meet with her."

More disappointment. "Thank you. Is she by any chance in Arancia?" Maybe she was visiting Vincenzo and Abby. Carolena should have called her friend, after all.

"No. She flew to Cyprus and left me in charge. I guess Valentino told you about me and Alexandra. The families are together now, discussing our plans to marry. We're thinking in four weeks."

It really was going to happen. "I'm very happy for you, Vito. I mean that sincerely."

"Thank you. I wish I could say the same for my brother."

"What do you mean?"

"It's my impression you're the only person who knows what's going on with him. He's not answering anyone's calls. This is a first for him. Our mother is worried sick about him."

Her eyes closed tightly. Carolena was the one responsible for him shutting down. She took a fortifying breath. "Now that I'm back, I'll try to reach him. Once I've contacted him, I'll tell him to get in touch with you immediately."

"I'd appreciate that. Good luck."

Fear clutched at her heart. Vito knew his brother better than anyone. To wish her luck meant she was going to need it. What if Valentino couldn't call anyone? What if he was in trouble? Her body broke out in a cold sweat.

"Good night, Vito."

"Buona notte, signorina."

As soon as she hung up, she phoned Valentino's number. Forget surprising him, all she got was to leave a message. In a shaky voice she told him she was back in Gemelli, that she loved him and that she was dying to see him. Please call her back.

Crushed because she couldn't talk to him, she got information for Tancredi's Restaurant so she could talk to Matteo. Maybe he'd spoken with Valentino. To her chagrin she learned it was his night off. If she'd like to leave a message… Carolena said no and hung up. The only thing to do was go looking for Valentino.

Again she rang for information and called the airport to schedule a commuter flight for seven in the morning to Catania airport. From there she'd take a taxi to the center where she'd been before. Someone would know how to reach Valentino if he still hadn't returned her call.

She went to bed and set her alarm, but she slept poorly. Valentino still hadn't called her back. At five in the morning she awakened and dressed in jeans and a T-shirt. After putting on her boots, she fastened her hair back in a chignon and left to get some food in the restaurant. Before taking a taxi to the airport, she knew she'd better eat first.

Everywhere she went was crowded with tourists. The commuter flight was packed and she had a long wait at the Catania airport before she could get a taxi to drive her to the institute.

Once she arrived, she hurried inside and approached the mid-twenties-looking man at the reception desk.

He eyed her with male appreciation. "May I help you, *signorina?*"

"I need to get in touch with Valentino Cellini."

The man smiled. "And you are…?"

"Carolena Baretti. I'm an attorney from Arancia who's been working with His Highness on a special project. I have to see him right away."

"I'm afraid that's not possible."

She refused to be put off. "Why not?"

"He's out in the field."

"Then can you get a message to him?"

"You can leave one here. When it's possible for him, he'll retrieve it."

This was getting her nowhere. "Would it be possible to speak to one of the pilots for the center? His name is Dante Serrano. He was the one who recently flew me up on Etna with the prince."

The fact she knew that much seemed to capture his attention. "I'll see if I can locate him." He made a call. After a minute he hung up. "Signor Serrano will be coming on duty within a few minutes."

"In that case, I'll wait for him in the lounge. Will you page me when he gets here?"

"Of course."

"Thank you."

Carolena hadn't been seated long when the attractive pilot walked over to her. She jumped up to greet him, but his expression was so solemn she knew something was wrong.

"Good morning, Dante. I was hoping to talk to you. I haven't been able to reach Valentino."

"No one's been able to reach him or his partner, Razzi. They were camped near a new eruption. The base camp received word that they were on their way back to it, but they lost contact."

"You mean th—"

"I mean, no one has been able to reach them yet."

"Then it must be bad," she cried in agony and grabbed his arms. "I can't lose him, Dante. I can't!"

"Let's not talk about that right now," he tried to placate her. "Half a dozen choppers have already taken off to search for them. This is my day off, but I was called in to help. Valentino's the best of the best, you know."

"I *do* know!" Carolena cried. "My life won't be worth living without him! I'm going with you!"

"No, no. It's too dangerous."

"I *have* to go with you. It's a matter of life and death to me. I love him. We're going to be married."

His eyes rounded before he exhaled a labored breath. "All right. You can come, but you'll do everything I say."

"I promise."

She followed him through the center and out the rear doors to the helipad. They ran to the helicopter. Once she'd climbed inside and strapped herself in the back, he found a gas mask for her. "When I tell you to do it, I want you to put this on."

"I will."

Another pilot joined them. Dante made a quick introduction, then started the engine. The rotors whined. Within seconds they lifted off.

At first, the smoking top of Etna didn't look any different to her. But before long the air was filled with ash. Afraid to disturb Dante's concentration, she didn't dare ask him questions. After ten minutes, the sky grew darker.

As the helicopter dipped, she saw the giant spectacular ash plume coming from a crater filling up with lava. She gasped in terror to think Valentino was down there somewhere.

"Put on your gas mask, *signorina*. We're going to land at the base camp."

She was all thumbs, but finally managed to do it after following his instructions. When they touched ground, Carolena thought there might be thirty geologists in the area wearing gas masks, but visibility was difficult.

"I want you to stay in the chopper until I tell you otherwise." By now he and the copilot had put on their masks.

"I will, but please find him."

"Say a prayer," he murmured. She bowed her head and did exactly that. To lose him now would kill her.

The two men disappeared. In a minute she heard the whine of rotors from another chopper. It set down farther away. People ran to it. She watched in agony as she saw a body being unloaded from it. Valentino's?

Forgetting Dante's advice, she climbed out of the chopper and started running. The victim was being transported on a stretcher to one of several tents that had been set up. She followed and worked her way inside the entrance, but there were too many people around to see anything.

The copilot who'd been on the chopper stood nearby. She grabbed at his arm.

He looked at her. "You weren't supposed to leave the chopper."

"I don't care. Is it Valentino?"

"I don't know yet, but I'll find out."

She held her breath until he came back. "It's Valentino's partner, Razzi."

"Is he…"

"Alive," he answered. "Just dazed from a fall."

"Where's Valentino?"

"The other chopper is bringing him in."

"So they found him!"

"Yes."

Her heart started to beat again. "Thank you for telling me that much." She hurried outside, praying for the other chopper to come.

The next minute felt like an eternity until she heard the sound of another helicopter coming in to land. She hurried over to the area, getting as close as she was allowed until it touched ground.

Carolena watched the door open, but there was no sign of Valentino. She was close to fainting, when Dante pulled her aside. Through his mask he said, "Valentino's head struck some volcanic rock. When they transported him out, he was unconscious but alive."

"Thank heaven." She sobbed quietly against him as they walked toward Dante's chopper.

"You can say that again. He's already been flown to the hospital. I'll fly you there now. Before long you'll be able to visit him."

"Thank you for bringing me up here. I'm indebted to you."

"He's lucky you love him enough to face danger yourself. Not every woman or man has that kind of courage."

She didn't know she had any until she'd been put to the test. It was only because of Valentino. He was her life!

"Razzi said they were eyewitnesses to an explosion that could have gotten them killed. I've heard that the footage they captured on film is the best that's ever been recorded at the institute. The guys are heroes."

They were. "So are you, Dante."

"Yeah?" He smiled.

"Yeah."

Carolena's thoughts drifted back to her conversation with Dr. Greco. He'd said it best. *And he's not the king, so what you're telling me is that he's still marvelous just being a man, right?*

"Your Highness?"

Valentino was lying in bed with his head raised watching television when a nurse came in. He'd been told he had a concussion and would have to stay in the hospital overnight for observation. Much as he wanted to get out of there, every time he tried to sit up, his head swam.

"Yes?"

"Do you feel up to a visitor?"

There was only one person he wanted to see. If she ever came to a decision and it was the wrong one, he wished his body had been left on the side of the volcano.

"Who is it?"

"This person wanted it to be a surprise."

It was probably Vito, who would have been contacted hours ago. He'd want to see Valentino for himself before he told their mother her firstborn was alive and well. But in case it wasn't his brother, Valentino's mind ran through a possible list of friends and colleagues. If it were Vincenzo, he would have just walked in.

"Shall I tell this person you're still indisposed?"

While he was trying to make up his mind, he heard a noise in the doorway and looked up to see Carolena come rushing in the room. "Val, darling—" she blurted in tears and flew toward him.

At the sight of her in a T-shirt and jeans she filled out to perfection, an attack of adrenaline had him trying to get out of bed. But she reached him before he could untangle his legs from the sheet and try to sit up. She pressed against him, wetting his hideous hospital gown with her tears.

"Thank heaven you're alive! If I'd lost you, I would have wanted to die."

He wrapped his arms around her, pulling her up on the bed halfway on top of him. "I'm tougher than that. How did you know I was in here?"

Moisture spilled from her fabulous green eyes. "I flew down to Gemelli last evening. When you didn't answer my call and Vito couldn't get through to you, either. I flew to Catania this morning and took a taxi to the institute."

Valentino was in shock. "You were there this morning?"

"Yes! I had to see you, but then Dante told me you were up on the volcano and there'd been no contact from you since the latest eruption, so I flew up there with him to the base camp."

His blood ran cold. "He took you up there?"

"He wouldn't have, but when I told him you and I were getting married and I couldn't live without you, he took pity on me and let me go with him to look for you."

It was too much to digest. His heart started to act up. "You're going to marry me?"

"As soon as we can." She lifted her hand to tenderly touch his head. "You're my man and I want everyone to know it." In the next breath she covered his mouth with her own. The energy she put into her kiss was a revelation.

"*Adorata*—" He could believe he'd died on Etna and had just awakened in heaven.

She pressed him back against the pillow and sobbed quietly until the tears subsided. His Carolena was back where she belonged.

"Did you know your mother is in Cyprus seeing about the plans for Vito's wedding to Alexandra? While they have their big day after all they've been through, wouldn't it be thrilling if we had our own private wedding with Vincenzo and Abby for witnesses as soon as possible? I'd love it if we could say our vows in the chapel at the palace.

"And while we're gone on a honeymoon, Vincenzo and Abby could stay at the palace with your mother so she could spend time with Michelina's little boy. I want everyone to be happy. The two of us most of all. What do you think?"

Tears smarted his eyes. She really understood what Valentino was all about. He shaped her face with his hands. "First, I think I want to know what has caused this dramatic change in you."

"A very wise doctor helped me get to the core of what was ailing me. He said I had a fixation on your royal person, which was true. He told me I was disappointed you were willing to forgo being king in order to marry me.

"But my disappointment really covered my guilt over your decision and it made me afraid. Then he asked me if I couldn't love the ordinary man instead of the prince. He said something about looking at you without your crown and battle armor. That question straightened me out in a big hurry and I couldn't get back down here fast enough to tell you."

"Battle armor?" Would wonders never cease? He kissed her lips once more. "Remind me to send the doctor a big bonus check for services rendered."

"I already wrote him one." She ran kisses along his jawline. "You've got a beard, but I like to see you scruffy."

"Maybe I'll let it grow out."

"Whatever you want. Oh—there's just one more thing. The doctor says my guilt will be cured after I've talked to your mother. Even though she'll never forgive me for ruining her dreams for you, I have to confront her."

"We'll do it together tonight."

"But you'll still be in here. The doctor won't release you until tomorrow. We'll talk to her then."

"In that case, come closer and give me your mouth again."

She looked toward the door. "Isn't this illegal? What if someone catches us?"

"Do we care? This is my private room."

"Darling," she whispered, hugging him to her. He was all she ever wanted. "What happened on the volcano? I have to know."

He let out a sigh and rehearsed what went on after the first lava fountain appeared. "When I saw that plume shoot into the atmosphere, I knew we needed to run for our lives."

She gripped him harder. "Were you terrified?"

"Not then. The sight was glorious."

"I saw it from a distance. I don't think there's anything in nature to compare to it."

"There isn't." He rubbed his hands over her back. "Do you remember when you were up there with me the first time and the ground shook?"

Carolena shivered. "I'll never forget."

"Well, try to imagine it so strong, neither Razzi nor I could stand up. That's when it started getting exciting. But the moment came when the force threw me forward. I hit the ground and lost hold of the things I was carrying. Then my gas mask came off."

"*Val—*"

"That's when I got scared because I couldn't find it in the darkness."

At this point she wrapped her arms around his neck and wept against his chest. "Dante says you're a hero for getting close enough to record the data. I adore you."

His breath caught. "You mean, you're not going to tell me I have to give up my profession?"

She lifted her head. "Are you kidding? Nothing could be more exciting than what you do. I plan to go up with you a lot. When we have children, you can introduce them to the mountain. We'll get the whole family in on the act."

A week later, Carolena sat in front of the same mirror in the same cabin on the yacht brushing her hair. She'd just showered and put on the white toweling robe hanging on the hook in the bathroom.

But there were differences from the first time she'd come down to this room. The first time she'd been on board, the yacht was stationary. Now it was moving. But the gentle waters of the Ionian carried it along like so much fluff. Their destination was the Adriatic. Valentino had mentioned Montenegro as one of their stops. To Carolena, it was all like part of a dream.

Only two hours ago the priest had performed the marriage ceremony in the chapel in front of loved ones and Valentino's best friend, Matteo. On her ring finger flashed an emerald set in white gold. She was now Signora Valentino Agostino Cellini, and she was nervous.

How strange for her to have been so fearless before marriage when she'd thought they were going to make love the first time. Now she really was a bride and her heart thudded with sickening intensity at the thought of it.

A rap on the door caused her to get up jerkily from the dressing table chair. When she turned, she saw that Valentino had slipped into the room wearing a navy robe. He moved toward her, so sinfully handsome her mouth went dry.

"I can tell something's wrong, *bellissima*. I know you missed your parents and grandparents at our wedding. I'd like to think they were looking on and happy. Let me be your family from now on."

It was a touching thing for him to say. She sucked in her breath. "You are. You're my whole life."

His eyes caressed her. "I thought you'd enjoy re-creating our first night on board, but maybe you would have preferred someplace else."

"Never. This is the perfect place."

"As long as you mean it."

"Of course I do."

She didn't know what his intentions were until he picked her up in his arms. "Then welcome to my life, *sposa mia*."

He lowered his mouth to hers and drank deeply as he carried her through the hall to the master suite. After he followed her down on the bed, he rolled her on top of him. "Never was there a more beautiful bride. I realize we've only known each other a short time, yet it seems like I've been waiting for you a lifetime. Love me, Carolena. I need you," he cried with such yearning, she was shaken by a vulnerability he rarely showed.

No longer nervous, her instincts took over and she began loving him. The rapture he created took her to a place she'd never been before. Throughout the night they gave each other pleasure she didn't know was possible.

"Don't ever stop loving me," she begged when morning came around. If they slept at all, she didn't remember. "I didn't know it could be like this, that I could feel like this." She laid against him, studying the curve of his mouth, the lines of his strong features. "I love you, Val. I love you till it hurts. But it's a wonderful kind of hurt."

"I know." He ran his hands through her hair. "Pleasure-pain is ecstasy. We have the rest of our lives to indulge in it to our heart's content." He gave her an almost savage kiss. "To think what we might have missed—"

"I don't want to think about it. Not ever. You set me on fire the first time you looked at me. Not everyone loves the way we do. It's overpowering."

"That's the way it should be when it's right."

She kissed his jaw. "Do you know who looked happy last night?"

"My mother."

Carolena raised up on her elbow. "You saw it, too?"

"She'd never admit it, but deep down she's glad her sons have found true love, something that was denied her."

Her eyes teared up. "After meeting you, I knew she'd always been a great mother, but the accepting way she has handled our news has made me admire her more than you could ever know. I'm growing to love her, Val.

I want to get close to her. She's missing her daughter and I'm missing my grandmother."

He hugged her tighter. "Do you have any idea how much it means for me to hear you say that?"

"It's so wonderful belonging to a family again. To belong to you."

"*You're* so wonderful I can't keep the secret Vincenzo wanted to tell you himself. When he springs it on you, promise me you'll pretend you knew nothing about it."

"They're going to have a baby."

His dark blue eyes danced. "If they are, I don't know about it yet. This particular secret concerns you."

"What do you mean?"

"Instead of handing you a check for invaluable services rendered to both our countries, he approached the latest owner of your grandparents' farm. After some investigation, he learned they're willing to sell it to you, but there's no hurry."

"*Val*— Are you serious?"

He rolled her over on her back and smiled down at her. "I thought that would make you happy. We'll use it as our second home when we fly to Arancia for visits."

"Our children will play in the lemon grove with Abby and Vincenzo's children."

"Yes. And when we get back from our honeymoon, we'll decide where we want to live."

She cradled his handsome face in her hands, loving him to distraction. "It's already been decided by Vito, but it's his secret. You have to promise not to tell him I told you."

His brows quirked. "My brother?"

"Yes. He said he's willing to be king so long as you're close by to help him. To quote him, 'The two Vs stick together.' He's already started a renovation of the un-occupied north wing of the palace where he says you two used to play pirates.

"I found out it has a lookout where you can see Etna clearly. It's the perfect spot for all your scientific equip-ment. He said the wing will be permanently closed off from the rest of the palace so it will be our own house with our own private entrance."

Her husband looked stunned. "You're okay with that?"

"I love the idea of being close to family. Think how much fun it would be for his children and ours, and they'll have a grandmother close by who will dote on them."

The most beautiful smile imaginable broke out on his face. "Are you trying to tell me you want a baby?"

"Don't you? After last night, maybe we're already pregnant."

"To make certain, I think we'll stay on a permanent honeymoon."

She kissed him until they were breathless. "You were right about the fire, darling. It keeps burning hotter and hotter. Love me again and never stop."

"As if I could…"

* * * * *

"I'd threaten you with a sexual harassment lawsuit but you flirt with everyone at the bar except me. Why is that?"

"You're the one pressed up against me." He shifted, somehow drawing her closer without pulling her to him. "Who's doing the harassing?"

He was right, but she could sense that his need matched her own. In the quiet intimacy of her apartment, it made her bold enough to ask, "Does this feel like harassment, Scott?"

"This feels like heaven," he whispered. "But I didn't come here for this. I'm no good for you."

"That's the point. I'm looking for a wild adventure and developing a new fondness for things that aren't good for me."

He took her arms and lifted them around his neck. Her head tilted and he brushed his lips against hers. Finally. It felt like she'd been waiting for this kiss her entire life.

And it was worth it.

A BREVIA BEGINNING

BY
MICHELLE MAJOR

Published in Great Britain 2014
by Mills & Boon, an imprint of Harlequin (UK) Limited,
Eton House, 18-24 Paradise Road, Richmond, Surrey, TW9 1SR

© 2014 Michelle Major

ISBN: 978-0-263-91289-0

23-0614

Harlequin (UK) Limited's policy is to use papers that are natural, renewable and recyclable products and made from wood grown in sustainable forests. The logging and manufacturing processes conform to the legal environmental regulations of the country of origin.

Printed and bound in Spain
by Blackprint CPI, Barcelona

Michelle Major grew up in Ohio, but dreamed of living in the mountains. Soon after graduating with a degree in journalism, she pointed her car west and settled in Colorado. Her life and house are filled with one great husband, two beautiful kids, a few furry pets and several well-behaved reptiles. She's grateful to have found her passion writing stories with happy endings. Michelle loves to hear from her readers at www.michellemajor.com.

To my grandmother, Ruth Keller,
for believing in me and my writing
from the time I was a little girl. I love you, Gram.

Chapter One

The street was deserted in the early-morning hours. Sunlight slanted over the roofs of the brick buildings as Lexi Preston huddled on the front stoop of a dark storefront. She rested her head in her hands and watched the wind swirl a small pile of autumn leaves. The air held a chill, but it felt good after being stuck in her car for the last day and a half.

Almost six months had passed since she'd set foot in Brevia, North Carolina. She couldn't imagine the reception she'd receive, but was desperate enough not to care. Her eyes drifted shut—just for a minute, she told herself—but she must have fallen asleep. When she blinked them open again it was to the bright sun shining and someone nudging a foot against hers. She scrambled to her feet, embarrassed to be caught so off guard.

"What the hell do you want?" Julia Callahan's voice cut through the quiet.

Lexi backed away a few steps. Yes, she was desperate, but Julia had every reason to hate her. Still, she whispered, "I need your help. I have nowhere else to go."

Julia's delicate eyebrows rose. Lexi wished she had the ability to communicate so much without speaking. She could almost feel the anger radiating from the other woman. But Julia's furrowed brow and pinched lips did nothing to detract from her beauty. She was thin, blonde and several inches taller than Lexi. The epitome of the Southern prom queen grown up. Lexi knew there was more to her than that. After all, she'd spent months researching every detail of Julia Callahan's life.

"You tried to take my son away from me." Julia shook her head. "Why would I have any inclination to help you?"

"I made sure you kept him in the end," Lexi said, adjusting her round glasses. "Don't forget I was the one who gave you the information that made the Johnsons rescind their custody suit."

"I haven't forgotten," Julia answered. "It doesn't explain why you're on the doorstep of my salon. Or what kind of help you need."

Lexi crossed her arms over her chest as her stomach began to roll. She should have stopped for breakfast on the way into town. "They found out it was me," she continued. "Dennis and Maria Johnson fired my father's firm as their corporate attorneys. Several of their friends followed. We lost over half our business."

Her voice faltered as memories of her father's rage and disappointment assaulted her. She cleared her throat. "In response, my dad made a big show of humiliating me in front of the entire firm. Then he officially fired and practically disowned me."

Lexi had worked for her father's firm since she graduated from law school six years ago. Following in his footsteps, doing whatever he expected, had been her overriding goal in life. She still lived in the apartment he'd paid for since college. Her eviction notice had come two days ago.

She drew a steadying breath. "He said he regretted the day I'd come into his life. That I'm nothing more than..."

"Your father is an ass." Julia's clear assessment almost made Lexi smile.

"True," she agreed, blinking against the sudden moisture in her eyes. "But he's all I have. Or had."

"What about other family?"

"I was adopted when I was six. I was in the foster-care system and barely remember my biological mother. My dad never married. He was an only child and my grandparents died years ago."

"Friends?"

"I have work acquaintances, country-club cliques and clients. I'm not very good at making friends."

"It's probably hard to be a backstabbing, underhanded, slimy lawyer and a good friend at the same time."

Although the words hurt, Lexi couldn't help but hear the truth in them. "I guess."

"Sheesh. That was a joke." Julia stepped past her and turned a key in the front door. "Lighten up, Lex."

Lexi followed her into the empty salon, the emotional roller coaster of the past week finally sending her off the rails. "Are you kidding?" she yelled. "I just told you that my life is destroyed because I saved you and your son. I have nothing. No job. No home. No friends. No family. And you want me to lighten up?"

Julia flipped on a bank of lights and turned. "Actually, I want you to tell me how I'm supposed to help. Other than playing the tiniest violin in the world in your honor. I appreciate what you did for me. But we both know you put me through hell trying to give custody of Charlie to my ex-boyfriend's family. That doesn't exactly make us long-lost besties."

"I want a fresh start."

"So make one."

"It's not that easy. As ridiculous as it sounds, I'm twenty-seven years old and my father has controlled every aspect of my life. Hell, he even handpicked a personal shopper to make sure I always projected the right image. The image he chose for me. Since the moment I came to live with him, I've wanted to make him happy, make him believe I was worthy of his love and the money he spent on me."

She ran her hands through her hair and began to pace between the rows of styling chairs. "I'd never done anything without his approval until I gave you that file. I don't regret it. You're a great mother and I feel awful about my part in the custody suit."

"You should," Julia agreed.

Lexi sighed. "If I could take it all back, I would. I know it was wrong. But helping you cost my father a lot. I thought he'd understand and forgive me."

"He still might."

"I don't know if I want him to. At least not on his terms. I don't want to be the same kind of attorney my dad is. I don't even know if I still want to be a lawyer. I need time to breathe. To figure out my next move. To make a choice in life for me, not because it's what's expected." She paused and took a breath. "I thought maybe you could understand that."

Julia studied her for a few moments. "Maybe I can."

Lexi swallowed her embarrassment and continued, "If I stay in Brevia for a few weeks, I could figure out my options. I don't want my father to find me. I don't think he's going to forgive me, but I do expect him to come looking. He likes the control and he's not going to give that up so easily."

She patted her purse. "I have five hundred dollars in cash. I don't want to use credit cards or anything to help him track me. Not yet."

"You're kind of freaking me out. Is he dangerous?"

Lexi ran her hand along the edge of a shelf of styling products. "Not physically. But I'm not strong enough yet to stand on my own. Who knows if I'll ever be. But I want to try. I liked Brevia when I was here. I admire you, Julia. Your fierceness and determination. I know you have no reason to help me, but I'm asking you to, anyway."

"And you couldn't have called on your way?"

"I'm sorry," Lexi said quickly. "I wasn't thinking. I just got in my car and started driving. This was the only place I could think of to go. But if you—"

Julia held up a hand. "This is probably more of my typical bad judgment, but I'll help you."

Lexi felt her knees go weak with relief. Julia Callahan was her first, last and only hope. She knew her father well enough to know he was punishing her. That when he felt as if she'd been gone long enough to learn her lesson, he'd pull her back. In the past, Lexi would have been scrambling to find a way to return to his good graces. Something had changed in her when she'd chosen her act of rebellion. From the start, she'd known he'd find out, and she'd understood there would be hell to pay. She also believed it couldn't be worse than the hell she called a life.

"Thank you," she whispered with a shaky breath. "I promise I won't be an imposition on your life. I could answer phones or sweep up hair—whatever you need."

"A job?" Julia looked confused. "I thought you needed moral support. You're an attorney, for Pete's sake. Why do you want to sweep the floors of a hair salon?"

"I'm licensed in North Carolina to practice, but if I register with the state's bar association, my father will find me. I told you, I need time."

"I'm going to make coffee. I need the caffeine." The stylist looked over her shoulder at Lexi. "Have you had breakfast? We keep a stash of granola bars in the break room."

Lexi followed her to the back of the building. "A granola bar would be great. And I really will help out with anything you need."

Julia poured grounds into the coffee filter and filled the machine with water. She turned back to Lexi, shaking her head. "We start renovations next week on the salon's expansion. I can't hire anyone right now."

"I get it. I appreciate the moral support. I guess."

"No wonder your father can manipulate you so easily. Your emotions are written all over your face. You need to work on a tough exterior if you want to do okay on your own. Fake it till you make it, right? I thought lawyers were supposed to be excellent bluffers."

Lexi slid into one of the folding chairs at the small table. "I'm not much of a bluffer. That's why I was usually behind the scenes. I'm good at details and digging up dirt."

"Yes, I remember," Julia answered drily.

"Do you know anyone who's hiring in Brevia? Just temporarily."

A slow smile spread across Julia's porcelain features. "Now that you mention it, I do know about an available job. One of the waitresses at the local bar had twins last night. They came about a month early and were practically born in the back of Sam's police cruiser."

"Are you thinking I'd make a good nanny?"

"I wouldn't wish that job even on you. I'm thinking you'd make a perfect cocktail waitress."

"I don't drink," Lexi said quickly.

"You have to serve the drinks. Not guzzle them yourself."

Lexi unwrapped the granola bar Julia handed to her, her empty stomach grumbling in anticipation. "I don't like those types of places."

"I don't like exercise," the other woman countered, "but I still run five days a week."

Lexi closed her eyes for a moment. Julia's quick wit and no-nonsense attitude were what she'd initially found so fascinating. Almost a year ago, Lexi and her father had been hired by their longtime clients Dennis and Maria Johnson to investigate Julia's life so they could try to take custody of her young son away from her. The boy's biological father was the Johnsons' son, Jeff.

Lexi knew if you threw enough money at a problem, it likely went away. But Julia had kept fighting. Sure, she had her problems, but Lexi had never seen someone stand up to people with so much power. Julia might have been faking her confidence some of the time, but it had made Lexi realize she didn't have to be her father's puppet forever.

Even if she owed him everything, didn't she still deserve to make choices in her own life? To live life on her terms? She had to at least try.

"Could the work last six weeks?"

"I think so. Amy is going to have her hands full, but I know she doesn't want to lose her job. She works at night, so she'll be able to manage around the babies once she gets back on her feet."

"It sounds good, although I don't have any experience as a waitress."

"Are you a quick learner?"

Lexi swallowed. "I made it through law school at the head of my class. I'm not sure how that applies to waitressing, but it's all I've got."

Julia watched her for another moment. "Are you sure you want to do this? It would be easier to go groveling to Daddy and beg him to give you back your cushy little life."

Lexi stood. "I want a real life."

"I know how that feels. I've got a place you can stay while you're in town. Let me text my receptionist to come in early, then we can get you settled." Julia took out her phone and began punching the keypad. "No offense, but you could use a shower and change of clothes."

Lexi looked down at her wrinkled pants and the stain of coffee on her collared button-down. "I stayed at a cheap motel off the interstate last night," she admitted. "The bathroom creeped me out too much to use this morning."

"Clearly." Julia finished her text, then grabbed a set of keys from a hook behind the door. "Are you ready?"

"As much as I appreciate your help, I can't possibly impose and stay at your house," Lexi argued.

"No doubt. You can have my apartment. With everything happening so quickly, I'm still on the lease. I've been subletting it to Sam's dad, but Joe and my mom got married a few weeks ago. The place is empty."

"Two family weddings in one year. Congrats, by the way."

Julia smiled. "Thanks. It's been a whirlwind but I'm happy."

"Your relationship with Sam really started as a fake arrangement to help with the custody case?"

"It did, but then it became so much more."

Lexi thought for a moment, then said, "I guess you could say that I'm partially responsible. Without the custody fight, who knows if or when you two would have gotten around to figuring out you're perfect for each other."

Julia laughed out loud. "Don't push your luck. I said I'd help you. I'll make sure you get the job, and sublet my apartment to you. I've got another three months on the lease. But as far as figuring out your life and growing a spine when it comes to your father, that's all you."

Lexi wondered if she'd ever be able to loosen her father's hold. In the past she hadn't realized how bad she wanted that. Now she did, and if this was her only chance to make it happen, she wasn't going to blow it.

She nodded, her throat tight with emotion. "I'm going to give it my best shot."

Scott Callahan heard the crash as he took another deep swallow from his glass of whiskey. He glanced toward the back of the bar as he jiggled the glass, determined to loosen every bit of liquor that clung to the melting ice.

"Sounds like she broke another one," he said to the waitress who brought him a third round. His instructions upon his first order were clear: as soon as his glass was empty, he was ready for another. No questions asked and there'd be a hefty tip at the end of the night. When Scott drank, he did it fast and he did it alone.

In his case, misery did not love company.

"New girl," the waitress answered. "The absolute worst I've ever seen." She put the fresh glass on the table and picked up his empty. "Julia vouched for her, but it's like she's never even held a tray. Luke is desperate for the help. Hell, he's desperate for a lot of things. But I don't know if we have enough glasses in the back to keep her around much longer."

Scott leaned back in his chair. "You said Julia vouched for her." He nodded toward the red-faced pixie who came around the back of the bar. "That little mouse is friends with Julia—uh, Morgan?"

"Julia Callahan now," the waitress corrected. "She married the town's police chief a few months back."

Scott nodded. "I'm happy for her. Do they make a good match?"

"Perfect." The woman's voice turned wistful. "Sam Callahan was the biggest catch this side of the county line. I never really pegged him for a family man. But he dotes on Julia's boy. It's true love."

"Good for them," Scott mumbled, not wanting to reveal his connection to Sam. He wrapped his fingers around the cool glass once more.

"How do you know Julia?"

He schooled his features into an emotionless mask. "Her hair salon."

"I haven't seen you in here before. You new to town?"

"Just passing through," he said and took a sip. "Thanks for the fresh drink."

"Sure." Realizing the conversation was over, the waitress walked away.

Scott had been in enough bars in his time to know that a good waitress could sense when a customer wanted to chat and when to leave him alone. He was glad he'd sat in the section he had. The little mouse waitress, cute as she was, didn't seem like someone who'd take a hint if you hung it around her neck. Not his type for certain.

He didn't know what he expected from Brevia, North Carolina. He looked around the bar's interior, from the neon signs glowing on the walls to the slightly sticky sheen on the wood floor. The bar ran along the back of the far wall although few stools were occupied. Not the most popular place in town, so no wonder there was a for-sale sign in the window. Still, the lack of customers suited him just fine. The watering holes he usually frequented in D.C. may have been classier and more historic. But as far as Scott was concerned, liquor was liquor and it didn't really matter who poured it or where.

He closed his eyes for a moment and wondered what had brought him to Brevia tonight. After the blowout he'd had with his brother, Sam, at their dad's wedding a few weeks ago, he'd vowed never to step foot in this town again. If he admitted the truth, he had no place else to go. No friends, no one who cared whether he showed up or not. His dad and brother might be the exception to that, but they were both too mad at him for it to matter now.

He drained his glass again. He liked the way alcohol

eventually numbed him enough so the dark thoughts hovering in the corners of his mind disappeared. Maybe it had led to some stupid decisions, but it also took the edge off a little. And Scott had a lot of edges that needed attention.

As a few more patrons wandered out, Scott's waitress came over to the table. "It's a slow night, honey," she told him. "I'm heading home. I could give you a ride somewhere or you could stop by my place for a nightcap."

She said it so matter-of-factly, Scott almost missed the invitation in her voice. He glanced up. "What's your name?"

"Tina."

He flashed the barest hint of a smile. "Tina, trust me. You can do way better than me on any given night. Even in a town like Brevia."

"I'm willing to take my chances." She surveyed him up and down. "I could wait years for a man who looks like you to walk into this place."

He took her hand in his and ran his finger across the center of her palm. "You deserve more than the likes of me. Go home, Tina." He pressed a soft kiss on her knuckles. "And thank you for the offer. It's a hard one to pass up."

She sighed. "Enjoy your night then."

He watched her walk away, then shifted his gaze as he felt someone watching him. The pixie of a waitress stood next to a table, her mouth literally hanging open as she gaped at him as if he was the big, bad wolf. A rush of heat curled up his spine. Maybe he should have taken Tina up on her offer. He was clearly in need of releasing some kind of pent-up energy.

He straightened from the table where he sat and lifted

his glass in mock salute, adding a slow wink for good measure.

The mouse snapped her rosebud lips together and spun around, sending another glass flying from the tray she balanced precariously in one hand.

Scott shook his head as the crash reverberated through the bar. That was her fifth for the night. A clumsy new waitress wouldn't last long.

He moved to a seat at the bar and ordered another round.

To his surprise, the bartender shook his head. "You've had enough, buddy."

"Excuse me?"

"I said I'm cutting you off."

Scott knew for a fact—almost a fact—that he never appeared drunk even when he was. It had been his downfall too many times to count. People assumed the idiot things he did weren't in direct relation to the amount of alcohol he'd consumed. "What the hell? I'm not making a scene. It's still early."

"It's 1:00 a.m."

"That means I've got an hour left."

"Not in my bar you don't. I own this place and I'm saying you're done here."

"What's the problem, man?"

The bar's owner was in his late forties, a tall, balding man with a lean face. Scott wasn't acting out of the ordinary, so couldn't figure out what was the problem.

"The problem," the bartender said as he leaned closer, "is that I saw you kissing my girlfriend's hand a few minutes ago. Now get the hell out of my bar."

Scott thought about the lovely Tina and cringed. "I

had no idea she was your girlfriend. She invited me over for a drink and—"

He didn't get to finish his sentence as the bartender grabbed at the scruff of his collar. Without thinking, Scott slammed the man's hand to the wooden counter, stopping just short of breaking it.

The bartender yelped in pain, then yanked his hand away.

"I told you," Scott repeated quietly, "I didn't know."

"Luke, is everything okay here?"

Scott turned and saw the tiny waitress standing at his side. She was even smaller up close, her big eyes blinking at him from behind round glasses. As far as he could tell, she didn't wear a speck of makeup, her pale skin clear without it other than a dusting of freckles across her nose and cheeks. Her red hair was pulled back into a severe ponytail at the nape of her neck. She bounced on her toes, looking warily from Scott to Luke.

"Everything's fine, Lexi," the bartender said coolly. "This customer has had enough. He's leaving."

"So Lexi's the bouncer?" Scott smiled at the mouse. "Are you going to throw me out?"

"You don't seem drunk," Lexi observed.

He knew the bartender was right even if he'd never own up to it. Scott wasn't much of a gambler, but he'd perfected a poker face. Nothing good ever came from admitting he'd had too much to drink. Especially at a bar. "I'm not," he answered, even though he knew it was a lie. "But I'd like to be." He settled into his chair and gave her a broad smile.

A streak of pink crept up from the neckline of her Riley's Bar T-shirt, coloring her neck and cheeks. A muscle in Scott's abdomen tightened. He imagined her entire petite frame covered in those sweet freckles and flushed pink with desire. For him.

Whoa. Where had that come from? He blinked several times to clear his head.

"Do you have something in your eye?" the mouse asked. "I have eyedrops in my purse if you need them."

So much for his charm with women. He was rusty these days. "No," he answered.

"He don't need anything," Luke interrupted. "He's on his way out."

"No wonder your bar is so run-down." Scott bit out a laugh. "If this is how you treat your customers…"

He saw Luke's eyes narrow a fraction. "My customers don't bad-mouth my bar. This establishment happens to be a local favorite."

Scott made a show of looking around at the nearly empty stools and tables. "I can see how popular you are. Yes, indeed." He glanced at the waitress, who gave a small shake of her head before dropping her gaze to the ground.

Somehow the disappointment he read in her eyes ground its way under his skin, making his irritation at being kicked out swell to full-fledged anger. He didn't know why it mattered, but suddenly Scott was determined not to let the bartender win this argument. Nobody in this one-horse town was going to get the best of him.

"I'm not leaving until I get another drink." He crossed his arms over his chest and dared the other man to deny him.

"Maybe you should just give him one more," Lexi suggested softly.

"No way." Luke reached for the phone hanging next

to the liquor bottles. "This loser is finished, one way or another." He pointed the receiver in Scott's direction. "I'll give the police a call. Tell them I've got a live one making a disturbance down here, and let them haul you away."

The last thing Scott needed was his brother finding him in a town bar tonight unannounced, let alone making trouble. Scott wanted to talk to Sam, but on his terms and in his own time frame.

Sam had moved to North Carolina several years ago and was definitely protective of his new hometown. Scott told himself he'd stopped caring about his brother's opinion years ago, but that didn't mean he wanted to go toe-to-toe with him tonight. He knew it would be easier to cut his losses and walk out now, but he couldn't do it. Not with Lexi and Luke staring at him. Backing down wasn't Scott's style, even when it was in his best interest.

His gaze flicked to the front door, then back to the bartender. "I noticed a for-sale sign in the window," he said casually.

Luke's eyes narrowed. "You in the market for a bar?"

"Someone could do a lot with this space. Make it more than some two-bit townie hangout."

"Is that so?" Luke crossed his arms over his chest. "Why don't you make me an offer, city boy?"

"Why don't you get me a drink and maybe I will."

A slow smile curved the corner of the bar owner's lips. He turned and grabbed a bottle off the shelf.

Lexi tugged on Scott's sleeve. "It's none of my business, but I don't think it's a good idea for you to discuss a possible business transaction now. You might want to wait until the morning."

"I think this is the perfect time," Scott said and leaned

closer to her, picking up the faint scent of vanilla. How appropriate for a woman who looked so innocent. "And you're right, it's none of your business."

The bartender placed a drink in front of Scott and clinked his own glass against it.

"Be that as it may," Lexi said, tugging again, "in order for a deal to hold up, there is the matter of due consideration. That won't apply if one or the other party is proved to be under the influence of drugs or alcohol."

Scott shrugged out of her grasp. "Honey, are you a waitress or a lawyer? Because you handle those big words a lot better than you do a tray of glasses."

"That's right." Luke's eyes lit up. "Julia said you were an attorney when she got me to hire you. Said you worked your way through law school waiting tables."

"She did?" Lexi had worked her way through law school clerking at her father's firm. She hadn't waited on anything other than an airplane before tonight. Still, she nodded. "I did. I am. An attorney, that is. I'm currently taking a break."

Scott eyed her. "As a cocktail waitress?"

Her lips thinned, which was a shame because he'd noticed they were full and bow-shaped. "For now."

Scott couldn't resist leaning closer again. "You might be the walking definition of the term 'don't quit your day job.'"

"You're a jerk," she whispered.

"Yes, I am."

Luke clapped his hands together. "This is perfect." He took a step back and flipped on and off the light switch next to the bar. "We're closing early, y'all," he shouted to the lone couple in a booth toward the back. "Clear out now."

Ignoring the groans of protest, he pointed to Lexi. "You can write up an offer for the pretty boy. Better yet, there's an old typewriter on my desk in the back. Grab it and you can make the contract."

She shook her head. "I don't think—"

"I'm not asking you to think," Luke barked. "You've broken a half-dozen glasses tonight. If you want to keep this job, get the damn typewriter."

She threw a pointed glance at Scott. "Are you sure this is what you want?"

Looking into her bright eyes, the only thing he could think of was that he wanted to kiss her senseless. But he sure as hell had a longer list of things he didn't want.

He didn't want the botched arrest at the U.S. Marshals Service that had taken his partner's life and put Scott on forced administrative leave. He didn't want the resignation letter burning a hole in his back pocket. He didn't want to go back to his empty condo in D.C. and stare at the yellow walls for days on end. He didn't want to feel so helpless and alone.

"Don't tell me you're all talk?" Luke slapped a wet towel onto the bar as he spoke. "I should have guessed you'd be willing to spout out big words but not follow up with any action. If you aren't serious, get the hell out of my bar. I've got better things to do than waste my time with this."

Scott spoke to the bar owner without taking his eyes from Lexi. "I'm all about action." He picked up his glass and drained it again. "Lexi, would you please get Luke's typewriter? We need to talk dollars for a few minutes. See how badly your good old boy really wants to sell."

Chapter Two

Scott felt someone poking at him, but couldn't force his eyes to open. "Go away," he mumbled.

A shower of ice-cold water hit his face. He sat up, sputtering and rubbing his hands across his eyes. Water dripped from his hair and chin.

"Rise and shine, Sleeping Beauty."

"I'm going to kill you," he said with a hiss of angry air, then looked around. He was on a worn leather couch in a small office, the shelves surrounding him dusty and lined with kitchen equipment. "Where am I?"

Sam handed him a towel. "You passed out. Luke Trujillo called me at three in the morning, laughing his butt off. He said he offered you a ride, but you insisted you wanted to spend the night in your bar. When did you get back into town?"

"Last night."

"You didn't call. Does Dad know you're here?"

"Not yet." Scott covered his eyes with the towel, under the guise of drying off his hair. "I didn't call because our last family get-together didn't exactly end on good terms."

Memories of the previous evening came back to him in full force. When he was certain he had his features schooled to a blank mask, he lowered the towel. "But I'm a big boy, Sam. You don't have to worry about me."

"Are you kidding?" His brother paced back and forth across the worn rug between the couch and an oversize oak desk on the far wall. "You didn't know where you were a minute ago."

"I was disoriented. It happens."

"What the hell were you thinking?"

"It was a misunderstanding. The guy was being a jerk about serving me, so I gave him a song and dance about wanting to buy this place."

Sam grabbed a piece of paper from the desk and shoved it toward Scott. "This isn't a song and dance. It's a contract for purchase and sale. You gave him a down-payment check for fifty grand. Luke has wanted to sell for over a year now. To hear him tell it, the place is a money pit. He's got family in Florida. Hell, he's probably already packing his bags."

As Scott read the words on the paper, his head pounded even harder. The contract had his signature on the bottom, along with Luke Trujillo's and one other. In neat, compact writing was the name Lexi Preston scrawled above the word *Witness* on the last line.

The pixie waitress-attorney from last night. Clear green eyes and the shimmer of red hair stole across his mind. Wanting to impress her. Wanting to keep drinking. His two main objectives from late last night. Now, in the harsh light of morning, he realized how stupid and impulsive he'd been.

Again.

Most of the trouble—and there was a lot of it—Scott had in life was a result of being impulsive. He led with his emotions, anger being the top of that list. Normally, he wouldn't let himself slow down enough to care about the consequences. But the botched arrest two months ago, a direct result of his poor judgment, had put him on the sidelines of his own life. It drove him crazy, although he wouldn't have that discussion with Sam.

"I know you're still getting a paycheck and Dad says you've done well on investments, but it's a lot of cash, Scott. What are you going to do when you go back to the Marshal Service? I don't want to see you throw your money away like this."

Sam was the by-the-book brother, the one who'd always done the right thing. The responsible Callahan. At least, that was how it had been after their mother died. But a lot of years had passed since then. Scott was a grown-up now and he wasn't about to admit that he'd messed up yet again.

"I bought a bar. So what?" He threw the towel onto the floor by the couch and combed his hands through his hair. "I can afford it."

"That's not the point," his brother argued.

"Sam, I'm a big boy. I know what I'm doing. Maybe it doesn't make sense to you, but you're going to have to trust me on this." He walked past his brother and down the short hall to the bar's main room. He couldn't let Sam see how in over his head he felt. He'd done a lot of stupid things in his life, but last night might take the cake. What had felt warm and inviting then now just looked in need of a good scrubbing. The wood floors were scratched and dull and the tables mismatched, several sporting a layer of grime years thick. The place definitely had more charm in the half dark.

"I don't have much of a reason to trust you, and I definitely don't trust Lexi Preston."

Scott spun around, then winced as the abrupt movement made his head hurt more. "What about Lexi?" he asked, not willing to address the issue of trust between him and Sam this early in the morning.

"She represented the family who tried to take away Charlie from Julia."

"I don't understand." Scott had immediately fallen for Julia's toddler son. He didn't know Julia well, but it was clear she was a natural mother. "I thought the ex-boyfriend's family was from Ohio. What's the attorney doing in Brevia? Julia got full custody."

Julia had been embroiled in the custody case when she and Sam were first together. Being with Julia had stopped Sam from taking a job Scott had helped arrange for him with the U.S. Marshals. It had been Scott's big attempt to repair his relationship with his brother, and it had felt like one more rejection when Sam had chosen Julia instead. Scott hadn't quite forgiven her for that, but it hadn't prevented him from forming a quick affection for the boy.

Sam shook his head, frustration evident in the tense line of his shoulders. "I don't understand, either. She got to town yesterday with some sob story about how she needs a fresh start. Julia may talk tough but she's a total softy at heart. She helped Lexi get the job and is renting the woman her old apartment."

"Keep your friends close and your enemies closer?" Scott asked, his mind suddenly on sharp alert. Julia was family now. He protected family, even if his methods were sometimes unorthodox.

Sam shook his head. "I want that woman to stay away from all of us. I don't like the fact that she was involved in this mess with you."

Scott bristled at Sam's condescending tone. "I told you, I can take care of myself. I don't know if she has ulterior motives coming to town, but Lexi Preston didn't influence my decision to buy this bar."

"She let you enter into a contract when you were drunk."

"Who said I was drunk last night? Maybe I bought this place as an investment. It's an historic building and—"

"You're not fooling me. I know the Marshals incident messed with your head. I know you've been drinking more than normal and your normal is pretty damn much." Sam took a step closer. "I think you need help."

Blood roared through Scott's head. He hadn't been back in Brevia twenty-four hours and Sam was already starting another referendum on how messed up he was. He couldn't afford to debate whether it was true. Not yet.

"Get out." He spoke the words slowly, without any of the emotion swirling through his gut.

"Scott, listen—"

"No, Sam, you listen." Scott began straightening chairs around the various tables, needing something—anything—to do with his hands. Needing to take some action. "The incident didn't mess with my head. It killed a good man. Maybe I use alcohol to dull the memories of that more than I should. But I'm not out of control.

I walked away when it was clear that part of the internal investigation meant me smearing my dead partner's reputation. I don't know right now if I'll go back. So I bought this place. It's an investment. Not one that you would make, but it's my money and my life. Back off. Go home to Julia and Charlie. I don't need you here."

The sound of the chairs scraping against the wood floor gave welcome relief to the silence that stretched between the brothers. Finally, Scott stopped and looked over. "I mean it. I'm fine."

Sam gave a curt nod. "I'm here, Scott. When you do need me, I'm here." He turned and walked out of the bar into the bright morning.

As the door swung shut behind him, Scott turned a chair around and sank into it, massaging his forehead with two fingers.

What the hell was he going to do now?

Lexi tried to ignore the pounding on the apartment door. As she stared, arms folded tightly across her chest, the noise grew. Had her father had a change of heart already, prepared to forgive her supposed lapse in judgment if she came home and continued to do his bidding? It was late morning and she'd already unpacked her few belongings and made a run to the local grocery for essential supplies. As silly as it seemed, she'd just gotten a taste of freedom and didn't want to give it up so soon.

She also didn't want her neighbors to worry or, worse, call Julia or Sam. Taking a fortifying gulp of air, she turned the knob and opened the door.

Oh.

Oh, dear.

Scott Callahan loomed in the doorway, irritation and

a healthy five-o'clock shadow etched on his handsome face. He was still wearing the same casual sweater and wrinkled jeans from the night before. She looked for the resemblance to Julia's husband, Sam, figuring it was too much of a coincidence to have two Callahans in the same small town.

She'd been shocked when he'd told her his name as she was putting together the contract for sale last night. Although Scott's hair was dark, the two men shared the same brilliant blue eyes, strong jaw and towering height that made them both intimidating and undeniably male.

She took an involuntary step back, hating the blush creeping up her cheeks. Why did this man rattle her so much?

That was easy enough to answer. Just the sight of him made her long-dormant imagination kick into high gear. His hair just grazed his collar, his blue eyes made brighter by the contrast to long lashes that any woman would envy. He was beautiful, the kind of handsome that would attract female attention wherever he went.

Men who looked like Scott Callahan didn't notice Lexi, and last night he'd certainly noticed her. At least it had felt that way. He'd leaned in and his eyes had caught on her mouth as if he wanted to kiss her. She'd imagined what that kiss would feel like as she lay in her bed in the wee morning hours, watching dawn through the curtains in her bedroom. She could almost taste his lips on hers even now.

Now.

She blinked and cleared her throat. "What are you doing here?"

He lifted one long arm to rest on the door frame, muscles bunching under his sweater. A smile played at the corner of his mouth. He seemed a lot less irritated than he had a few moments earlier. "What's your story, Lexi Preston? You look shy and talk like an academic, but you've got a wild side. I can tell."

She hugged her arms more tightly around herself. "You can tell no such thing."

"I can tell you want me to kiss you."

She sputtered, "I do not."

"Liar." He took a lazy step toward her. "But that's not going to happen. Yet."

Lexi was shocked by the ripple of disappointment that rolled through her. "What do you want?" she repeated. "I'm guessing this isn't an official employee meeting."

He pulled a sheet of paper out of his back pocket. "I want to know why you let me sign this damn contract."

"You told me to write it up. I didn't let you do anything. In fact, I advised you not to sign it."

"I was drunk."

She cocked her head to one side and studied him. The rumpled clothes, the hint of bruising under his eyes. "You said you weren't."

"I hide it well."

No wonder he'd been flirting with her. It was the alcohol, not attraction. Of course. A guy as hot as Scott would definitely need beer goggles to flirt with her. "I warned you about due consideration. You assured me you were in full control of your faculties and able to make a rational decision."

"I want out." He came all the way into the apartment, filling it with his large, muscular body and…sheesh, she had a one-track mind.

"The bank has to draw up the final contract. Maybe you won't be approved for the loan."

"I can guarantee I'll be approved, so I want out now."

A whistle sounded from behind her. "It's not that easy." She turned on her heel and padded to the kitchen, pulling two cups from the cabinet. She dropped a tea bag in each and poured the hot water. Turning back, she handed one to Scott. He eyed it suspiciously. "What's this?"

"Green tea. It helps me think." She took a small sip. "Explain to Luke Trujillo that you were inebriated last night. The contract won't hold up if you signed it under the influence. I'm sure Tina will vouch for how many drinks you had over a normal limit."

"That's the problem. No one can know I was drunk."

"Why not?"

He brought the mug to his mouth, sniffed and made a face. "You're kidding with this, right? Where's the coffee?"

"I don't drink coffee. Green tea is full of antioxidants."

"You're an attorney and a health nut? That's some combination."

"My father says... Never mind." She took another drink. "Don't be a baby. It's just tea." She studied him intently. "Why do you want to hide that you were drunk?"

"I'm not a baby," he said and took a huge gulp of tea. "That's disgusting."

"You're avoiding my question."

"You're such a lawyer." He shook his head and reached around her to place the mug on the counter. "My brother's already given me grief about last night. I don't need him on my back for anything else."

"Are the two of you close?"

"Not a bit."

She raised the cup to her lips again, then lowered it as her mind raced. "If you're not close, why do you—"

"It's complicated."

Lexi could just imagine. She'd known him for less than twenty-four hours, but Scott Callahan was already the most intriguing man she'd ever met. At first glance he was all alpha-male bravado, but she sensed something more. His eyes had a haunted look that wasn't related to a hangover, but might have everything to do with a bone-deep loneliness. The kind of lonely people felt if they thought no one in the world truly loved them. As if they had no home.

The kind of lonely Lexi often saw reflected in her own eyes.

She had nothing in common with this man, but she wanted to reach out to him. She yearned to understand what made someone who appeared so sure of himself at the same time give off waves of uncertainty.

She wanted to really know him.

As if he could read her intention, his eyes turned cold. "Never mind. I'll figure something out." His voice cut through her thoughts. "Luke gave me a fair price and I've got the time and money to deal with it. Maybe I'll redo the whole thing and sell it for a hefty profit." His words were sure but his tone still held a hint of uncertainty.

"If you didn't want to own a bar, why did you buy it?"

"I don't know." He ran his hand through his almost-black hair. "I'm known for being impulsive. It's my trademark."

There must be more to the story, but as much as she wanted to know, it wasn't any of her business. Yet. "I never do anything impulsive."

"That's not how I heard it." He glanced over her

shoulder at the tray of half-full glasses sitting on the kitchen table. "Here you are, a fancy-pants corporate attorney, renting my sister-in-law's apartment, practicing to be a bar waitress in this sleepy Southern town. Are you telling me this is some sort of master plan?"

She almost smiled. "I guess you're right. I've been pretty impulsive in the last couple of days."

He shook his head. "That wasn't a compliment."

"I'm going to take it as one, anyway." She placed her mug on the counter. When she turned back, Scott had stepped closer. Too close. Close enough that she could smell toothpaste on his breath and the musky scent of last night's cologne on his shirt.

"If you want to get impulsive, I can help." He reached his hand up and trailed the pad of his thumb along her jaw. "I'm an expert at impulsive."

"I'm not that kind of girl," she whispered, hating that he broke straight through to her earlier longing.

"I can't figure out what kind of girl you are." His mouth turned up at the corner. "But I know you're the worst waitress I've ever seen." He straightened, dropping his hand. "I'm the boss now. So you'd better practice all day with those glasses. Because you helped get me into this mess and I'm not going to let you cost me more money every night. Luke may have owed Julia a favor, but I don't owe anyone anything."

Lexi sucked in a breath. "Are you threatening to fire me?"

"It's no threat," Scott told her. "I'm sure you've got a corner office waiting for you somewhere. I don't care why you're slumming it in a bar. But it's mine now. I don't play favorites. Show up a half hour early for your shift tonight. We're having an employee meeting."

He turned and headed for her door.

"This is because you're mad that I wrote the contract. You want to blame me. It's not fair."

He held up one hand and ticked off several points. "I'm mad that I signed the contract. I blame myself for that, but I don't appreciate you being a part of that moment. And if you haven't realized it before, life isn't ever fair. Deal with it."

Without looking back, he strode from her apartment, slamming the door shut behind him.

Chapter Three

By five o'clock that night, Scott's headache was way beyond a hangover. He'd driven down to Charlotte to pick up some updated electronics the bar needed right away, along with a few extra clothes until he had time to get to his condo in D.C. for his stuff. He'd noticed a bathroom and shower off the office in back, where he'd bunk until he could figure out what to do with his new investment.

Damn. His plan hadn't included staying in Brevia for more than a few days, and definitely not in this run-down bar. He didn't know why he'd come in the first place, other than wandering around D.C. and watching ESPN in his place had been driving him crazy.

He and Sam hadn't been close in years, and he knew his brother still didn't trust him after Scott's part in breaking up Sam's first engagement. He pressed two fingers to the side of his head as the pain of regret mingled with the dull pounding inside his brain.

He'd thought they were going to put the past behind them when Sam was planning to take the job with the Marshals, but the relationship with Julia had ended that. Scott had been mad as hell. He'd stuck his neck out to get Sam the job. Although he didn't want to admit it, he'd craved a second chance at a relationship with his brother.

He knew Sam didn't want him here. Maybe that had been part of the motivation for making this stupid deal. He'd always had a talent for getting under his brother's skin.

Hefting another box of beer bottles into the large refrigerator in the back room of the bar, he spun on his heel as someone cleared his throat behind him.

Scott slammed the refrigerator door and faced a craggy-looking man whose thin blond hair was pulled back into a ponytail at the nape of his neck. He looked to be in his mid-forties and wore faded jeans and an army-green canvas jacket over a white T-shirt.

"You ain't Luke," the man told him.

"Great observation." Scott eyed the stranger, clearly ex-military by the way he held himself. "I'm Scott Callahan, the new owner of this place."

"New owner?" The man's eyes narrowed. "I didn't hear nothing about a new owner."

"It's a recent development." He'd also met earlier with Luke, who'd been thrilled to hand over his keys. He'd offered to stick around for a few weeks to help, but Scott had declined. From what he'd seen this morning going through the bar's accounts and ledgers, Luke hadn't known much about running a business. Scott had certainly spent enough time in bars. He figured he could pick up most of what he needed to know from the staff. As long as he kept the beer cold and the liquor flowing, how hard could it be?

"You can't be any worse than Luke. That guy could barely tap a keg when he got here."

"I've tapped plenty of kegs in my day," Scott assured him. "I didn't catch your name."

The two of them stared at each other for several moments. Finally, the man said, "I'm Jon Riley."

"As in Riley's Bar?" Scott tried not to look surprised.

Joe nodded. "My dad opened this place almost twenty years ago. Luke took over when Dad passed a few years back."

"I'm sorry. You work here?"

"Unfortunately." When Scott didn't reply, Jon continued, "I've worked in restaurants most of my life. Trained as a chef up in New York. But I got hurt over in Iraq and, well...ended up back here."

Scott had noticed the full kitchen, although from the looks of it, nothing had been cooked there for years. "Riley's doesn't serve food."

"Used to when my dad had it." Jon shrugged. "Now I wash glasses, clean up, handyman stuff. Whatever needs doing. You gonna change things around?"

"I've owned the place for less than twenty-four hours. My head is still swimming." And pounding.

"That didn't answer the question."

"You've still got a job if you want one."

"I do." Jon stuck out his bony hand and Scott shook it. "Nice to meet you, boss."

"You, too, Jon."

"I got one more question for you." Jon nodded toward the unused kitchen space. "My apartment's only an efficiency. I can't cook anything worth eating. I clock in here at six-thirty most nights. Would you mind if I brought in some supplies and made myself dinner before I started? I'll keep it clean."

"Is that what you've been doing?"

"Nope." His gaze dropped to the ground. "Luke didn't want to deal with it or have customers smelling my meals, but—"

"I don't care what you do in the kitchen. I'm not using it. We're having a staff meeting in a few minutes. Be great if you could be there."

"Thanks." Jon shrugged out of his coat. "I'm going to get started moving last night's empties."

Scott nodded, feeling overwhelmed by the task in front of him. He liked the fact that he was moving, at least. It gave him less time to think about what he couldn't do. Like his real job.

He heard voices at the front of the building. He glanced out to see four women, including Lexi, come through the entrance. He'd contacted the five waitresses and two male bartenders from the employee records he'd found in the desk. One of the women had just had a baby, which explained Lexi's hire. Both of the guys had come in right after lunch to go over things. Scott had asked the waitresses to meet just before they opened tonight. He had no idea what he was going to say to them. Should he give a football-huddle pep talk or beg for help? He'd never been an employer. Never had to worry about anyone on the job but himself. That was about to change. He had his first employee meeting to run.

"Hello, ladies," he called with more confidence than he felt. "How is everyone doing tonight?"

All four women stopped and stared at him. He recognized Tina from last night, her gaze still an open invitation. Lexi looked wary, making eye contact with everything except him. The other two women he didn't recognize. He'd left messages for both of them earlier, so he didn't know what they thought of the change in ownership.

He stepped forward. "I'm Scott Callahan, the new owner of Riley's Bar."

"I'm Misty," the first woman told him. She was older for a bar waitress—early fifties if he had to guess. Her jet-black hair curled on top and was held back by a shiny clip. She couldn't have been more than five feet tall. It was hard to imagine her hefting a tray of glasses. But that remained to be seen.

"I appreciate all of you coming in."

Tina gave him a slow smile. "I didn't know you were going to buy the place."

Scott returned her smile. "I didn't know Luke was your boyfriend when you invited me for a drink."

She shrugged. "We're on a break."

"I'm single." The fourth waitress piped up. "My name's Erin." The young woman sidled up to him. "I've been here awhile, so I can help you with anything you need." She wrapped her long fingers around his wrist. "Anything."

He heard Lexi snort as he unhooked his wrist and stepped away from Erin. He felt like more of a fraud as he tried to think of what they'd want a new boss to say. "I'm going to do my best to make Riley's Bar the spot for nightlife. I think there are a lot of opportunities for improvement."

"You can say that again," Misty agreed.

"First and foremost, we need to take care of our customers—both current and potential. I'm going to be making some changes that will help with that."

"What kind of changes?"

"Making this place look a little better for one thing. Nightly specials, more events to get locals and visitors in the door. It's your job to keep them happy once they're here. I want good customer service. Be attentive but not overbearing."

"Do we let them hit on us?" All the women but Lexi giggled. She looked horrified.

"Only if you want them to." He smiled. "But I'd prefer you kept your time here professional."

The three experienced waitresses nodded, while Lexi continued to look straight ahead. She seemed as nervous as a deer at a shooting range.

"What about tips?" Tina asked. "Luke used to take part of what we got because he made the drinks."

"He skimmed your tips?" Scott didn't know why this surprised him. He'd checked the liquor on the shelves earlier and found several bottles watered down. Apparently, Luke hadn't been cutting corners only on the alcohol.

"He said it was his fair share," Misty offered.

"What's fair is that you keep the money you make." Scott stepped behind the counter. "Most nights I'm going to be handling the bar. Max and Jasper, the other bartenders, will fill in as needed."

"You know how to mix a decent Tom Collins?" Misty asked.

Scott nodded. "I can mix almost anything." He had spent time as a bartender when he'd been younger and had picked up a thing or two from his favorite haunts in D.C.

They watched him as if they expected more. He'd called them in here, but now had no pearls of wisdom to dispense. Basically, he'd wanted to see what he was working with. Other than Lexi, they all looked competent and at home in the bar.

He pulled shot glasses down from a shelf and grabbed a bottle of Jack Daniel's. He needed something to take the edge off. Just one. He turned to the man standing in the doorway. "We're going to have a round to welcome the new owner. Join us?"

Jon Riley shook his head. "No, boss. I'm five years sober."

Scott's hand paused in pouring. "Sorry. I didn't know."

"It's fine," Jon said quietly and disappeared through the door.

"I don't want one, either," Lexi told him when he pushed four of the small glasses forward.

"You on the wagon, too?" Tina asked.

"I don't think it's a good idea to drink while working."

Scott felt a hot burst of irritation skim along his spine. He didn't need to be judged by his little mouse of a waitress. "It's a special occasion," he told her. "Maybe if you relax, you won't have so much trouble keeping the glasses on the tray instead of the floor."

She narrowed her eyes. "I'll be fine. Thanks." With a huff, she followed Jon.

"Anyone else got a problem?"

In response, the remaining waitresses each picked up a shot glass. They toasted and downed the whiskey. It burned his throat, but after a moment the familiar warmth uncurled in his stomach.

"Thanks, boss," Misty told him and headed toward the back behind Lexi.

The other two women left the glasses on the bar and after a bit of small talk, meandered out the front door. Lexi and Misty were the two working tonight.

When he was alone again, Scott cleaned up the glasses and wiped down the top of the bar. He stared for a moment at the whiskey Lexi hadn't drunk. It seemed a shame to waste perfectly good alcohol, so he quickly downed it before putting the glass in the stack to be washed.

He turned to see Lexi watching him from the side of the bar. "Do you think that's a good idea?" she asked quietly.

"Sweetheart, none of this is a good idea." He returned the bottle of Jack to the shelf. "Luckily, I'm not much one for caring. If it feels right, I go for it."

"And drinking on the job feels right to you?" She took a step closer. "It seems to me that's what got you this bar in the first place." She pulled the apron in her hands over her head and reached behind her back to tie it, causing her breasts to push against the soft material of her light pink T-shirt.

Scott sucked in a breath. Hell, the T-shirt wasn't even formfitting and its conservative crew-neck collar practically covered half her throat. Misty was wearing a low-cut, skintight number that barely held in her ample chest. But it hadn't had any effect on him. Unlike Lexi's buttoned-up outfit.

He walked around the edge of the bar and took her arm, spinning her away from him.

"What are you doing?" she said with a gasp.

"Helping you," he answered and tied her apron strings

together. "It seems to me the reason I'm in this mess is because of you and your contract."

"You wanted to buy the bar," she argued.

"I wanted to pick a fight with Luke," he countered, resting his hands on her hips, unable to resist circling his thumbs against the place where her shirt hem met the fabric of her black dress slacks. Attorney clothes, clearly made of expensive material. Not the sort of pants someone wore to serve drinks.

Which reminded him that Lexi wasn't the sort of woman who should be waitressing in a bar. "If it wasn't for your ever-helpful legal skills, we would have exchanged some big talk and called it a night. Now I've got a business I don't want in a town I don't want to live in."

She went perfectly still, whether because of his words or his touch, Scott didn't know. But her voice was breathless when she spoke. "Maybe you should have stopped to think before you agreed to anything. Maybe if your ego wasn't so big you would have left when he told you to go."

Ouch. Scott didn't want to admit how close to home that hit. The phrase *if you'd stopped to think* could have saved him so many different times in his life.

"I never do," he said quietly. "Stop. Or think."

Because then he might remember how lonely he always felt, how afraid he was of needing someone and being left alone, the way both his parents had done when he was a kid.

"You should try it sometime," she said, her voice just a whisper.

"What's done is done." He pulled her closer to him and whispered against her ear, "It's easier to do what people expected of me—which isn't much."

* * *

Lexi felt her heart squeeze tight. It was so quiet in the bar at the moment. She was surrounded by Scott, the warmth of his chest against her back and his spicy, soapy scent mingling with the tangy smell of liquor on his breath.

That was what did it, brought her back to her right mind. The alcohol was the only explanation for why he seemed to want to touch her as much as she wanted to be touched by him.

She drove her elbow back, surprised at how quickly he moved to block the shot. "You're messing with me—"

She stopped when the front door opened and half a dozen men walked through. One called out, "There's an under-new-management sign in the window. What's that about?"

Another gave a long whistle. "Hey, there's a flat screen now. Is that new?"

"I'll be watching you tonight," Scott whispered to her. "Just remember that."

Her mouth went dry as he turned away.

"Put it up today, boys," he answered. "Got cable set up, too. Have a seat and we'll find a game to watch."

A round of cheers went up and the men came over to shake Scott's hand. They moved toward a table, but he pointed to the other side of the room. "You're going to have a better view over there, fellows."

He'd moved them from her section to Misty's, but only smiled as Lexi glared at him.

She spilled one glass the entire night, a huge improvement from her first shift. She didn't have the natural gift of gab that Misty did, flirting and making small talk with the customers. But Lexi did her best to keep up, making sure she got every order right and moving as quickly as her legs could carry her.

She was getting used to the noise and the smell of the bar, the customers who got more boisterous as the night wore on. Lexi didn't have a lot of experience with boisterous. Her father's idea of out of control was playing opera music instead of something mellower during dinner. Even in college, Lexi had stayed away from bars, worried there was something in her, some sort of predisposition for addiction, like her biological mother had had.

Her dad had told her in great detail about how she would have to overcome the deficiencies in her gene pool throughout her life. He'd made her believe that if she got too close to the wild life that had killed her mother, she might end up down that same dark path. She had only a few snippets of memory of her birth mom. The scent of her musky perfume and being left alone in their small apartment for long periods of time. But she was curious about "the other side of life," as her dad called it.

Being in Riley's Bar, serving customers, was a revelation to Lexi. She didn't really have a desire to drink, but the energy from the people around her made her feel more alive than she ever had.

Scott took a shot with another customer. She didn't know how much he'd had tonight and it wasn't any of her business. He didn't seem wasted, although he hadn't last night, either. She still knew he was trouble. He tempted her to be different than the person she'd worked so hard to become. The way he made her feel could be dangerous to her very soul. She wanted an adventure, but how far was she willing to go to get a real one?

The bar emptied soon after the football game was

over, which she figured was normal. She took off her apron and hung it in the back hall, counting the money from the front pocket. She'd made twenty dollars in tips. Not a lot, but the cash meant more to her than any paycheck she'd ever received from her father's firm.

"You did better tonight."

She turned to see Jon Riley in the doorway that led to the unused kitchen. "I practiced carrying drinks around all day," she said with a grin.

"It worked." He returned her smile. "You're not a natural but you'll get there."

"My mom was a waitress her whole life," Lexi said, then wondered why she'd shared that.

"There's worse ways to make a living."

She thought about her father and the underhanded legal deals he'd gotten into the habit of arranging to keep his firm on top. Maybe that was a type of addiction in its own right. She'd never made a connection between her adoptive father and her biological mother, and the thought made her skin crawl the tiniest bit.

"She was an alcoholic," Lexi blurted. "Lost custody of me when I was six. Working in bars killed her."

Jon shook his head. "The booze killed her. You're not like that."

"How do you know?" Lexi asked, suddenly needing reassurance from this virtual stranger.

"I've been down that road," he said simply. "I can recognize a person battling demons. Sometimes it's easier to drown yourself than work on what's really wrong."

She heard Misty's laughter ring out from the front of the bar, followed by the deep tone of Scott's voice.

Jon jerked his head toward the sound. "That boy has

a war waging inside him. He's got a good heart but he's going to have to do some digging to find it again."

"Can someone like him be helped?"

The man shrugged. "Maybe. But they've got to want it. And you've got to risk that if they don't, you're gonna be real hurt trying for 'em."

She thought again about her mother, wondered what her demons had been and if anyone had tried to help her.

The door to the front of the bar swung open and Misty's head popped through. "Scott poured an extra glass of wine. Want to join me for a drink?"

Lexi turned her head. "I think…" She paused and glanced back over her shoulder. Jon had disappeared into the kitchen again. "I'm going to head home now."

Misty shrugged. "Your call. Nice work tonight. Scott thinks you're too slow but I could see you busting your hump the whole time."

Lexi felt color rise to her cheeks. Scott thought she was too slow. She'd been worrying about how to help him, and he'd been talking trash about her. She swallowed against the embarrassment rising in her throat. "Have a good night, Misty," she said. Grabbing her purse from the hook, she headed for the back door.

She wrapped her arms around herself against the cool night air. Fall temperatures were dipping, even here in the South. She hurried to her car, and once back in her apartment, slipped off her shoes. Her feet ached, her shoulders were sore. Most of her body hurt from using muscles she'd never dealt with before. She wore heels as an attorney but never spent hours standing.

Even though it was late, she ran a bath and slipped into the warm water, letting it soak away some of her aches and pains. She liked to be clean. That was one thing she did remember from the time before Robert Preston had adopted her. She'd spent a lot of time dirty.

The bathtub in Julia's apartment might not be large or fancy like the deep soaker she'd left behind, but it did the trick. By the time she put on her soft cotton pajamas, she felt relaxed again.

She'd padded to the kitchen for a glass of water before bed when she heard the soft knock on the door. This time she didn't worry that it might be her father. From the way her stomach dipped, she knew who was waiting on the other side.

Chapter Four

"It's late, Scott." She hated that her voice sounded breathless. "What do you want?"

"I need a place to sleep."

His tone held none of its usual teasing or cocky certainty. But she kept the door open only a crack, not yet willing to let him in. "I thought you were staying at the bar."

"Too damn quiet after everyone leaves. Too empty. And it smells like a bar."

She smiled a little. "You smell like a bar."

"I could use a shower." He lifted a black duffel bag into view. "I brought a change of clothes."

She shook her head. "You should stay with Sam and Julia."

"They're a family. I don't belong there."

"You don't belong here."

He shrugged. "I don't belong anywhere." Lexi knew it was the first wholly honest thing he'd said since they'd met. The smallest bit of vulnerability flashed in his eyes and she was a goner.

Jon Riley's words about being hurt echoed in her head, but she pushed them away as she reached out and took Scott's hand. Pulling him to her, she brushed a wayward lock of hair away from his forehead. Her finger traced the side of his face, much the same way he'd done the last time he touched her. Did it have the same effect? His heated gaze gave her hope that it did.

He looked as if he wanted to devour her, but didn't make a move. He only watched as she explored his skin with her hands, his chest rising and falling with shallow breaths.

"Misty said you think I'm too slow," she told him softly, the words stinging her pride as she repeated them.

"The customers don't seem to mind," he answered. "You made good tips tonight."

"So you're not going to fire me?" She tried to make her voice sound teasing.

"Not yet," he answered.

"I'd threaten you with a sexual-harassment lawsuit but you flirt with everyone at the bar except me. Why is that?"

"You're the one pressed up against me." He shifted, somehow drawing her closer without pulling her to him. "Who's doing the harassing?"

He was right, but she could sense that his need matched her own. In the quiet intimacy of her apartment, it made her bold enough to ask, "Does this feel like harassment, Scott?"

"This feels like heaven," he whispered. "But I didn't come here for this. I'm no good for you."

"That's the point. I'm looking for a wild adventure and developing a new fondness for things that aren't good for me."

He took her arms and lifted them around his neck. Her head tilted and he brushed his lips against hers. Finally. It seemed as if she'd been waiting for this kiss her entire life.

And it was worth it.

His mouth felt delicious, the pressure sending sparks of desire along every inch of her skin. She lost herself in the sensations, reeling from the onslaught of need he aroused in her.

His strong arms wrapped around her, pulling her more tightly against him until she could tell how much he wanted her. She wanted him with the same need, like a drug she couldn't get enough of. She was quickly tipping out of control and the unfamiliarity of that made her push away.

Lexi Preston never lost control. She knew the dark and dangerous path where that might lead.

"You're right," she said around a gulp of air. "I'm slow." She covered her still-tingling lips with her fingers for a moment and stared at the floor. "I'm not one of your usual barflies."

"I never thought you were."

She pulled her shirt hem down where it had bunched around her waist. "You can stay here tonight." She still didn't meet his gaze. "On the couch. There's no furniture in the second bedroom right now. Use the shower,

whatever you need. I'm going to bed." She squeezed her
eyes shut tight. "Alone."

Before he could answer, she turned and retreated to
the bedroom.

Scott watched her go, willing his heart to slow and
his body to settle down.

What the hell was he doing in Lexi's apartment?

He'd told her the truth—he'd come here to sleep.
After the last stragglers had gone home, he'd sat alone
at the empty bar with a glass of Jack Daniel's in his hand,
ready to blot out the memories that flooded him when he
closed his eyes. But he couldn't lift the drink to his lips.

Sam was right—he'd been doing more self-medicating
with alcohol than he should lately. Since his partner had
been killed, it was the only thing that numbed the pain
and the thoughts that raced around his brain. He'd always
enjoyed a good buzz, but he'd never needed it the way he
did now.

He'd already lost control in so many areas of his life.
How much was he willing to give up? He'd poured out
the glass of whiskey and paced the length of the building. There was nothing more depressing than an empty
bar after closing, when the lack of body heat and voices
made it feel like a sad, lonely shell of broken dreams.

A lot like his life.

He'd gotten in his truck and driven here. Sure, he
could have called Tina or even Misty and found a warm
welcome and a warmer bed. Instead he'd craved the
lightness he felt radiating from Lexi. She was the pur-
est person he'd met in a long time, someone good and
innocent and everything he hadn't been in years.

He didn't understand his need for her. He'd never been

attracted to the buttoned-up type before. But her straw-berry hair, big luminous eyes and creamy skin made him want to fold her into him and not let go.

Except he knew he'd destroy the goodness in her. That was what he did to the people he needed. As much as he might want her, he'd keep his distance. He'd stay on the couch, stay away from her bed. As self-destructive as he could be, he still had a deep need to protect the peo-ple around him. Too bad he was the person Lexi needed protection against the most.

Scott slept better on the overstuffed couch than he had in years. He woke, showered and dressed, feeling halfway human again.

By the time eight o'clock rolled around, Lexi still hadn't made an appearance. He knocked softly on her bedroom door. "I know you're awake. I hear you mov-ing around. You can come out—I won't bite."

He heard something bang behind the closed door.

"I bet you have to go to the bathroom pretty bad by now."

The door opened and Lexi appeared, fully dressed in jeans and a shapeless T-shirt that nonetheless gave him a little thrill. She tried hard to hide her petite figure and he couldn't understand why.

"Why are you still here?" she asked warily.

"It's cheery."

"There isn't a lick of decoration in the place," she said and nudged him out of the way, slamming the bathroom door behind her.

He chuckled and moved back toward the kitchen, call-ing over his shoulder, "It's a hell of a lot cheerier than the bar."

He opened several cabinet doors. "There's got to be coffee here somewhere," he said as she came into the kitchen behind him.

"I told you I don't drink coffee. Tea is your only choice."

He made a choking sound.

"There's a bakery around the corner." She rolled her eyes. "Have at it."

"I have a better idea," he told her. "Let's grab breakfast. That diner in town is always crowded."

Her eyebrows shot to the top of her head. "I'm not having breakfast with you."

"Why not? All you've got is yogurt and fruit here. That's not going to do it for me."

"What does it for you isn't my concern." She put her hands on her small hips. "I let you stay here."

"Consider it a thank-you, then." He winked. "We'll discuss our future living arrangements. The couch is great but I'm going to need to get a bed."

She shook her head. "This is my apartment."

"Actually," he said slowly, "it's my sister-in-law's apartment. I have more rights to it than you."

Lexi's mouth dropped open and he found himself wanting to kiss it shut. "She's renting it to me."

"I don't like staying at the bar. I'm family." He grabbed her purse from the back of the chair and handed it to her. "My brother doesn't trust you after what you and your father tried to do."

She sucked in a breath.

"Don't make me use the family card."

"I'm ordering everything on the menu," she mumbled and headed out the door.

They drove in silence the few minutes to the restaurant. Scott could feel her frustration. He knew Julia didn't think much of him, and the truth was, his sister-in-law might very well rather rent her apartment to Lexi than him. He wasn't letting on, though.

He didn't want to stay at the bar. Although he would never admit it out loud, he didn't want to be by himself right now. He'd been living alone since he'd left home at eighteen. By nature, he was a loner. Even with girlfriends, he'd never been much of a stay-the-night snuggler. But he'd felt a strange sort of comfort knowing Lexi was sleeping down the hall last night. He had about a decade's worth of decent sleep to catch up on, and he was determined to make it happen.

She didn't order everything on the menu, but did ask for both an omelet and a stack of pancakes, plus granola on the side.

"Where do you put all that food?" he asked after their waitress had filled the table with plates. "You're no bigger than a minute and you've got enough calories on that plate for an NFL quarterback."

Reaching for the syrup, she answered, "It's going to be my dinner, too. I'll get a take-home box."

"So you conned me into buying you two meals?"

"I gave you a place to sleep last night." She took a big bite of pancake.

"Why do you need to hoard food? You don't strike me as someone hard up for money."

"I don't want to use my credit cards while I'm here." She stopped chewing midbite and stared at him, as if realizing she'd shared too much. "I'm trying to save money."

"You're hiding." He took a drink of coffee and studied her, the mystery that was his little pixie mouse falling into place. "From a boyfriend?"

She rolled her eyes. "No. My so-called boyfriend is probably relieved to get a break from me. My father set us up and I'm pretty sure he's only with me to improve his chances at making partner in the firm."

"Then he's an idiot." Scott held up a hand when she would have argued. "Don't change the subject. It must be your father. What happened between you and dear old dad?"

"Nothing," she muttered. "I just want some time on my own."

Scott shook his head. For an attorney, she was a terrible liar. "Tell me," he coaxed, extending his leg so he could brush against hers under the table. "Secrets are better when you share them."

She put down her fork. "It's not really a secret. I gave Julia some information about her ex-boyfriend's family that ensured they'd end the custody suit. They found out and dropped my father's firm. In turn, he dropped me."

"Not for good."

She shrugged. "From the moment I came to live with him, I've done everything he wanted me to. This is new ground for both of us."

"You're adopted?"

"When I was six. I'd been put into the foster system and shortly after, my mother died." Lexi drew in a breath and stared at her plate. "She was an alcoholic. I'd already been in two homes when my father found me. I owe him my life, really." When she looked up, tears shone in her big eyes. "But it's my life and I've never once made a decision just for me. He's mad now, but you're right, it's not forever. He's going to expect me to come back. Before I do, I need a little freedom. I'm going to see what it's like to do what I want to for a change."

"Why go back at all? If you want freedom, take it."

"It's not that simple."

"You're making it complex."

"I owe him."

"He's your father. That's not how it works with parents." Not that Scott had a lot of experience with unconditional love. His mother had died when he was a boy, killed in a car accident when she'd been driving after drinking. Her death had made his father pull away emotionally for years.

"When my father decided he wanted to adopt, he had fifteen kids in the foster system IQ tested. I happened to be the smartest of the bunch. That's how he picked me."

The thought made Scott cringe. "Is that even legal?"

"It doesn't matter. He made it happen." Lexi took a drink of juice, holding the tiny glass in front of her like a shield. "I always understood that I'd been given a great opportunity. And that I'd be a fool to jeopardize it. So I didn't. I was perfect, exactly who he wanted me to be. Up until seven months ago, I was more Stepford daughter than real person. I'm grateful for everything he did for me and I love him." She put down the juice and gestured with her hands. "This is all pretend to me. He made me the person I am and I can't change that. I'm going to take this time and enjoy it."

"Then what?" Scott almost didn't want to hear the answer.

She bit her bottom lip. "Then I go back to regular life. Or I go a different way. I need time to figure that out."

The waitress came to the table. "Could you box all

this up for us?" Scott asked, gesturing to the three plates still sitting in front of Lexi.

"Sure thing, sweetie." As she picked up the dishes, she smiled at him. "Aren't you the new owner over at Riley's?" she crooned.

He returned her grin. "Guilty as charged."

"I've always preferred Cowboys," she told him. Scott knew the other bar in town had loud country music, a huge dance floor and a mechanical bull. His version of hell. "But," she continued, leaning closer to him, "it might be worth a change of venue one of these nights."

"We'd love to see you over there."

Lexi cleared her throat and nudged the waitress's arm with one of the plates. "You forgot this."

She turned, as if noticing her for the first time. "Thanks," she muttered before walking away.

"I don't get why you're such a magnet for women." Lexi huffed out a breath. "What's so special about you?"

"Where do I begin?" he asked with a laugh, enjoying how bothered she was by the other woman's attention to him, even if he couldn't quite explain why. "But you're changing the subject again. You think by not using your credit cards, your father won't find you? What about when you use your cell phone?"

"I haven't yet." She fidgeted in her chair. "I don't expect you to understand. I need time, that's all."

He understood better than she knew. After everything he'd seen and done, if he could take a break from his messed-up life for a time, he'd gladly do it. Maybe that was why he'd made the impulsive offer to buy the bar in the first place. It was an expensive way to keep himself busy while he regrouped, but that was what he needed. After the incident, his superiors had wanted him to see a counselor while the internal investigation ran its course. According to his boss, it was standard when a marshal was killed in the line of duty and part of the requirement to have his administrative leave lifted.

Not that it mattered. Scott wasn't sure he'd ever go back. He still had the resignation letter he'd drafted. Any day now he'd get around to sending it.

He grabbed Lexi's hand as she made to stand from the table. "Not so fast. I bought you enough breakfast to feed a fire station. But we haven't talked about our living arrangement."

Lexi stared at him as a shiver ran down her spine. He couldn't be serious. "You can't live with me," she whispered.

"Why not?"

"People will talk about us."

"You think so?" he answered as the waitress came back to the table with a large bag of to-go cartons and the check.

She slid the small piece of paper toward Scott with a wink. "My phone number's on the back. When you get a night off, give me a call."

"How can she do that?" Lexi said with a hiss as the woman walked away again. "I'm sitting right here. It's like I'm invisible. For all she knows, we're on a date. We could have spent the night together and she's propositioning you while I watch."

"If I was staying at the apartment with you, maybe the flocks of women would back off." He wiggled his eyebrows.

Lexi did a mental eye roll, but at the same time her stomach fluttered. Scott Callahan was exactly the kind of man her father had warned her about for years. A bad boy to the core. Maybe that was part of the reason she found him so appealing.

She knew it was a bad idea, but said, "If I let you stay there, I don't want any more talk about me being fired."

He chuckled. "You're a terrible waitress. You know that, right?"

"*Terrible* is a strong word."

"You break more glasses than drinks you serve."

"I'm getting better," she argued.

"True, but you'll never be a natural."

"Those are my terms." She grabbed the bag of food and made her way toward the door.

Scott caught up to her easily as she rounded the street corner. "How long are you planning on staying here?" He grabbed her elbow and swung her around to face him.

She stared at him, not sure how to respond. "A month. Six weeks? However long it takes."

"I won't fire you for a month. You let me stay at the apartment for four weeks and I'll let you keep your job. Deal?"

She watched the fall breeze play with the waves of his hair. His hands were shoved in his pockets and he looked as if he didn't have a care in the world. His jeans hugged the strong muscles of his legs and his faded flannel shirt was unbuttoned enough to reveal a small patch of hair on his chest. Every part of him was the essence of cool.

But his eyes told her a different story. A tale of loneliness, loss and a need that called to her own secret, lonely heart.

"Okay," she said quickly, before she changed her mind. "I mean, since you're Julia's brother-in-law, she certainly wouldn't mind you crashing there, too."

He tried to hide the smile that played at the corner of his mouth. "You won't regret it."

"I already do," she muttered. "You need to get your own bed. By tonight."

He nodded. "I can do that."

"Would you really have fired me?"

His grin widened. "You'll never know. I have to be at the bar for some deliveries. I'll give you a lift back to your apartment first."

"I need to do some things in town, so I can walk back later. It's not far. I'll have an extra key made and leave it under the front mat." She lifted the bag. "Thanks for breakfast. And dinner."

She was brushing him off, but Scott didn't want to push the first good luck he'd had in ages. He reached forward and tapped his finger on the tip of her nose. "Have a good day, Lexi."

She pushed her hair behind her ears and watched him walk away. Her stomach gurgled and she hoped it was from the food rather than her reaction to Scott.

Halfway down the sidewalk, she noticed a light on in Julia's salon. The place was closed until noon, according to the sign in the window. But the front door was unlocked, so she let herself in. Closing the door behind her, she heard the patter of feet, then a dog was in front of her. He was big and gray and barked several times before showing his teeth.

Lexi pressed her back against the wall of windows at the front of the building. "Good doggie," she whispered.

The animal's lip curled back even more and she could have sworn he snarled at her. Lexi felt her recently eaten breakfast threaten to make a repeat appearance. At least that might distract the dog long enough for her to get away. She concentrated on breathing without passing out.

"Casper?"

Lexi heard Julia's voice from the back of the salon. "Julia," she called softly. The dog came a step closer to her. "It's Lexi. I, uh, your dog… Can you come…?"

"He's friendly." Julia walked toward her, hands on her hips.

"Really?" Lexi's voice was a high-pitched squeak. "Why is he snarling at me?"

"He smiles." The woman placed a hand on the dog's broad back. "Casper, sit."

He plopped to the ground.

"Pet him," Julia suggested. "He'll love you."

Lexi swallowed and held out a hand. She ran her palm along the animal's silky head. He immediately flipped on his back, wriggling in ecstasy as Lexi rubbed him with more enthusiasm. "He's a sweetie."

"Told you so."

"How well do you know Sam's brother?" Lexi asked, keeping her attention focused on the dog.

"Not very," Julia admitted. "He and Sam aren't close. They never have been. Has he been giving you trouble at the bar?"

Lexi shook her head, straightening. "He's been okay. It's just…weird, right? That he bought the bar and is staying in Brevia."

"There's more than one person in Brevia who doesn't belong right now."

Lexi felt herself blush. "I'm sorting things out. This is a little detour, that's all. Does it bother you that I'm here? I put a lot on you and maybe it didn't feel like you had a choice but to help." A thought crossed her mind. "I don't want to make it uncomfortable for you. Scott said Sam doesn't like me."

"Can you blame him?"

"No," Lexi admitted, cringing. She loved her work and the law, but hated some of the things she'd had to do as part of her job. Her father had so many powerful clients and Lexi had spent a lot of her time digging up dirt on their enemies, often people with a lot less money and influence. It made her feel like the stereotypical unethical attorney, and she wished it could be different.

"Actually, I like thinking I'm getting back at your dad in a way." Julia smiled at her. "Not that I'm vindictive or anything, but he and the Johnsons made my life difficult. You know what they say about payback." She absently straightened one of the styling bays. "Don't worry about Sam. He's protective of me. But it's all good."

Lexi noticed Julia's dreamy smile. "You're lucky to have someone who loves you like that."

"Agreed," Julia said. "How is the apartment? Other than the basics, I didn't leave a lot of stuff there."

"It's great. Thank you again. I get paid at the end of this week so I should be able to get you more than the deposit, but…"

"Don't worry about it," Julia told her. "I know you're good for it. It's not too weird in a strange place by yourself?"

Lexi thought about Scott sleeping on her couch and shook her head. "I'm fine." She should tell Julia about their new arrangement, but the words wouldn't form. "I noticed a few dog toys in the closet."

"I found Casper when I was living there." Julia bent

forward to scratch between the dog's ears. "Or I should say, he found me."

"So the building is pet friendly?"

The stylist studied her. "You don't seem like a dog person."

"I don't know," Lexi admitted. "My father never let me have pets. Dogs make me nervous." She gave a small laugh. "Almost everything makes me nervous. But this adventure is all about trying new things."

"An animal is a big commitment. It's not just something you try out for a little, then dump when you go back to your real life."

"I know that." Lexi's resolve suddenly got stronger. She'd never experienced unconditional love, but was sure she had it in her to give. She'd always wanted a pet, but had been afraid that even a dog or cat might not think she was good enough. She didn't know anything about caring for an animal. Suddenly, it was very important to prove it to herself. "What time does the animal shelter your mom runs open?"

Julia glanced at her watch. "Not for another hour. But I have an in with the owner, if you know what I mean."

"You don't have to help me with this. You've done more than enough already. I'm not here to take charity from you."

"I've got a good instinct for matching dogs with their forever people." Julia grabbed a leash off the hook on the wall. "But you can return the favor. One of the girls is going through a divorce and she's feeling uneasy about the filing. Frank Davis is her attorney, the same one I used. He's not giving her the time she needs. I'll take you out to the shelter, and in return, you look over the paperwork for her."

Lexi had run away from her life and her job, but she still loved the law. Maybe giving legal advice to someone here could start to make up for all the things she'd done as an attorney that weren't helpful.

She nodded, loving the sound of the word *forever*. She wanted to be a forever person, even if only to an animal. Plus, it would be good to have a distraction in the apartment when Scott was there.

"You've got yourself a deal."

Chapter Five

Scott arrived at the bar in the late afternoon, after spending the day in Charlotte buying more supplies and a mattress set to take to the apartment. At this rate, he was going to run through his savings within the month.

He was tired and, strangely, wanted to return to Lexi's. The two-bedroom apartment was nothing special and not nearly as stylish or comfortable as his condo in D.C., but he felt more at home there than anyplace he'd been in years.

He had work to do at the bar first. As soon as he walked into the building, the smell of spices and roasting…something…hit him. He followed his nose to the kitchen and found Jon Riley at the stove with four men sitting around the small table in the corner.

"Hey, there," he called to the group.

All four men jumped up, turning toward him with

varying degrees of mistrust in their eyes. "He invited us," one of them offered.

"We're allowed to be here," another insisted.

"Who are you, anyway?" a third asked.

Jon turned from the stove. "It's okay, guys." He motioned them to sit back down. "This is Scott Callahan, the bar's new owner. I told you about him. He's cool."

Scott didn't feel particularly cool at the moment. "Uh, Jon? What the hell is going on here?"

"I'm making an early dinner."

"You asked if you could use the kitchen to make yourself food. You forgot to mention company."

Jon turned the heat down on one of the burners and pointed to the hall. With a wary glance at the strangers sitting at the table, Scott turned and followed him there.

"I won't make a habit of it," he said with a shrug. "But these guys are like me. They don't have much and they've given a helluva lot more to this country than they've gotten back."

"They're ex-military?"

Joe nodded. "They need a break and a decent meal. I didn't think you'd be here this early. Thought I could get them fed and out before anyone noticed." He gave Scott a sheepish smile. "Sorry."

Scott scrubbed his hand across his face. His life was so far from the norm, he didn't know which way was up anymore. He was used to action, a mission and constantly moving. He was used to being on his own. Now he'd gotten himself a roommate and had a kitchen full of hungry men waiting for a meal. He shook his head. "Do you have enough for one more?"

Jon's grin looked out of place on his somber face. "You bet."

Scott walked back into the kitchen and sat down with the men, feeling an odd camaraderie with this misfit band of soldiers. They asked him a few questions about his military career, but mainly enjoyed the meal in a companionable silence he could appreciate. Then he took his first bite from the plate Jon placed in front of him and could barely stop himself from moaning out loud. He looked around at the other men, whose faces reflected the same food rapture he felt.

He met Jon's gaze. "This is beyond amazing," he said, then took another large bite. "I'm talking four-star-restaurant good."

"It's only a chicken potpie," Jon said with a shrug. "I like simple food that tastes good."

"It's a little bit of heaven," Scott agreed.

One of the men shook his fork at Jon. "Everything he makes is like this. I look forward to my weekly Jon fix like I used to crave the bottle."

"That's quite a comparison," Scott said with an uncomfortable laugh.

"Denny is in my AA group," Jon explained. "Like I said, I worked as a chef in New York, but the big-city lifestyle didn't exactly agree with me."

"Didn't you say Riley's used to serve food?" Scott asked.

He nodded. "It's where I got my start."

Scott looked around the large kitchen. "What would you think about putting together a menu?"

"Are you serious?"

"Nothing fancy, but a step up from normal bar food. Like you said, simple food that tastes good. If we could tap into part of the lunch and dinner crowd, it would expand the bar's reach in a great way. Riley's Bar & Grill. What do you think?"

"I think it's the best offer I've had in years," he answered, his voice thick.

A round of applause and several catcalls went up from the men.

Scott felt a smile spread across his face. He stood, shook hands with Jon, then grabbed his plate. "I'm glad you agree. Get something to me by end of day tomorrow. I'd like to get the new menu implemented by early next week."

"Will do, boss."

"I've got to put away some boxes out front, so I'm going to take my dinner to go." He turned to the men. "It was nice meeting you guys." He paused, then added, "If any of you are looking for work, let me know. There's a lot of odd jobs to be done around here, painting and the like."

"There aren't a lot of opportunities for guys like us," Denny answered. A couple of the men nodded in agreement. "Some of us got arrest records, pasts we're not too proud of."

"I know all about that," Scott answered. He pointed to Jon. "If he vouches for you, that's enough for me."

"Thanks, Mr. Callahan." Denny stepped forward and shook his hand. "You're a good man."

Scott smiled. "I don't know about that, but I'm a man in need of good help. Come in tomorrow morning and we'll talk work."

He finished the meal as he unloaded bottles into the cooler. He walked from the back with more beer and heard the front door open. Annoyance crept up his spine at his hope to see Lexi, who was on the schedule tonight, coming in early. He knew his interest in her would lead nowhere for either of them, but couldn't put a stop to it. Instead, his father and Sam stood inside the entrance.

"To what do I owe the honor?" he asked, setting the box on top of the bar.

"Scotty, it's so good to see you." His dad came forward and wrapped Scott in a tight hug, ignoring the way he stiffened in response. Joe Callahan had been the consummate Boston cop for years, both before and after his wife died. He'd dedicated his life to the force, even when he'd had two young sons at home grieving the loss of their mother. Joe's ability to cut off his feelings had been ingrained early in both his boys, which was just fine by Scott. Recently Joe had rediscovered his "emotional intelligence" as he called it, and was on a mission to make sure Sam and Scott came along for the ride.

Joe had traveled south last spring to reconnect with Sam, and in the process had gotten a second chance at love—with Julia's mother, Vera. Now both Sam and Joe called Brevia, North Carolina, home. Scott was happy for them, but he had no desire to be part of Joe's lovefest. He thought Sam had gone soft, and although he liked Julia and her little boy well enough, the thought of being tied down with a wife and kid felt totally foreign to him.

"Good to see you, old man. Married life is treating you well so far." He pulled back from Joe's tight hug. "Jeez, Dad, what's up with the tears?"

Joe swiped a hand across his face. "I'm happy to see you, son. Nothing wrong with showing my emotions."

"He's a regular watering pot," Sam added, clapping a hand on their dad's broad back. "How's it going here?"

"Coming along," Scott answered, stepping behind

the bar and out of Joe's reach. "Is this a social call or something else?"

"I've got a buddy who's a local Realtor specializing in commercial property," Sam said. "I can make a call and get him over here within fifteen minutes."

"Why do I need a Realtor?"

Sam exchanged a look with their father. "We thought he could help."

Scott pointed a finger at Joe. "You're in on this, too?"

"I want you to be happy, Scotty." He stepped forward. "You've been through a lot. You deserve it."

"It was an impulsive decision to buy this place," Sam said. "We get that. But Mark can help you unload it before things go too far."

"You think you know me so well," Scott muttered, transferring beer bottles into the cooler behind the bar.

"I know you love being a marshal, the action and adrenaline of it," his brother countered. "I know life as a bar owner can't give you that."

"I thought the same thing when you left the force in Boston to take the police chief's job in this Podunk Smoky Mountain town. It's worked out all right for you. Why not me?"

Sam shook his head, but Joe stepped between them. "Is this what you want, Scott? This kind of life change? Because I'll support whatever you want to do, whether it's going back to D.C. or staying in Brevia. Hell, I'll wipe bar tables for you if it would help."

"Dad, he's not staying in Brevia."

Scott felt his temper flare. Why didn't anyone around him think he could stick? "Is it so hard to believe I could make a life here in your precious town? I get that you don't want me here."

"It's not that, although could you blame me if it was?" Sam let out a breath. "The last time we were living in the same place, you slept with my fiancée. That's a hell of a breach of trust."

"You know why that happened. She'd already cheated on you and you wouldn't believe it. I had to prove it to you."

"By going after her yourself? That's not my definition of brotherly love."

Scott squeezed shut his eyes to ward off the dull pounding inside his head. When he opened them again, he saw Lexi standing just inside the front door. By the look on her face, she'd heard his conversation with Sam and the awful thing he'd done. He'd wanted to protect his brother, but ended up betraying him in the worst way possible. Sam was right—he'd made a huge alcohol-induced mistake when he'd taken Sam's former fiancée, Jenny, to bed.

Buying the bar had also been impulsive and alcohol-induced. Whether it was a mistake remained to be seen. Sam certainly thought it was, and probably their dad, as well. Scott met Lexi's gaze, surprise in her eyes, but not the judgment he'd come to expect from everyone around him. Maybe that would appear later. He couldn't say. But the absence of it bolstered his resolve.

He turned to face his brother and father. "I messed up, Sam. Royally. I'm sorry for what I did, but you have to believe that my intentions were good. Or don't believe it. It doesn't matter anymore. I'm here now and I'm staying in Brevia until I decide it's time to go. I'm not going to make a mess of the bar. I won't embarrass you in front of your wife or your neighbors. You have a life here. I get that."

He expected Sam to argue, but instead his brother gave a curt nod.

Joe put one arm around Sam's stiff shoulders and reached for Scott, hugging both men to his chest. "All three of us together again. I couldn't ask for anything more." He gave a loud sniff and Scott saw Sam roll his eyes. At least they were in agreement in not liking their father's emotional mumbo jumbo. "We should celebrate."

Scott looked over his father's shoulder to Lexi, who was gesturing wildly. He nodded as her meaning became clear. "We should celebrate the fact that both of you bozos were dumb enough to get caught in the marriage net. I'll throw a party here for you—a joint reception with all your friends. As big as you want it to be."

Sam shook his head. "I don't think so."

"It's a great idea." Joe clapped Scott on the back. "When are you thinking?"

"I need a few weeks to get everything running the way I want. How about a month from Saturday?"

"Perfect," Joe answered.

"No way," Sam said. "Julia won't agree to it."

"Nonsense," Joe argued. "Vera will be thrilled and Julia will agree to anything that makes her mother happy."

"I'm sure you want to make your mother-in-law slash new stepmother happy, Sammy-boy."

Joe nodded. "If Vera's happy, we're all happy."

Scott got a good bit of satisfaction in watching his brother's jaw clench. "Why are you doing this?" Sam asked.

How did he answer that? Because his old life held too many reminders of the partner he'd lost. Because he couldn't stand to be alone anymore. Because he had to keep moving, stay busy to keep the demons at bay. His chest tightened but he held Sam's gaze. "I want to make things right between us. At least let me try."

"Fine." Sam looked over his shoulder at Lexi, then back at him. "I thought you were going to fire her."

Scott felt that unfamiliar surge of protectiveness wash over him again. "Leave her alone, Sam. We've come to an understanding."

"She's trouble and I don't trust her."

Scott watched Lexi walk forward until she stood directly behind Sam. Scott had a couple of inches on his brother, but Sam was broader, making Lexi look even tinier so close to him. "I can hear you talking about me," she told Sam.

"I don't particularly care," he said, glancing at her again.

"Do you work here with Scotty?" Joe asked, oblivious to the tension between Sam and Lexi. "I'm Joe Callahan, his proud father."

Proud father? Scott groaned. Next Joe would be handing out cigars to customers, as if Scott's being in Brevia was cause for a real celebration. It was too bad his dad hadn't been around like this when he was a kid. Joe had been a workaholic cop, leaving the raising of his two young sons mostly to their mother, so he could put his life on the line for the force. And after Scott's mom died, things had gotten even worse, with Joe working extra shifts so he could bury the pain of his loss. Unfortunately, Scott had been stuck with his own pain and loss, but too young to know how to deal with them. Maybe things would have turned out differently if his mom was still around, but he'd never know. All he had was the present moment. "Dad, this is Lexi Preston. She's one of the waitresses here."

"Nice to meet you, Mr. Callahan."

"Call me Joe." He took her hand and brushed his lips across her knuckles. "If all the waitresses are as pretty as you, this place should do a bang-up business."

"Dad, inappropriate." Scott felt his jaw drop as Lexi giggled. He hadn't heard her laugh before. The sweet sound washed over him and made him crave more.

"I don't mind," she said, tipping her chin down as a blush crept up her cheeks.

Scott sucked in a breath as she smoothed her hands across the fabric of her dark miniskirt.

Sam nudged him. "Be careful, little brother. I still don't trust her."

Joe turned to Sam, frowning. "You're being rude, Sammy. I didn't raise you to disrespect a lady like that."

"It's true, Dad."

"Thanks for the compliment, Joe." Lexi met Sam's angry stare and swallowed. "But your son has good reason to mistrust me. I worked on the custody case against Julia Morgan. I put her and Sam through a lot and I'm sorry for that."

Joe crossed his arms over his chest. "Is that so?"

"I also gave Julia the information that helped her get the lawsuit dropped, if that makes a difference." She glanced toward the front of the bar as if she wanted to bolt, then turned back to the three men. "I know I have to earn your trust, and I'm going to do that, Sam. Julia has given me a chance and I'm very grateful to her."

"A chance at what?" Joe asked.

"A chance for a fresh start." Lexi took a deep breath. "I'm going to live by my terms and that means helping people instead of hurting them. I learned a lot in the past couple of months. I've gotten a second chance and I'm going to make the most of it."

Joe studied her with his best hard-nosed cop stare. Scott knew the look well, as he and his trouble-making buddies had caved under it many times growing up. Lexi didn't look away and Scott realized that his little mouse had a lot more backbone than he'd given her credit for. Suddenly, Joe reached out a hand and pulled Lexi into one of his trademark bear hugs.

"You've got to be kidding me," Sam muttered under his breath.

"It takes a lot of guts to admit you've made a mistake. I'm proud of you, Lexi. We'll be here to help you every step of the way."

Joe released Lexi and she stepped back, looking a little dazed, much like Scott felt. "That means a lot, Joe." She quickly swiped at her cheeks and kept her eyes to the ground. "I've got to clock in now. I'll, um… Thank you."

With that, she raced through the door that led to the back of the bar.

Scott wanted to follow her, but turned to his father. "What was that, Dad? You made her cry."

"When are you going to learn there's nothing wrong with tears?"

"Excuse me, but you were the one who told me to man up after Mom died. I was seven, and as I remember, there was a strict no-tears rule."

Joe wiped at his own eyes. "I'm sorry, boys. I know I made big mistakes. But we're all together now and things are going to be back on track with the three of us." He pulled Scott to him and let out a shuddering breath.

"Okay, Dad, sure." Scott looked at Sam. "Is he always like this now?"

"Yep. Welcome to Joe Callahan 2.0." Sam nudged their father. "Come on, old man. Scott has work to do."

"I'll have Vera call you about the details of the reception. She'll be thrilled."

Scott's eyes widened at the thought of dealing with his spirited new stepmother. For the first time today, Sam smiled. "Be careful what you wish for," he cautioned, then turned for the front door.

Joe stopped and looked back at Scott. "Do you have a place yet? You're welcome to stay with Vera and me."

"I'm set. Thanks, though."

Sam's eyes narrowed, but Scott ignored him. "See you, boys," he called, then turned back to his cases of beer.

Lexi entered another order into the computer and turned away from the bar as a hand clamped down on her wrist.

"You're avoiding me," Scott said, leaning toward her.

"I'm hustling so you don't have a reason to complain about me."

"I wasn't aware I needed a reason."

"Don't you have bottles to open?" She blew a strand of hair out of her eyes, then stilled as he brushed his thumb across her face.

"I'm an excellent multitasker," he said, somehow making the words sound like foreplay.

She shrugged out of his grasp and stepped away from the bar, his quiet laugh flustering her even more. She still hadn't recovered from the emotions that had bubbled to the surface when Joe Callahan said he was proud of her.

Never once since she'd been adopted had her own father said anything like that to her, despite the fact that she'd made it her life's mission to make him proud. Instead, the more she'd tried, the more he seemed to expect, until she felt more like a machine than a real person. Now, by her simply admitting she wanted to do better, Scott's dad had given her the validation she craved. How weak and pathetic did that make her?

She was totally off-balance, which may have explained why, when Jon poked his head out of the back of the bar and told her she had an emergency call, she automatically took the cordless phone and held it to her ear.

"Hello," she said into the receiver.

"Lexi." Her father spoke her name like an admonishment. It was a tone she recognized all too well.

She sucked in a breath. "How did you find me?"

"The better question is why are you hiding from me?"

"I'm not hiding," she said softly, holding the phone close to her ear to hear over the background noise in the bar. Although it was a weekday night, a decent crowd had trickled in to watch the evening's game on the big screen. "You fired me. I left. That's how it works."

"No need to be snippy, Lexi," her father said, his voice clipped. "I acted in a moment of anger. I think your leave of absence has gone on long enough. I'll expect to see you at the office Monday morning."

Lexi bit down on her lip until she could swear she tasted blood. She'd known this was going to happen, that her father would reel her back in eventually. She was too valuable a commodity for him to truly let her go. But she'd hoped to have more time. "I'm not ready."

"Excuse me?"

"I want to stay," she said, trying to give her voice a confidence she didn't feel.

"To spend your nights in a bar in that backwoods Southern town? I don't think so. With your biological history, that's a very bad idea. I'll see you Monday and—"

"No!"

Silence greeted her outburst. "I'm taking a month. I have the personal days." She spoke quickly so as not to lose her nerve. "I'll let you know then if and when I'm coming back. Goodbye, Daddy."

With trembling fingers, she clicked off the receiver and held it tight against her chest, her stomach turning. She'd never disobeyed her father before. Yes, she was twenty-seven years old, but when it came to her relationship with Robert Preston, she felt more like a schoolgirl, afraid of his dissatisfaction, disappointment and ultimately his rejection. Her biggest fear was that the man who'd rescued her from her awful childhood would leave her with nothing and no one in her life. She knew he had the power to do that, at least as far as her career went. Still, she couldn't give up now. She needed to know she could make it on her own if she had hope of going back to her old life with any shred of dignity intact.

She felt someone watching her and looked up to see Scott standing stock-still next to the bar, the waitresses a flurry of activity around him. Lexi tried to throw him a casual smile, but her mouth wouldn't move in that direction so she fled to the back of the bar. With a calming breath, she headed into his small office at the end of the hall and returned the phone to its cradle. Scrubbing her hands across her face, she turned and ran smack into Scott's rock wall of a chest.

"Who was on the phone?" he asked, holding her upper arms to steady her.

"It was personal. None of your business."

"You look like someone called to say they'd shot your puppy."

"That's awful." She tried to step way, but he held her in place, one finger tracing small circles on her skin, as if he was trying to soothe her. She hated to admit that it worked, but felt herself sagging a bit, the conversation with her father draining what little energy she had left from the day.

"I'm guessing you got the call from dear old dad?" Scott asked softly.

She nodded. "I blocked the firm's and his personal numbers from my cell and haven't been picking up callers I don't recognize. It was sneaky of him, phoning the bar."

"He's an attorney—what do you expect?"

"Lawyer jokes. Funny." But she smiled a little. "He wants me in the office on Monday."

Scott's fingers stilled on her arm, which made her glance up into his suddenly unreadable eyes. "Are you going?"

"No. Not yet, anyway. I like it here, the apartment, the small town." She gave a tiny laugh. "Even this crummy job. The boss is a jerk but the customers are great."

"Boss jokes. Funny." One side of his mouth kicked up before drawing into a tight line. "Will your father come looking for you?"

"I don't think so. I told him I needed a month."

"What happens in a month?"

"I'm not sure, but it gives me time to figure it out."

"You can take care of yourself, you know. You had

my dad eating out of the palm of your hand minutes after you told him you'd tried to take his grandson away."

"Your dad's a big teddy bear."

Scott grinned. "I've never thought of him that way."

His smile disarmed her, made her breath hitch. She wanted him in a way she couldn't explain and barely understood. Clearly, she wasn't his type, and he was way too much…man for her. But it didn't stop her body's response to him. He met her gaze, and the way his blue eyes darkened made her think he might feel the same. She knew her time in Brevia would eventually come to an end, and she wanted to experience everything she could while she was here. Maybe that was what made her blurt, "Have an affair with me?"

Scott's grip on her arm loosened. His fists clenched and she thought he might walk away. "You can't want that."

"I do." She licked her lip and felt the electricity of desire charge between them. "More than you know."

His hands smoothed up her arms and across her shoulders to her neck, his fingers burning a path along her heated skin. He cradled her head in his hands as one thumb traced the seam of her lips. "You should be gentler with this mouth," he told her, soothing the spot she'd bit down on earlier. "I've grown to like it quite a lot."

She could hardly manage a breath, but whispered, "What if gentle isn't what I want?"

He cupped her face, tilting her chin up and leaning in so they were so close she could smell the peppermint scent of his breath. "You don't know what you're asking, Lexi."

"Show me."

Heaven help her, he did. His mouth covered hers, igniting a fire in her belly that quickly spread out of control. Which was exactly what she wanted: to lose control with this man. Right here, right now. As his lips teased hers, she lifted her arms around his neck, pressing her body against him.

Scott groaned low in his throat and deepened the kiss, his mouth making demands that she tried her best to meet. His hands moved down, just brushing the outline of her breasts, making her gasp. He took the opportunity to tangle his tongue with hers and she lost all coherent thought, so caught up in the physical sensations that were flooding through her.

When he pulled back she thought she might melt into a puddle on the floor, that was how boneless and weightless he'd made her feel. "Don't stop," she said, reaching for him again.

"No."

That one word brought her back to reality like a swift kick to her stomach. She blinked several times to clear her head. "You don't mean that. The way you were just kissing me, you can't mean that."

He shook his head, his hands clenched at his sides. "You're not thinking clearly and you want to get back at your father. I understand that. But I'm not going to take advantage of your weakness."

"I'm not weak."

"I didn't mean—"

"I get to make my own decisions." She adjusted her shirt where it had bunched around her waist, embarrassed that she was still reeling from the kiss, when Scott could clearly pull away with no problem. "Good or bad, the point of me being on my own is to live on my own terms."

"Which involve a relationship with me?"

She crossed her arms over her chest. "Not a relationship. An affair. You know…"

"Sex?" he offered.

"Well…yes. Casual. Fun. Easy. All things that have been missing from my life since…forever, really."

"You don't strike me as the casual-sex type."

"That's the point." She wanted to stomp her foot in frustration. Why was he making this so complicated? Couldn't he just go back to kissing her and see where that led?

"My answer is still no," he said quietly.

Tears of embarrassment clogged her throat. Here she was, all but throwing herself at his feet, only to be rejected. "Because I'm not your type."

"Because of a lot of reasons. I don't—"

"It's fine." She held up a hand. "There's no need to go on. We both need to get back to work."

He shook his head as he watched her. "It's a slow night. Take the rest of it off. You look like you could use it."

Lexi felt a blush burn her cheeks. He was going to reject her, then tell her she looked like hell? Great. Insult to injury, why would she expect anything else?

"What I need," she said, straightening her shoulders and setting her jaw so he wouldn't see how his words stung, "is a drink. It works for you. Why not me? I'm going to have an adventure with or without you, Scott. Just wait and see." Mustering every ounce of dignity she could grasp, she walked past him back toward the bar.

Chapter Six

Scott put his key in the lock, then leaned forward to listen for any sound coming from the apartment. It was late, past 2:00 a.m., and thankfully, things seemed to be quiet here. He wasn't sure if he could keep his temper at Lexi's ridiculous proposition, not to mention his desire for her, in check if she was still awake.

He wasn't sure how things had gone bad so quickly. Not that they'd ever been particularly good between them, but he'd thought they'd reached an understanding. Then he'd seen her take that phone call, shock and misery evident on her face. He'd known it was a mistake to follow her back to his office, but he'd had to make sure she was okay. She wasn't, and after minutes spent kissing her, neither was he. Holding a woman in his arms had never affected him the way being with Lexi had.

When she'd made the offer of an affair, parts of his

body had literally jumped to attention. But he couldn't agree to it. He had a track record of hurting the people he cared about, and although he'd known her only a short time, he felt an undeniable connection to Lexi. Whether it was his mother or Sam or his late partner at the Marshals, Derek, Scott's need and desire to protect them turned to poison.

It had become easier to keep people at arm's length. He'd also become an expert at avoiding the pain of rejection or having someone he cared about not believing him. Lexi was a good person, pure of heart in a way he could never hope to be. For once he was going to do the right thing, even if it killed him.

It just might, he thought as the door opened to reveal Lexi asleep on the couch in nothing but a tank top and boxer shorts. Her legs curled under her, the skin creamy all the way down to her bright red toenail polish. Legs he could well imagine wrapped around him.

A low sound coming from the other side of the couch distracted him. A moment later there was a flash of brown fur accompanied by several high, yippy barks, and a small dog sunk its teeth into the toe of Scott's work boot.

"What the—" He shook his foot but the tiny dog had clamped on tight.

Lexi sat up, rubbing her eyes. "What's going on? What time is it?"

She wiped a hand across her mouth and Scott was momentarily distracted from the dog attack by the fact that Lexi wasn't wearing a bra. Was she trying to kill him?

The small animal holding tight to his boot was certainly intent on the job.

Lexi's sleepy gaze met Scott's, then dropped to his

leg. "Oh, no. Freddy, no. Come here, sweetheart." She moved around the side of the sofa, then dropped to her knees on the carpet. "Come, Freddy," she said, and with one last growl, the small pup jumped into her arms.

Scott closed the door behind him and contemplated the picture of Lexi on her knees in front of him. The couch in his office at the bar was suddenly looking more appealing.

"What is that thing?" he asked, dropping his keys on the table next to the door. He went to take a step into the apartment, but the dog turned and barked.

"It's not a thing. It's a dog. He's my dog." She picked him up as she stood, the small animal licking her chin with its pink tongue. "His name is Freddy."

Scott shook his head. "That's not a dog. You could make a case for an overgrown rat, or a football with legs, but it's definitely not a dog."

Lexi cradled the animal close to her chest, covering its ears at the same time. "Don't say things like that. He has a bit of a Napoleon complex. You're going to make it worse."

Scott couldn't imagine this night getting much worse.

"Where did he come from?"

"The Morgans' animal shelter, of course. Julia helped me pick him out. Freddy and I bonded right away. He's a Chihuahua mix."

"Mixed with rodent I'd bet." All Scott wanted was to go to sleep, and now he couldn't get past the apartment's entrance without mini-Cujo gunning for him.

"Scott, please. My father never let me have a pet, not even a goldfish. I love Freddy. He needs me." Lexi's voice was a plea. "He's obviously a good watchdog.

That's important when you're a single woman living alone."

"You don't live alone. I live here, too."

She tilted her head. "You never know what I might need protection from."

That was the truth if he'd ever heard it, especially with one thin strap of her tank top sliding down the smooth skin of her upper arm. He refocused his attention on the dog. "He's going to have to get used to me."

"Come sit down on the couch with us."

Areas low in Scott's body tightened. The last thing he needed was to be sitting close to Lexi on the soft couch. "I'm tired. I want to go to sleep."

"In a minute," she argued and reached for his hand, lacing her fingers through his. "I want you to see how sweet Freddy is."

Her smile, both excited and tentative, did Scott in. There was nothing he could do to resist her.

She led him to the sofa, Freddy still nestled in her arms, and they sat side by side, the length of her bare leg pressed against his thigh. Even with his jeans between them, he could sense how soft her skin was. Knew it would feel like silk against his hands, his mouth. With a shake of his head, he looked at her holding the dog. "What do you want me to do?"

"Don't move," she answered. "I'm going to let him go so he can check you out. Don't make eye contact with him."

"Seriously?"

"Julia's mom told me that's how you start when a dog is nervous." Lexi smiled at Scott again. "Just close your eyes."

"Can I fall asleep?"

"No, but close your eyes."

He sighed and did as she asked, letting his head fall back. Despite how tired he was, there was no chance of him falling asleep sitting this close to Lexi. She smelled like heaven, and as she spoke softly to the dog, Scott imagined her soothing words were for him. That was until she let go of the animal, who promptly stepped into the middle of his lap. Scott let out a grunt of pain and the dog growled.

"Don't move," Lexi commanded, using her hand to push Scott against the cushions once more. "You'll spook him."

"If he bites me, all bets are off."

"He's not going to bite you, but don't open your eyes yet."

Her arm pressed into his shoulder as she spoke to the dog. "Good boy, Freddy. You make friends."

Scott felt a wet dog nose press against his neck. "That tickles," he whispered.

"Don't be a baby," Lexi answered.

"Me or the dog?"

"You, of course. Oh, look at that."

He opened his eyes just as the dog curled into a ball on his lap. Scott's gaze lifted to Lexi, her head tipped forward so close all he had to do was move the tiniest inch to taste her again. He craved her more than he'd ever wanted a drink. More than he could remember wanting anything.

"They say dogs are a good judge of character," she whispered. "Freddy likes you."

"I still think Freddy is more rat than dog."

"Don't be mean. I love him."

"You've had him less than a day."

"It only takes a moment to fall in love."

Scott's mouth went dry. He could say with certainty he'd never been in love. After his mother's death, he hadn't wanted to feel the pain of losing someone he loved again. Sitting here on the couch with Lexi, he could imagine what it would feel like to be in love, to truly let another person in. The crazy part was he'd bet it would feel a lot like the pitch in his heart right now.

Needing to bring the conversation back to a safer subject, he said, "I saw you talking to a few different guys tonight at the bar."

He'd wanted to engage her temper, but she smiled at him instead. "I know. I flirted a ton."

Scott tried not to groan. "Do you think that's a good idea? You don't want to give them the wrong impression."

"I do, though." Her smile grew wider. "Not give the wrong impression," she added quickly. "I want to meet new people, try new things. Flirting is one of them."

"Heaven help the men of Brevia."

She swatted his arm. "One of them asked me out, you know."

The hand Scott was using to pet Freddy clenched into a fist. "Who asked you out?"

"I doubt you know him. His name's Mark. He's a teacher at the high school." Lexi's eyes dropped to Scott's mouth and awareness traced a long path down his spine. "He seemed nice enough."

Nice. Lexi deserved *nice,* a word that had never been in Scott's vocabulary. He thought of her pressed against him in his office earlier, how open and responsive she'd been and how much it had affected him. Would she melt against Mark the same way?

The thought made Scott crazy. He wanted to pull her to him now, brand her as his so she was ruined for anyone else.

But that wasn't his right, because he had nothing to offer her and they both knew it.

The dog stirred on his lap, a welcome distraction. "Do you have a leash?" Scott asked.

"On the counter."

"Go to bed, Lexi. I'll take the rat out one more time to do his business." He lifted Freddy off his lap, tucking him under one arm. He grabbed the leash from the kitchen.

Lexi stood next to the sofa, arms crossed over her chest. "You're okay with me going on a date?" Her voice was strained.

"It's your life, sweetheart," he answered, not adding how much he wanted to be a part of it. He clipped the dog's collar to the leash and headed out the door.

Lexi walked along the path around the park, Freddy trotting ahead of her. She'd taken to morning walks during the past week to make sure she had as little to do with Scott as possible. Of course, she still saw him every night at the bar, but other than putting in orders, she had almost no contact with him.

She hated to admit how embarrassed she was about her behavior, practically begging him to sleep with her, only to have him reject her. And when she'd told him she was going on a date with another guy, the stupid, girlie part of her had hoped to make Scott jealous. Relieved was more like it, she realized now.

She was so busy wallowing in self-pity she didn't

notice someone walk up behind her until she felt a tap on her shoulder.

"You look a million miles away," Julia said, handing Lexi a steaming to-go mug.

"Kind of…. What's this for?" Lexi took the cup, watching as Julia bent down to scratch between Freddy's perky ears.

"I've seen you the past couple of mornings, walking around the park like the hounds of hell are nipping your heels. I thought you could use someone to talk to."

Lexi made a face. "It's supposed to look like I'm out for exercise."

"Sam told me you let Scott move into the apartment."

"It's hard to believe anyone has the power to let that man do anything." Lexi took a sip of the hot tea and sighed. "But, yes, he's there with me. I didn't think you'd mind. It's okay, isn't it?"

"Of course. How's that going?"

"I've been in the park every morning. Do I need to say more?"

"I'll take a lap with you." Julia began walking in the same direction as Lexi. "I also heard you were at Cowboys last night."

"Word travels fast," Lexi muttered.

"Welcome to a small town." Julia sighed.

"It was my night off."

"And you decided to spend it in the only other bar in town? That doesn't seem like you."

"You don't know me very well."

Lexi tried to make her tone sound dismissive, but Julia only laughed. "I also heard you were putting the moves on several different guys."

"What the…? Are you having me followed now? As

thankful as I am for your help, it's none of your business what I do with my time, Julia." Lexi looked down at the ground, cursing the blush she felt rising to her cheeks.

"I know. And I know you're here to taste freedom, have a grand adventure, whatever. But I can tell you from personal experience that once you get a reputation, it can stick for a long time."

Lexi stopped to untangle Freddy's leash. The dog nuzzled against her legs and tears sprang to her eyes. "It's a lot of work, being totally on your own." She wiped at her cheek and looked at Julia. "I really admire you for taking care of yourself the way you did."

As part of the custody suit, it had been Lexi's job to delve into Julia's past, trying to dig up dirt that could be used against her. There had been a fair bit of it, mostly stemming from bad decisions Julia had made while trying to hide the learning disability that plagued her most of her life. But Julia was strong and kept fighting. In the process of her investigation, Lexi had come to respect her and understand that there were choices in life beyond doing what people expected of you. Once Julia had started living life on her terms, things had worked out for her. Lexi only hoped she could have an ounce of the woman's personal success.

"You're doing a fine job of taking care of yourself, Lexi." Julia smiled at her. "But you can't hold your alcohol."

Lexi snorted. "I know. But I don't have friends other than the girls at the bar. I didn't want to be alone in the apartment on my night off. That seemed too pathetic."

"There's nothing wrong with being alone if the alternative is hanging out with the wrong people."

They started walking again when Freddy tugged on

the leash. "My stylist, Nancy, said you were a big help to her with her divorce case."

"It's not my area of expertise," Lexi said with a shrug, "but her case is pretty cut-and-dried. I'm not sure why Frank Davis couldn't be of more help to her."

"Frank's been Brevia's main attorney for decades now. I think he might be slipping a bit. People are waiting for him to retire or at least bring in a junior associate, but he hasn't done it yet."

"I know from my dad there can be a lot of pride of ownership in having your own practice."

"People still need lawyers. Good ones." Julia pointed her coffee cup toward Lexi. "Like you."

"I'm not practicing law in Brevia."

"But you're certified in North Carolina?"

Lexi hesitated, then said, "I'm taking a break."

"Right. For the grand adventure." They'd done a full turn of the park and Julia stopped at the same place she'd met up with Lexi. "I have another friend who could use some legal counsel. Or at least a second opinion."

Lexi shook her head. "Grand adventure, remember?"

"She's a longtime client and needs help with an estate inheritance."

"Not my area of expertise, either."

"Please. It's a bad situation. She needs someone she can trust. We both know how that feels." Julia raised her eyebrows. "Don't make me beg, Lexi. It's not in my nature."

Lexi threw her cup into a nearby trash can. "Fine. Give her my cell number, but I'd like to go to that attorney's office and give him a piece of my mind."

"I'd like to see that." Julia tipped her cup in Lexi's

direction. "By the way, I'm having a girls' night in the salon tomorrow night. Are you off?"

"I can get off." Lexi fiddled with the leash, trying not to show too obviously her excitement at being included. "Are you sure? You don't have to ask me just to be nice."

Julia threw her head back and laughed. "Everyone knows I don't do anything to be nice. Some *nice* girls work at the salon, though. A couple of them are new to town. It would be a better place than a meat-market country bar to make friends."

"Great, then," Lexi said with a grin. "Thank you." She paused, then added, "I have a date."

"With Scott?"

Lexi ignored the wave of disappointment that rushed over her. "No. His name is Mark Childs. He's a teacher at the high school. He moved up from Charlotte last year. He's nice, too." She took a breath. "Sorry, I'm babbling."

"I'm glad for you. That sounds like a good addition to the adventure." To her surprise, Julia leaned forward and gave her a quick hug. "See you tomorrow, then."

"Okay, I'll see you." Lexi turned away quickly, surprised as well that her throat was suddenly a bit scratchy. But she felt better about her life. Funny how one quick conversation could do that. She leaned forward to pet Freddy, who flopped onto his back, always glad to have more attention. After a minute, when she had her emotions in check once more, she headed down the path and toward home.

"Don't even think about taking advantage of that girl."

Scott looked up from the new bar menu at the woman standing, hands on hips, just inside the front door.

Jon Riley stood quickly. "I'll be in the back, boss. Call me when you're through here." In a quieter voice he added, "Or when she's through with you."

"Chicken," Scott muttered as Jon made his escape, clucking over his shoulder.

"To what do I owe the honor, Mrs. Callahan?" Scott stood, rubbing his palms down the front of his jeans. "Or should I call you sis?"

Julia rolled her eyes. "You know who I'm talking about. She's fragile right now."

"You don't give her enough credit."

"She gives you too much."

Scott's jaw tightened because Julia was right. Even though Lexi had avoided him the past week, he'd seen her watching him when she thought he wasn't looking. Sometimes she'd catch him watching her. Either way, instead of the wariness she should have for him, her gaze showed nothing but trust. That was dangerous for both of them. He wasn't someone she could trust, and he didn't trust himself around her. Which made working and living with her a form of torture. But he couldn't walk away.

Not willing to admit any of this to Julia, he shrugged. "In case it matters, your little ray of sunshine propositioned me. I said no."

Julia's eyes narrowed. "Bull."

"It's true, ask her. Despite the fact that you and my big brother think I'm the bad seed of the Callahan clan, I don't want trouble in Brevia."

"You're nothing but trouble."

"From what I understand, you were a bit of the same back in the day."

"I've grown up."

"Who says I can't?"

She studied him, literally looked him up and down. After a moment, she said, "Stay away from her."

"I have every intention of staying away."

"You moved into my apartment."

"You and I are family. I have more right to it."

"I sublet it to her."

"That's right, you rented an apartment and gave a fresh start to the woman who tried to take your son away."

"I'm giving her a second chance."

"Maybe I'd like one, too."

"You betrayed Sam," she said after a minute. "In the worst way possible. He doesn't trust you."

Scott nodded. "I know that. What I did was wrong and I can't apologize any more than I have. That woman was bad news. The way I went about proving it to him was a mistake. But I don't regret breaking them up. She would have hurt him more than I ever did."

Julia's delicate features went soft. "He's a good man."

"And I'm happy he's found you. I'm glad you have each other."

"You were mad he didn't take the job with the Marshals because he wanted to stay in Brevia."

Scott nodded. "I was frustrated. I thought working with him would give us a chance to put the past behind us. But after meeting you and Charlie, I understand why he made the choice he did. I'm not mad anymore." Scott sighed. "I'd still like things to be better."

"He told me you're hosting a reception for us."

"He said you'd be against it."

"I'm not. I hated this town for a long time, but I'm

happy here now. Why not celebrate that?" She offered a small smile. "Will you come to dinner this weekend? I'll invite my mom and Joe, too. Vera is thrilled about the party. We can make plans then."

"Sure," Scott said, returning her smile. "I'm not so bad once you get to know me, Julia."

"Maybe," she answered, eyes skimming the bar. "This place looks a lot better."

He followed her gaze to the newly polished floor and the fresh coat of paint on the main wall. He'd put in a lot of hours this week fixing things up where he could. He liked the hard work and couldn't help but feel proud of how much he'd accomplished. "Thanks. We're going to start serving food in a few days. Open for lunch, too."

She nodded. "Anything that brings more people into downtown is good as far as I'm concerned." With a last look around, she turned for the door. "I'll see you later, Scott."

"A pleasure talking to you, sis."

She laughed and walked out into the late-morning sunlight.

Scott glanced at his watch. It was close to noon, which meant he didn't actually have to be here for nearly five more hours. Suddenly, another day of being cooped up in the bar was too much for him.

He poked his head into the back hallway. "Jon?" he called out.

"Yeah, boss." Jon came from the kitchen, wiping his hands on a towel.

"Do you think you can take care of things here for a few hours?"

A smile broke across the man's ruddy face. "I'd be happy to. I used to watch over the place for my dad."

Scott nodded and grabbed his jacket from a hook on the wall. "I'll be back before we open."

Chapter Seven

Lexi tossed the book she was reading onto the coffee table. Freddy yawned and stretched next to her. She had a whole day in front of her before she needed to get to work, but couldn't muster the energy to make decent plans.

She heard keys in the apartment's door and turned as Scott walked in. She'd thought he'd already gone to the bar for the day or else she would have been holed up in her room.

"Let's go," he said, pointing a finger at her.

"Go where?" She reached again for her discarded book, ignoring the fact that her heart had picked up its pace. "I'm kind of busy."

He gave her a lopsided smile. "Liar. Come on. We're going to have some fun."

"Can you clarify how you define *fun?*"

"Nope." He leaned over the couch and took her hand to gently pull her to her feet. Freddy stood up, tail wagging. "We'll see you later, buddy."

"Do I need to change clothes?" Lexi asked, smoothing her hands across her T-shirt and jeans. "It would help if I knew what to prepare for."

"We're going on an adventure," Scott replied, his eyes traveling up and down her body like a caress. "You look perfect."

Lexi's mouth went dry but she forced herself to smile. "Somehow that doesn't reassure me."

The truth was she was excited to go with him, wherever they ended up. She knew Scott was bad for her, or at least that was what he kept saying. But she trusted him to keep her safe no matter what. Lexi had never felt that with anyone in her life. It was an oddly freeing sensation.

"Grab a jacket and gym shoes. We don't want to be late."

After gathering her things, Lexi followed him out to his truck and climbed in, both excited and a little bit scared. She wondered if Little Red Riding Hood had felt the same way when she'd gone through the woods to Grandma's house. Scott drove through town and turned onto the highway heading into the mountains.

As the truck climbed the curvy road, Lexi gazed out the window to the forest below. Brevia sat in a valley nestled at the base of the Smoky Mountains. Although mornings were crisp this time of year, by noon the sun was bright in the sky, bathing the tips of trees in a golden light that made the whole area look more alive. She'd grown up in the city, gone to college there, too, so she found herself transfixed by the beauty of nature surrounding them.

Scott didn't say much as they drove, but the silence was companionable. Lexi was used to silence. Other than discussing current cases or other legal matters, her father didn't talk much to her. She often lived in her head and now found her mind wandering along paths of memories that were better left untraveled. Her father's harsh criticism and her fear that she'd never have the courage to truly live life out from under his thumb.

"Don't go there."

She jumped as Scott drew his fingers across her hand where it rested on the seat between them.

"Whatever you're thinking about, let it go today. We're going to have fun, leave the problems for later."

"It's hard not to think about things," she admitted.

"Have you gone on your date yet?"

She was taken aback by his question. "I can't talk about that with you."

"One of the other waitresses mentioned that Mr. High School Science Teacher is considered quite the catch."

Lexi shrugged. "We're supposed to go to a movie next weekend."

"You don't sound too excited."

She glanced at him from under her lashes, but his eyes were fixed on the road. "I'm very excited."

"Do you have a long list of qualifications for a potential suitor?" he asked, and she heard the smile in his voice.

"Actually, being with someone my dad didn't pick out for me is my top priority." She sighed. "My last…current…whatever boyfriend is a fourth-year at the firm. He wants to make partner in the worst way."

"He thinks making it with the boss's daughter will help his chances?"

"I can't imagine another reason he'd be so serious with me."

"Then he's an idiot." Scott said the words with such conviction that a little ball of emotion began to unwind inside Lexi's chest.

"Do you have a girlfriend?"

"Nope. I don't do relationships." He glanced over at her and winked. "I'm a bad bet, remember?"

"What about your brother's fiancée?" Lexi asked and saw his fingers tense around the steering wheel. "Did you fall in love with her?"

"I fell into bed with her," Scott answered candidly. "Not the same thing."

"Oh."

"I don't believe in love, Lexi. I'm not made that way."

She shook her head. "Everyone is made for love."

"For an attorney, you're kind of an idealist."

"It's not an ideal. It's true. There's somebody for everyone."

"Whatever you say." Scott pulled into a long gravel driveway and slowed to avoid divots on the well-worn track. A sign that read Smoky Mountain Adventures greeted them from the side of the property. They pulled up to a small cabin with several picnic tables in front.

"What are we doing?" she asked again, eyeing the row of shiny Jeeps and ATVs sitting next to an oversize garage. A corral of horses was situated on the side of a long barn, with a few parents and children milling about outside.

"We're going zip-lining."

Lexi clenched the door handle. "You're kidding, right?"

"Have you ever been?" Scott pulled into a parking

spot and turned the key, looking at her as the truck went quiet.

"I'm afraid of heights," she whispered.

He squeezed shut his eyes. "I didn't know that."

"If you'd told me our destination back at the apartment, I could have filled you in."

"That's okay," he said after a moment. "Even better, actually." He opened the driver's side door and hopped out.

Lexi would have followed him, but she was paralyzed in her seat. Her stomach churned as a bead of sweat made a slow trail down her back. She concentrated on moving air in and out of her lungs at a normal rate. She might have understated her fear of heights. Petrified was more like it. She could barely walk up an open-air flight of steps.

The door to her side of the truck opened and Scott leaned in. "Ready?"

"No."

"You can do this."

"I'm going to puke," she said, her voice a croak.

He smiled and raised his mirrored sunglasses onto the top of his head. His blue eyes looked into hers, total confidence in her radiating from their depths.

"You left your job, your home and moved to a tiny town hundreds of miles away where the only person you knew was a woman who hated you. You found a job, albeit one you're no good at and totally overqualified for, but it's a job. And for reasons unknown to me, everyone you meet loves you. Customers, the other staff, even the guy who delivers the beer asks about you."

"He does?" Lexi shifted in her seat. "That's so sweet."

"Sweet as pie." Scott reached across her waist and

unbuckled the seat belt. "If you can manage all of that in a couple of weeks, sliding down a cable is going to be a cinch."

Lexi dug her fingernails into the seat. "No way."

Scott's fingers found hers, easing them from their death grip on the leather. "You can do this. It's part of the adventure. Once-in-a-lifetime, bucket-list adventure. That's what you want, right?"

"I can't," she whispered miserably.

"Yes, you can." He dropped a soft-as-a-feather kiss on her mouth. "I believe in you, Lexi Preston."

She breathed him in, the crisp, male scent and the taste of mint on his lips. "I believe in you, too, Scott."

He tensed for a moment, then eased back. "Prove it. Let's take our mutual-admiration society to the zip line. I'll make sure you're safe the whole time."

She met his gaze and saw both a challenge and promise there. Sometimes she felt as if she'd spent most of her years avoiding the parts of life that scared her the most, whether it was something physical such as her fear of heights or, more terrifying, feelings and worries. Suddenly, this step represented so much more, and she needed to take it. She wanted to prove that she was worthy of his faith in her.

"Okay," she answered, her voice shaky with nerves.

She let him lead her to the front office, her knees stiff with fear as her insides churned. Scott filled out the paperwork and spoke to the tour operator, a tall man in his early forties with sandy-blond hair and a full beard. Lexi paced back and forth, reviewing legal briefs in her head to stop the panic from consuming her. She could overcome this. Look at how much she'd done in the past few weeks. This was just one more part of her adventure.

"Zach's going to take us out personally," Scott told her as the man disappeared into a room off the side of the main waiting area. "He's the owner, so it will be fine."

Lexi bit down on her lip.

"You can do this," Scott said again and wrapped one arm around her, his fingers tracing circles on her biceps.

"I thought you didn't want to hang out with me," Lexi said softly, grasping on to anything that would distract her from the thought of careening through the forest tied to a metal cable. "Why the change of heart?"

"I never said I didn't want to hang out with you," Scott corrected. "I said having an affair with me was a bad idea."

She looked up at him, searching his pale blue eyes. "So you want to be friends?"

"I don't really have friends, Lexi." He shrugged but kept his eyes on her. "I'm probably as bad at friendship as I am at dating."

"I don't have many friends, either. It would be new territory for both of us." She couldn't help the smile that curved her lips. "I think I'd be pretty good at it, though."

He studied her for several moments. Once again, everything else disappeared as she lost herself in him. "I bet you will." Taking a breath, he added, "We're friends."

Lexi's stomach tightened as she swayed the tiniest bit closer to him. She felt more than friendship for Scott, but she'd been honest about not having many friends. Hearing him say they were seemed like a good step "You know, friends don't try to kill each other by making them do a zip line."

He took her hand in his and led her toward the front door. "I'm broadening your horizons," he said as they walked outside into the warming air.

Zach, the owner, was waiting in a four-person open-top Jeep. "Y'all ready?" he asked as they came down the steps.

"Sure are," Scott answered.

At the same time Lexi whispered, "Heck, no."

She climbed into the backseat and they headed up a dirt road behind the property. Lexi didn't realize how much Scott's touch had bolstered her confidence until it was gone. She wrapped her arms tight around her middle, trying to quell the panic that rose to the surface once more. Scott looked back several times and gave her a smile or wink. She wanted to climb up between the seats and bury herself in his lap.

After a few minutes, she began to see a web of cables attached to what looked like oversize telephone poles between the trees.

"Scott tells me you're nervous," Zach called back. "We're going to start with one of the shorter lines so you get used to the feeling."

Lexi nodded, but her fingernails dug into her back. When he said *going to start,* she got the distinct impression he expected her to do this more than once. She wondered briefly what would happen if she passed out or literally threw up. There were countless ways she could embarrass herself today, and she figured she had a good chance of hitting them all.

In another moment the Jeep stopped and Zach jumped out and began gathering harnesses and other equipment from the cargo hold. Scott offered her a hand to help her out of the backseat. She snatched hers back when he commented on how cold it was.

"It's going to be fine," he said softly, taking her hand again and warming it between his.

She was a ninny, no doubt about it. She bet the women he knew from his time in the military and the Marshals did stuff that would make this look like a walk in the park. She wanted him to know she was up for the challenge, even one that was so small in the grand scheme of things.

"Let's do this," she said and charged after Zach.

Scott couldn't quite believe the woman careening down the cable, whooping with joy, was the same person he'd practically had to drag out of the car a few hours earlier.

Lexi came to a stop on the landing of the last line and pumped one fist in the air. "That was awesome," she yelled and threw her arms around Zach. "Thank you so much for this," she said, hugging him hard.

As Zach's big hands moved a wee bit lower than was appropriate, Scott cleared his throat. "It was my idea, if you remember."

She turned to look at him, her smile widening. "Did you see me? I was flying. It felt like I was literally flying."

She came toward him and he grinned, thinking of her launching herself into his arms the same way. Instead, she punched him lightly on the shoulder, then danced in front of him, just out of reach. "I was so scared at the edge of the first zip line, but it was such a rush. That was the best day. Ever."

Scott's best day would actually include her pressed up against him, preferably naked. He inwardly shook his head. "I'm glad you liked it," he told her. "But we should head back."

They gathered the gear and walked toward the Jeep,

Lexi and Zach taking the lead as the older man regaled her with stories of other adventures he'd had.

"Maybe I'll try skydiving next," Lexi said with a laugh.

Scott wondered if somehow he'd created an adrenaline junkie, and it made him crazy to think that Zach or any other guy would be with her on subsequent escapades.

His eyes dropped to Lexi's jeans, specifically her hips swaying as she walked. He was a fool, he realized, to think that he could be her friend without his desire for her getting in the way. The more he told himself she wasn't his type, the more drawn to her he became.

He'd wanted to get away from town today, to forget everything from his conversation with Julia to the bar to his family and their expectations of him. The only person he wanted to spend time with was Lexi. She'd been avoiding him and he knew he should have left it at that.

Seeing her face down her fear today and come out on the other side of it more confident and proud had made him want her all the more.

If he could, he'd like to bottle up the light that radiated from her and save it for his darkest moments, like a perfect Scotch he could savor at his own pace.

It had killed him to watch both Zach and the younger man who'd helped them gear up flirt with Lexi, all the while knowing he had no right to stop it. She'd offered herself to him with no strings attached and Scott had been a fool to turn her down. Now the young guide, Matt, jogged up to Lexi. He leaned down to whisper something in her ear. She glanced back at Scott, then shook her head. Matt handed her a small piece of paper, grinning like an idiot until Zach shooed him away.

He watched Lexi tuck the paper into the back pocket of her jeans, looking over her shoulder and giving Scott a thumbs-up before turning away again.

Scott gritted his teeth. This friendship was going to be the death of him.

Lexi knocked on the door of Frank Davis's law office for the third time. She knew someone was in there because she'd seen the blinds move after she'd first knocked.

Finally, the door opened, revealing the older attorney, his button-down shirt wrinkled and a spot of what looked like mustard staining his polka-dot tie. He'd lost weight since she'd last seen him, but not in a good way.

"Hi," she said, holding out her hand. "You may not remember me but—"

"I remember you. You're the little girl who made a fool out of me on the Julia Morgan case."

Lexi stepped forward to prevent him from shutting the door in her face. "I'm sorry about my actions around the custody suit, but I think we can both agree that things worked out for the best in the end."

"I had it under control," he muttered.

"Like you do Nancy Capshaw's divorce and Ida Garvey's latest estate plan? Her will hadn't been updated in almost ten years, Frank. She had no living trust, nothing to protect her family's inheritance of her more recent investments."

His round eyes widened even further. "Listen here, missy, don't you go trying to steal my clients. You have no right. I could report you to the bar association for that."

"I don't want to steal any clients," Lexi said. She

glanced over his shoulder. "Could I come in for a few moments?"

"I'm busy right now."

Lexi might not have been the most assertive person in the world, but she pretended she was working for her father once again. Her fear of failing in his eyes always made her more forceful when dealing with people who didn't want to talk to her. Fear was a powerful motivator.

"I'll be quick," she said and easily slipped past him. She looked toward the receptionist's desk in the small lobby, which looked as if it had been deserted for months. A sad houseplant sat on the windowsill behind the desk, leaves brown and shriveled. "Where's your secretary?"

Frank let the door shut and turned to her. "She quit a while back. I don't need her, anyway. Brevia doesn't generate a lot of law business, not like it used to."

"Really?" Lexi found that hard to believe. In the past two days, since her meeting with Ida Garvey, she'd had a half-dozen messages from locals wanting help on a variety of cases. "Is there another law office nearby?"

He scoffed. "Of course not. I've been the main attorney in these parts for over twenty years. I built my life in this town. I've worked on every major case this county has seen." His finger jabbed into the air as if underscoring his importance. He looked around the office and sighed. "It isn't like it used to be. A whippersnapper like you wouldn't understand."

She glanced toward the inner office and sucked in a breath at the stacks of manila files lining the walls. It appeared that Frank hadn't put anything away since his secretary had left. "I understand your clients need an attorney who can keep up with their cases." She stepped forward. "I could help if you want."

His lips pressed into a grim line and she continued quickly, "I don't mean take over. But I'm licensed to practice in North Carolina. I've got time during the day...before my shift starts."

As she said the words, she realized how much she still wanted to work as an attorney. Yes, the bar was a fun diversion, something totally different than what she'd been doing. She was proving that she could take care of herself, and facing some of the demons left over from her childhood and what had happened to her mother.

But despite choosing to become a lawyer to please her father, in her heart she loved working with people and having the opportunity to help fix their problems. She'd lost sight of that in Ohio, when most of her work had been fighting for people who didn't deserve her help. People unlike the ones she'd met here in Brevia.

She realized she felt at home here, and the feeling didn't scare her. Even if it was for only a short time, she wanted to make a difference, pay it forward in her own way. Maybe that would give her some confidence for believing she could do the same thing once she returned to her own life.

"What do you think, Frank?"

"Are you crazy?" He slammed a fist into the wall, making her jump. "I see what you're doing here! You think you're the first young lawyer to walk into this office and pretend you want to help me?"

"I'm sorry, it's just—"

"I don't need your help. You think anyone in this town would ever trust you, with your background?"

"But you do need assistance." She took a calming breath, trying not to let his words hurt her.

"So what if I've slowed down a bit? I can keep up. Maybe I like to play golf a little more than I used to. I get the work done. And I'm my own man. I built this practice from the ground up. I'm not someone's puppet. I never did my daddy's dirty work, digging out every tiny bit of nastiness about the people I was working against."

"I didn't—"

"You're not the only one who can look into someone's background, Ms. Preston."

Lexi swallowed. "I did things I'm not proud of. I'm trying to make a better life here. I'm trying to start over, to learn from my mistakes."

He walked to the door and held it open. "Then you'd better learn it someplace else. You're not welcome here."

She clenched her fists, both from frustration and embarrassment. Her intentions here had been so good.

"What am I supposed to do when someone comes to me for help? I won't turn them away."

"Run along home to daddy, Ms. Preston. You don't belong here."

"I… You… This isn't…" Frank did nothing but stare at her, arms crossed over his chest.

Blinking back tears, Lexi fled from the office back into the street. She felt as if she were a young girl again, wanting nothing more than her father's approval, but being continually denied no matter how hard she tried to please him. She knew her past wasn't perfect, but wondered if she'd ever get to a point of being able to outrun it.

* * *

"What do you think of sweet-potato fries verses regular ones to go with the burger selection?"

Scott finished his inventory of bottles and turned. "Whatever you want, Jon. It's your kitchen."

Jon grinned at him. "We'll be open for lunch on Monday."

"Great. The sign guy is coming tomorrow to change the wording on the marquee to Riley's Bar & Grill." Scott picked up the stack of mail from the bar and began to leaf through it. "We need the bump in revenue to offset all the cash I'm…" His voice trailed off as his eyes settled on a small white envelope.

"You okay, boss?" Joe took a step closer.

"Yeah, sure. I'm just thinking of when the new barstools are going to be delivered."

He picked up the envelope, his fingers holding it so tight that one corner began to crumple. "Can you give a call to the food supplier and confirm we'll need the fresh ingredients Monday morning? I don't want anything to go wrong with the rollout."

Jon studied him, but didn't call Scott out on his quick mood change. "Got it. I better get to work." He turned and hustled toward the kitchen.

Scott walked around the bar and sat on one of the high stools. He didn't have to open the letter to know what it contained, but he did, anyway. The short memo indicated that he'd have an official review in D.C. at the end of the month. It was scheduled two days before the reception for Sam and their father. The timing couldn't have been any worse, but Scott knew if he didn't show for it that his career with the Marshals was over.

He wasn't sure what he wanted his future to be, but he

didn't want the decision to be made for him. At the same time, he wasn't ready to talk about what had happened.

As if on cue, the front door of the bar banged opened.

"This day stinks," Lexi announced as she stalked through. Scott could almost see the smoke rising from her ears. "I try to help someone and he wants nothing to do with me. Totally ungrateful for my offer. It's ridiculous."

Scott wasn't sure if she was talking to him or about someone else, but her words hit home. "Not everyone wants to be helped," he muttered.

"That doesn't make sense," she said, her big eyes narrowing as she met his gaze. She took in the letter in his hand and came forward. "What's the matter? What happened?"

It bothered him more than he was willing to admit that she could read him so easily. "Nothing happened for you to worry about." He folded the letter and tucked it into his shirt pocket. Scrubbing his hand across his face, he forced his mouth into a smile. "What's got your cute panties in such a bunch?"

"You have no idea if my panties are cute or not."

"We're roommates." He winked at her. "You left a basket of folded laundry in front of the TV last night. I especially like the little pink ones with bunches of cherries on them."

Her mouth dropped open. "You shouldn't look at my panties, folded or not."

He'd like to do a lot more than look. He'd like to peel them from her hips and...

"I know what you're thinking," she said, pointing a finger at him.

"Honey, if you knew what I was thinking, you'd run out that door right this minute."

He loved the hint of pink that flushed across her cheeks. "Don't distract me. What was that piece of paper you stuffed in your pocket?"

"You're the one who came in here all hot and bothered."

"I had an awful conversation with Frank Davis. He won't admit he can't keep up with his caseload or why. I offered to help and he was rude."

"Offered to help? You want to practice law in Brevia?"

"Not forever. But I can ease some of his backlog. People are already coming to me. It's strange that there are no other law firms in town. It's like he's hoarded all of the business for himself but can't manage it anymore." She shook her head. "You're getting me off track again. Why are you upset?"

"I'm not upset," Scott said, standing and turning back toward the bar.

She grabbed his arm and pulled him around to face her. "There's a muscle pulsing at the base of your jaw. You're mad as heck about something. Maybe I could help if you told me what it was."

"I doubt it." He glanced at his watch. "Besides, your shift doesn't start for another hour. You shouldn't be here."

"I'm too worked up to go home. I came in to start on the plans for the reception. I need to burn off some energy."

"I know how you can burn off some energy."

She looked straight into his eyes. "I've already asked you for an affair. You said no."

"What if I've changed my mind?" he said, reaching out and pulling her close.

"What's in the letter?"

As fast as he'd drawn her to him, he pushed her away at those words. He walked from the bar to his small office, wishing for a way to burn off some of his own energy. As sunshine-sweet as she appeared, he knew Lexi could be worse than a dog with a bone. She wouldn't give up until he told her something.

As he expected, she followed him back. "You can tell me," she said quietly. "It's okay to let me in."

She was wrong. Scott wouldn't let anyone in, not even Lexi. But he answered truthfully, "It's a summons for a review from the Marshals office in D.C."

"To review what?" She lifted one hip onto the corner of his desk, clearly making herself comfortable. "I thought you were on a leave of absence?"

"An administrative leave," he clarified. "My partner died during a botched arrest. He was one of my few real friends at the agency. We'd gone through the academy at the same time."

"I'm sorry, Scott."

He hated sympathy. "It was my fault. Derek Sanchez was a good officer, a family man with a pretty wife and two small children waiting for him at home. The pressure of the job was bad enough, but trying to balance a normal life would take its toll on anyone."

"What happened?"

"He put himself in the line of fire instead of waiting for backup. It was stupid, a rookie mistake. He knew better but…"

"But?"

"Derek had been drinking the night before. We'd been

on a stakeout for days. Sitting around with nothing to do but think can drive you nuts, even in the field."

"He was drinking on the job."

"Technically, we had the night off. But it made him careless the next day."

"How is that your fault?"

Scott shook his head, stopped in front of her. Suddenly, he needed to tell someone…to tell Lexi…the whole story. "I should have stopped him, but he'd been griping for weeks about how his wife was busting his chops, pressuring him to take a desk job with the agency. I knew he needed to blow off some steam, so I didn't stop him."

"He was a grown man," she said softly. "You weren't his babysitter."

"I should have been his friend. I knew Derek had been drinking more than usual in the months before he died, but I wasn't much of a role model. I was trying to protect him, but as usual my methods left a lot to be desired. I fell asleep and left him alone. He drank a lot more than I'd realized. When things went down the next morning, he was in no condition to handle it."

"You think he was still drunk?"

"I sure as hell hope not, but I don't know. I never said anything. If it came out that he was at fault, it could've messed up his life insurance and pension. His wife… she needs that money."

Realization dawned in Lexi's eyes. "So you walked away from your career rather than expose his issues."

"It doesn't matter," Scott said, shaking his head. He balled his fists at his sides, the familiar frustration returning. "I let him down. Like I let everyone down."

She straightened, and Scott expected her to reach for

him, felt his whole body stiffen as he both feared and longed for her touch and the way it made him feel. She walked past him instead. He glanced over his shoulder, unable to help himself watch her walk away. Just like his mother had done to a seven-year-old boy who'd needed her more than she could handle.

Chapter Eight

But Lexi didn't leave. Her hand reached out and turned the lock on his office door. She returned to him and took his clenched hand in hers, trailing her fingers across his palm the same way he'd done to hers when she'd been frightened of zip-lining. His awareness of her almost overwhelmed him.

"Have you changed your mind, Scott?" she asked softly, her eyes still on their intertwined fingers.

He shook his head, forcing himself to ignore his need for her. "I'm not going to tell them anything about Derek. Even if it means I'll never work for the agency again."

She looked up at him now and her eyes held none of the judgment he expected to see there. "I meant about my offer."

He sucked in a breath and jerked back his hand, but she held tight.

"Do you," she asked, lifting his arm to place a whisper-light kiss on the inside of his wrist, "want to be with me?"

He nearly groaned. "It's not about what I want," he said with a ragged breath. "It's about what's good for you. I'm trying to protect you, Lexi."

"I don't need you to protect me." She stepped closer, taking his other hand in hers, then running her fingers up his arms until they curved around his neck. "I want you, Scott."

He knew he should walk away, but for the life of him, he couldn't move a muscle. "Don't do this," he whispered.

"What?" Her smile belied the innocence in her voice. She reached up and pressed her mouth to his. "Do you mean this?" Her body leaned against his as her scent wound through his mind, filling his head with the most amazing pictures of her moving underneath him. "Or this?" Her tongue traced the seam of his lips like an invitation.

He knew it was wrong, but he couldn't take any more of her sweet torture.

His arms tightened around her and he slanted his mouth over hers, taking control of the kiss. He felt her smile against him and melt into him even more, her desire stoking his until it was difficult to tell where he stopped and she began.

"Don't say I didn't warn you." He ground out the words before lifting her into his arms and carrying her to the couch pushed up against the far wall.

"This is all my fault," she agreed, tugging at the hem of his shirt even as he lay her against the cushions.

He stripped off the shirt and almost smiled at the way her eyes widened. "Having second thoughts?" he asked, sitting up a bit. If she was smart enough to stop this beautiful madness, he had no choice but to let her.

To his surprise, she leaned forward and lifted her own shirt over her head. "Not a single one," she said, watching him from eyes full of need and wonder. "I just hope I don't disappoint you."

Desire unfurled low in his stomach at the sight of her creamy skin under a peach-colored lace bra. "Seriously, how does a woman who dresses like a nun half the time have such great lingerie under her clothes?"

She rewarded him with a saucy smile. "It's my little secret and there's no one to tell me that I can't."

"If anyone tells you to stop, send them to me and I'll break all of their fingers." Scott placed his hand on her neck, feeling her pulse race. "You are so damn beautiful," he whispered.

"You don't have to say that." Some of the light in her eyes dimmed. "I know it isn't true."

When she would have turned her head, he cupped her face between his hands. "Lexi Preston, you are beautiful, desirable, smart and too kind for your own good."

Lexi wanted to believe him. Looking into his eyes, she almost could believe him. The desire she saw there made her bold. With trembling fingers, she eased her bra straps along her arms. Scott sucked in a breath as he reached behind her to unhook the clasp. The small bit of fabric dropped to the floor, suddenly making her self-conscious again. She covered her breasts with her hands until he gently pushed them away.

"I want to look at you," he whispered, his voice filled with something that sounded like reverence.

Lexi groaned softly as his hand covered one sensitive tip, rolling it between his fingers. "So beautiful," he repeated softly and lifted his head to flick his tongue across her heated skin.

She sucked in a breath and at that moment his mouth found hers, melding to her, and he pressed her bare skin along the length of him. He touched her everywhere, running his hands down her back, flipping her over and, in the process, easing her jeans and underpants down her hips. His clever fingers slid up her thigh and she gasped for air, his mouth over hers taking in her tiny moans as he touched her in ways she hadn't imagined.

He continued to kiss her as his fingers stroked her to a frenzy she couldn't control. All her inhibitions seemed to melt away until there was nothing left but sensation and feeling, her entire body throbbing with need.

"Let me hear you," he said against her mouth, speeding the rhythm of his fingers against her.

As if at his command, her body arched and bright pleasure tore through her, shattering her senses. He held her close as her arms and legs trembled, finally coming back to herself and settling under him once more.

He kissed her softly, nuzzling her neck with his mouth and whispering gentling words to her. "You are amazing."

"We didn't…" she began, embarrassed at her body's intense reaction to him. "You didn't…"

"Not here," he told her, raising himself onto his arms above her. "You deserve more than a roll on my office couch."

She looked toward the ceiling and mumbled, "I like your office couch."

He laughed, dropping a kiss on her forehead. "Then you'll love my bed."

She glanced at him then. "So this isn't over?"

He straightened, his eyes heating once more as his gaze traveled across her body. "We haven't even gotten started."

A knock at the door had Lexi jumping, grabbing for her clothes.

Oh...no.

She was naked in her boss's office. How much more clichéd could she be? "This is bad. What was I thinking?"

Scott picked up her shirt and handed it to her. "You weren't thinking. Neither of us were." He pulled her to him, kissing her once more. "We're going to do more not thinking together later." Then he unlocked the door, slipping out before whoever was on the other side could see that he wasn't alone.

Lexi took a steadying breath as she pulled on her jeans, then smoothed her hair back into a ponytail. She felt terrified and elated at the same time. Good-girl Lexi Preston having a go at it on the job. She put a hand over her mouth to suppress a nervous giggle. Finally, it felt as if her adventure was really beginning.

Lexi took another order from a table of regulars. They were a group of guys from a local construction company who came in for a weekly boys' night out. She liked the harmless flirting, and when one of them grabbed her hand and loudly kissed it, she laughed before drawing back.

She'd been in Brevia for two weeks and still reveled in how invigorating her new freedom made her feel. A few nights earlier she'd indulged in a dinner of chips, soda and cookie-dough ice cream, savoring the choice to do something her father wouldn't approve of, even it was a tiny stake in the ground of her independence.

She'd been embarrassed when Scott had walked in midfeast, then surprised when he'd grabbed a spoon from the kitchen and helped her polish off the pint while watching some cheesy reality TV show on cable. He hadn't tried to kiss her or made any kind of move, but hanging out with him had been so easy and right that her heart had opened to him even more.

But she'd been avoiding Scott since the encounter in his office, too afraid of her own feelings to pursue anything more with him. Realizing she needed to keep better control on her emotions, she turned away now to collect the table's drink orders, but Misty hauled her off to a corner of the bar.

"What's going on with you and Scott?" the other waitress asked on a hiss of breath.

"I... We... Nothing," Lexi answered quickly. "Why?"

"He just about came over the bar when that guy grabbed you." Misty shook her head. "He looks like he wants to throw you over his shoulder and carry you off."

"A little too caveman for my taste." Lexi laughed as her pulse started to race.

"I wouldn't mind being carried off by that man," Misty said with a knowing smile.

Lexi's gaze tracked to the bar. Scott handed two beers to a couple sitting at the stools in front of him before his eyes met hers. One side of his mouth curved up and the promise in his gaze made Lexi's knees go a tiny bit weak.

"That look isn't nothing," Misty said, whistling softly under her breath. She chucked Lexi on the shoulder. "I don't know how you did it, girl. Most of the waitresses and half of the female customers have been angling for a way to catch Scott Callahan since he got to town."

"And you think I've caught him?"

Misty smiled. "I think you're darn close." She winked at her. "I just hope you know what to do with him once you've got him."

Lexi swallowed hard as Misty walked away. She had no idea what to do with Scott. The things her imagination conjured made her tingle from her toes to the top of her head.

She waited until he was busy at the other end of the bar to retrieve the drinks for a table up front. She'd gotten them balanced on her tray when a familiar voice spoke behind her.

"I can't believe I raised a common barmaid."

She managed to hold the tray steady as she turned to face her father. "What are you doing here, Daddy?" She glanced behind him to see Trevor Montgomery, her onetime boyfriend, standing in the wings. "And you've brought reinforcements. How lovely. Grab a table and I'll get your order after I deliver these drinks."

Her father reached for her. "You'll speak to me now, Lexi, and not to take my order. You're coming home."

"I'm working right now," she said, her spine stiffening. "We're busy tonight and I can't keep the customers waiting." She held her tray in front of her, pushing past her father and Trevor. She brought the drinks to the table, then motioned to Misty. "Could you cover my section for a few minutes?"

Misty looked to where Robert Preston was glowering next to the bar. "Sure thing, sweetheart."

Lexi made her way back to her father, dread making her legs feel as if they were encased in cement. Lord, how she wanted to just run out the front door. She knew her father was serious about her coming home, but she'd never thought he'd actually show up in Brevia to collect her. She'd been stupid and naive to think he'd actually respect her decision. Respect for her wasn't part of Robert Preston's makeup.

"I have return tickets on the late flight out of Charlotte," he told her when she stood in front of him. "We're leaving now."

"You just got here," she answered weakly, pretending not to understand

He shook his head. "Let's go, Lexi. Trevor will drive us to Charlotte, then return to Columbus with your car. You're lucky he's willing to take you back after the way you deserted him. You're lucky we both are."

Trevor's eyes darted to her father before returning to her face. "I've missed you, Lex." He gave her a placating smile.

"Give me a break, Trevor. I doubt you noticed I was gone, besides the fact that you had to find a new way to brownnose my father." She shook her head. "Dad, I'm not going back yet. I told you that on the phone. I want a few more weeks."

"That's ridiculous."

"You're the one who sent me away."

"You ruined the relationship with one of our best clients." He looked around with clear disdain. "What is it about this town that attracts you?"

Lexi forced her gaze to remain on her father. Out of the corner of her eye she could see Scott with a group of men at the far end of the bar. "People are nice here. It feels real. I feel real."

"Nonsense," her father scoffed. "Your life is in Ohio

with me. The firm needs you. I didn't pull you out of the gutter only to have you return there."

"This isn't the gutter, Dad, and you didn't pull me out of anywhere."

"Your birth mother was a common bar whore, Lexi. A stereotype of the worst sort. I saw something more in you." He paused, his eyes narrowing. "The adoption agency thought I'd be happier with a boy, but I chose you. I invested in you. Don't make me regret my decision."

"I'm not a piece of property." Her voice caught and she swallowed, trying to get ahold of her emotions. Robert Preston could smell weakness in an adversary and would gladly use it to his advantage. She knew that better than anyone. "I'm your daughter."

"Which is why I can't understand how you could disobey me in this way."

"I'm not trying to disobey you," she argued. "I just need time."

"Time is up and you're coming with me."

She shook her head and backed away. "No."

He reached for her arm, but someone stepped between them.

"She said no." With Scott looming in front of him, her father took a step back, his eyes wide with disbelief.

"This is none of your business," her father said on an angry breath.

"Anything that happens in my bar is my business."

"It's okay, Scott."

He glanced at her. "Are you sure?"

She nodded, wiping at her eyes.

Scott turned to Lexi, his thumb smoothing a tear off her cheek. "You're safe here, you know."

"Safe?" her dad sputtered. "I'm her father, you idiot. I'm the one who keeps her safe."

"I'll take care of this," Scott told her. "You can go in back and get yourself together."

She nodded. "I'll let you know my decision about my future in a few weeks, Dad. Don't contact me again before that."

"Come back with me now or I'll make sure you have no future. Not in the legal community, anyway." He pointed at Trevor. "Do something, you oaf. Ask her to marry you."

Trevor looked visibly shocked, but stepped forward. "Lexi, would you…?"

Her head started to pound. She knew Trevor was her father's henchman, but hadn't realized how far his loyalty went. "You don't have to do that, Trevor. I'm not going to marry you. Now or ever."

He sighed, probably with relief. "I'm sorry, Lexi," he whispered, and it might have been the first honest thing he'd said to her the whole time they'd been dating.

She turned away, expecting her father to follow, but found herself alone, leaning on the hallway wall outside the kitchen. She stifled a sob, then jumped when Jon popped his head out of the kitchen. "You look like hell."

"I feel worse," she answered.

He shifted uncomfortably, then offered, "I made an apple pie earlier."

She smiled, grateful for the simple gesture. "A slice of pie is just what I need."

Scott turned to Robert Preston. "Leave her alone."

Preston's eyes narrowed. "I know you, Callahan, and you aren't the Boy Scout your brother turned out to be."

"This isn't about you or me. It's about Lexi."

"I think you're part of the reason she doesn't want to come home."

"I don't give a damn what you think."

"You should." Preston smiled, but it was a mean look on him. "I have contacts in D.C., you know. Some with the U.S. Marshals agency."

Scott felt a muscle clench in his jaw. "So what?"

"I know why you're hiding out here. Based on your history, I'd guess running a bar in Brevia, North Carolina, isn't going to cut it for you. You need action. I can help you."

"You don't know anything about me."

"I know you have a snowball's chance of getting back to active duty without a recommendation from the review board." Preston's smile widened as Scott flinched. "I want my daughter back. I didn't realize how serious she was until tonight. I'm not used to seeing Lexi with a backbone."

"It looks good on her."

"In your opinion. But she belongs with me. Her life is in Ohio, not down here." Preston sighed. "I'll give her the month she wants. I'm not stupid. But at the end of the next few weeks I want her to return home. I want you to make sure she does."

"She can make her own decisions," Scott answered, tension balling low in his gut. This guy was a real piece of work. No wonder Lexi needed to take such drastic measures to gain some sense of independence.

Preston nodded in agreement and reached in his wallet to hand Scott a card. "Let's make sure it's the right one. Call me when you come to your senses."

Scott pocketed the business card. He didn't plan to do

anything with it, but Preston didn't need to know that. Right now, he just wanted him out of his bar. "If you knew me at all, you'd know I can't be bought."

Robert Preston only smiled, then turned and walked out of Riley's Bar. Scott hoped it was the last time he'd ever lay eyes on the man.

He looked around the crowded room, surveying the changes he'd made, as well as the groups of people laughing and mingling throughout. In truth, he hadn't missed the action of the field as much as he thought he would. Renovating the bar had taken his time and energy and given him an outlet that was more satisfying than he'd thought it could be. He liked belonging somewhere, getting to know the regulars and making this place part of the community.

The menu was already a success, with local business people coming for lunch and families in the early evening. He'd talked to a couple of local bands and musicians about hosting an open-mic night, and he'd put some events on the calendar to draw people in during the week. Carving out a place in Brevia was good, but he also wondered how long his desire to stay would last. Scott had a long track record of leaving people and places behind. After things were stable, would Brevia still hold his interest? Preston was right that this wasn't the life he'd imagined for himself.

Lexi took another bite of the apple pie, then washed it down with a long drink of milk. "This is fantastic," she told Jon from her seat at the large work island in the middle of the kitchen. "You're a genius."

"Don't plump up his ego too much," Scott said from the doorway. "I've already given him one raise."

Her eyes darted to Scott. "Is my father...?"

"He left, Lexi."

Both disappointment and relief rolled through her. "I guess that's good."

"He's giving you the time you want. He's going to leave you alone for a month."

She nodded. "But he's not interested in me until I come back to Ohio."

Scott didn't answer and his silence told her everything. She took another bite of pie, swallowing back her emotions.

"It's his loss," Scott said quietly.

"Thank you," she answered. She pushed away the half-empty plate and stood. "I need to get back out there. Misty can't cover everyone."

"It's thinned out. People are going home early. She'll be fine."

Lexi took her plate to the sink, then turned to give Jon a small hug. "Thanks for the pie and the company. Your food is going to make this place a huge success. I bet your dad is smiling down on you right now."

A broad grin stretched across the older man's face. "I'm glad you think so. You're a good person, Lexi. I hope your father comes to his senses."

She tried to smile, then swiped at her eyes. "I need to pull it together," she said with a shaky laugh.

Scott took her hand as she came into the hall, tugging her toward the back exit. "Where are we going?"

"Home," he answered, pulling harder when she would have stopped.

"You have a bar to tend and I can't just leave because my dad's a jerk," Lexi argued. "I'm going to pull up my big-girl panties and—"

"Max will finish up the night behind the bar," Scott told her as he opened the door to the alley. "He'll appreciate the extra tips. Misty and Tina can cover the floor. You've had the rug yanked from under you and my day wasn't much better. We're taking the night off. I'm picking up carryout and you can choose the movie."

She dug in her heels as the door shut behind her. Scott turned.

"You don't have to do this."

She squared her shoulders as he studied her. She tried to look brave and tough and unbreakable. All the things she didn't feel.

"I want to," he answered softly. "I want to be with you, Lexi. God help us both, because I know I should leave you alone. I knew it that first night I banged on the apartment door. I can't offer you much, but you deserve your adventure or whatever you call it. Especially if you're going back to make nice with that nasty old coot you call a father. I'm going to make sure you have some fun before that happens."

She hated that her lip trembled at his words, that what he said touched some deep, hollow place inside her. It didn't matter that Scott couldn't offer her much, because living with her father had made her believe she wasn't worth anything. She tried to lighten the mood by asking, "How about a Hugh Jackman movie?"

"As long as he's not singing."

"Let's go for the first *X-Men,* then. It's my favorite."

"You like superheroes?" Scott looked doubtful.

"Only on the big screen," she promised.

He drew her closer, but instead of kissing her he wrapped his arms around her and buried his face in her hair.

"I'm sorry your father is a schmuck."

She laughed despite the emotion welling in her chest. "That about sums it up. But I stood up to him. That's something, right? I'm still here whether or not he wants me to be."

"You are," Scott agreed. "Now let's get that food."

Hours later, Lexi glanced up into Scott's sleeping face. His long lashes rested on the smooth skin of his cheek, while a shadow of stubble covered his jaw, making his perfect features more human. With his eyes closed, his face had a sense of vulnerability he made sure to keep hidden most of the time. He was strong and tough and so alone.

She understood that last part. Despite all her plans and pledges about a big adventure, she was scared to death to be by herself. She didn't know who she was and she wondered if she'd like the person she'd find at the end of her journey.

She was tucked in the crook of his arm, where she'd been through most of the movie. They'd shared Chinese takeout and a couple beers before settling in to watch Professor Xavier and his crew save the world.

If Scott's intention had been to give her some distance from the pain of her father's rejection, it worked. She still felt the hurt, but it wasn't so raw. It was like a prism she could hold out in front of her and study, see the sharp edges and places where feeling unlovable had torn at her soul. But now she could place it on the shelf, add it to her collection of emotional scars.

Maybe that was what someone who'd been physically abandoned by one parent and emotionally rejected by the other did. Lexi was a pro at compartmentalizing her feelings, on tamping them down until she could be in control enough to do what everyone around her expected.

Scott was different. He bulldozed through his emotions, trying to run fast enough that they couldn't touch him with their demanding tendrils. The two of them were so different and yet alike in many ways. That could explain the connection she felt for him. She didn't have to polish herself to a glossy shine for Scott. He'd take her as she was, broken parts and all.

That final thought gave her the courage to lean up and trace his face with her fingers, then press her mouth to his. After a moment he stirred, moaning softly.

She lost her nerve at the sound of his voice. This was stupid. Women like her weren't meant for seduction. But when she would have scrambled away, his arms came around her, grabbing her tight to him and pulling her across his lap. His hands wound through her hair, his mouth devouring hers. She couldn't get enough of him and she pressed herself along the length of his body, straddling him so she could feel his desire for her. She needed him so badly. He made her feel whole and right. She wanted to capture that feeling and carry it with her all her life.

He gripped her face until she looked into his eyes. "I want you, Lexi. I want this. Now."

"Now," she agreed with a soft intake of breath.

He lifted her easily and she clung to him, ripping at his shirt as he made his way down the hall to her bedroom. He tore away the quilt and lowered her gently onto the bed. She lifted her blouse over her head, then watched as he stripped away his shirt. His jeans and boxers followed a minute later. She felt her mouth drop open at the sight of him. Muscles bunched and rippled across his chest, and her eyes caught on the tattoo banding one firm biceps. His whole body was strong, hard and ready. The breath whooshed out of her lungs as desire pooled low in her belly.

She'd had a couple boyfriends over the years, but nothing had prepared her for the sight of Scott Callahan.

A hint of a smile played around his mouth as he watched her watching him. "You can't leave me standing here all alone like this. Aren't you going to join me?"

She reached for the waistband of her pants, then stilled. "I don't know... I'm not you—"

"Thank the Lord for small favors," he said with a laugh and came toward her. The look in his eyes could only be described as predatory.

Slowly, he moved his hands up her legs to the top of her cotton pants, then bent forward to kiss the tip of one nipple through the lace fabric of her bra as he slid her slacks down her legs. He leaned back as he reached her knees. "Each part of you is perfect," he whispered. "And I plan to become intimately familiar with every inch."

"I hope you're not disappointed," she said, then shut her eyes, embarrassed that he might think she was fishing for a compliment.

"Nothing you do could disappoint me, Lexi. I want to touch you. All of you. But only if you're sure." He bent toward her once more, his kiss soft and exploratory, as if giving her time to change her mind.

"Open your eyes," he said against her mouth.

He sat back and she couldn't help reaching out to run her palm across his taut stomach muscles and up the hard planes of his chest. She could feel his heartbeat, strong and steady under her hand. A small grin curved her lips as she watched his blue eyes darken with desire the longer she touched him.

He swallowed and let out a ragged breath that was almost a groan as she grazed her fingernails along his skin. He was giving her time, she knew, to get her bearings...to take control of this moment between them. His ability to understand her needs, even at a time like this, melted her heart. The knowledge that he wanted her as much as she did him gave her the courage she needed to pull him to her again.

But when the tip of her tongue touched his and her legs wrapped around his body, his mouth turned hot and demanding.

She put out her hand to pull the sheet over them, but Scott ripped it away. "We don't need that."

He trailed his mouth down her neck, along her collarbone and over the swell of her breast. At the same time his hand traced a path up her thigh until his fingers found her core. He teased her until she almost lost control.

"Wait," he whispered into her ear. "Not yet."

He grabbed his jeans from beside the bed and pulled out a condom, ripping it open with his teeth. A moment later he balanced above her once more, and his mouth captured hers at the same time as he entered her. She couldn't tell if the groan of pleasure came from her lips or his.

As if their bodies were made for each other, they moved together. A sensation built low in her stomach as the rhythm intensified. For the moment, they were one, and she reveled in the feel of his body over hers, the sparks of pleasure firing through every part of her. After several minutes, she couldn't hold back any longer and her release echoed through her, followed by Scott's harsh intake of breath. He whispered her name and then his head fell to the pillow next to her, nuzzling against her ear as he said words of endearment.

She'd never known anything like what she and Scott had just experienced together. She knew now what true freedom meant. And that no matter what her future held, she'd hold this night close to her heart for the rest of her life.

Chapter Nine

Lexi was able to keep her feelings about her father at bay for the next week. Her feelings for Scott were another story. Things seemed to speed up, both at the bar and between them. They worked to finish renovations, then spent every night together.

As much as she loved being in Scott's arms, her favorite times were the morning. They'd take turns making breakfast, then walk Freddy through the park, talking about everything and nothing. Scott told her about his mother's death, his stint in the army and the work he'd done for the Marshals Service. His life had been an adventure already. He'd seen so much of the world and had to take care of himself in a way she couldn't imagine. Her life up until now had been so structured.

But he seemed just as fascinated with her life as she was with his. She realized, for all the moving around and excitement, what Scott lacked was a sense of being grounded. She thought maybe the bar did that for him, gave him a sense of purpose. She hoped their time together gave him a sense of home. But if she delved too far into sticky emotions, she could feel him pull away. It didn't matter, she told herself. Her time was ticking, anyway, and she'd have to make a decision about her life.

It was becoming clear that going back to the way things had been wasn't enough for her anymore. She didn't want to give up her law career, but working for her father would suck her down the same black hole she'd finally clawed her way out of. She put together a résumé and began to send it out, using contacts she had from the law community and law school. She applied for positions both in big cities and smaller towns, although nothing in her hometown of Columbus, Ohio. She was too afraid of her father finding out and sabotaging her plans. Several of the openings were in D.C. And Charlotte. She knew it was stupid, but hoped that being in one of those cities might enable her to continue to see Scott after her time in Brevia was done.

She also continued to advise locals, despite Frank Davis's not wanting her to. She couldn't turn away people who needed her help, and she was learning which aspects of the law were most appealing to her. She liked the variety that being a general counsel in a small town afforded her, liked using her skills to help people with their problems.

Scott told her she was being taken advantage of again, since all the work she'd done so far was pro bono. But she didn't care. It was important for her to believe she was making a difference.

She'd just finished up a meeting with Ida Garvey in

one of the back booths at the bar when the front door opened and Julia, her mother and her sister, Lainey, walked in.

It was late afternoon, so other than Lexi, Ida and Scott, the place was almost empty. The reception to celebrate the two weddings was only a couple weeks away, so Lexi expected they'd come in to discuss that. She sank down in her chair a little. Scott had asked her to help with the plans for the reception from a logistical end, and she'd actually enjoyed discussing everything with Julia. But she'd managed not to be around when Vera had come by previously. While Lexi had made amends with Julia, she had a pretty good idea how the rest of the family felt about her, and it sure wasn't friendly.

"Don't let Vera scare you," Ida said with a knowing smile. "She's mostly bluster."

Lexi looked at her client. She'd come to enjoy her weekly meeting with the older woman. Sometimes they discussed her estate, but often Ida filled her in on local gossip. She knew everything that was going on in Brevia. Julia had warned her that Ida was a busybody, but Lexi liked hearing her stories.

She watched Scott greet the three women, then his gaze met hers and he motioned her over.

She groaned softly. "I've got to be a part of this. It was good to see you, Mrs. Garvey. I'll get those motions filed, but you should really talk to Frank. I know he doesn't want me working with his clients."

"He'll deal with it," Ida said with a scoff. "He's gotten plenty of my business and more of my money. If his practice was so important, he'd spend more time on it."

"He's a good attorney," Lexi offered. "I still think you should talk to him."

"Too nice for your own good," Ida mumbled. "Go see to those Morgan women, dear."

Lexi stood and walked toward them. Vera was talking to Scott, pointing to something in a file she'd laid across the bar. Julia smiled, but her sister, Lainey Daniels, narrowed her eyes as Lexi came closer. She'd met Lainey only once, when she and her husband, Ethan, had come in for dinner. Lexi had seen some promotional photos Lainey had taken of the bar for a marketing campaign focusing on the tourist season in Brevia.

"Everything looks good for the reception," Lexi said to Julia. "I confirmed the time with the band yesterday and asked Scott to order the champagne you wanted for the toast."

"Thanks, Lexi." Julia smiled again and turned to her sister. "She's making me look totally on top of things with Mom."

"I still don't understand why she's in charge," Lainey answered, keeping her eyes trained on Lexi. "We all want to trust her but are you sure about this?"

"It's different now." Julia gave Lainey a pointed look. "You should know people can change."

"I agree with your sister," Vera interjected, taking a sip from the glass of water Scott had placed on the bar. "Julia, you've always been too trusting of people. It's gotten you into trouble in the past."

Lexi shook her head. "I'm not here to cause trouble, Mrs. Callahan. I want everything to be perfect for your celebration."

"Besides," Julia added, "I trust her a lot more than I do Scott."

"He's making changes to this place that are going to help the local economy for years to come." Lexi looked at Julia. "You know bringing more people into downtown is good for all the businesses here, including your salon."

"He's a loose cannon." Julia crossed her arms over her chest. "I don't trust him."

Scott cleared his throat. "I'm standing right here."

"I see you," she said. The look she threw him made Lexi smile. "I'm hoping you'll leave."

He tossed down the towel he'd been holding. "Gladly." His gaze met Lexi's, warming her from her toes up. *Good luck,* he mouthed to her before disappearing into the back.

"If you do anything to hurt my daughter, you'll have to answer to me," Vera said, turning her full attention on Lexi.

Before she could sputter out an answer, Ida Garvey's shrill voice rang out. "Vera Morgan, give the girl a break. It wasn't too long ago that your daughters were practically duking it out in the middle of town. Everyone deserves a second chance."

"Since when did you become anyone's champion, Ida?" Vera asked.

Lexi felt like repeating Scott's comment that she was standing right in front of them. But Julia caught her gaze and shook her head slightly.

"She's been helping me with changes I'm making to my estate plan. You know Frank Davis hasn't been up to snuff for a while now. That's what makes me her champion," the older woman said with a smirk. "I'm in it for what's best for me."

"Same old Ida," Vera muttered.

"But she's working for you, too," Ida retorted. "You'd see that if you weren't so hardheaded. She's got a whole file with the details of your reception. She's put a lot of thought into it. Half the town is going to be here to celebrate with you. Lexi's the one making sure it will be a night everyone will remember. Give her a chance, Vera."

With a small pat on Lainey's back, Ida shuffled out the front door. Lexi wasn't sure why it meant so much to her to have a woman she'd known for only a few weeks come to her defense, but it did.

Vera's gaze moved to Lexi. "Is this true?"

She nodded. "Yes, ma'am. I hope so."

Julia's mother motioned her forward. "Let's see what you've got then."

Lexi opened up the file where she kept her plans for the Callahan and Callahan reception. She'd never put together a party of this size before, but the organizing and details appealed to her analytical side. Plus, the busier she kept, the less time she had to spend worrying about her future. So when Scott had asked her to handle the celebration, she'd jumped at the chance.

As she pulled out her notes, her excitement overtook her nervousness regarding Vera's reaction. Most of what she was showing her Julia had already approved, so Lexi felt a bit more confident. "Julia told me your favorite color is yellow and hers is blue, so that's what I went for with the color scheme." She took out samples of fabric from the tablecloths and napkins. "Obviously, we're in a bar, and the whole event is a casual, homey family affair, but I still wanted it to be elegant." She glanced at Vera from under her lashes. "Because you seem like a very elegant lady."

"Agreed," she answered.

Julia and Lainey both laughed.

"There will be fresh flowers and candles at every

table—understated, but they should look beautiful in the light. I contacted the microbrewery over in Asheville, and they're supplying beer for us. They've agreed to brew a special Amazing Animal Ale for the event and donate a portion of their profits back to your shelter."

Vera nodded. "I like it."

"Congratulations on your wedding, by the way. Joe seems very nice."

"That's why I married him."

"It means a lot to Scott to be here with his dad and Sam." She looked at Julia. "They're all hanging out, you know."

"I know."

"Joe loves his boys," Vera stated. "He'll do anything to make up for how things used to be. He wants it to be right between them."

"Scott wants that, too. He's worked hard on the reception. I think he sees it as a way to prove to both of them that he's changed."

The older woman studied her. "You seem to know Scott pretty well."

"I work with him almost every day," Lexi said quickly, hoping nothing on her face gave away her true emotions.

"And they're roommates," Julia said.

Lexi saw Lainey choke back a laugh. "You're sharing the apartment with Scott?"

"It's not like…"

"Like what, Lexi?" Julia leaned forward and whispered, "Are you sleeping with him?"

Lexi tried to no avail to stop a blush from creeping up her cheeks.

Lainey shushed Julia, then put a hand on Lexi's shoulder. "Julia doesn't have good personal boundaries."

"And you're one to talk, little sister."

"You've obviously put a lot of work into the reception," Lainey continued, ignoring Julia. "I appreciate your help." She glanced at their mother. "We all do. Right, Mom?"

Lexi blinked back tears as Vera smiled.

"Julia's right that we believe in second chances. We also take care of our own around here. You're included in that now. Scott's family, too. If the two of you make each other happy, we're happy for you."

"I'm not staying in Brevia." Lexi choked on the words, but knew she owed these women the truth. "Scott knows that. What we have…whatever it is, it's temporary."

"You aren't staying?" Lainey looked confused. "But you fit."

"I don't know where I fit. That's what I'm trying to figure out."

Lainey gave her a quick hug. "I know how that feels, so I hope you do." She turned to her mother. "Come on, Mom. I want to show you the dress I picked out for the reception."

"Thank you for everything you've done." Vera pushed away Lexi's outstretched hand and gave her a hug.

"Oh." Lexi breathed out the one syllable, overwhelmed with emotion that these women could forgive her so easily for what she'd put Julia through. That they could accept her with her faults and all.

When Vera and Lainey walked out, Julia turned to her. "That wasn't so hard, was it?"

Lexi swallowed. "You're lucky to have the family you do."

"It took me a while to realize it." She nodded. "But you're right. Speaking of families, have you spoken to dear ole dad lately?"

"He was here a few nights ago. He ordered me to come home with him."

"And yet you're still here." Julia chucked her on the shoulder. "You have more backbone than I gave you credit for."

"You and me both," Lexi agreed. "I'm coming into the salon to see Nancy before my shift starts, by the way."

"She's grateful for all you've done to help with her divorce."

Lexi shrugged. "It wasn't that much. But she offered to give me a complimentary cut and color as a thank-you."

"Hallelujah!" Julia reached out and tugged on Lexi's ponytail. "It's about time you stopped wearing it pulled back."

"It's professional," Lexi argued.

"It's boring." Julia's eyebrows wiggled. "I bet Scott likes it down."

"He says… Never mind." Lexi blushed under the other woman's scrutiny. "I'm a total fool, starting something with him. I know it already so you don't need to tell me."

"You know as well as anyone that I've had my share of romantic missteps. Big ones." Julia glanced toward the back of the bar. "I know Scott has had problems in the past, but maybe he'll surprise us all. Either way, you're a big girl. You get to make your own mistakes."

Lexi nodded. "But it wasn't a mistake coming to

Brevia. Thank you, Julia, for giving me a do-over. No matter what happens, I'll always be grateful."

"No mushy stuff. Just buy me a drink if I ever get a night out on the town again." She shrugged at Lexi's questioning look. "My mom and Lainey help with Charlie during the week, but I haven't found an evening sitter he likes."

"What about me?"

"What about you?"

"I could watch him. I'm off tomorrow night. I can come over or you can bring him by the apartment."

"I wouldn't want—"

"Please, Julia. It's the least I can do. I swear you can trust me with him. You and Sam can have a date night."

Julia took a deep breath as Lexi found herself holding hers. Suddenly it was very important to her that Julia trust her enough to babysit Charlie.

"That would be great," Julia said finally. "I'll see if Sam can get off, and text you about the time."

"Perfect." Lexi glanced at her watch. "I need to get to my appointment. Are you walking back to the salon?"

Julia nodded. "Let's hit it."

"I need to..." Her eyes strayed to the back of the bar.

"Oh." Julia rolled her eyes. "Give lover boy a kiss goodbye for me."

"It isn't like that."

"I'm kidding, Lexi." She smiled broadly, then laughed. "Sort of. Either way, I'll wait for you outside."

Lexi walked to Scott's office, but stopped just outside the doorway. Suddenly she felt nervous, wondering if Scott would even care that she was going. Sure, they'd spent every night together for the past week, but it wasn't as if they were dating. More like roommates with benefits, which she supposed should make her feel cheap. But it didn't.

She peeked her head in as Scott looked up from the paperwork on his desk. "Hey there, gorgeous."

Lexi glanced behind her to see if Julia had followed her down the hall.

"I'm talking to you, Lexi." Scott came around the desk and toward her, as if he meant to replay their previous interlude on his couch.

Her breath caught in her chest and she held up her hands, palms out. "I have a hair appointment," she said quickly. "I just wanted to say, um…goodbye, and…"

Her mind went blank for a moment as he reached out and drew her to him, his mouth claiming hers in a deep kiss. After a moment he asked, "How did it go with Vera and Lainey?"

It took a few seconds before Lexi could even remember who Vera and Lainey were. "They're happy with the plans, I think."

Scott cupped her face with his hands. "That's because you've done an amazing job of organizing everything."

"Vera doesn't seem to hate me anymore."

"If she's happy, my father will be over the moon."

"Would you believe Ida Garvey came to my defense?"

"You have the ability to wrap just about anyone around your little finger," Scott said, kissing her again.

"Are you wrapped around my finger?"

"What's it look like?"

She thought about that for a moment. "Like I'm a convenient place to land at night."

He stilled. "You think I'm with you because you're convenient?"

"It's easy for both of us, right?" She didn't like the

sparks shooting from his blue eyes. "It's not as if we're dating."

His eyes narrowed. "So it's just sex for you?" His tone was incredulous.

"I didn't say that. But we haven't exactly been out to dinner or a movie or the stuff people do when they're dating. I'm not complaining. We're friends." She smiled to try to lighten the mood. "Like you said, the kind with great benefits."

"Friends," he repeated ominously.

"I need to go," she said, backing out of his arms. "We can talk about this later. Or not."

"Tomorrow night." He crossed his arms over his chest. "You're off. I'll get someone to fill in for me. We're going out."

"I'm busy tomorrow night." She bit down on her lower lip. "And that wasn't a very nice way to ask me on a date."

He shook his head. "Busy with what? And if you say a date with the high-school teacher, we're going to have a problem."

A little butterfly danced through Lexi's belly. "I canceled my date with Mark. I... It wasn't the right time for me." Was it possible that Scott Callahan was jealous over her? The mere thought made her want to giggle. "I'm babysitting. For Julia and Sam."

"Whoa. Didn't see that coming." Scott looked absolutely stunned and Lexi couldn't blame him.

"I owe Julia a lot." She paused, then added, "And I like kids. You've met Charlie. He's adorable."

Scott nodded. "Another time, then."

She nodded, but wondered if she'd freaked him out so much that there wouldn't be another time. The thought made her heart sink a bit, but she forced a smile. "I'll see you later, then."

He nodded and she turned to go.

"Lexi?"

She glanced over her shoulder.

"Don't do anything crazy with your hair," he said softly. "I like it just the way it is."

More butterflies took flight and she hurried out the door.

Scott knocked on the door to his brother's house, then wiped his damp palms across the front of his jeans. This was ridiculous. He'd seen combat zones, drug takedowns and everything in between. This night was nothing in comparison.

So why was his heart beating like crazy?

Before he could come up with a reasonable excuse, the door opened to reveal his brother in a pale blue button-down, striped tie and khaki pants.

"A tie?" Scott asked, whistling softly. "That's laying it on a little thick, don't you think?"

Sam huffed out a breath, then pulled at the collar of his shirt. "It's called making an effort, numskull. You should try it sometime."

Scott laughed. "Too bad I won the genetic lottery in our family. With a face like mine, showing up is all the effort I need."

"Is that so?" Sam looked unimpressed. "Then tell me why you're here tonight."

"I thought Lexi could use some help." He kicked his toe at an imaginary rock. "She practically begged me to come with her."

"There are different kinds of effort, Scott." Sam tugged at his collar again. "But I'm glad you're here."

"Because you still don't trust her?" Scott's fists clenched at his sides. "That's not fair if you—"

"Simmer down, bro. I trust her well enough. Lexi Preston is suddenly Julia's new best friend, and from what I've seen, she's making up for lost time, being helpful and kind and all that stuff." Sam stepped back and motioned Scott through the door. "I'm glad you're here because it's about time my son got to know his uncle. Julia's brother-in-law, Ethan, has quite a head start, so you've got some work to do."

Scott felt his nerves sound off like soldiers in a battle line. "I don't do kids, Sam."

"You're here."

"Obviously my first mistake." He shook his head. "Don't get me wrong. I'm happy for you. I'm sure you're a great dad. You were always so damn responsible and honorable and, well, everything I'm not. I think you'd be smart to stick with Ethan to play the doting uncle."

"We'll see. Charlie's pretty irresistible."

"I'm immune to cute." At Sam's raised eyebrows, Scott amended, "Kid cute, that is."

"Lexi's not your usual type."

"She's not."

As if sensing his sudden urge to bolt, Sam backed off. "I like her, Scott. You're obviously happy with her and you deserve some happiness."

"I don't want—"

"You can deny it all you want, but it's written all over your face. It's not a bad thing to care about someone. It took me a long time to realize that. Dad, too. We Callahans are kind of stupid in the face of scary things like love and emotions. But it's not so bad once you get the hang of it."

Scott couldn't help but laugh. "You missed your calling as a poet."

"You'll see," Sam said, giving him a light punch on the shoulder. "Come on in. They're back in the kitchen. Julia and I have a reservation awaiting us."

Scott followed Sam through the Craftsman-style house, wondering if he could be happy with a regular life. He hadn't been there since he'd first come to Brevia. Most of the time he'd spent with Sam or their father had been at the bar, either having lunch or watching a game. He couldn't believe how domestic Sam had become, his home filled with overstuffed furniture and framed photos on the bookshelves. It made Scott's body ache in a way he didn't understand.

This was never what he'd wanted for himself. He liked the thrill of the chase, the adrenaline high he got from putting himself in danger through his work. He would have never guessed that Sam could make a life for himself in a town like Brevia, and he certainly didn't understand the longing he couldn't seem to shake.

That need intensified as he walked into the kitchen to see Lexi seated in front of a high chair, talking softly to Charlie as the boy ate small mouthfuls of macaroni and cheese. She looked so beautiful with the early-evening light reflecting off her strawberry-blond hair. She looked as if she belonged there.

He wanted to belong, too.

"Daddy," Charlie yelled when he noticed Sam. "I got macan for dinner."

"Looks good, buddy." Sam walked over and bent to kiss the top of Charlie's head, a gesture so natural it made Scott's throat burn. "Miss Lexi is going to have help with you tonight. Buddy, do you remember meeting your uncle Scott?"

Charlie gave Scott a toothy smile, then held up a spoonful of macaroni noodles.

Lexi turned, the blush that was now so familiar to Scott creeping up her neck. "What are you doing here?"

"Reinforcements," he answered simply.

"Sam, we need to go if we're going to…" Julia came in through the back door, but stopped when she saw Scott. "Well, well. What have we here?"

"Be nice, Juls," Sam said quietly.

"One of the bartenders wanted to pick up an extra shift so I…I'm here." Scott crossed his arms over his chest, hating the feeling of being the center of attention in this cozy scene. "If it's a problem I can leave."

Julia flashed a knowing smile. "I don't have a problem. Lexi, do you have a problem?"

Lexi shook her head, but kept her attention focused on Charlie.

"Then let's go, hot husband of mine." Julia crooked a finger in Sam's direction. "I have plans for you." She bent forward and kissed Charlie's cheek. "Be good for Lexi, my little peanut. Mama loves you."

"Bye, bye, Mama. Loves you," Charlie answered and offered her a spoonful of macaroni.

"I love you, too, sweet boy." She looked at Lexi. "We won't be late. Bedtime at seven with a bath first and—"

Sam wrapped one arm around her waist and steered her toward the door again. "You've left a detailed list. They've got our numbers. It's all good."

"Have fun, you three," he called over his shoulder as the door shut behind them.

Charlie raised himself in his high chair to watch them walk out. "All gone," he announced and went back to scooping up his dinner. "Charlie thirsty."

Lexi straightened. "How about some milk, sweetie?"

The boy nodded.

Scott stepped forward, needing to be occupied with something. "I'll get it. Is there a bottle or...?"

"He's almost two," Lexi said with a small laugh. "There's no bottle." She went to the cabinet and pulled out a plastic cup with a lid. "He uses a sippy cup. They don't spill."

"I have some customers who could benefit from one of those."

Lexi filled the cup with milk, tightened the lid and gave it to Charlie. Then she turned to Scott. "I'm going to run the bath. Bring him upstairs when he's finished with dinner."

Scott grabbed her arm as she went to move past. "You're not leaving me here with him. Alone."

She smiled sweetly. "Reinforcements, remember?"

The way she studied him, Scott knew she was well aware of how uncomfortable he was. What had he been thinking? It was true that one of his bartenders, Max, wanted to make extra money. But there was plenty at the bar to keep Scott busy even when he wasn't serving drinks. Not to mention that several single women came on a regular basis and made no secret of flirting with him. If he'd wanted to occupy himself, there were better ways than babysitting for his brother. In truth, what he wanted more than anything was to be near Lexi. He'd do just about anything to have more time with her.

He had no intention of letting on, though. "Sure. Right. We'll be up in a bit."

With a small shake of her head, she left him alone in the kitchen with Charlie. His nephew. Scott sat on the edge of one of the chairs and watched the toddler as he would have a key witness, not wanting anything to go wrong when he was in charge.

"Relax," Lexi whispered as she peeked into the room once more. "He's a little boy, Scott. He won't bite."

"He might."

"Just have fun with him."

She disappeared again and Scott thought about all the ways he'd had fun in his life. Babysitting had never once been on that list.

Julia's dog, Casper, came to sit next to him, his gray snout almost level with the high-chair tray.

"Good doggie," Charlie said and threw a piece of macaroni in the air. Casper promptly jumped up and caught it, his stubby tail wagging. Charlie exploded into a fit of giggles.

"Um…" Scott said slowly. "I don't think you're supposed to feed the dog your dinner."

Charlie laughed again and threw another noodle, which the dog caught. More laughter erupted and Scott found himself smiling.

He picked up a noodle off the tray. "I once knew a dog who could do a special trick, Charlie. Let's see if Casper knows this one.

"Casper, stay," he commanded, then carefully placed the noodle on the tip of the dog's snout. "Wait," he said slowly, then gave the "Okay" command. Casper flipped the noodle off his nose and caught it.

Charlie squealed with delight. "Again, Unc-le. Do it again."

Scott's heart clenched the tiniest bit at the word *uncle*.

As much as he didn't want them to, that word and the boy who spoke it meant something to him. Reconnecting with his dad and Sam meant something. Something more than simply proving he wasn't the schmuck they both assumed him to be. Scott wanted to make it right with his family. He wanted to be the man no one believed he could become.

No one except Lexi. Since that first night in the bar, she'd seen more in him than he'd seen in himself. It made his gut clench to think he had only a couple more weeks with her. For just a moment he entertained the idea that it didn't have to end. What would it be like to make it really work with Lexi? Could he give that much of himself?

He didn't know for sure, but right now he wanted nothing more than the chance to try.

He did the treat-on-nose trick with Casper until there were no more noodles left on the tray.

"Up," Charlie said, raising his arms above his head.

Scott took a breath. Okay, he could do this. He carefully placed his hands under Charlie's arms and lifted, then cradled the small boy against his chest. Charlie immediately wiggled to be let down, and when Scott put him on the floor, he headed for the stairs.

"Baaf-time," the toddler announced as Scott followed on his heels.

"Would you grab a couple of towels from the hall closet?" Lexi called as they got to the second floor.

He did, then made it to the bathroom as she lowered Charlie into the tub. "Have you ever done this before?"

"No," she answered, her eyes never leaving the boy. "But I think I can manage." She handed Charlie an assortment of rubber toys and squeezed excess water out of a duck-shaped sponge.

Scott leaned against the counter and watched Lexi in action. She and Charlie sang several verses of "The Wheels on the Bus" as the little boy sat in the tub.

It was strangely intimate in a heart-tugging way to be a part of such an everyday routine in his nephew's life. Scott thought Lexi had never looked so beautiful. Her hair was pulled back in a loose ponytail, with several tendrils escaping to curl around her face. It was lighter since she'd been at the salon today, highlighting her pale green eyes even more. She laughed as Charlie splashed, leaving the front of her pink T-shirt sprayed with water.

"You'll be a great mother one day," Scott said softly, not realizing he'd said the words out loud until she turned to gape at him.

"I hope so," she said after a moment, her eyes so full of tenderness he wished he could stop time so that she'd always look at him that way.

Still, it scared him. Lexi made him want things he never expected to have and couldn't believe he deserved. He'd always managed to ruin the relationships that meant the most to him, so why did he expect anything would change now?

"I'm going to clean up the kitchen," he said and left the bathroom before she could see how much she meant to him. How much he longed for the stability and caring she represented. How he couldn't bear the thought that he was bound to ruin her, too.

Chapter Ten

Lexi finished putting Charlie's dump-truck pajamas on, pulling the bottoms over his diaper. She picked him up and snuggled her face into his neck for a few seconds, reveling in the scent of clean boy. Scott hadn't reappeared since he'd practically run from the bathroom earlier. She knew there wasn't much to clean up in the kitchen, so figured this whole night had freaked him out beyond the point of no return. She half expected that he'd left a note downstairs and already escaped to the bar, where he was much more comfortable.

She bit down hard on her lip to avoid tearing up again when she thought of Scott telling her she'd be a good mother. It surprised her how natural the role felt. She had so little memory of her own mom and found it hard to believe that she had any genetic instincts for parenting. But taking care of Charlie gave her an indescribable joy, while at the same time it left a deep ache in the core of her heart. It was one of many revelations from her time in Brevia. She now knew that, one way or another, becoming a mother someday topped her list of priorities.

She sat down in the rocking chair in the corner and read two books to Charlie, then turned down the lights and slowly swayed around the room with him in her arms, singing softly. When she felt his head grow heavy on her shoulder, she placed him in his toddler bed, dropping a soft kiss on his forehead before turning to go.

Scott stood in the doorway watching her, his eyes cast in shadow so she couldn't read them. He held out his hand and she laced her fingers through his, closing Charlie's door most of the way before following Scott down the stairs.

"I can't believe I'm saying this, but hanging with Charlie is almost fun." He led her to the living room and sat on the couch before pulling her down next to him. His arm wound around her shoulders and he dropped a kiss on her hair, a gesture so unconscious it made her feel they'd been a couple for years instead of weeks.

"He's amazing," Lexi agreed. "You must have quite a knack, too, because I could hear him laughing the whole time I was running the bathwater."

"Kid whisperer. Just one of my many talents."

She laughed and snuggled in closer. After a moment she asked, "Do you remember much about your mom?"

She felt Scott's breath hitch, but he didn't pull away. "I was so young when she died, there's not a lot of details. Mainly random snippets. I can recognize the perfume she wore, and she loved the Beatles, so certain music brings her back to me." He drew his fingers up and down Lexi's arm. "But I try not to remember that it was my fault she died."

Lexi tried to sit up so she could turn around and look at him, but he held her tight.

"My dad doesn't blame me. I think Sam used to. Either way, it's the truth."

"You were seven. She died in a car accident, right? How could it be your fault?"

"My dad worked all the time back then. His whole life was the force. It scared the hell out of my mom. I think she was afraid of being left with two boys to raise alone. She drank every night. My dad either ignored it or didn't want to admit there was a problem. But Sam and I knew, even as young as we were. I could see she wasn't right. Sam compensated by being the perfect kid. He tried to anticipate her every need, make life easier for her, to take away the stress."

"He was just a boy," Lexi said sadly.

"It was his nature." Scott gave a humorless laugh. "Not me. I was mad and I pushed all of her buttons. There was only room for one of us to get the attention from being a good kid, and Sam had that locked up. I went the opposite way. But I still didn't want her drinking. I don't remember my exact thinking, but I knew the bottle wasn't helping her cope with life. She'd hide the liquor and I'd find it and dump it. It would make her so angry, but I couldn't stop. I thought if the alcohol wasn't around then maybe she'd have a chance to get better."

"You were trying to help in your own way."

"The night she died she and my dad had a big fight. She went to get another drink, but I'd poured the rest of the bottle down the sink. That's part of why she drove off that night, to make a liquor-store run to replenish her stock. She wasn't far from the house when the accident happened. If she'd just been at home, she would have been safe."

He said the last words with a ragged intake of breath.

Lexi turned, looking into his eyes, so full of pain and guilt. "You were a kid," she said gently, wanting to reach out and touch him, but too afraid of breaking this moment and scaring him away. "You wanted her to get better."

He looked miserable as he said, "My good intentions didn't save her. If I'd just left her alone, maybe she would have stayed home that night. Maybe she'd never have died."

"It wasn't your fault," Lexi told him. "Children aren't responsible for the actions of their parents. Trust me, I know that better than anyone."

He lifted her hand off his cheek and placed a kiss on the inside of her wrist. "Do you remember your mom?"

"Only a little. An image here and there. But not much more than that. My father—big surprise—sent me to a psychologist when I was younger to 'process' what had happened to me. Basically, I was told not to dwell on the past and to be grateful for my new life and the second chance I'd been given." She sighed. "Which I was. I still am. But there are questions I wish I could have answered about her. I never knew my biological father and sometimes I wonder where I came from, who I'd be if Robert Preston hadn't molded me into his perfect, obedient daughter."

"You're more than the person he tried to make you." Scott said the words with such conviction, Lexi couldn't help but believe them. "You have a good heart and a kindness that has nothing to do with your father. You're stronger than he knows. If nothing else, you must have learned that since being here."

She swallowed around the lump in her throat. "I never thought of myself as anyone besides Robert Preston's daughter. But now I do. Holding Charlie tonight made me see that I have more to give than I could have imagined."

"But you still plan to go back to Ohio?" Scott asked, as though he'd read her mind.

She stood, the familiar feeling of nervousness coursing through her body. "It's like my time here hasn't been real. I've told myself it was just a break, something temporary, which made it not quite as scary. The thought of really being on my own, that's terrifying." She paced back and forth in front of the couch. "My dad is the only family I have. That's important to me. What would it be like if I had no one?"

"You have me," Scott said quietly.

She stopped and turned to him. "Do I really? What if I told you I was applying for jobs in Charlotte and D.C. so I could stay close to you? Would you stick around if you thought I wanted more than a couple of weeks of fun? You've made it clear you don't have anything more to give."

"You deserve something—someone—better." A muscle ticked in his jaw. "Of course I want time with you. But I've told you before, I mess things up for the people who care about me. Your life is just starting. I'm not going to ruin it for you."

"I don't believe that," she said, feeling her temper rise. "I think that's an easy out you've given yourself because you don't want to do the hard work a real relationship takes."

His eyes went dark. "I can't give you what you want. Isn't it enough—"

He stopped midsentence as the front door opened. Sam and Julia came into the living room, holding hands.

"We're back," Julia called out. She paused, her gaze traveling between Lexi and Scott. "Rough night?"

Lexi shook her head. "Charlie was wonderful. It all went great."

Sam watched the two of them, then threw a pained look at Julia. "She's totally lying."

"I'm not," Lexi protested. "Did you have a good dinner? You're back so early."

Now Sam's expression turned soft as he gazed at his wife. "Dinner was great, but…"

"We're so boring," Julia finished. "We just wanted to come home and watch a movie on the couch."

Scott stifled a yawn. "How old are you two, anyway?"

"That doesn't sound boring," Lexi argued. "It sounds perfect."

"Would you like to join us?" Sam asked after a moment.

Julia elbowed him in the ribs. "Ignore him. He's being polite." She turned and planted a deep, wet kiss on Sam's mouth.

"She's right," he agreed, his arms tightening around Julia. "You should go now."

"Um…right." Lexi grabbed her purse from the side table.

"Get a room," Scott muttered.

"We have a whole house," Julia countered. But she turned and placed a hand on Lexi's arm. "Thank you for watching Charlie tonight. We needed this."

"It was my pleasure," Lexi answered.

"If you stay in Brevia awhile, we'll try a long week-end." Sam laughed when Lexi's eyes widened and Scott groaned. "Think you can handle it?"

"Have a nice time, you two." Scott put his hand on the small of Lexi's back and guided her out onto the porch.

She kept walking down the steps and toward her car, suddenly feeling exhausted. She yearned for the kind of love Sam and Julia shared, but was afraid she'd already given her heart to a man who could never let himself feel the same thing back.

"Hold on," Scott said, tugging on her hand. "Don't leave mad, Lexi."

"I'm not angry." She pulled away and kept moving. "I'm tired. I'll see you back at the apartment."

"Is this our first fight? Should I sleep at the bar to-night?" His tone held a hint of teasing she couldn't return.

"I'm not sure what this is, Scott. I know what I want, but it's up to you to decide whether you can give it to me." She unlocked her car, then looked back at him. "When you figure it out, let me know."

She pulled up to the curb outside her apartment build-ing. Scott had disappeared shortly after they'd left Sam and Julia's street. She wondered if he really planned on sleeping at the bar. There were bound to be several women willing to let him warm their beds if he needed a place to stay. The thought filled her with a hollow feel-ing of disappointment.

He'd told her he was bound to disappoint her, so who was truly to blame?

She'd hoped for something more even though it was foolish. He hadn't made any promises, but he'd smiled when she told him she was applying for jobs in D.C., answering her unspoken question about their future with a kiss. The way he looked at her, the way he held her close every night made her believe they could have one. He might not say the words out loud, but she knew he cared for her.

Every morning for the past week he'd warmed her towel while she was in the shower, leaving it ready for her on the sink when she got out. It was a small gesture, but to her it represented the essence of Scott. He could be cool and detached on the outside, but he had the softest heart of anyone she'd ever met.

Now her own heart ached at the thought that she wanted things Scott would never be able to give her.

She sat in the car for several minutes before climbing the steps to her apartment. The wind blew cold as darkness fell. A light mist that promised more rain enveloped her, giving the air a heavy weight that matched the pressure in her heart.

This evening had started out with so much promise and now here she was, alone again. Just as she put the keys in the lock, a noise behind her made her turn. Scott stood at the end of the hallway, a bouquet of fresh flowers held out in front of his chest.

"I thought you'd gone to the bar," she whispered.

"I'm sorry," he said as he walked toward her. "I'm sorry I don't have all the answers, that I'm not a better man."

"I like you just the way you are." Her voice cracked as he handed the bouquet to her. She knew suddenly that she didn't just like him. She loved him. The vulnerability and need in his eyes called to a place inside her, and there was nothing she could do to resist the pull.

He scooped her into his arms and she clung to him as he carried her into the apartment, kicking the door shut. His mouth captured hers with a kiss so possessive, so commanding, it stole her breath. But she met his desire with all the emotions she'd banked up inside. Everything she wanted to tell him but was too afraid to say out loud she tried to show him through their embrace. He seemed to be filled with the same hunger she felt for him. The flowers dropped to the floor as they tore at each other's clothes and he carried her to her bedroom.

Her breasts tingled as he slid his hands over them, over her entire body, trailing kisses in the wake of his skilled fingers. When he moved over her, inside her, she knew that in embracing her freedom she'd also lost her heart to this man. Whether or not he could ever truly be hers didn't matter as they found a perfect rhythm, a connection she knew she'd only ever find in his arms.

He whispered endearments into her ear, coaxing her to the highest peaks of pleasure before finding his own release. He continued to kiss her, lightly and softly. He nuzzled her neck and threaded his fingers through her hair, pulling her close as he sank back against the pillows.

Her head lay on his chest and she could hear his heartbeat, as wild and erratic as she knew hers to be, until it finally settled to its normal pace. She wondered for a moment if anything would ever be normal inside her again.

She knew he wasn't sleeping because he continued to run his fingers lightly over her bare back.

She tipped up her head after a moment. "I've never had make-up sex before."

He grinned wryly. "So I guess now you're going to want to fight all the time."

"Only if you promise to bring me flowers and apologize so enthusiastically."

He shifted her onto her back once again. "Enthusiastic? You haven't seen anything yet."

And for hours more, he proved to be a man of his word.

Scott whistled as he loaded cases of beer into the big refrigerator off the kitchen. It was midmorning and the bar was quiet, his favorite time to get work done.

"Someone's in a great mood today."

He turned to Jon Riley with a grin. "It could be because I just ran the numbers for last month. We're doing better than I ever expected on revenue. I think that has a lot to do with your menu drawing in new customers. I appreciate everything you've done, Jon."

The older man shrugged, looking embarrassed to be singled out. "You've made some great changes here. My father would be happy to see his place thriving again." Jon made a show of checking supplies in the food pantry. "But I'd guess your attitude has more to do with a certain tiny redhead."

Scott went back to stacking boxes. "We're trying to keep it quiet, you know. She's only here temporarily, but I'm the boss and I don't want it to look..." No matter how he tried, he couldn't stop the smile that played across his lips. "Truth is, I don't care how it looks. She's amazing."

"Everyone can see that you two belong together."

"The hell they do."

Scott's back went stiff as he glanced to where Robert Preston stood in the doorway of the kitchen.

"I assume you're talking about my daughter," Preston said through clenched teeth, "and I'm here to tell you she belongs back home with a man who is worthy of her. Not with some washed-up ex-combat soldier stuck in this town."

"Your daughter gets to make her own decisions now," Scott argued. "You don't own her anymore. You never really did." He stepped toward the man. "You have no business here, Preston."

"I want to check on Lexi. Make sure she's doing okay. I assume she's ready to come back. If you've kept up your end of the bargain in making sure she knows what's best for her."

"She told you she'd make her decision at the end of the month. You agreed to leave her alone until then."

Preston glanced around the kitchen, derision clear in his gaze. "If her choice is the life she left behind or this, I know what she'll choose. I didn't raise her to settle for someone like you. I can offer her safety, security and a guarantee that she'll have a decent future."

Anger coursed through Scott. "Your problem is you underestimate her. Does the name Reid and Thompson mean anything to you?"

"It's a D.C. firm started by one of my old partners. So what?"

"What if I told you Lexi had an interview with them?" She had said she wanted to keep her interviews quiet until she got an offer, but Scott knew she'd get hired and couldn't help but gloat to her father. He enjoyed seeing Preston's face turn blotchy.

"You think you're her only option, but what you forget is Lexi is a hell of an attorney in her own right. There are plenty of places that would be glad to hire someone with her talent. I'm not saying that I'm worthy of her. She's better than either one of us deserves. Maybe now that she's out from under your thumb she'll have enough confidence to believe in herself." He paused, then drove the final nail in the coffin. "Maybe you've already lost her."

Preston stalked toward him, looking as if he was ready for a fight. As much as he'd enjoy pummeling this man who'd caused Lexi so much pain, Scott wasn't that stupid.

"You think you know her so well." Preston spit the words, his face only inches from Scott's. "She needs me. I'm her only family and that means something to Lexi. She'll come to her senses one way or another." His mouth curved into a nasty grin. "And what about you? Hiding out here from your past. This isn't what you want. You need to be where the action is. Do you really think it's all going to work out so easily for you?"

"Maybe this is enough for me." Scott forced his voice to remain even. "You don't know who I am."

"We'll see about that." Preston turned and walked from the room.

Scott stood there, his fists clenched tightly. Robert Preston had hit the heart of Scott's biggest fear. That he was going to mess up this chance he'd gotten at a new life, that the broken part of him would bubble to the surface and cause him to destroy the connections he'd built. That was why he'd chosen to be a loner in life. It was easier to take care of only himself, leaving less chance of collateral damage for the people around him.

He may have been only a boy when his mother died, but he knew he was the one who'd driven her away, even as he'd wanted to save her. When he'd tried to show Sam that his fiancée was no good, Scott had ended up almost ruining his relationship with his brother. And he'd wanted to protect his partner to the point that he'd turned an unintentional blind eye to the drinking that had eventually killed Derek.

He'd opened up to Lexi, let her into his life and heart because he'd believed it was a temporary arrangement. But he knew she wanted more from him, and he desperately wished he could give it to her. She filled the dark corners of his body and soul with her light. She'd become a lifeline back to the world for him, away from the isolation he'd lived with for so long. What would he risk if he fell for her completely? There was a good chance he would eventually hurt her. Scott wasn't sure if he knew another way, despite his best intentions.

Even if he couldn't hold on to her, he knew for damn sure he wasn't going to let her father reclaim her.

"He's intense," Jon said, pulling Scott back to the present.

"He's like a poison to her," he answered. "Toxic."

"Lexi certainly seems happier and more confident than when she first arrived." Jon laughed softly. "She doesn't drop glasses anymore."

Scott felt a smile play at his lips as he thought back to her first bumbling shifts at the bar. "This isn't where she was meant to be, either. It's just a short-term stopping point on her journey."

"What if the path leads to her father again?" Jon asked.

"She can't go back there."

"Maybe you should give her a reason to stay."

Chapter Eleven

The bead of sweat that trickled between Lexi's shoulder blades had nothing to do with the sun beaming through the clouds. The weather was growing colder, but this morning felt almost perfect. Leaves shimmered on the trees in the park and Freddy played with a pinecone, batting it around with his nose as she sank onto the park bench.

She held her cell phone in her palm, still staring at it, unable to believe the conversation she'd just had. When the Human Resources department from one of the firms where she'd applied had called earlier this morning to tell her she hadn't gotten the position, Lexi had been surprised but not too disappointed. She had several leads on open positions at reputable law firms. But after that first call, her phone had rung almost on cue every fifteen minutes, with all the openings suddenly drying up or the positions going to other applicants.

The final call had come in from the senior partner at Reid and Thompson, her father's former colleague, who'd informed her that they had no room for her at their law firm. When she'd questioned him about the reason, his answer had been cryptic, but he'd eventually suggested her best option might be to head back to Ohio to try to patch things up with her father.

She dialed her dad's private line now, the sinking feeling in her chest expanding as he answered on the first ring.

"Are you ready to come home?" he asked, cutting right to the heart of the matter.

"How did you know I was applying for other jobs? Are you having me followed?" She bit her lip as emotion threatened to overtake her. She wouldn't give him the satisfaction of hearing how upset she was. "Why, Dad? Why sabotage my chance at a fresh start?"

"I want you here with me."

"I have to learn to live on my own."

"You're all I have, Lexi." She heard him draw in a breath, as if he was shocked he'd admitted that much to her.

"I'm your daughter and I love you," she whispered, willing him to accept her right to choose her own life. "Where I live won't change that."

"You don't belong there. Especially not with him."

"Are you talking about Scott?" She adjusted the phone in her hands, realizing her fingers were shaking. "Leave him out of this, Dad. He cares about me."

Her father barked out a bitter laugh. "Always so naive. That's part of the reason you still need me. The man you think cares about you is the one who told me about your job prospects."

Lexi shivered from the ice that suddenly ran down her spine. "When did you talk to Scott?"

"I paid another visit to Brevia and Riley's Bar. Your boss was very interested in how I could help him return to his real life as a marshal. I still have quite a few contacts in the Justice Department, you know."

"What did you do, Dad?"

"It's time to come home, Lexi. Your little adventure is officially over."

She hung up, stunned to think that Scott would have betrayed her this way. He'd been encouraging her to apply to law firms in the region, bolstering her confidence and making her feel as if she could really contribute if given a chance. He still wouldn't talk about a future with her, insisting she needed to worry about herself before she made any relationship a priority. But Lexi had continued to hold out hope that his feelings for her, or the ones she believed him to have, would be enough to make him realize their relationship was worth taking a chance on.

Now any future they could have had together was ruined, so much collateral damage—just like her heart. She knew he didn't love her; he couldn't with what he'd done. She also knew that as much as she loved him there wasn't a way to repair this kind of betrayal.

Still, she had to know why.

Her hands were shaking as she started walking, Freddy trotting along at her side. She didn't stop until she was in front of Riley's Bar & Grill. Part of her wanted to keep going, to return to the apartment and pack as much as she could fit in her suitcase. She wanted to escape this place and the sad, desperate promise she'd believed it held for her.

She couldn't outrun her past, couldn't pretend it wasn't waiting to swallow her again. She'd gotten what she came for—adventure and a taste of freedom. But now that was done and nothing could change the future she'd tried so hard to avoid.

Scott stood behind the bar, his full attention captured by whatever he was reading. He looked up as she walked through the door, tenderness shining in his eyes. Their light made her heart break even further, creating a wide chasm so painful she clutched a hand to her chest to tamp down some of the pain.

It didn't work. Nothing could lessen the hurt she felt. Nothing but the truth.

"You're not going to believe this," he said, coming around the bar. "The Marshals office has reinstated me. Apparently, their investigation has been satisfied without my review." He reached for her, but she stepped away. Freddy, traitorous canine, wiggled at Scott's feet.

"Was it worth it?" Her throat was so dry the words came out as croak.

"Hell, yes, it was worth it." His smile brightened and he crouched down to pet Freddy. "I didn't have to rat out my partner. I didn't ruin his family. I'm in the clear."

His words were another blow, so much like a punch to the gut that she bent forward with the force of it.

"Lexi, what is it? Come sit down."

"Don't touch me," she said with a painful hiss of breath when he tried to gather her close. "You ruined me. You destroyed us. And you're telling me it was worth it?" She shook her head. "You're no different than my father. I thought—"

"What are you talking about?"

How could he look at her as if he gave a damn? Her

pain turned to anger, which gave her the strength she needed to straighten her shoulders. "You told my father about my job applications. He came to see you and you gave him the information he needed to ruin my chances at being hired on at any of the firms where I'd applied."

Scott looked confused for a moment, then shook his head. "No. I mean, yes. He showed up here and I told him that you weren't coming back, that you were going to find your own way in life. It wasn't so that he could interfere."

"But he did," she said, her voice cracking. "I told you he would. I asked you not to say anything until I had everything settled. He's basically blackballed me in the legal community. I guess I could get in my car and drive to California. That sounds like a great option, right?"

"I didn't—"

"And now you've been reinstated. Do you think that's a coincidence, Scott? According to the conversation I just had with my dad, it isn't. He said he offered you a deal—help limit my options and he'd use his contacts at the Justice Department to have your review abandoned. I guess you both got what you wanted." She drew herself up and asked, "So tell me again, was it worth it?"

"It was a mistake, Lexi." Scott ran his hand through his hair, a gesture so familiar to her now it made pain slice through her once more. "You have to believe that."

"Was it?" she countered. "You've told me over and over how you sabotage your own life. You destroy the connections you have with people."

"Not you—"

"You're a coward." She wanted the words to hurt him. She needed him to feel some of the same pain she did, as if she could hold on to him with any kind of desperate connection.

"Excuse me?" He said the words through clenched teeth.

"I got too close. I think your feelings for me scared the hell out of you and you dealt with them the only way you know how—by pushing me away. Guess what? It worked. I've had a great time, but some things weren't meant to be. I'm not a fighter by nature. I don't want to spend my whole life looking over my shoulder, waiting for the next time my father sticks his nose in my affairs. I'm stronger than I was when I left, and I can go back now, hopefully on my own terms."

She raised her chin, biting down on her lower lip to keep it from trembling. "Tell me I'm wrong." She tried not to let her voice sound as if she was pleading with him. "Tell me there's another way."

For a moment, the pain in his eyes matched her own. He looked as miserable as she felt. She knew that if he reached for her now, told her he loved her and they would figure out another way, she'd believe him. If he could be honest, they might work through this.

But he didn't give her that chance.

He took a step toward her, then stopped. His eyes closed for a second and when he looked at her again, the mask was back in place. The man who cared only about himself had returned. Lexi wondered if he'd ever really left in the first place.

"Don't say I didn't warn you," he told her, his quiet voice a knife across her soul. "I didn't want to hurt you, Lexi, but we both knew it was inevitable. That's the guy I am. It's who I've always been. Maybe you are better back with your father. At least he's an enemy you know."

"And you'll leave Brevia? Leave behind everything you've built here to go back to the Marshals?"

He bit out a harsh laugh. "What have I really done here? I've put a shine on a two-bit bar. Come on, that's no future."

"It's more than that and you know it. It's your family, the friends you've made in this community. Riley's Bar & Grill is a part of the town because of you. You've made a difference. How can you turn your back on that?"

"The town will go on without me. Sam and my dad will do just fine. They were doing fine when I came back into their lives, and it won't take much for things to return to normal."

She wanted to turn and walk away, but something inside her made her keep pushing. "What about you, Scott? What about your pain? Being in Brevia has healed what was broken inside of you. I know that it has."

"When are you going to get it? It's not a piece of me that's damaged. It's the whole thing. I'm broken and there's no fixing it." He paced back and forth in front of her. "I can get on with my life." He stopped, pressed his lips together, then said, "We both can. This was a fun ride while it lasted. You got the adventure you wanted and I had a distraction while I was waiting for things to work out. But it's not real. It never was."

The unexpected rush of sorrow almost brought her to her knees. Wasn't she repeating the same mistakes she'd made with her father? She'd tried to guess what Scott wanted from her. Attempted to meet his expectations without ever knowing what they truly were. She'd hoped their relationship meant something to him, but was too afraid of being rejected to share her feelings. And now when things were difficult, when she wasn't making it easy on him, he shut her out. Just as her dad had done.

She shook her head, not bothering to wipe away the tears that streamed down her face. "It was real for me," she whispered.

Scott's eyes narrowed and she thought he might respond, believed she might have finally found a crack in his armor. But when he said nothing, she finally turned and walked away.

Forever.

The bar was loud and crowded several hours later. It was a Friday night, and in the few short weeks he'd been in Brevia, Riley's Bar had become a favorite hangout for locals and tourists alike. Scott surveyed the room, knowing he should feel pride in what he'd accomplished. All he could see was how he'd ruined things once again.

He poured a round of shots for a group near the front celebrating someone's promotion, then added an extra glass for himself. He hadn't taken a drink of hard liquor since the night he'd moved in with Lexi. The bourbon burned his throat, but nothing could burn away the memory of Lexi's tortured face as he'd watched her heart break in front of him.

It had killed him to see her like that, but he couldn't seem to stop himself from lashing out once she'd accused him of conspiring with her father. Scott was used to people believing the worst about him and meeting their low, low expectations. She'd been different, or so he'd thought. He'd had the crazy idea she'd seen a better side of him, the man he wanted to be. He'd been stupid enough to hope that he could do right by her.

He'd been waiting for her to leave him, but that didn't

make it hurt less. When it was clear he'd once again messed up, he made sure the door shut behind her for good. His whole body felt the loss of her.

Now he had to live with the gaping hole that hours ago had held his heart.

He put down the empty shot glass and noticed Sam standing at the edge of the bar.

"Busy here," Scott shouted, indicating the jumble of people in front of him.

"Make time," Sam replied. "Now."

Scott grabbed the arm of the second bartender. "Max, can you handle this for a few minutes?"

The younger man smiled. "More tips for me."

Scott followed Sam down the back hallway and into his office. He swore Lexi's scent lingered in the air, making him catch his breath.

A half-dozen large garbage bags were piled in front of the desk.

"Your stuff from the apartment," Sam said flatly.

Scott's gut tightened. He hadn't planned on going back there tonight. But to know she'd already packed and shipped him off still got under his skin, even though he knew everything was his fault. As usual. "Is that what you pulled me away for?"

"I know all about making things harder than they need to be," his brother said, instead of answering the question. "I think a Callahan invented the concept. Did you do it on purpose?"

Scott knew Sam was talking about the information he'd given to Lexi's father. "I don't know." He scrubbed his hands across his face. "I was mad and I didn't want to answer the questions he asked. I wanted him gone. I'm not exactly an expert on thinking before I speak.

Lexi is better off without me. Maybe this was the only way to show her that."

"You love her," Sam told him, using his best big-brother voice.

"You don't know anything about me," Scott countered. "You never have. I'm not like you, Sam. I'm the black sheep, the one who messes up. I always have been. Why should this be any different?"

"It's different because you love her. You're different."

"You know what happened, I assume. So you know it's over."

"Do you remember when we were little, before Mom died?"

Scott gritted his teeth. He and Sam rarely talked about their mother's death, about life before that. Hell, they'd had a hard enough time getting through their childhood, with their father gone most of the time. They'd dealt with the pain and loss in different ways. Yet it remained a common bond they shared, pushing them apart while at the same time keeping them tethered to each other.

"You were a fighter, the most stubborn kid ever," Sam told him. "When her drinking got bad, I'd make excuses or try to coddle her through the bad nights."

"You also made a lot of ramen-noodle dinners and sack lunches when she wasn't in any shape to do it herself."

"I tried to gloss it over."

"You were making the best of the situation." Scott closed his eyes for a moment. "I couldn't."

"Not you," Sam agreed. "You'd get in her face, dump the liquor bottles, play games, sing and dance, whatever you could do to keep her engaged with her family.

You made her step up a lot more than she would have otherwise."

"Look where that got all of us. She went out to replace what'd I'd poured down the sink and died because of it."

"She died because she was driving drunk. That wasn't your fault."

"Well, it sure as hell wasn't yours."

"It wasn't any of ours," Sam told him. "Even after that, you kept fighting. Half the reason you got in trouble was to get Dad's attention, to pull him back into our lives."

"It took twenty years for that to happen, and now he's turned into Dr. Phil. I don't think I had anything to do with that."

"Of course you did," his father said from the doorway.

Scott groaned and rolled his eyes in Sam's direction. "Not him, too."

Joe Callahan stepped into room. "Sammy's right. You were a fighter back then. So what happened, son? What made the fight go out of you?"

"The fight didn't go out of me," Scott said through clenched teeth. "If you both remember, I joined the army, I became a marshal. I've spent my whole damn life fighting." He threw out his hands. "Other than these past few weeks. Maybe that's my problem. I'm going soft." He pointed a finger at Sam, then his father. "Just like the two of you. I let this town make me forget my priorities."

Joe came forward, placing his big hands on Scott's shoulders. "This town and that woman gave you priorities. She made you whole."

"She made me think I could be someone I'm not," Scott said quietly. "Lexi and I both learned our lesson there."

"You need to fight for her," Sam countered.

"She doesn't want me to. It's better for both of us if I let her walk away."

"Are you kidding?" His brother slammed his hand down on the desk. "I saw you with her. I know that look. Hell, I avoided that look in the mirror for ages. But I'm telling you that for the rest of your life you'll regret it if you don't try to make this right."

"It's the truth, son." Joe brought his face close to Scott's. "I'm sorry that your mother drove off that night. I'm sorry I left her with no options and that I didn't do right by the two of you after she was gone. I messed us up real good." He drew in a shaky breath.

"Dad, don't cry." Scott's head began to pound. "I don't need this."

"What you need is to have your butt kicked into next week."

Shrugging out of his father's embrace, Scott turned to Sam. "I suppose you're the guy to do it?" His hands curled into fists. He was angry at himself, but if he could take it out on Sam, that worked, too. He wouldn't pass up the opportunity for a decent release of frustration. "Bring it on."

Sam shook his head. "No, thanks. Hitting me isn't going to make you feel any better."

"I think it might." Scott stepped forward. "Because it sure as hell feels wrong that my brother isn't on my side."

"I'm on your side," Sam answered. "Just like you were on mine when you slept with Jenny."

"That's not the same thing."

"I said I'd never thank you, but I am now. Your method was crazy, but you were right. I would have been miserable married to her. If you hadn't shown me her true colors, I might not have come to Brevia. Julia and Charlie might not be a part of my life. Sometimes bad things that happen are for the best in the end."

"And sometimes they aren't. That's how it works with me." Blood thrummed through Scott's head, making it hard to get the words out. "I pushed Mom until she left that night. I should have found a way to convince you that Jenny was the wrong woman. Instead, I took her to bed, making you look like a fool and guaranteeing that you'd cut me out of your life. I didn't confront my partner when I knew he was drinking too much and too often, and he got killed because of it. Try telling his wife and kids that things will work out in the end for them." Scott drew in a ragged breath. "Now I've given Robert Preston the information he needed to make sure Lexi feels like she has no options but to go back to him."

"You aren't responsible for the fate of everyone around you," Joe said sadly. "When are you going to realize that, Scott? You do the best you can and so does everyone else."

"My best is pretty awful, Dad." He turned. "You might be right, Sam. I hate what happened with Lexi and her dad, but it could work out for the best when she moves on with her life and I'm not a part of it."

"That's not what I mean and you know it."

"I'm sorry," Scott said after a long moment. "I want you both to know that."

"You don't need to apologize," his father told him. "We're your family. We love you no matter what."

Scott glanced at Sam. "I bet Julia wants to kill me."

"She'll get over it. Quicker than you will."

"We'll have to see," Scott answered. "I need to get back to the front now."

Joe pulled him close for another hug. To his surprise, Scott felt some comfort in the gesture, but still he shrugged away. "Go home, you two. There's nothing more to be done here."

He walked into the hall, sagging against the wall for a moment before he continued. He was going soft. That must be the reason all of this was hitting him so hard. Normally he could leave his mistakes behind, keep moving so that things didn't catch him. But now he felt weighed down, as if he'd swallowed a load of boulders and was sinking into a deep pool of misery. In a way he welcomed the darkness. It was familiar, and right now Scott clung to that to keep from totally drowning.

He straightened his shoulders and went back to the bar, jumping on top as he put two fingers to his mouth to whistle for the crowd's attention.

"I got some good news today," he shouted, "and everyone here is going to celebrate tonight. This round's on me!"

A loud cheer went up from his customers and he climbed down to a chorus of congratulations and back slaps. The blackness in him expanded until it blotted out all of the light he'd known this past month. He sucked in a breath and forced his mouth into a smile. This was what he knew, and he was going to relearn to live with faking happiness.

Chapter Twelve

"You're running away."

"I was running away when I came to Brevia." Lexi folded another shirt and placed it in the suitcase. "Now I'm going home. That's what most people do after they run away."

"You don't want to go back there." Julia plucked the shirt out of the pile and shoved it back in the drawer as Lexi turned away.

"Quit doing that," she said, shaking her head. "I don't know what I want. Not with the options I have left. I came here to find my independence, and instead I traded being dependent on my father with being dependent on Scott. Those jobs I was looking at—their appeal hinged on keeping me close to D.C. so I could be near him. That was stupid."

"That's love. It makes you do stupid things." Julia shrugged. "Trust me, I know."

"I'm going to be smarter now."

"Smarter isn't going home to be your father's puppet."

"I'm going back on my terms."

"You're going back because that's the easy way out."

"Easy? I've been miserable for the past three days. What part of my swollen face and bags under my eyes looks easy to you?" Lexi growled in her throat as Julia put away another sweater. "Stop unpacking me."

"You don't want to leave. Brevia sucks you in until you're a part of the community. I know you like it here."

"Of course I do," Lexi said miserably. "But what am I supposed to do to make a living? I'm not going back to the bar and...I like being an attorney."

"So be one. In Brevia." Julia pointed a finger at her. "You have a half-dozen clients already. Find some cheap office space and hang out your shingle or whatever it is lawyers do."

"I have a handful of people I've helped on a pro bono basis. I can't be paid with free highlights and apple pies."

"Your hair looks a lot better since Nancy got ahold of you."

Lexi couldn't help but roll her eyes. "Not the point."

"The point is you're afraid to try."

"I did try. And I failed. End of story."

"You didn't really. You told everyone that you were having 'an adventure.' That this was just a short vacation from reality. That's not putting yourself out there for real."

"I left my job, my father, everything I knew behind. How is that not real?"

"You didn't leave them. You said 'I'll be back.' You could be someone different because it was a costume you were trying on. Why bother with the guts to make it work? You knew you could go running home to Daddy."

"Running home...!" Lexi said with a sputter. "I was applying for other jobs. I didn't plan to go back."

Julia shook her head. "I don't believe you."

"How dare you—"

"I don't believe you and I don't think you intended to stay with Scott, either."

"You can't be serious. He's the one who betrayed me."

"He did you a favor."

Lexi felt her mouth drop open. "You're crazy. I don't know why I came here in the first place."

"You came here," Julia answered, "because I'm the only person you know who would let you live your own life. But you can't do it. You're not brave enough. I thought you had it in you, but I guess I was wrong."

"Had what in me?"

"The courage to really stand on your own two feet. Not just take 'a break' from life. Your dad interfered with your job applications. So what? Big deal. Stuff happens. Move on. Apply for more jobs, smaller firms. Start your own firm. Right here. What's stopping you?"

"And what would stop him from interfering again?"

"You will. You're the only one who can stop him. But you have to stand up to him once and for all and be willing to deal with the consequences, no matter what they are. You haven't done that yet. You've told him you 'need time.' To him that's an open door. If you really want to live life on your own terms, you have to force him to let you go."

"That's easier said than done."

"Maybe," Julia agreed. "That's why Scott did you a favor. Eventually your father was going to find out you'd applied for jobs. Did you really have any intention of taking one of them, or was it just a ploy to prove to him you were ready to move on?"

"Yes... No... I don't know, when you say it like that." Lexi sat down on the bed, suddenly tired now that the edge was taken off her anger. "I knew he was going to be mad, but I still haven't proved anything to him. I've shown I can live on my own for a few weeks. So what? I wanted to get a job without his help. Everything I've done in my life has been because my dad has been holding the strings. I went to his alma mater. I worked for his firm on the cases he assigned me. I needed a change. I thought a month would show him that there was more to me than he thought. I wanted to prove it to myself, as well."

"And it did, right?"

"I suppose. But you're right, taking a break and making a fresh start for real are two different things. I'm scared of being alone. I'm afraid to be on my own when it's permanent."

"You're not on your own in Brevia," Julia said softly. "You have friends here. You have Scott."

"I don't." Lexi shook her head. "I have friends and I'm grateful for that. Grateful to you. But I don't have Scott. He's going back to the Marshals. He doesn't want anything long-term with me."

"He loves you," Julia told her. "I can see it."

"I don't think he knows how to let himself love someone." Lexi wiped at her damp eyes with the T-shirt in her hands. "We both knew it was temporary. He made sure of that when he told my father about my plans." She shook her head. "I don't think he did me a favor, but either way, we're done. You're right about one thing, Julia."

"I'm usually right about everything," the other woman corrected with a smile.

Lexi mustered a watery grin in return. "I haven't learned to stand on my own two feet," she said softly. "I didn't take control of my future. I only postponed the future my father has planned for me."

"It's not too late." Julia placed a hand on Lexi's shoulder. "Take it from one who knows, it's never too late. Do you know what you want to do with your life?"

Lexi thought for a minute, then nodded.

"Then go do it."

Lexi took a deep, soul-cleansing breath. "You're right. This isn't over until I say it is." She stood up, then smiled as she looked at the empty suitcase on the bed. "Did you unpack everything?"

Julia shrugged. "I basically threw it all into a drawer, so I'm not saying you'll be able to find what you need. But it's here, Lexi. You belong here."

Lexi nodded. As if the clouds had parted after a heavy storm, her path appeared before her, suddenly clear as a blue sky. "I know what I want. And I know just the person to help me get it."

An hour later, Lexi stood on the steps of Frank Davis's office once again. She raised her hand to knock, but Ida Garvey pushed her aside.

"It's a good thing you called me to meet you. After all, I practically paid for this building," the older woman told her, turning the knob and walking right in. "Frank," she called out. "I know you're hiding out in here."

Frank Davis came forward from the main office. "Ida," he said, his voice dripping with Southern hospitality. "To what do I owe the honor of…" He trailed off when he noticed Lexi standing behind Ida. "Why is she here with you?"

"She's my attorney," Ida said simply.

Lexi couldn't help the smile that curved her lips. Listening to Ida ramble on during the short drive downtown, she'd questioned the logic of including the older woman in this confrontation. But she knew she'd get further with Frank Davis if she had his best client in her corner.

"I'm your attorney," he argued now.

"You were for many years," Ida agreed. "And you did a good job. Mainly. Adequate, anyway. Well, except for that time—"

"What's your point, Ida?" The sweetness had dropped from his tone.

"Something's wrong with you, Frank." Ida pointed a fleshy finger at him. "I don't know what, but I smell trouble on you. You're ignoring clients, messing up filings, generally dropping the ball across the board. I want to know why."

"That's not true." Frank's hand shot up in the air. "It's this…Yankee. She's put these notions into your head."

"Yankee?" Lexi asked. "Did you really just call me that?"

"Hush, girl." Ida turned to Frank. "No one puts any notions into my head and you know it. Spill the beans, Frank."

He puffed himself up as if to argue, then let out his breath in a large burst. Frank Davis sank into the chair behind the secretary's desk and ran a hand across his face. "I'm in love," he said with a loud moan.

Ida looked back at Lexi, a question in her eyes. Lexi

wasn't sure if the question was *Is this guy crazy?* but that was what she was thinking.

"Well, good for you, Frank," Ida said slowly. "Doris has been gone awhile now and the boys are grown and out of the house. You deserve some happiness."

"Happiness," Frank wailed. "There's nothing happy about loving this woman. She torments me every day. Her expectations, her needs. I'll be sixty-three years old next month. There's only so much this old body can handle, even with them little blue pills."

"TMI," Ida said quickly, then, at his odd look, explained, "Too much information, Frank."

"Maybe this was a mistake," Lexi whispered.

Ida ignored her. "Who is this gal?"

A look of pained adoration crossed Frank's ruddy face. "Miss Lucy St. Louis from down in Atlanta."

"Atlanta, Georgia?" Ida asked. "You've taken up with a woman who lives three hours away? Frank, you're a bigger fool than I thought."

"I love her, Ida." Frank dropped his head into his hands. "She loves me, too. But the distance is part of the problem. She wants to see me every weekend, and I've been driving back and forth. Sometimes in the middle of the week, too, if she wants…"

"A booty call?" Lexi couldn't help but ask.

Frank turned red, but mumbled, "She can't get enough."

"Then move her up here." Ida threw her hands in the air. "This isn't rocket science."

"It's not that easy." Frank leaned back in the chair, hands pressed to his temples. "She's got a little sister in private school down there she takes care of, and she makes good money at her job."

"I don't even want to know what someone named Lucy St. Louis does for a living," Ida muttered.

"Probably not," Frank agreed, then sighed. "I'm sorry, Ida. I haven't been giving my clients my all. I'm distracted and tired and…"

"Then why didn't you take my help?" Lexi asked.

"After what you did last year with Julia's son?" Frank shook his head. "I may be an old fool, but I'm not stupid. I don't trust you and I'm sure as hell not entrusting my clients to you."

"I trust her," Ida said firmly. "Lots of other people around town do, as well. Vera Morgan being one of them."

Frank's bug eyes narrowed in on Lexi. "Is that true?"

"It is." Lexi stepped forward. "I want to do right by the people of Brevia, Mr. Davis. Just like you. I know my introduction to the town was poor at best, but I'm a good attorney."

"Can't deny you there," Frank muttered.

"I'd like to stay in town, but I'm not a waitress."

The lawyer raised his head. "I heard you haven't been breaking as many glasses recently."

Lexi bit out a short laugh. "That's true. But I'm a better attorney than the best waitress I could ever be."

"I could use someone working with me," he admitted, scrubbing his hand across his face again. He looked expectantly at Lexi. "I'm going to be retiring here in a few years. If Lucy doesn't kill me first."

Lexi nodded, her mind such a jumble she could barely form a coherent thought. This was really happening. She was going to stay in Brevia. For good.

"It's settled, then," Ida said.

Frank stood and walked around the desk, grabbing

Lexi's hand and shaking it. "Welcome to Davis and Associates." He turned to Ida. "Could you give Lexi and me a few minutes alone to discuss salary and benefits?"

"No way." Ida crossed her arms over her chest. "I'm staying for that part of the conversation."

"You can't leave now."

"It's only for a couple of days." Scott handed Jon Riley a piece of paper. "I've put together a list of deliveries and the schedule for the week with each person's contact information. If you need anything, call my cell phone."

"I'm the cook, not a bar manager," Jon argued, holding the paper tightly.

"You'll do fine." Scott clapped him on the shoulder. "I trust you." *More than I trust myself at this point,* he added silently.

"How can you run away?"

Scott's head began to pound again. "I'm not running away. I have business in D.C."

"Your old job."

He nodded.

"Are you going back to it?"

"I need to discuss some things with them first." Scott rubbed his temples. He wished he was running right now. Away from questions he couldn't answer, away from prying eyes every night at the bar. It had been almost a week since he'd gotten his reinstatement letter, and only three days until the reception for his dad and Sam. Riley's was crowded every night, with many people coming in for dinner and to hang out with friends or family. He'd gotten to know a number of locals, the majority of whom wanted to remind him what a fool he'd been to "fire" Lexi. No matter how many times he explained that she'd quit, the result was the same—everyone telling him how badly he'd messed up.

As if he didn't know that already. He felt the loss of her through every fiber of his being, from the moment he woke up until he dropped to sleep again. His back was killing him from nights on the couch in his office. Sam had offered him a place to stay, and so had his dad, over the objections of both of their wives, he'd guess.

But Scott wasn't going to be a burden to his family, especially not when they were treating him like some fragile doll who'd break in two if not handled the right way. He'd explained over and over that even if he went back to the Marshals, he'd find a good manager for the bar and come back to visit whenever he could. But it didn't seem to be good enough. They wanted him to promise to stay, and he couldn't do that.

He told himself it was because he had too much to lose if he gave up his job, but his heart felt as if he'd already lost everything important when Lexi walked away. Whether he stayed in Brevia or went back to D.C. and the Marshals wasn't really important. All that mattered was that she was gone. His mind might know it was for the best. Hell, he'd almost forced her to leave, but that didn't make it hurt any less. If anything, the ache only intensified, because if he wasn't such a self-destructive fool, he could have prevented it. That part hurt the most.

"You're not leaving, are you?" Misty walked into the kitchen. "Jon says he's going to be in charge now."

Scott rubbed two fingers against his temple. "He isn't in charge. I'm going to D.C. for a few days to wrap up some stuff with my old job."

"Are you coming back?"

He hesitated for the briefest second and she stomped her foot on the floor. "You can't desert us here."

"I'm not deserting anyone," Scott muttered. "I have business to take care of out of town. Jon is going to be running the place for a few days."

"I never agreed to that." Jon slammed the refrigerator door shut.

"The waitresses will never agree to it," Misty repeated. "You'd better make one of them the manager."

Scott wanted to hit something. "Fine. You're in charge."

"I don't want to be the manager," she argued. "Those girls can't get along."

"You two are killing me!"

"We need you, Scott." Misty's voice softened. "I know you don't want to be needed. I know you've been in a terrible mood since Lexi left, but this bar is yours. Like it or not. Take it or leave it."

He saw the expectation in her face, felt it in her tone of voice. It weighed on him, just as it had with Lexi and his family. Why couldn't anyone see that he wasn't a person to depend on? He'd tried to be honest about what he could and couldn't give. It wasn't that hard to understand.

He'd reached his breaking point. This was how it happened with him. People pushed him further than he could manage, always thinking that he'd step up to the challenge. But he never did. As much as he wanted to, he couldn't make it work.

Now was no different.

He grabbed his duffel bag from the floor next to the desk.

"Leave it," he said quietly and walked out the door.

Chapter Thirteen

Lexi heard the fire truck before she saw it. The big red engine came screaming around the corner of Main Street. She stopped midstride walking out of Julia's salon, riveted by the noise of the siren. Then her heart leaped into her throat as the truck pulled up in front of Riley's Bar & Grill.

Scott wasn't there. Julia had told Lexi he'd left town for D.C. Lexi didn't know why the news had shocked her. Even after he'd told her he wasn't going to stick, some part of her had still held out hope. She told herself it didn't matter. It was enough that she'd found a place to call home. If Scott had to keep looking for his happiness, that was no business of hers.

She hadn't been back to the bar since she'd walked out. But she cared about the people there. She'd had lunch with Misty just yesterday, and Jon had stopped by her new office at the end of the day to bring her a take-out dinner. It was concern for her friends that had her running toward the bar, following two firemen inside.

The scene inside stopped her in her tracks. Water gushed through the doorway to the back half of the building. At least two inches covered the floor of the main room, the legs of chairs and tables standing in it.

"Oh, no," she whispered. Jon waded out from the back, a look of pure panic on his face.

"What happened?" she called to him, not wanting to step farther into the wetness.

"Water line broke, I think." He shook his head. "I got here about twenty minutes ago and this is what I found."

"Why is the fire department here?"

"Dave Johnson, a local plumber, is also a volunteer firefighter. I called him first and he brought the truck. I guess they were worried about an electrical fire or something."

A man dressed in a black T-shirt and yellow over-alls up behind Jon. "We've turned off the water. It's going to be tomorrow morning before I can get the parts here to fix it for real."

"What about tonight?" Lexi asked. Thursday was a popular night out in Brevia.

"Unless your customers have rubber boots," Dave told Jon, "they're not going to want to be in the place."

Lexi took off her shoes and rolled up her jeans, slosh-ing through the water to get to Jon. "Did you call Scott?"

"At least a dozen times," he answered. "He's not tak-ing my calls." The older man shook his head. "With how he tore out of here, I'm not sure he means to come back."

"Of course he's coming back," Lexi answered with

more conviction than she felt. "The reception for Joe and Sam is Saturday night. He's not going to miss that."

"I don't know. He stormed off in quite a huff. Looked to me like he was done with Brevia." Jon shook his head sadly. "Wouldn't surprise me."

A shrill cry had both of them turning toward the door. Misty stood at the entrance. "Did someone forget to turn off a faucet? Why is there a fire engine out front?"

"We have a small situation," Lexi explained. "A water line broke." She turned to Dave Johnson. "What are the options here?"

"Start swimming," he suggested with a smile.

"Not funny."

"Like I said, I'll have the pipe fixed by tomorrow. You're lucky it's fresh water, so that's a plus. Basically, you need to get a team in here to clean things up. I'm guessing it will take a week or so."

Lexi shook her head. "We don't have a week. This place needs to be ready for a party on Saturday night."

"That's right," Dave answered, nodding. "This is the big shindig for Sam Callahan. Sorry, lady, ain't going to happen."

"Who knows what will happen if Scott doesn't get back," Misty called out. "At this point, maybe we should start looking for other work."

"No way," Lexi argued. "We can't leave this place like this. If we don't get this water up quickly, the floor will be ruined. It needs time to dry out. There's got to be something we can do."

"Why do you even care?" Misty asked her. "I thought you were done with this place. Done with Scott Callahan."

"I am done. But I can't let it end like this. Scott poured

his time, energy and money into revitalizing Riley's. I know you all have been making more in tips in the past month than you have in ages."

The waitress nodded slowly.

"We can't just give up on it now."

"What are we supposed to do?" Jon asked.

Lexi turned to Dave. "You said you can get the pipe fixed tomorrow morning?"

"First thing," he promised. "I can make a call to the guys who work on flooded buildings and the like."

"Good." Lexi racked her brain for what to do next. "I'll get ahold of Sam. If anyone can rally the troops around here, it's the police chief."

Jon put a heavy hand on her shoulder. "I'm serious, Lexi. I doubt Scott's coming back. At this point, it might be better to walk away and let him hash things out with the insurance company."

"I don't believe that, Jon." She pointed a finger at him. "He gave you a chance when no one else would, and hired a couple of your buddies for odd jobs around here, right?"

"Yes."

"He's made an investment in Brevia. This place and this town mean something to him. Even if he doesn't re-alize it yet, he's going to. We have to show him…" Her voice lowered, became shaky. "I have to show him that even if he doesn't believe in himself, I still do. I'm not giving up." She felt her throat tighten with tears. Jon was probably right. For all she knew, Scott wouldn't care what happened here or what she did to make things right. But she had to try. That was what she'd want some-one to do for her, and she had to believe her faith would pull him through.

Jon drew her into a tight hug. "You're a good woman, Lexi Preston."

"Let's hope I'm good enough."

Scott thumped his hands on the steering wheel as he drove into town. He'd been calling Jon Riley every fifteen minutes for the past four hours, but Jon hadn't answered his cell. That seemed ominous to Scott, and ominous was the last thing he needed this morning. He'd been delayed an extra night in D.C., wrapping up loose ends. He'd expected to make it to Brevia last evening, but now had only half a day until the reception, and there was so much to do.

If he even had a bar to get back to.

He'd left messages with directions for who to call and how to manage the cleanup. The one time he'd been able to reach Jon, after the man's many messages, their conversation had been cryptic at best. Jon had told him he wouldn't believe what had happened—something about a flood, a miracle, and to return as soon as possible. Then he'd hung up. Scott understood why Jon had been mad. Scott hadn't picked up the phone on Thursday. He'd left his cell in the car while he'd met with his former boss at the U.S. Marshals. That conversation had been bad enough, without having more distractions piled on top.

Now he worried that his carelessness may have put his future in jeopardy once again. It didn't matter, he told himself. He'd get through the reception without letting anyone down. He was going to stick this time. Whatever he found when he got to the bar, he was determined to make it right again.

He came to a screeching halt at the curb and threw his truck into Park. Bolting for the door with his heart in his throat, he rushed through, then stopped, shocked at the scene that awaited him.

The whole bar was decorated in shades of cornflower-blue and lemon-yellow. Linen cloths covered the tables. A mason jar filled with flowers sat in the center of every one. On each corner of the bar was a bouquet of balloons floating into the air. Poster-size photos of his dad and Vera, Sam and Julia, stood on tall easels off to one side. The place looked beautiful and, more importantly, ready for the reception.

"How did this happen?" he whispered, unable to believe how good everything looked. Of all the scenes he could have walked into, this was the last one he'd imagined.

His father was standing inside the front door, surveying the brightly decorated room. "Glad you made it, son." Joe wrapped him in a tight hug. "Did you get everything taken care of in D.C."

Scott nodded numbly. "Where's the water?"

Joe laughed. "You can't very well have a party when people would be getting their feet wet, right?"

"Why didn't anyone pick up when I called?" Scott pulled back from his dad's embrace.

Sam came over and chucked him on the shoulder. "We were kind of busy around here, with your building flooding and all."

"But Lexi had a plan," Misty told him as she finished tying more balloons to the edge of the bar. "She can be quite the mini taskmaster when she sets her mind to it."

"Lexi?" Scott felt his mind go blank.

"She's over at the salon with Julia, Vera and Lainey right now," Sam announced. "Julia insisted that she take a break. Otherwise, she'd still be here working."

He threw his hand out in a sweeping gesture. "All of this is her doing."

"She was convinced something had delayed you in D.C.," Joe explained.

"I went to see Derek's wife. I wanted to explain to her what had happened that day. She needed to hear it from me."

Joe nodded.

"We were ready to give up on you," Misty told him candidly. "Not your dad and brother, I guess. They didn't know about the water damage until Lexi called them. But the other waitresses, Max, Jon—we all thought you'd deserted us and we were ready to return the favor."

"I told you—"

"Everyone knows what you said." Jon came out of the kitchen, an apron tied around his waist. "We also know what you did. You left us behind. You don't have a reputation as someone who sticks. Why would we think this time was any different?"

"Maybe because I told you I'd come back."

"Past actions mean more than words." Jon shrugged. "You should know that."

"But Lexi believed in you," Misty told him. "Even when the rest of us didn't have faith, she never actually gave up on you." The waitress clasped him in a quick hug. "Who knew she'd be right?"

"Are you here for the party or to stay?" Sam asked quietly.

Scott hesitated, his mind a whir. For the first time in as long as he could remember, he didn't feel alone. Someone had his back. He'd done his best to push Lexi away, but she'd stayed true. Even though he didn't deserve it.

He was going to change that. If this time had taught him anything, it was that he didn't have to be a prisoner to his own doubts and fear. He could make things right and he had every intention of doing that.

Starting now.

Chapter Fourteen

Her nails drying, Lexi tried to feign interest in the latest magazine gossip. Her eyes drifted shut as she listened to Julia, Lainey and Vera talk, and wondered what it would be like to have grown up with sisters and a mother. The easy camaraderie and obvious closeness was something she'd never experienced. But she'd learned there was no use wishing for things that couldn't be. That might have been the biggest lesson from her grand adventure this past month.

She'd spent her whole life trying to make the people around her happy. Her only goal had been to live up to everyone's perfect image. Each time, the expectations had changed, when she got near enough to believe she might actually accomplish what she'd set out to do.

Now she knew she could only do her best and keep moving forward. She had to be true to herself and what she knew was right. That was what she'd told her father last night on the phone when she'd explained that she wasn't coming back to Ohio. He'd yelled and threatened, and although she'd been shaking with emotion, she'd held steady to her path. Eventually, he'd calmed down, and although he hadn't liked what she was saying, she'd gotten him to agree to stop interfering in her new life. She'd invited him to visit, offered him a chance to get to know her as her own person. He hadn't accepted, but hadn't outright refused, either.

She'd also done all she could for tonight's reception. Part of it was for Julia and Vera. They'd taken her into their circle even though she'd once tried to rip apart their family. They accepted her for who she was now and helped her gain the confidence to believe in herself. No one had given her a second chance like that before.

It taught her a great deal about how to live. Her heart still ached every day for Scott, but her belief in him had been a big part of why she'd stepped up to the plate. She knew that no one had ever given him a second chance when he needed it. That might have been because he'd never stuck around long enough to earn it. But it didn't matter. She believed in him, in who he was deep in his soul. She'd caught glimpses of the tender, honorable man he was inside. Yes, that man was buried under layers of pain and fear, but he was still the essence of who Scott was.

Even if he didn't come back for the reception, she knew he'd eventually talk to Joe or Sam. She wanted Scott to know that he could count on her when it mattered most. Because to her that was what love was, and even if he couldn't return her feelings, that didn't lessen what she felt for him.

A hush fell over the salon and she opened her eyes, wondering what had caught everyone's attention. Scott Callahan stood in the doorway, looking tired, beautiful and directly at her.

Julia strode forward at the same time Lexi rose to her feet, as if something in him pulled her closer.

"You've got a lot of nerve coming here," his sister-in-law told him, her finger wagging. "After—"

"I know," he said, holding up a hand, his eyes never leaving Lexi's. "I'm sorry and you can lay into me later. I need a few minutes to talk to Lexi."

To her surprise, Julia stepped back to let him pass.

Lexi felt her breath begin to come out in short, nervous puffs of air. "I wasn't sure you were coming back."

He nodded. "It may be the first non-idiot move I've made in the past couple of weeks. I'm sorry, Lexi."

He was standing in front of her now, so close she could see that he needed a shave. She could pick out the bright flecks of gold in his blue eyes. She could feel the warmth radiating from him, smell his soap and minty gum. Her whole body tingled, as if telling her how badly it had missed him.

"You hurt me. A lot."

"It won't happen again," he whispered. "I promise."

She glanced around at all the women staring at them and knew that she'd remember this moment, no matter how it ended, for the rest of her life.

"I'm staying in Brevia. I talked to my father and told him he can't run my life anymore."

"I talked to him, too."

Her heart sank. "To thank him for getting your job back?"

"To tell him I wasn't going back to the Marshals. That

even if he wanted to make the lies he told true, there was nothing he could offer to make me betray you again."

Lexi's mouth dropped. She didn't know how to answer.

"You're not going back?" she finally asked.

"I want to make my life in Brevia, Lexi." His eyes looked hopeful. "With you, if you'll have me again. I know I pushed you away. I broke your trust and it kills me that I hurt you."

He reached forward and laced his fingers in hers. "I'm nothing without you. You make me the person I was meant to be. I want to spend our whole lives together."

"What about action and adventure? What about adrenaline and the thrill of the chase?"

"Building our life together is all the adventure I need." He raised her fingers to his lips and kissed the tip of each one. "Every time I look at you is a bigger rush than anything else I could imagine. I want to let you into every part of my life. I want to know all there is to know about you. Good and bad. I love you, Lexi. With everything I am and everything I have. Give me a chance to prove it to you."

She heard several women sigh. "If you don't take him back, I'm coming after him," one lady said from underneath a dryer.

A smile broke across Lexi's face. "Oh, I'm taking him. He's officially off the market," she whispered and threw her arms around his neck.

Scott kissed her deeply, holding her tight against him for several minutes.

Then Julia moved closer. "Do I get to kick your butt now?" she asked him.

Lexi laughed. "Do you still want to?"

Julia hesitated, then smiled. "I guess I'll give you a pass. Since you're family and that was a pretty good speech."

Scott looked at Lexi. "I meant every word of it." He took a step away from her. "But there's one more thing."

Lexi's eyes widened as he dropped to one knee.

"Lexi Preston," he said, pulling a small box from his jacket pocket, "will you marry me? I want to know you're mine forever."

"Yes," she breathed, and he slipped a perfect pear-shaped diamond onto her finger. "Yes, yes, yes."

She looked at him and knew the happiness she saw in his eyes was reflected in her own. He stood, pulling her close once again. Then he looked over his shoulder at Julia and Vera, both of whom were wiping at their eyes.

"Could we expand tonight's celebration to include an engagement?"

"That's a perfect idea," Vera said, and Julia nodded.

Scott turned back to Lexi. "What do you think? Do you mind going public so soon?"

She nodded in turn, happiness filling her completely. "I think all three Callahan men have finally found a place to call home."

Epilogue

"Who wants pie?"

Vera Morgan Callahan came into the dining room with Joe following her, a pie plate in each hand.

"Me do," Charlie shouted from his seat at the end of the table.

Lexi smiled as Julia ruffled his hair. "Are you sure, buddy?" his mom asked. "You practically ate your weight in mashed potatoes."

Charlie grinned at her. "Want more pie and more taters."

Sam laughed. "You get your healthy appetite from your uncle Scott. As a kid, he could put away more food on Thanksgiving than anyone has a right to without puking."

"You eat pie, too." Charlie pointed a chubby finger at Scott.

Scott stretched an arm across the back of Lexi's chair, fingers tickling her shoulder. "You betcha, Charlie. Let's have a couple of pieces and head out back. I want to show you how to throw a football the right way."

"Like I haven't already?" Sam tried to look offended, but his big grin ruined the effect.

Ethan cleared his throat from his seat across the table. "Did you forget you have a real-life former quarterback in the room?"

"You want to prove you've still got your skills in a friendly game?" Scott asked.

Ethan smiled in return. "I've got my hands full here." He glanced down at the baby sleeping in his arms and dropped a kiss on the top of his daughter's head.

Ruby's adoption had been finalized a month ago, and Ethan and Lainey had brought her home. Ruby was a chunky cherub of a baby, sweet and smiley. Lexi knew they'd had a long road to finally have their own baby. It was clear that Ruby completed their family, and everyone in the whole town seemed to dote on her, including Scott.

His eyes softened and he gave Lexi's arm a little squeeze. "That's a good excuse, Daniels." He leaned close to Lexi's ear and whispered, "I can't wait until I have one of my own."

His voice sent a quick shiver down her spine. He kissed the side of her neck and the shivers traveled south. They'd been married only a couple months and weren't even trying for babies yet. Scott was busy with the bar and Lexi was building her practice and taking on more clients as Frank transitioned to more part-time work. But they were certainly practicing, as Scott called it, quite a bit. He joked that he wanted to get it right when they were finally ready. And there was no arguing that he got it very right.

"Lainey, take that baby from your husband." Julia stood and picked up her plate. "I'm either going to suffocate from all the testosterone in the air or lose my tasty turkey watching the newlyweds over here." She waved her hand in the direction of the backyard. "You boys take it outside while we clean up. You can have pie later."

Sam reached for her plate. "You should go sit down, Juls. I'll help with the dishes. In your condition—"

"I'm pregnant. I can still carry plates."

He placed a protective hand on her round belly. "I don't want you to get worn down."

She kissed his cheek. "You didn't seem too worried last night."

Ethan groaned and pushed back from the table. "Enough already." He transferred Ruby to Lainey's arms. "Joe, do you think you can help me whip your sons?"

"Absolutely." Joe turned to Vera. "Mind if we postpone dessert?"

"Go for it." She took the pies from his hands and set them on the table. "Just take it easy on these boys. Even though they're younger, I doubt they have your stamina."

Joe wrapped her in one of his trademark hugs. "Only for you, sweetheart."

Scott made a face. "That's my cue to get out of here."

Lexi giggled as he scrambled from his seat.

Sam helped Charlie climb out of the high chair and the three other men followed them toward the backyard.

"I'm happy to clean up the dishes," Lexi said, collecting plates and glasses. "You three can have a seat."

"Look at you, putting your month as a bar wench to good use," Julia teased.

Vera shook her head. "You don't have to do it by yourself." She waved her hands at her two daughters, clearly shooing them away. "You girls take Ruby to the living room. Lexi and I will take care of this."

A grin broke across Lainey's face. "Do you hear that, Ruby honey? Not only are you the best baby in the whole wide world, but now you've earned me a hall pass from kitchen duty."

"Don't just stand there." Julia scurried around the table. "Let's get out of here before she changes her mind."

As the two sisters disappeared through the doorway, Lexi turned to Vera. "I'm fine to take care of this on my own. It's the least I can do." She felt emotion rise in her throat and swallowed it down. "This is the best Thanksgiving I've ever had."

"I'm a decent cook," Vera agreed, "but not that good."

Lexi shook her head. "The meal was amazing, but it's everything about it. It's having all of you around me, feeling like I'm part of a family. I can't tell you how much I appreciate it."

"I don't mind the cleanup," Vera said as she picked up several plates and led Lexi into the kitchen. "If you haven't noticed, I'm a bit of a control freak." She laughed when Lexi didn't respond and began stacking plates in the dishwasher. "I'm sorry your father couldn't make it down."

Lexi sighed. "Me, too, but he's still having trouble adjusting to me living my own life. I'm glad he came to the wedding, and he promised to fly down for a few days over Christmas." She picked up a casserole pan and dunked it into the sink filled with hot, soapy water. "We're taking small steps, which is more than I ever thought I'd get from him."

"And you're happy still?" Vera asked quietly.

"So happy. I couldn't imagine anyplace feeling more like home than Brevia." She rinsed the pan with clean water and lifted it out of the sink. "I feel lucky to have all of you in my life, especially Scott."

"I'm the lucky one."

Lexi felt Scott's arms wrap around her waist. He took the pan from her hands and stepped to her side. "I'll dry."

"How are the boys doing out there?" Vera asked.

"Charlie's scored two touchdowns. We may have a future football star on our hands."

Vera smiled. "I have to see that. Can you two handle the rest of this mess?"

"Absolutely," Lexi answered. "We're almost finished, anyway." She loaded the last of the glasses into the dishwasher as Vera disappeared into the backyard.

Lexi straightened, to find Scott watching her, his gaze warming her from the inside out. He held out his hand and she stepped into his arms, his familiar scent still making her heart dance as he pulled her close. "I love you," she whispered.

His lips brushed against her forehead. "You are everything to me. You're my home, my heart, my whole life. I love you, Lexi. Everything about you, who you are…who I am when I'm with you. I can't imagine anything better than where we are right now."

His words filled her soul, though Lexi couldn't help but laugh. "In Vera's kitchen?"

"In a kitchen, a dining room. Standing in the middle of the street. It doesn't matter as long as we're together."

"Always." She brought her mouth to his, sealing the promise with a kiss.

* * * * *